HEARTLESS BELOVED

NORTH SHORE STORIES BOOK TWO

LOLA KING

Cover art by Wild Love Designs
Editing by Angie at Lunar Rose Editing
Alpha reading by Lauren Pixley
Beta Reading by Ratula Roy

FOREWORD

Dear readers,

You will notice some Arabic words in here! I've had an awesome time creating a character who speaks like my mother's side of my family. You might speak Arabic and notice that the expressions or words are different from the ones you use. I just want you to keep in mind that my characters speak Darija, which is the Moroccan Arabic.

Also, please keep in mind that it is quite a challenge to write Arabic words using the Latin alphabet and that some spellings might differ from the ones you know as there is often multiple ways to spell those words with the Latin alphabet.

Lastly, traditions and ways of speaking are borrowed from my own experience with my family. Everyone's experience is different, and by no mean is it a general representation of Moroccan and Algerian households—just mine, which was an amazing mix of cultures. ☺

Enjoy!

Don't blame me, love made me crazy. If it doesn't you ain't doing it right.

Taylor Swift

This book is for all my girls out there who have dark desires.

Haters will hate women writing dark books and the empowered women reading them. Let them.
Lose yourself in the dark fiction, enjoy the ride, and feel the freedom.

ACKNOWLEDGMENTS

This is a special acknowledgement to all my readers who kindly shared their favourite Taylor Swift song with me.

As you already know, I couldn't put every song in there as they didn't all fit the story. Regardless, thank you for being part of this book!

(this is in no particular order)

Jess, Pau, Kasey Bridges, Kiley Baker, Ann, Vanessa, Anusha, Alexandra Yordanova, Barb Walker, Tracey, Cheryl, Eni, Keely Witham, Iskra, Kimberly, Jordan Triplett, Amber Kuehn, Gina Stallone (Gigi), Veronica Ramos, Magon Brindley, Dena Coles, Kayla, Madelyn, Amber Pate, Stephanie, Crystal Stewart, Mindy Bormann, Daniella, Melanie, Ari, Beth Webb, Theresa Derwin, Jennifer, Christina, Amina, Mariam Allen, Lauren Donley, Erin Mcmanis, Lori, Diana

Thank you!

PLAYLIST

TOXIC PARADISE - Oliver Francis
Not Another Rockstar - Maisie Peters
I Knew You Were Trouble - Taylor Swift
fuck this town - glaive, ericdoa
Get Stüpid - bülow
Pursuit of Happiness - Kid Cudi, MGMT, Ratata, Steve Aoki
No Romeo - Dylan
Sparks Fly - Taylor Swift
Anti-Hero - Taylor Swift
sex scenes and video games - Grady
Falling Slowly - Vwillz
Ghost (Dark Version) - Confetti
Lavender Haze - Taylor Swift
Bad Ones - Call Me Karizma
I GUESS IT'S LOVE? - The Kid LAROI

Manipulate - Mxze, Clarei
I Chose Violence - iamjakehill
Falling - Trevor Daniel
Style - Taylor Swift
Wonderland - Taylor Swift
Better - Gracie Abrams
Hate The Way - G-Eazy, blackbear
Fearless - Taylor Swift
Flatline - 5 Seconds of Summer
Love Story - Taylor Swift
Shake It Off - Taylor Swift
Mirrors on the Ceiling - mike.
I Know Places - Taylor Swift
Hazel Eyes - Ollie
Without You - Lana Del Rey
Mine - Taylor Swift
Eyes Off You - PRETTYMUCH
Better With - Friday Pilots Club
5,6,7,8 - LØLØ, girlfriends
traitor - Olivia Rodrigo
I fucked up - convolk
White Horse - Taylor Swift
NEVER BREAK - Ethan Ross, Luga, Lames
Satin Black - iamjakehill
ARSON - Chri$tian Gate$
I Did Something Bad - Taylor Swift
Blank Space - Taylor Swift
From Hell With Love - Ryan Caraveo
Sober - Josh A, NEFFEX
i hope ur miserable until ur dead - Nessa Barrett
Young, In Love, & Depressed Af
Mastermind - Taylor Swift

The Heart Wants What It Wants - Selena Gomez
Vigilante Shit - Taylor Swift
The Night We Met - Lord Huron
Afterglow - Taylor Swift
Miss Americana & The Heartbreak Prince - Taylor Swift

CONTENT WARNING

This book is a dark romance for 18+ readers only. It contains scenes that may be triggering to some readers, including on-page dubious consent, kidnapping, torture, murder, panic attacks, PNES, hazing, domestic abuse, dealing with trauma, death of a parent, and mention of terminal illness. Like in all my books, this couple is toxic, my MMC close to non-redeemable, and oh so manipulative. I do not approve of this in real life, and in fact, actively tell you to keep this to fiction.

This book includes kinks such as CNC, very light pet play, and degradation/humiliation. My books are *not* guides to BDSM. There is *no* real BDSM in this book.
This book is for people who want to dive into their fantasies safely, on the page. Please, be aware that the fantasy starts on the next page, and you are entering at your own risk—there will be no further warning and no safe word.
The only safe word/gesture at your disposal is to close the book.

Always play safely and consensually.

Lots of Love,

Lola

PROLOGUE

ALEXANDRA

Toxic Paradise – Oliver Francis

I startle awake.

"Don't scream."

The coldness of the gun against my forehead forces me to inhale sharply. My body freezes as my eyes dart around.

He's wearing a balaclava, dark eyes looking down at me.

The moon is shining into my room, tracing the outline of his body and keeping him in the shadows as my breathing accelerates.

My mouth opens, but his head shakes. "Not a sound." He presses his weapon harder against my forehead, and my eyes squeeze shut.

This is a nightmare. It must be.

I remember falling asleep tonight. I struggled from the excitement, knowing that when I would wake up, it'd be my eighteenth birthday. Before I kissed my boyfriend, Chester, goodbye at the door, I took a Polaroid of us with my camera. It's sitting on my desk right now. My last evening as a seventeen-year-old in the arms of my high school sweetheart. Tomorrow is Valentine's Day. My birthday.

I had a warm shower, got into a sexy nightie, and video-called Chester as soon as he got to his house. He promised me he had a day full of surprises tomorrow.

So, I know this man in my bedroom in the middle of the night *has* to be a product of my imagination. It wouldn't be the first time I dreamed of someone breaking into my room.

But my dreams usually excite me. My body tingles and I wake up wet. This one feels different, almost like a nightmare.

When I open my eyes again, he's still here.

"I'm not going to hurt you. I'm just here for the money. As long as you do what you're told, you'll be fine. Got it?"

I struggle to fathom what is darker, the room or his low voice.

I nod silently, not having the courage to do anything else. He pulls the gun away from my head while still pointing it at me.

"Sit up," he orders.

My nightie is a fuchsia color, with see-through lace around my breasts that turns into satin just under and barely covers my behind. A perfect mix of sexiness and innocence, just like I know Chester loves.

I sit up slowly, keeping the sheet to my chest. I can't get myself to look at him, too scared to accidentally take in details that might make him recognizable. The less I know, the better. I stare at my shaking knees which are covered by my bedding. "Please, don't hurt me," I whisper. "I-I can take you to the safe."

I know there is no other reason this man would be in here. He said so himself.

My parents are rich. Billionaires. Mom comes from old

money, and this man broke in to get his share. Whatever is in the safe won't matter to us; he can have it all.

"I said not a sound," he snaps harshly, making me jump. "You can talk when I ask questions. Not before."

I nod, feeling my throat tightening.

"Put your hands behind your back."

My eyes flick to his. "There's no need. Please..." I open my mouth to keep going, but he presses the weapon to my right temple. I take the hint and clamp it shut.

Grabbing something in the pocket of his black hoodie, he throws it at me. My eyes dart to the white plastic on my lap, and a whimper escapes me.

"Tie your hands behind your back."

I'm forced to let go of the covers, and the second I do so, his gaze goes to my tits. The pale globes are so obvious in the darkness of the room, barely protected by the flimsy lace.

I watch his mouth twist. "Do all the Stoneview bitches sleep like they're gonna pose for Playboy in the morning?"

Stoneview. The reason he's in my house tonight. A town only inhabited by billionaires and millionaires. Where the average income is higher than all the other cities in the state of Maryland combined.

Our cars are unaffordable to the usual rich person, and our houses are too expensive to sell by average real estate agents. Our prep school is so pricey only we can afford it.

We're the elite of the elite. The richest of the rich. Closed off from the outside world, the kings and queens of nepotism and privilege.

Our crime rate is next to zero, our town inaccessible, our mansions gated and protected. I have never heard of a home invasion in Stoneview.

Until tonight.

"See," he taunts, "Now I asked you a question, so I expect an answer."

I gulp and shake my head. "N-no."

"Just you, then?" he keeps going as I struggle to slip the zip ties around my wrists. It's awkward in this position and my hands are starting to shake.

"It was for my boyfriend," I whisper back. Why do I feel the need to justify myself to him?

"Lucky boy. You should keep doing what you're told, since I'm sure he'd love to find you alive tomorrow morning."

I finally slot the zip tie in place and pull. "I am," I say to placate him, making sure not to tighten too much.

He gets closer to me, slides his hand along my arm, grabs the end of the plastic, and pulls harshly, making me wince.

"Bad girl," he whispers in my ear. "That was way too loose."

I shiver as his warm breath caresses my neck. He steps away, and the hand holding his gun comes to rest against his thigh. "Where's Mommy and Daddy's room?" he asks in a mocking tone.

"They're not here."

His eyes narrow, and he crosses his arms. "I'm gonna be very mad if you're lying to me. You don't want to find out what happens when I'm mad."

"I promise they're not here," I squeak past my taut throat. "They're on vacation. I'm alone."

"Any brothers and sisters?"

"I'm an only child."

He nods, and the moment he does so, my bedroom door opens, startling me. Another man dressed in all black and wearing a ski mask enters.

4

He's holding a handbag, *my* handbag, in his right hand and a torch. He's pointing it at my driver's license in his left hand.

"There's no one else here," the new incomer confirms as he walks in. "But, man," he laughs. His voice is much lighter than the person who's been with me till now. It flies through the air while the other crashes into you heavily. "You'll never guess what I just found."

No.

I already know what he's so happy about.

"Not money, that's for sure," the one next to me answers unhappily.

"Oh no. Much better." He walks toward my bed. "Tell my friend here your name, sweetheart."

My heart kicks into a panic. Nothing will be smooth from here on out.

"Elisabeth."

The one holding my driver's license laughs again, knowing I purposely didn't say my last name. I'm delaying the inevitable. "Yeah," he nods. His eyes drop to the plastic card in his hand. "Elisabeth Alexandra *Delacroix*."

He butchers my last name. Pronouncing the 'x'. *Delacroyx*, like the La Croix drink, instead of *Delakwa*. It doesn't matter. Either way, the effect is the same.

I look at the man next to me in a panic. I can already tell he's the leader of the two. "As in Senator Delacroix?" He pronounces it perfectly, surprising me.

"Yep. I can confirm he's in all the family pictures. Just him, his wife, and lovely Elisabeth here."

I haven't gone by my first name in forever. I'm so used to being called Alexandra that Elisabeth feels foreign to me.

"Man." The guy with my driver's license smiles. "You know what that means, right?"

The one who's been with me since the beginning brings an index finger to my cheek, tracing the outline of my jaw with his knuckle. The soft gesture stops when he wraps his entire hand around my jaw and pulls my face so I'm staring up at him.

"Yes," he says calmly. With his other hand, he puts his gun in the back of his jeans. "It means we're going to get a hefty ransom for Elisabeth."

The entire weight of my body drops into my stomach, and I feel the blood draining from my face.

"No!" I yell as I pull away from him. Then I start to writhe, my wrists burning as I fall onto my mattress and attempt to crawl away.

"Tell the others to get the car ready. She's coming home with us."

The others? How many people are in my house?

I watch the guy with my driver's license leave my room as I try to roll onto the floor so I can get up and run away.

"Come here." A hand clasps around my ankle, and I'm pulled back to the other side of the bed. The movement makes my nightie run up to my hips. Despite wearing something sexy for Chester, it's not like he saw underneath it while we were on FaceTime, I still have on some cotton panties. How glad I am of that as I'm being dragged on the mattress. At least there's some protection from his eyes.

"Help!" I scream even though it's futile. The closest neighbor is a ten-minute walk away. We like our privacy in Stoneview; no one can hear me from here.

But he doesn't know that, and it angers him.

"Shut the fuck up," he hisses. He's right on me, and after a shift in the air, a hand crashes against my ass.

I shriek as I feel him climb on top of me.

I'm not scared of the gun anymore. He won't kill me now that he knows he can get millions out of me.

But I am terrified of all the other things he could do.

"No. Please...please!" I tear the skin at my wrists from trying to escape the zip ties.

His jeans are harsh against my exposed skin and a wave of fear courses through my body. "Please, don't hurt me..."

His hand is in my hair next, and he pulls harshly until my head snaps back. Before I can beg anymore, he shoves some material in my mouth. Some sort of cloth. He lets go of me, and I hear the telltale sound of tape being unrolled.

I shriek from being scared, the cloth in my mouth swallowing the sound. I try to push it out with my tongue, but I'm too late. Tape is plastered on my skin, wrapping around my head multiple times before he cuts it.

My voice is muted now, my cries for help impossible. He gets off me, grabs my hips and flips me around.

"I thought you were going to be a good girl for me, Elisabeth. I'm not happy with this behavior of yours." The mockery in his voice makes it all worse.

I shake my head, my body trembling.

He grabs my phone on my bedside table and smiles. "Your daddy is going to have the call of his life."

He puts my phone in the back pocket of his jeans and grabs me by the upper arm, pulling me up until I'm on my feet. "Come on. Time is money."

Time?

What time?

It becomes a concept I don't understand as he drags me down the stairs and to the three other men waiting in our grand foyer, as my knees buckle at every step.

The moment we pass the last step, there's a pause as the other three look at me.

"Holy shit," one says. "Look at those tits."

"Fucking hell," the other adds.

Their comments force a whimper up my throat. I retreat, turning to my right to hide my body and end up bringing myself closer to the man holding me. I press against his body in an attempt to shield mine, and one of the three behind me bursts out laughing.

"The girl thinks she's gonna get protection out of the worst of us."

The hand around my upper arm tightens, his leather glove warm against my skin, and I gaze up as his dark gaze looks down. He's so imposing I feel the need to take a step back even while perfectly knowing I can't. I'm average height, but the top of my head barely reaches his shoulders, my eyes in line with his broad chest.

For the few seconds our eyes lock, I sense the pity in them. Almost like he feels bad for what he's doing to me. It's gone as soon as it came, though. He pushes me away from him, shoving me into the others.

"Get her in the car."

Outside, the air is freezing cold, being that it's mid-February, and I'm only wearing a nightie. My feet hurt from the way they drag over the cobblestones of our driveaway.

When he said the car, he meant our car. Someone beeps open my mother's G Wagon and pushes me inside. They're quick. Like they've done this before. Two sit on either side of me, and two at the front. I keep my eyes on the one who pointed the gun at me, the one who was in my room from the beginning. Despite the ski masks, I recognize him clearly. He's the biggest out of all of them. He has the stance of a leader, and they all distinctly follow whatever he says.

Our gazes cross in the rearview mirror. "I'm sorry,

Elisabeth. But unfortunately, you don't get to see where we're taking you."

I feel my eyes widen a split second before a cloth is pressed to my nose. I shriek against my gag and attempt to fight them to the best of my ability.

It's no use.

Not when my wrists are tied behind my back and four men surround me.

Whatever is on that cloth chokes me, bringing tears to my eyes from the strength of the product. I cough for a few seconds before feeling my eyelids drop.

Please, God. I don't want to die.

Nausea awakens me. My stomach is churning, and my head is pounding. My tongue feels heavy in my mouth, and I groan as I hear some noise around me.

The events come back to me quickly. Despite the fog in my brain, the fear of what happened is still so evident that I can't forget it.

I'm on my side, my hands still tied behind my back. I groan from the pain in my shoulders and the feeling of sickness. The moment I stir, the voices come closer. A flash is in my face as I try to open my eyes, making it impossible to do so.x

"Elisabeth," a voice taunts me. It's him, their leader. I know it. "Say hi to your daddy. We're taking a video for him."

That's when I realize the gag is gone. I shake my head, trying to bury myself against the mattress.

Mattress.

I'm on a mattress.

There are no sheets, nothing. Just bare padding and

squeaking springs. It smells of piss, sweat, and God knows what else.

A hand pulls at my hair, bringing me onto my back. Fear takes a hold of me so tightly that I freeze. The flash is in my face. "Beg him to come get you from the bad men who took you."

I manage to open my eyes slightly, squinting, only I can't see much bar a bright white light in my face.

I shake my head and close my eyes again. Taking a deep breath, the fear dissipates slightly as I try to recall my training.

I'm the daughter of the present-day majority leader of the Senate, who is mainly known because of his elitist wife. My father was so thirsty for power when he married my mother that he took her billion-dollar last name. They also made sure to give it to me.

I've had countless talks about what to do in case of a kidnapping, though I never thought I'd have to put it into practice.

The hand in my long hair tightens, making me hiss from the sharp pain. "Tell him," the voice behind the light growls. "Tell him how scared you are."

Trying to take control of my trembling voice, I say, "My father doesn't negotiate with terrorists."

The light finally turns off, allowing me to open my eyes and look around the dark room. I'm on a single mattress on the floor, and three men are towering around me while the fourth is crouching next to me.

He lets go of me and gets up, now completely silent.

"Terrorists," one of them snorts. "A bit extreme."

They're still wearing their balaclavas, and the light is too dim in the room for me to make out any of their features. I only recognize the leader because of his physique. None of them are restless or anxious. None of them are taking this too seriously or are scared to get caught.

They're real criminals who aren't afraid of the law.

The leader has his back to me now, tapping something on the phone he was using to record me. He takes a while, his gloves probably not helping. His strong back and broad shoulders aren't even tensing. The man kidnapped me, and he is wholly relaxed about it.

I struggle into a sitting position, my head still pounding from whatever they made me inhale. Settling my back against the brick wall behind me, I look around the room.

"Kidnapping the daughter of a politician makes you a terrorist. My father doesn't negotiate, and he doesn't give in to ransom. The moment he knows I've been taken, you will have the FBI after you. And when they find me, because they will, you will all be arrested and locked up in a maximum-security prison. The U.S. government doesn't joke around when it comes to the senators and their families. I don't know you, and I haven't seen your faces. You're better off taking my credit card and letting me go. There's no limit, and I will give you the pin. All you have to do is—"

"All *you* have to do is keep that mouth shut." The leader turns around, his hard eyes on me. "Unless it's to ask your father to give us the money or beg for mercy on camera, we don't need to hear your exposé on the U.S. government."

I narrow my eyes at him. "Good luck. Because that man will not be paying one penny of ransom."

He walks back to me, goes on his haunches beside me, and brings his gloved thumb to my lips. He traces the outline before pulling the bottom one. My heart kicks against my chest, my breath getting shallow. For a second, the headache dissipates. This close, I can see the depth in his brown eyes. I can see the specks of gold around his irises. They literally take my breath away.

"We'll see about that. Won't we?" In a swift gesture, he backhands me so hard I fall back on the mattress in a shriek.

I drag air into my lungs and taste blood on my tongue, the warm liquid spilling from the corner of my mouth.

"Sorry," the leader shrugs as he steps back. "We won't be taken seriously if you're not bleeding a little. It's a whole process. Make sure you add some tears to that."

He grabs the phone in his back pocket and throws it at one of the other guys. "Go for it. I saved her dad's number on there before throwing her phone away."

I'm back on my side on the mattress, and the camera flashes in front of me again. I look up at it but don't say anything. I will not play into their games. If they get one thing out of me, they'll know they can get anything.

I shake my head and close my eyes as they film the state I'm in. Curling onto myself, I refuse to say anything.

The flash goes away, and I'm assuming they've stopped recording.

"Come on, Elisabeth," the leader says as he nudges me with his foot against my ass. "If you don't perform, I'm going to have to hurt you. Why make it hard on yourself when you could go through this entire thing unharmed."

"Unharmed?" I hiss back. "You took me from my house and hit me. Do you call that *unharmed*?"

He rolls his eyes at me and chuckles. "I barely touched you. That could change, though. We're going to film you again so we can send it to your dad. Let's try something else, okay? I want you to state who you are and explain that you were taken from your house tonight. And then you're going to say we want two point four million dollars in hundred-dollar bills. It'll fit in a twenty-five by eighteen by four suitcase. That's exactly what I want. Nothing more, nothing less."

Not even three million dollars. My mother is a billionaire with enough money to last generations. Two point four million dollars is nothing to us.

Yet it's the principle. My father will not give them that money. I know it. Because he knows no one wants to be the person who murdered the daughter of a senator. And he also knows he can find me.

"Elisabeth," the leader calls again. I'm sick of hearing my name on his lips. It makes my heart jump and drills a hole of anxiety in my stomach. There's so much derision in it. He's having the time of his life while I'm tied up on a dirty mattress, practically naked. He presses the sole of his shoe against my right ass cheek, shoving me again. "Do you think you can remember what I just said?"

"Yes," I seethe. "I'm not an idiot."

"That's still to be proven," he laughs softly. "Alright, film her again."

The light flashes in my eyes and I'm forced to look to the side. I watch one of the men behind the one filming me.

"My..." I try to swallow, realizing how thirsty I am. "My name is Elisabeth Delacroix. I..." My throat tightens as reality hits me. "I was taken from my house during the night." My eyes burn with tears, but I swallow them back. Their leader wants them, and I will do anything but give them to him. I squeeze my eyes shut, opening them to find the same image before me. Everything is tilted since I'm lying down on my side. "My ransom is two point four million dollars in one-hundred-dollar bills. It fits into a twenty-five by eighteen by four-inch suitcase."

There's a long silence before the man holding the phone turns the camera off.

"No tears, then?" he asks.

The leader chuckles. "They'll come, don't worry. Send that to her dad with the coordinates of where he should drop off our money. Tell him he's got forty-eight hours."

Forty-eight hours. *And then what?*

My father will have found me before then. He must.

The guy with the phone taps for a minute and sends the message. "Done."

"Nice. Let's go for some food. We can come back when we hear from him."

My heart stops. They're just going to leave me here? I press my lips together and take a deep breath through my nose. Just before he leaves, the leader comes by my head, grabs my shoulders, and rolls me onto my back.

"I love to have those nice tits of yours on display."

My nostrils flare, knowing how noticeable my boobs are through the transparent lace. He looks down at them, and I want to die at the fact that my nipples tighten.

It's the cold. We're in the middle of winter and this is clearly an abandoned house. That's why.

He seemingly thinks otherwise in the way his mouth twists into a sick smile. He doesn't say anything, however. He just leaves me alone on the bed and walks away. The lock clicking tells me there's no reason to even get up and try to get out. I'm stuck here.

I'm not sure for how long they're gone. It feels like less than an hour. I'm dozing in and out of sleep when the door slams open and they all walk back in in a hurry.

"Daddy's calling," the leader tells me. "Be a good girl and show him how frightened you are."

One of them grabs me by the hair to sit me back up,

making me wince in the process. I'm sick of being manhandled by these brutes.

The telltale of a video call being answered shocks me. I thought it was a voice call, but it's my father's hard face on the screen.

Everything I remember about the training kicks in at once. I take a deep, long breath as I assess my father's stern eyes. I know what he expects of me.

"I'm in an abandoned house. Red bricks. Boarded windows. There are four of them. Their leader has an American accent, broad build, brown eyes. Armed. They're wearing—"

That's all I get in before the one holding the phone hangs up.

"Stupid bitch," he shouts at me. He rears his arm back, ready to slap me. I close my eyes, waiting for the brutal hit, but nothing comes. When I open them, I see the leader holding his wrist in a tight grip.

"It's alright," he says calmly. "I'm sure Elisabeth simply didn't understand how serious we were being. She thinks this is a little game. After all, two point four million is nothing to her, right?"

His brown eyes flick to me, and I can't stand his stare, dropping mine to my lap.

"You don't understand," I whisper, my voice trembling. "He won't give you anything."

"Not if you make it look like you're on a fucking vacation to Cabo, no." He gives a look to two of the others and they leave the room.

"See," the leader says as he comes to stand right by my side. "This isn't our first rodeo, but I have a feeling it's yours. You're being brave. You're the daughter of a politician, and you were probably trained for this since you were a little girl." Still standing, his hand comes to caress my hairline. "Forget about what they told you. Nothing can prepare you for this. Nothing can prepare you for me. I asked you to do something, and you didn't. I told you I wanted tears and fear, and you denied me. Now I have no choice but to hurt you. It truly is unfortunate, Elisabeth. We could have done this the easy way."

I can feel the way my heart is begging to be let out of my chest, and I can't seem to calm it down. Cold sweat starts pearling at the back of my neck as I look up at him.

"I know my father," I push past my tight throat. "Tears won't convince him to give you money. At this point, he will only care about destroying you."

The door to the room opens again, and two of them come in carrying a giant bucket. They put it right next to the leader's feet. I eye the water and the ice floating in it.

My wide eyes snap back up. "W-what—"

"It's okay. You just stay there and be pretty. We'll take care of convincing your dad."

He grabs my long hair and pulls me until my knees crash against the dusty rundown carpet.

"Take a deep breath, Elisabeth." The flash comes back on and the next second, my head is plunged into the iced water.

I choke on it, full gulps invading my throat from the shock. The coldness rings in my ears, putting pressure on my brain and making me feel like my head is going to explode.

My body is tensing as I try to fight my bonds in vain.

It feels like an eternity when he finally pulls me back up. I choke on air as I try to bring it into my burning lungs. My whole body is on fire, and I'm shaking so hard my teeth are chattering.

The flash is so harsh in my eyes my head rears back. But the leader's grip on my hair is tight.

I keep coughing as he hisses, "Ask your daddy for help, Elisabeth."

When I don't, he forces my head back into the bucket. I'm a little more prepared this time, and my lips stay sealed until my body spasms from the cold and the lack of air. Water gets into my nose and he brings me back up only for me to cough some more.

"S-stop!" I retch.

"Why don't you tell him to make it stop, huh? It'll only cost him two point four million dollars."

I don't. That would make me weak, and my father didn't raise me to be weak.

My head is pushed back into the freezing water. I don't thrash around this time. I keep my eyes and mouth shut and let the cold burn my face. And because I don't fight, he holds my head in there long enough for me to feel the darkness enveloping me.

When he pulls me back out, I'm barely able to breathe. Everything around me is dark, and my muscles are so weak I fall back against his legs.

"Two point four million, Senator." I'm assuming he's talking to the camera now. "We'll give you ten hours before we start playing new games with her."

The flash disappears, and I know they're not recording anymore. The leader pushes me back onto the bed and one of them puts something on the floor next to me. A clock.

"Here. Just so you can judge for yourself how much your dad gives a shit or not. Count the minutes."

They all leave the room as I look at the time. It's four a.m.

I'm so cold. My muscles spasm and my entire body is

shivering. I cry as I attempt to breathe, and oxygen feels like needles in my throat and lungs. A sob wracks my chest and I'm glad none of them is here to see it. These men will not see me break.

Because if they do, my father will break me harder.

As time passes, my eyes only open to check the clock next to me. I watch minutes turn into hours without any of them coming back. Four a.m. becomes eight a.m., and I notice the winter morning light passing past the wooden panels blocking the window.

My mind is awake but so foggy. My eyes are closed when I hear them walk back in. My hair is still damp, but the rest of my body has dried.

"I have good and bad news, Elisabeth," *his* voice spreads into the room, crashing against the walls and punching me in the stomach. It's so heavy and dark. It's perfectly manly in every sense of the term, and yet I hate it so much.

He comes to the mattress, and from lying on my side, all I can see right now are his shins in front of me. I don't want to look up into his eyes again. I don't want to see the nightmarish ski mask that will haunt me forever.

The fact that I still haven't seen their faces tells me I'm going to make it out alive, although I'm not even sure I want to right now. My body is weak, my mind giving up. The thirst is the worst. I keep coughing, feeling like there's sand in my dry throat.

I close my eyes when I feel him lower himself to his haunches.

Breathe, I hear my dad's voice. *Keep control of yourself because that's all you have control of.*

"The good news is you've just survived ten hours since almost being drowned in icy water."

A shiver hurts my back as it crosses my muscles. His hand is in my hair, caressing the blonde strands. His words are a contrast to his gesture. "The bad news is your daddy hasn't given us the money. And now we have to hurt you some more."

I can't stop the whimper that escapes me. Everything is already hurting so much. My wrists are bleeding. My chest is burning and I just want out of here.

"That's it." His hand on my hair is almost reassuring, coaxing me into giving in to his commands. "Give me some tears, Elisabeth."

My heart skips a beat when I hear the shift in his tone. The threatening voice has given way to something else. Something dark and lustful. When he talks about my tears and about hurting me, there's an excitement he barely seems able to contain. Something terrifying and electrifying.

I want to cry and give him what he wants. For it all to be over. But I have to be stronger than him. Because none of this is up to him or his friends. This thing ends when my father decides to give the money or find me.

"Open your eyes."

My lids flutter open as I force myself to look up at him. He smiles down at me as he keeps caressing my hair, pushing dirty strands away from my face. "Maybe a video call with your dad would help? You could beg him to come get you like I told you to do."

My throat is too dry to speak, so I just shake my head.

He sighs, faking disappointment. "Alright, then. Let's keep playing."

"I need the bathroom," I rasp. It's true, and it'll delay whatever sick thing he has in store for me.

"Someone will take you." He straightens up, takes a step back, and lets another one of the men grab my arm and pull me up.

The man guides me outside the room and across a hallway. Everything is dusty and broken.

"This way," he pushes me forward, letting go of my arm. "It's at the end of the hallway."

The wallpaper has been ripped off the walls or covered in spray paint. It smells of cold cigarettes and mold. I hiss when my bare foot catches on something. The old wooden flooring is split in many places, and I just walked on multiple splinters.

The pain disappears the moment I see the stairs. We're about to walk past them. This is my chance. Now or never.

Without even looking or giving him a hint, I change trajectory the moment we walk past the stairs. Going down two at a time, I fly off the last few. I'm slower than I would like to be with my hands tied behind my back, but I still manage to crash into a wall downstairs before he registers what happened.

"She's running!" I hear shouting upstairs. A second later, heavy steps are after me. I hear them all descending the stairs, but I don't stop. I have to find a way out of here.

I run to what should have been the front door, but wooden boards are blocking it. They must have come in another way. Running off to the rest of the house, I panic when all I find are boarded windows, barely letting any light in.

No, no, no. That's impossible.

Which way did they come in?

Running into a different room, my heart accelerates

when I notice a back door that hasn't been condemned. I sprint, knowing my life depends on this.

But I'm not quick enough.

A hand lands in my hair, dragging me back and making me cry out from the violence.

"No!" I wail, refusing to process my escape was cut short so easily. I feel my body flying as he grabs me and throws me over his shoulder.

"Oh, Elisabeth." It's him. That mocking voice. Their leader. "And here I was thinking we were starting to warm up to each other."

"Let me go!" I scream. "Let me..." A sigh leaves me as I give up mid-sentence. He won't. Why even waste my breath?

The moment we're back in the upstairs bedroom, he throws me on the dirty mattress.

"Didn't they teach you to save your energy and wait for a safe opportunity? That was reckless. Stupid, really."

I'm panting from the run, and I stare daggers at him. "And now you've pissed me off," he growls low. "And turned me on."

My heart stops completely. Did he just say...

"Lucky for you, I've got a solution to all our problems."

I gulp and shift on the bed. "No," I attempt.

He pulls out the phone again and gives it to one of the others. "You've been tempting me with your slutty nightie. That mixture of innocence and sex is truly fucking working on me."

I shake my head violently despite knowing it won't change anything.

"Your boyfriend is a lucky guy, Elisabeth."

"Don't," I squeak. "Whatever...whatever you're thinking. It'll only make things worse for you. Kidnapping is one thing but—"

"You worry about calling out for help. I'll worry about myself."

The next second he's on me. I scream as he straddles my hips, writhing underneath him.

"Those fucking tits," he rasps as he rips the top of my nightie. "They should be illegal."

My ample breasts have been the talk of my school for years. I was an early bloomer, and they're definitely hard to miss. I'm used to people noticing them and loving them. They're beautiful, and Chester is crazy for them.

But Chester and I never do anything.

What I tell him is that I'm not ready. For nothing more than kissing.

The truth is I know he can't give me what I need.

I know it in the way he treats me and kisses me. He's kind and gentle. The perfect boyfriend, the future son-in-law my parents adore. We're perfect together.

Apart from the fact that I crave darkness and depravation. That I touch myself to sick videos of humiliation. The kind where women are degraded so severely it makes me ashamed to even know these things exist. Things I keep to myself, secrets I would never even tell my closest friends.

So no, my sweet boyfriend has never even touched my boobs before.

This man? He will be the first, and he doesn't even know it. Why would he? He only cares about using me to get his own pleasure. Only his ultimate goal matters.

"Stop," I cry out as he grabs my tits and crushes them in each of his hands.

It would seem there is a difference between watching fake videos of women being turned on from being assaulted and experiencing it. My brain can feel that so clearly. It makes me want to scream and fight. It makes me scared.

Completely and utterly terrified.

I pull at my binds, grunting from the pain it creates. "Stop," I screech as I lose complete control of my reactions.

Twisting doesn't do anything.

I try to throw him off.

I scream.

But there's nothing I can do when he undoes his black jeans and pulls out his cock.

"Don't..." The more I swallow back the tears, the more they choke me. They mix with the dread stuck in my throat, turning me into a squeaking mouse.

The flash to my left brings a new wave of panic. I wheeze as I try to take another breath and freeze when he spits between my boobs.

"I'm going to fuck these tits until they're bruised. You just stay there and act like the pretty victim you are. I'm sure that'll kick your dad into action."

He shuffles closer to my chest, sitting on my stomach and stopping me from breathing. He crushes my tits together with his gloved hands as he pushes his hard dick between them. Forward and back, he keeps going violently. I gasp when his fingers start playing with my nipples. He doesn't relent, though it does add a new feeling to the mix. He rolls the tips between his fingers, and a sharp exhale escapes me. Our eyes cross. The balaclava hides his face, but I don't need to see every single one of his features. It's so clear in his eyes that he knows what he's doing.

"Elisabeth." He taunts me as he thrusts between my tits again. The movement shoves me higher on the mattress. "Look at the camera, baby." He presses harder on my tits and his violence increases. "We want to catch the fact that you're loving this."

"I-I'm not," I groan, but I realize too late that it sounds like I'm moaning.

Another slips past my lips, and my eyes widen.

It *is* a moan.

Oh my God. I'm moaning.

I suddenly become hyper-aware of my body and the way my writhing movements have become chasing. Every time he moves, I follow. My chest is burning from his rubbing and the lust that has started to spread through my veins. He keeps sending electric spikes from my nipples all the way to my stomach and lower.

It feels the same as when I touch myself. Only better.

That's impossible.

That's...*no.*

"Stop," I choke. "Please...please, stop."

He accelerates. "How can I stop when I know how much you're loving this?" His words are strained now, his breath shortening.

I'm too late to understand what's going on. One hand lets go of my boobs to grab his dick as he straightens up. He lets go of my left tit to lift his top, probably so he doesn't dirty himself.

That's when I notice them. Three scars on his stomach. Amongst the ridges of his perfectly defined abs. His skin is darker than mine, a light brown that seems almost golden. And there are three thick places where the tissue has hardened and turned white against his skin.

Don't forget, I command myself.

Three deep scars.

Do. Not. Forget.

I gasp when I feel the warmth of his cum on me and ribbons land in my mouth.

"Fuck," he pants. "You're one hot fuck toy, Elisabeth."

I shake my head, looking away from the flash blinding me. I feel him get off me, naively believing the nightmare is over. That's until I feel him pushing up the hem of my nightie.

No is at the tip of my tongue, and yet it doesn't come out. I wish I could say it's because I'm scared. I wish I could say it's because I don't want it.

The truth is much scarier than that.

The truth is the excitement and lust running through my veins is what scares me the most.

"Give me the phone." His order is curt. He has no patience in him. There's tension in his tone. Hunger.

I feel a gloved finger press against my panties. He's at my entrance, and it's wet.

It's so wet I can feel it all over my crotch.

"Holy shit," he chuckles. "You're so turned-on."

"I'm not!" I scream. There's a rage inside me. The shame is pushing anger through my limbs. "You got what you wanted. Just stop."

How could I possibly be enjoying this?

Didn't my body get the memo when my brain decided this was a terrifying and traumatizing experience?

Or did it get it and is indeed loving these exact facts?

"See, I think you didn't listen to what I wanted. I said give me tears and begging. I said convince your daddy to give us the money. Right now, all I'm seeing is a little slut enjoying herself."

Without moving my panties, he presses harshly against the damp material, pushing it past my entrance.

I cry out, and my legs instantly close as I turn to my side and curl in on myself.

"Tsk, tsk," he tuts me. He grabs my legs and rolls me on my back again. Spreading my thighs, he settles between them so I'm unable to close them anymore. My wrists are crushed under my back, and my entire body is trembling.

"Do you cry when someone makes you come, Elisabeth?" he asks with genuine curiosity.

I don't answer. I won't give him the pleasure. Mainly, because I don't know. No one but myself has ever made me come before.

I don't think it feels the same when someone else makes you orgasm. I can only imagine.

"So stubborn," he laughs, pressing against my entrance again. He's pointing the camera at me, making the humiliation that much worse. "I guess we'll just have to check for ourselves, won't we?"

I shake my head so hard the room spins. I can hear the other men snickering behind me. I can feel the shame. It's so sticky on my sweaty skin.

This time, he pushes my panties to the side, exposing my pussy to the camera.

"You're so wet, Elisabeth," he growls.

I honestly wish he'd stop calling my name. It makes it all so *real*. It stops me from escaping the moment.

I sense the tip of his gloved finger pressing against my entrance and the fright sends another wave of confusion through my body. I feel the exact moment I get wetter. He doesn't miss it, either.

His mocking laugh is deadly as he looks up at me. "That was caught on camera," he murmurs. The desire is evident in his voice. It's raw and hits me with force.

He starts pushing in, my wetness allowing him easy access. But I twist and try to pull back.

"Please," I plead in a desperate rasp. "I don't...I've never...just don't."

He freezes when he understands. "Did that boyfriend of yours never touch you, baby?"

I shake my head. "I wasn't-wasn't ready."

And now I so shamefully am.

A soft laugh escapes him. "And he listened to your words instead of your body?"

My body doesn't react like this to Chester, is what I don't say.

He moves further inside me, and I feel the way my pussy clamps around his finger. The cold sweats have been replaced by a fire licking at my skin, making me squirm from pleasure.

"Change boyfriends, Elisabeth. Because if you were mine, I wouldn't be able to keep my hands off you, no matter what you said."

His finger retreats only to come back more roughly. It's impossible to stop my body's reactions; the staggered breaths, the whimpers of pleasure, and the way my hips start to follow his movements.

I'm not even used to the thickness of one finger when he adds another. My mouth falls open, yet no sound comes out. I simply gasp for air as he fucks me into oblivion with two simple fingers.

"You're so hot," he pants with me.

"Wait," I panic as I feel myself losing control completely. I'm on the edge of a cliff, and this man is going to push me off. "Stop..."

"Are you going to cry from loving this? When will it hit

you that you're coming on the hand of the man who kidnapped you?"

It hits me the moment he says I'm coming. Like I hadn't realized before that. It's as if my body decided to wait for him to spell it out before letting my brain know. I explode on his fingers, hotness spreading in my limbs, snapping sharply in my lower belly.

When he stops, my body slumps against the bed, and my head falls to the side. Finally, I give him exactly what he wanted, my tears falling freely.

Not from the kidnapping or from the fact that he tried to drown me. Not from the violence or the pain.

I'm crying from the shame. From understanding I'm truly disturbed. Something in me is broken and my kidnapper isn't even the one who broke it. He just took advantage of it. He found the vile piece of me and exposed it.

It's heartbreaking when you're forced to see who you truly are.

A sob wracks my chest as I feel him move around, and the flash comes right in front of my face again. I look down.

"Please." I sniffle as more tears run down my face. "Just stop."

"Have you had enough, Elisabeth?"

Scrunching my eyes shut, I nod, unable to stop the flood.

"Do you want your dad to give us the money so we can let you go?"

"Please," I weep. I can't control my breathing anymore. The need to go home is too intense. I just want out of his clutches.

"Please, what?" His hard voice forces more tears out of me.

"Please, Dad, give them the money," I say to the camera. "I want to go home." Another sob shatters through me, and I struggle to breathe more air into my lungs.

The flash turns off and his hand comes to my damp hair. Water, cum, sweat. I feel utterly disgusting, but still, he strokes me like he doesn't care. "Well done, baby," he says softly. "You've been a very good girl. This will be over soon."

I hate the way he calls me baby. Like he's entitled to it now that he was the first man to ever touch me.

"Please, don't send this to my dad."

His hand comes to wipe some of his cum on my face, rubbing it on my lips and making his eyes light up.

"Don't worry, the moment he sees your tits, he'll give it to someone else to watch. No father wants to witness what we did to you."

He finally lets me go. As he stands up, I feel something around my ankles.

"What are you doing?" I snap in alarm as I twist again. Two strong hands immobilize my legs while another pair slides plastic around my ankles. They tighten the zip ties until they're digging into my skin.

"Can't risk you trying to escape again when we're so close to the goal, can we?" the guy tying my ankles says.

The leader gives the phone to the fourth one. "Send it with the note: *Four hours before we do worse to her.*"

I whimper at his words. I can't do this again. I need out.

They all head toward the door and lock it behind them.

I need this to be over.

I know the moment they're going to walk back into the room, because my eyes haven't left the clock. Dread seeps through my bones when I see three hours and fifty-nine minutes turn into four hours, making it six p.m.

I feel beaten. Abandoned.

If they're back, my father hasn't given them the money. I've never had a good relationship with him. Then again, my dad has always been a bit obsessive over me. He loves me in his own strange way. I'm his only child, his miracle. He expects anything and everything from me, and I must never disappoint. The fact that he hasn't rescued me or paid the ransom has taken a toll on my mind.

What about my mom? She must be in a state of panic, broken.

Why am I still here?

My dad knows how to find me. If he isn't here, it's because he doesn't want anyone to know his dirty secret. He doesn't want anyone to know he tracks his daughter like a crazy man.

Darkness envelops the room again. A day has passed since I've been taken, and things are only worsening.

How long until I'm broken beyond repair?

I already know I'll never be the same person again. Joyful Alex is gone. The girl who goes on dates with her boyfriend, who wins cheerleading competitions, and who rules Stoneview Prep with her friends is gone.

Now I'm the whore who came when her kidnapper told her to. My dad will know. I can't imagine the disappointment.

How can I ever live a normal life again?

"Who wants to play some more?" their leader taunts me as they walk in. I curl more tightly in on myself, remaining silent.

My ankles are hurting now. Not as much as my bleeding wrists, though it's slowly becoming unbearable too. I can't feel my toes, and I'm not sure if it's from the cold or the zip ties cutting the blood flow.

He comes to squat next to me, pushing my dirty hair away from my face. "How are you, Elisabeth?"

"Thirsty," I croak out. I've already pissed myself and come to the realization I wasn't the first person they've tortured in this room. No one appeared when I screamed that I needed the bathroom. Not after I tried to run the first time.

I'm dehydrated, coughing from the dryness in my throat.

"Do you want water?"

I nod slowly, my energy wholly depleted. Silently, he gets back up. A second later, freezing liquid crashes all over my body.

I gasp, crying out as I roll around.

"Gotta clean you, baby. You pissed all over yourself and it stinks in here."

Another full bucket is spilled all over me.

"Stop!" I shriek.

"It's water. You asked for it."

Who becomes that evil in life? And why am I the one who has to suffer from it?

A phone rings in the room. It's not the one he's been using to contact my dad because I can see it in the hand of another one of the men.

The leader pulls the different phone out of his pocket and puts it to his ear. That must be his personal one.

He doesn't talk, but I notice the way his body tenses.

"When?" he says. His mouth twists and his gaze snaps to mine. Fear grips me when I see the fury rising in his eyes. "Don't worry, they won't find anything. Thanks for letting me know."

He hangs up and strides back to me. "How?" he hisses in my face. He grabs me by the throat and drags me up until I'm sitting with my back against the wall.

"I've just been told there are six FBI police cars and two Swat trucks entering our town. How?"

Hope blossoms in my chest. They found me. They're coming. A smile spreads on my lips and his grip on my throat tightens.

"This entire fucking house will be gone by the time they arrive. I've got enough men on the streets to slow them down and for me to torture and kill you before they reach this place. So be smart, Elisabeth, and tell me how they found you."

I cough from the pressure on my throat and push words out. "Enjoy prison, asshole."

He drags me to the side and slams me on the floor. "Answer the fucking question or die. So close to freedom? That would be a shame."

He straddles me and uses both hands to strangle me. The panic is back when I feel my head swimming. Everything tilts as my vision narrows. I can't talk. So how does he expect me to tell him?

My eyes wildly stare down as I feel my oxygen run out. I do it again, and again, trying to make him understand, and I see the moment he gets I'm pointing at the necklace he's currently crushing.

"Fuck!" he snaps as he lets go of me. He grabs the heart locket and rips it off me. "Rich assholes. She's being fucking tracked!"

I'm desperately gulping air as he throws the necklace on the floor and destroys it with his boot.

"We're outta here," he growls.

And just like that, they're gone.

For good this time.

I hear a ruckus downstairs. They didn't close the door and I can hear a few of them laughing. They're so sure they won't get caught. And I bet that's true.

The house goes quiet and long minutes pass, but I'm not scared anymore. I'm going to be rescued. I've always hated home, but I've never wanted to return so badly.

I'm at peace until a smell I didn't expect reaches me.

Smoke.

Forcing myself to listen past my rising heartbeat, I hear crackling downstairs. And when my eyes start to sting, I understand.

Fire.

They set the place on fire.

For the first time since this whole thing started, I'm not so sure I will survive.

"No," I cry out. After surviving this man for almost twenty hours, I'm going to die from carbon monoxide poisoning.

"Help!" I scream. "Help!"

Thick smoke starts to make its way into the room and the fear doubles. I'm on the floor, my wrists and ankles bound, but I still begin to crawl across the room and to the only window. It's boarded up, but I'm hoping there's enough air coming through.

"Help! Please! I'm stuck in here!" A sob makes me tremble as the tears come back.

I don't want to die. I am a few months away from moving away to college. My life hasn't even started.

Pushing my back against the wall, I manage to slide up. I hop back a step before throwing myself against the board. "Please, help me!"

I bounce and fall back onto the floor, first on my wrists

which take most of the crash and then my shoulder. The pain that radiates makes me scream harder.

I struggle to take a breath through the agony. Something's wrong. Something's broken, and I wail to the empty house.

"Please," I cough, even though no one will hear me. I can barely hear myself anymore. I can't open my eyes. The smoke is too much. "Help me..."

There's a loud noise beside me, but I can feel myself slipping into the darkness.

Two arms grab me, keeping me conscious. The ache from my shoulder and all the way to my left wrist is keeping me alive.

"I got you."

It's his voice.

The leader.

Brown eyes. Plump lips. Three thick scars.

I mustn't forget.

The smoke becomes thicker, and burning heat blankets us. I bury my head against his chest as I feel him starting to run.

"Hold on. We're almost there."

The moment I can drag fresh air into my lungs, I choke on it. I cough until I can't breathe anymore. My head is spinning, the world around me blurring.

He puts me down on the asphalt. I think we're on the other side of the street now. I catch the sound of sirens in the distance.

My eyes squint open as I feel his hand stroking my hair. "You're gonna be okay. It's all over now."

He's still wearing his ski mask, but I recognize his voice and his eyes. The browns are beautiful despite the monster he is.

34

I try to look around, except all I see are ashes and the gray sky. I turn my head toward him. There are some trees to my right and an abandoned building.

"W-where..." I rasp.

"I hope you enjoyed your stay on the North Shore, Elisabeth. Come back anytime."

The sirens grow louder, and he's gone just before everything goes black.

1

ALEXANDRA

Seven months later...

"*Hi, baby!*" Peach's voice resonates loudly on the other side of the line. In the background, I hear. "*When is she getting here!*" That'll be my other best friend, Ella.

"Hey," I giggle into the phone. "I'm just packing the last box into the truck. I'll be another hour or so, probably."

"*Alex!*" Peach whines. "*Why are you so slow? We've been here since ten a.m. It's almost three, and we're still waiting for you. Seriously, how much stuff did you pack?*"

I look around my room, and then at the last box our butler still has to put in the car. "Honestly, not even that much. I was waiting for my parents to get home so I could say goodbye. They're here now."

"*Who cares about them right now? You're going to college! We're not even that far.*"

It's true. Silver Falls University is less than a forty-minute drive from Stoneview. It's basically a continuation of our prep school. It's one of the best private colleges on the East Coast, and the pricey tuition fees make it as elitist as our town. Most Stoneview Prep students end up there because it's so close to the billionaire town, yet it gives us a sense of independence.

SFU is on the south bank of Silver Falls and it's an easy drive from here. I didn't really need to wait for my parents, but I would rather that than receive an incendiary text from my dad later.

I walk to my desk to grab my purse and look at the Polaroid pictures I left. I have a hundred and three of them exactly, and I couldn't take them all. My parents gifted me the Polaroid camera, and I've been taking one picture a month, every single month, since I turned ten. I'm no artist, but I'm a lover of life. Every month gets a special memory I capture in a picture.

I sigh as I look at the stack I left on my desk. "Sorry, guys." I grab the shoebox on my desk and start putting them in there, a nostalgic smile on my face as I go through all of them.

My heart stops when I grab the one from February.

I wish I'd taken a different picture to represent my birthday month. This one marks the day my life changed forever. I gulp as I look at Chester and myself, grinning. It was taken only a few hours before the nightmare.

A shiver runs down my spine and I shake my head. Chester and I weren't meant to last. Sadly, it took being kidnapped and assaulted to come to this conclusion, but we would have broken up one way or another. We're better as friends, and we're both going to SFU, so we have many more years of fun together. Just not as a couple.

He could never give me what I needed.

No one can.

Except your kidnapper. That's someone you never stop touching yourself to.

I shut down the irrational voice in my head and take a deep breath.

"Miss Alex," a voice rises behind me, startling me.

"Yes?" I ask as I put the picture in the shoebox along with the others.

"May I take the last box to the car?" Jordan asks. My butler has seen me grow, and it's making me feel emotional to leave him behind. My mother never took care of me, while my father only cares about the image I bring to this family. Jordan likes me for me.

"Yes, please." I smile as I turn around. I undo the tight bun in my hair and let it fall to my waist.

"Excited?" he asks as he squats to grab the box.

"Does scared count as excited?" I chuckle.

"It does." He winks at me as he stands back up. "I'll be outside. Your father is waiting for you in his study."

My stomach recoils as I fake a smile. "Thanks for letting me know." He leaves the room and I follow him, although he goes for the front door when we're down the stairs while I take a left toward my father's study.

"Knock, knock," I fake a cheery voice as I push the door open.

"Alex," my father calls in his serious tone. "Come here." My eye twitches but I keep the grin on my face, bracing myself for a life lesson, or two.

I walk to his desk and sit in front of him like a kid who's been called to the principal's office.

"God," he chuckles to himself before getting up and walking to the globe that serves as an alcohol cabinet. He pulls out an old whiskey and pours it into a tumbler. "My daughter is off to college. I'm starting to feel old."

My father has always been a handsome man. Women fall over at his feet constantly. My mother wasn't his first wife. She's the young, second one. His gray hair is peppered with whatever is left of the black he used to have. He's always clean-shaven, wearing perfectly tailored suits and an expensive watch from his collection of Rolexes and others. He doesn't look his sixty years of age one bit, but I can only imagine what it's like to see your only baby off to college.

He walks back to his chair and takes a sip of whiskey before leaning back.

"You're lucky you got into Silver Falls University, Alexandra. I don't think you worked as hard as you should have, but I'm glad they accepted your application. Maybe our name had to do with it. I don't know."

He swirls the whiskey in the glass as I clench my jaw. Or maybe it was because of my outstanding GPA, or the fact that I was my year's valedictorian. The volunteering? My compelling resume? Perhaps the great essays, recommendations, and letters of application.

No, according to him, it's my name and *luck*.

"The point is," he keeps going, "you got in." He takes another sip, puts the glass down, and leans toward me, aiming his finger in my direction. "You're going to work hard, Alexandra. I am not going to accept you bringing any shame to this family. It's embarrassing enough you can't compete in any sports anymore."

I look down at my left wrist and the scar that goes from there to the inside of my forearm. It's not like I chose to stop competing. I was great at swimming and a nimble cheerleader. Not possible anymore since my birthday.

I nod and tuck my dirty blonde hair behind my ear. "Of course, Dad. That's why I'm going."

"I know your mom wants you to join the sorority she

was a part of. I agree, as it brings valuable connections, but you will behave yourself. No drinking, no boys, no losing sight of goals. Work, Alexandra. That's the only thing that pays."

"Yes, Dad."

"Have you done the required reading? The essays your tutors gave you? I've not seen any of that on my desk."

"You were away for work," I tell him. "I've done them all."

Spelling bees, private tutors, math summer camps, English literature retreats. I've done it all. I even tried drawing and painting. My mother's family is known for their grandfather being a renowned painter. She's an amazing artist herself and owns the only art gallery in Stoneview. She tried to teach me as a kid, and those were our best times together. However, that stopped when my dad realized I was having too much fun and lacked talent. No fun is ever allowed in the Delacroix house. No rewards come without hard work. In fact, no rewards ever come, no matter what. Never a well done or a great job. Even less a desperately needed *I'm proud of you.*

"Come here, show me your wrist." He turns in his chair as I stand up and round his desk.

His fingers come to my right wrist and toy with the diamond bracelet he gave me the day after my eighteenth birthday. He couldn't stand that my tracking necklace had been broken and stolen.

There's a silver heart locket attached to this bracelet too. He undoes it and slides it off my wrist. My eyebrows lift from the shock.

Is he going to let me go to college without it? The hope of freedom blooms in my chest as the corner of my lips tips up. "Dad," I exhale. "Thank y—"

"I've thought about your request to not have your bodyguard come with you to college."

"Really?" I can feel my eyes lighting up with hope. Everyone in my family has a personal bodyguard. My mother has Vincent, who is one of the politest and most handsome men I know. I have Julian, who is on the older side but still perfectly good at his job. He doesn't stay at home like Vincent, but he does come with me everywhere I go. And my father has three. Two with him at all times, and another who has all his work passwords, codes to safes, and other secrets like that. That's in case something happens to Dad.

I've been begging my father all summer to let me go to college without Julian. Silver Falls University is the safest college in the country. It's completely private, gated, and security drives around campus at all times. I probably wouldn't be the only person on campus with a bodyguard. Most of the students from SFU are from influential families at risk of being targeted. But having someone follow you everywhere is so suffocating, especially when I know they report everything to my father.

"Yes, really," my dad confirms. "I will let you move away from home without Julian. On one condition."

Anything! I scream so loudly in my mind I'm sure he can hear it.

He puts my bracelet on his desk, tracing the circle of diamonds with the tip of his index fingers.

"I noticed you keep forgetting to charge this one." His low voice forces the smile off my face quickly.

"Oh," I stammer. "I just...I just forget."

I just forget to charge the tracker so I can have some time away from you and your insane obsession.

"It's unacceptable behavior, Alexandra. And extremely

disappointing." He doesn't need to raise his voice to make me feel like a scolded child. That's the kind of power he has over me.

"I'm sorry," I whisper as my gaze falls to my feet.

"College is a whole new life experience. Anything could happen to you."

Something already happened to me.

He can read my answer in my eyes, despite my best efforts to hide it.

"We have to be twice as careful."

"Yes, Dad," I agree meekly.

He twists in his chair and grabs something on his desk. "That's why I got you this new one." He shows me the gold bracelet in his hand. I recognize the kind right away. It's the "Love Collection" by one of my favorite jewelers. This one is paved with diamonds on the sturdy cuff. He's got a small jewelry-type screwdriver on the desk and takes hold of it as well.

"See, I need to unlock it with this," he tells me condescendingly. He unlocks it and grips my wrist again. "It's the only tool that can be used." He closes the cuff around it, and I startle at how tight it is. A little more, and it would cut the blood flow.

"It's a bit small." My gaze goes to his, and hard eyes stare back at me.

"It's perfect. I know your size. That way you can't slide it off." He locks it with the screwdriver, and the reality falls onto me.

I can't unlock it or take it off. And I doubt he's going to give me that screwdriver.

"Dad," I murmur shyly. "This isn't necessary. We've learned from experience that it doesn't matter if you know where I am at all times. Something can still happen."

He ignores my pleas and keeps talking. "This one has a long-lasting battery. Months. And when it's almost out, I get a notification on my phone. The tracker is much smaller, so you don't need a locket or anything. It's more discreet."

"Dad, please. This is too much."

His hand slams on his desk, making me jump back. "For God's sake, Alexandra. I don't know many eighteen-year-olds who would complain so much when their father gifts them a forty-thousand-dollar bracelet." His voice is even, but the gesture is enough.

"I'm sorry," I finally comply.

"That's what I like to hear. You've been spoiled rotten your entire life. A bit of gratitude would do you well. This is the condition. You always keep this bracelet on, and you won't have to take Julian with you."

"I understand." My lips break into a tight smile. "Thank you."

"Do you have time for one game before you leave?"

I should be getting to my friends, but the truth is, our games are the only time I enjoy with my dad. So I nod. "Just one."

My dad has always been protective of me. There is no other way to put it. Over me, my brain, my body. It's not so much that he's worried about *me* but what I represent. Him.

If I fail classes, it's a reflection on him. If I sleep around, it's because he didn't raise me right. If I'm not pretty, polite, lady-like, intelligent. This is all Senator Delacroix's legacy. I must never mess it up. I must never disappoint.

I'm used to it, and growing up the way I did, it never bothered me.

But then came the tracker. I fought tooth and nail against it. Not only because it's completely insane but because he wanted to put it on my grandmother's locket. I'd had this necklace since I was a baby, wore it all the time. He had it torn apart and put back together just so he could follow me everywhere. My mom just went with it like she does with everything. She's not a leader or a fighter. She likes being taken care of. She likes someone to take charge and for her to sit back and relax. She's never had to work a day in her life, never had to fight for anything. Everything was always handed to her on a silver platter, and she couldn't care less that Dad married her for her name and money.

Because of that stupid tracker, my grandma's necklace was ripped off of me, broken, and destroyed in a fire. But just like everything else, I got used to it. I got used to how protective he is, to the pressure, to the extra work I constantly have to do, and to having to wear a mask around everyone so I can pass as the perfect daughter.

Our games have always been the only way for me to pretend he cares about me, not just how I make him look. They're games. Games are fun.

"Alright," he looks up, racking his brain for the first word. "What does *prudhomme* mean?"

"A trustworthy citizen. Unless you're spelling it p.r.u.d. apostrophe h.o.m.m.e. Then it's the labor court where disputes between management and workers are settled."

He nods. When I'm right, I don't hear anything from him. Only when I'm wrong. "What is noctambulism?"

"Sleepwalking." *Easy.*

"Origin of the word, Alexandra," he asks, unimpressed, as if I should have known to add it.

"It comes from noctambulation. Nocti comes from the Latin *nox*, which means night. Ambulation comes from *ambulationem* from the past participle stem of *ambulare*, which means to walk."

45

He scratches his cheek, the rough sound of nails against an invisible, slowly growing stubble he will have to get rid of again tomorrow morning. "Antipode?"

I open my mouth and close it again. I tuck my hair behind my ears before looking down. "Um..."

"*Um,* is not an answer."

I bring my index to my hairline, rubbing where the skin meets the soft strands. "I know, I'm thinking."

And here comes the most hated response he always gives me. "You shouldn't think about these answers, they should be instinctive. *Thinking* is for essays and debates. Definitions require no thinking at all."

I pinch my lips and look down as I bring my hands in front of me, twisting my fingers.

"Disappointing," he concludes gravely.

"I'm sorry." I'm not sure I really am. However the response is automatic.

"Instead of being sorry, be more intelligent."

There's a lump in my throat as I nod silently. I hate disappointing him.

"You should get going."

I step away, not expecting a kiss or a good luck from him. Moments later, I'm by the door when he calls me back.

"And Alex..." I turn around, foolishly hoping he will say something nice to me, or maybe that he'll miss me. "I hope you packed your dictionary. God knows you need it."

I swallow the lump in my throat and nod. "I did," I murmur, walking out of his office. Like every time I step away from him, I feel my shoulders relax as if I can finally take a deep breath.

And people wonder why I'm a know-it-all.

2

ALEXANDRA

Not Another Rockstar – Maisie Peters

"Alex, are you sure you're okay to drive on your own? Can't Dad drive you?" my mom insists as I get into my car. It's a two-seater sports car, a Porsche 718 Cayman, so Jordan already left with all my boxes in the big car.

"Mom," I groan. "I'm a big girl, come on." I get in the car, but she stops me from closing the door.

"Honey, you didn't even hug me goodbye."

"Sorry," I huff. I get back out and hug her tightly. I get my beautiful blonde locks from my mother, and I bury my face in hers, holding her against me. She's got beautiful blue eyes, though, and I get the hazel in mine from my dad.

We separate, and I'm out of our driveway in a split second. Unsure how to get to SFU, I turn the GPS on and just keep going.

Almost forty minutes later, I'm finally entering Silver Falls when Ella calls me.

"You've reached your best friend in the whole world," I cheer as I press the green key on my car screen.

"*Ugh, Peach is killing me. Where are you?*"

I look down at the GPS and my brows furrow. "Uh, I just entered Silver Falls, but it says another twenty-five minutes? Maybe there's traffic."

"*There's some road work,*" my friend explains. "*Your GPS might fuck up, but there are some detour signs.*"

"This is so long. I want to be there already," I complain.

"*So, the uniforms are worse than Stoneview Prep, but Peach is certain the skirts are shorter. Can you explain to her that's just dumb thinking?*"

A laugh escapes me, and I shake my head. Because SFU is affiliated with Stoneview Preparatory School, it's the only university in the U.S. that has a strict dress code, aka a uniform. The college has such a respectable reputation that it doesn't deter any of us from applying and dying to get in.

"*It's weird to see the postgrads walking around in day clothes while we have to wear the uniform,*" Ella continues.

I drive onto a street I don't know and look around. I've never been this way and my GPS keeps trying to send me back to the closed road.

"*We bumped into some Xi Epsilon girls, by the way. If we don't all get in, I'm burning their house down.*"

I see a temporary sign that says *diversion* and indicate left to follow it.

"I'm so confused," I murmur to myself.

"*I mean, you're going to get in anyway because of your dad. But my dad is currently bringing himself all sorts of unwanted attention.*"

"Wait, Ella," I say, peering around me. "I'm completely lost."

There are no more detour signs, and I have no idea where to go. The road stretches out in front of me, and I don't know if I should turn left or right at any point.

"*Are you on the main road?*"

"I think I'm on the road that leads to the Silver Snake River, though that's not the way to SFU. The campus is much closer to the falls, isn't it?"

"*Yeah, but all the roads leading to the falls are closed because of the flooding last week. They're redoing them. Just keep going to the river and you'll see the diversion sign again.*"

Taking a deep breath, I keep driving. I just told my mom I was a big girl, and now I'm panicking because I can't find my way around Silver Falls. I'm moving here, and I'm bound to get lost at some point.

By the end of the road, I finally notice the diversion and my heartbeat calms. I take a left, the opposite way to where I'd assume SFU is located.

"This is the worst diversion in the history of Silver Falls," I groan. "I just want to get there."

"*Don't sweat it. We're excited to see you but keep driving safely.*" The sound of her voice lowers as she seems to pull away from the phone. Then she talks to me again. "*Peach says she just got an alert on her phone saying they closed another road so the way to campus might have changed from this morning.*"

Traffic slows down and I notice the sign directing me right. I pull away from the line of cars, wondering why everyone is sticking to the left when there's clearly a quicker way to the right. Someone beeps at me, and I look their way. A lady with her kids in the car shakes her head at me.

I'm confused; I didn't do anything wrong.

"*Everything okay?*"

"I don't know. People are being weird, I swear."

"*Idiots don't deal well with changes.*" She pauses, and I hear her talk to Peach. "*She's fine, don't worry. Right, Alex? You're feeling alright?*" I love my friends; they know I've had

49

issues being alone in the last few months. I believe Peach and Ella are starting to worry I'm going to have a panic attack, although I feel fine now. I'm not worried, just eager to get to them.

The men who held me hostage were never caught. They were from the North Shore, after all. Criminals there know their town inside out. They escaped, and I never saw their faces. Their leader had been sure to wash his cum off me with those buckets of water, and there was no DNA to find.

This is what scares me the most. The reason for the panic attacks. They could come back anytime. I wake up at night in sweats because I can swear I heard someone enter the house or a shadow walk past my bed.

College will change that. Being away from my house will help.

I indicate right to follow the sign.

"Yeah, I'm totally fine. People are all queuing and causing traffic when they could just take the way I'm taking right—"

I slam on the brakes, my heart jumping to my throat. "Oh my God," I gasp.

"What's wrong?"

The sign in front of me forces the hair at the back of my neck to stand with attention.

YOU ARE ENTERING
SILVER FALLS
NORTH SHORE

I glance around me, noticing I'm on the red truss bridge that leads to the North Shore of Silver Falls. How did I end up here? In less than ten seconds, cold sweats dampen my skin from my neck to my lower back.

No one goes there. The North Shore belongs to dangerous criminals. It belongs to the two crews that rule it, and no one dares enter that part of town.

I've only been once. When *they* took me.

Some girls in Stoneview would die to be invited to their parties. They wanted to leave the rich parties behind and go with the bad boys from the North Shore. Some of them even went in their uniforms because they wanted to flaunt to the North Shore guys that they went to Stoneview Prep. My dad wouldn't even let me go to parties in Stoneview, let alone on the North Shore.

That's the only thing I'm grateful for regarding his controlling behavior. After that fateful night, I never wanted to be anywhere near this part of Silver Falls.

And now I'm on the bridge that leads right to it.

"*Alex, what is going on?*"

"I-I..." My heart starts beating loudly in my ears. "Ella," I panic.

I need to do a U-turn, but this bridge is so tight, it's impossible. I can drive to the end and just turn around there. I look in my rearview mirror and a small whimper escapes me. They've blocked the other way and made the bridge a one-way system for the time being.

"*Alex, talk to me, babe.*"

"I'm on the bridge to the North Shore. The sign...I don't understand."

Someone beeps behind me before circling around me at a dangerous speed.

"What do I do?" I panic. "I can't." I shake my head even though she can't see me. "Ella, I can't go there."

"*It's okay, take a deep breath. Can you turn around?*"

"They made it one way."

"*Alright, that means you just have to cross the town and go out from the other side. That's okay. You can do it. Just keep breathing.*"

"I can't breathe!" I practically shout.

"*You can, babe. You just need to focus on one thing at a time. You know how it works. Build a pearl necklace one pearl at a time.*"

I attempt a deep breath, my lips trembling as I do so. Ella has this technique to deal with anxiety that often works on her and sometimes on me. She pretends she's building a pearl necklace and that each pearl is a small task. One pearl at a time, and before you know it, you'll have a whole necklace.

"*What's the next pearl?*" my best friend asks softly.

"To...to get to the other side of the bridge," I murmur. "But I can't do it."

"*It's dangerous to stop on the bridge, Alex. Anyone could be coming full speed and not see you. I think the next pearl is taking the foot off the brake and pressing the gas pedal. Can you do that for me?*"

Slowly, I lift my foot off the brake pedal and start moving again. "Yeah, okay." I nod to myself and start driving to the other side of the bridge. Passing the sign makes me feel sick. Is that the way they took me when I was unconscious? They must have. It's the quickest way to go from Stoneview to their town.

Quickly, the truss bridge turns into the North Shore. There are no houses on that side of the river. Only a road and the woods that line the bank.

"*Are you by the woods?*" Ella questions in a calm voice.

"I am, yeah."

"*Okay, then the next pearl is to turn right. Don't take the road that goes through the woods.*"

"Wouldn't the woods be quicker to cross town?"

"*It's better to go the long way.*"

"I don't want to go the long way, El's," I panic.

"*I know, sweetie, but the main roads are safer. We never know what really happens in those woods. Just take the long way. Turn right.*"

Now scared of the woods, as much as I'm scared of the rest of this town, I decide to listen to my friend and avoid them.

"Okay, okay." I turn right and drive along the river until the road leads left and into town.

Everything here is the opposite of Stoneview. Rundown houses and abandoned buildings line the road. I stick out like a sore thumb in my expensive sports car. Stoneview truly is a bubble. We move from our billionaire town to SFU, avoiding real life and pretending society is only about us. It's only because I'm being confronted by poverty that a tinge of guilt runs through my stomach. We are so privileged in everything, and at no point do we ever think of what's outside our luxurious world.

Girls in our town think of coming here as a game. They like to play with fire and get close to the criminals, knowing perfectly they would never be able to handle a third of what they go through here.

I gulp when a group of men and women stare at me as I drive past them. One of the girls cocks an eyebrow and shakes her head.

I look exactly like I feel: lost.

"*How are you holding up?*"

Ella's voice startles me. I forgot she was there.

"I'm okay," I lie. "My GPS has found its way again. It's

taking me to the other side of town, and then I guess I'll get on the highway back to the entrance of Silver Falls."

"Perfect. We'll stay with you, Alex. Everything's fine."

"We love you, Alex," Peach shouts in the background. *"You're the strongest."*

"I love you too, guys." A soft smile spreads on my lips. "Tell me about our apartment," I ask as I look at the road ahead. North Shore is just a small part of Silver Falls. It's not a big deal, which means I don't have to be so scared.

I'm not going to talk to anyone. I'm just crossing in my car. Everything is fine.

"Is it that bad?" I laugh at their silence. "We're paying tons of money for this college. They better have put us in a great apartment."

The lack of response makes me check my phone. The screen is black.

"Girls?" I tap my screen and my heart drops.

My phone's dead. The GPS is gone, and so are the girls.

"It's okay," I try to say cheerily. "It's fine. I'll just put on the car's GPS."

I type *Silver Falls University* on my car's GPS and keep going straight as it calculates.

"Turn around as soon as you can," the car voices out.

"No, the road is one way, you stupid thing," I groan. It's trying to make me go back to the bridge.

I keep going forward, but I can only go left or right when I reach a crossroads. The GPS is telling me to do a U-turn and go back to where I came from.

"Are you for real? Just...ugh," I sigh.

My phone needs to charge, except my charger is somewhere in my boxes.

Jordan has probably arrived at SFU by now.

Not knowing where to go, I turn right. The GPS

calculates the route again, and I watch as it reroutes me back to the bridge.

"Come on," I grunt. This, right here, is why I never use this thing. It's never up to date.

Giving up on trying to find my way, I exit the road into the first parking lot. There's a convenience store here, so maybe I can buy a charger or ask them if I can charge my phone.

I will buy a whole new phone if that's what it takes to get me to leave this godforsaken town.

I park and turn the ignition off, but my hands go back to the steering wheel.

Come on, Alex. You can do this.

Instead of letting go of the wheel, my grip tightens.

What if I see someone in there?

What if they attack me?

Kidnap me?

Take me back to that house?

Cold sweats run down my spine, my muscles spasming as my throat closes.

One pearl at a time.

Just open the car door.

I let go of the wheel and open my door. Taking another deep breath, I get out. There's no one in the parking lot and that already makes me feel a little better. Walking to the store, I push the door open, startling slightly when an electronic bell rings.

It's the kind of store you find at a gas station. They probably have everything in here. There's a large man behind a counter. He's drinking from a can of Pepsi as his gaze scans me up and down.

I feel like I have *Stoneview Rich Bitch* written all over my face and that's a sure way to be hated around here. If not that, then at least severely unwelcomed. My mind races, thinking of everything I wish I didn't have on me right now. I'm in denim shorts and a white silk blouse, but it's clear they're the designer type. Not only that, but I'm wearing Jimmy Choo sneakers that I know for certain I paid over five hundred dollars for. My entire outfit is probably more than this man earns in a month, without even counting the forty-grand bracelet my dad forces me to wear. While I would fit in perfectly at SFU, it's awakening how unnecessary it is to wear these things when confronted with someone who couldn't afford them.

I force a weak *hello* past my throat, though I don't know if he hears it. If he does, he clearly doesn't care. I watch his throat work for a few seconds as he gulps down his Pepsi, and I disappear into an aisle where he can't see me. It's only me in here, and I hurry to the small electronics section at the back corner. I look for my phone charger but can't seem to find it. Wanting to check if it fits with the only chargers they have here, I tap my pockets to find my phone.

But it's not there.

I left it in the car.

Anxiety makes me self-sabotage, and I hate myself for it. I throw my head back, huffing and trying to calm myself. That's when I notice my charger on the top shelf.

Thank God.

I go on my toes to grab it, but I can't quite reach. It's not like I'm a small girl, but damn, why would they put it so high?

A few other chargers fall off as I try to grab the box I need, causing me to let out a loud sigh.

"Come on," I huff.

I freeze when I feel a presence behind me. I watch helplessly as a large hand appears, the fingers grazing the back of mine until they reach the box, grab it, and disappear.

Time stops for a split second. I feel someone's breath at the back of my neck, their body practically touching mine, and I could swear that I feel them inhale the perfume I sprayed on this morning. A shiver descends down my spine until it turns into a full-on tremble.

Close.

Too close.

I press myself against the shelves, and they must sense my discomfort because they finally take a step back. I flip around instantly, my blonde hair slapping against my face, as my breath becomes shallow.

It stops altogether when I face the handsome man in front of me. I press my back against the shelves, looking up at his beautiful face. His sharp jaw is relaxed, and I bet it could still cut glass right now. It's not what makes my heart speed up, though. His eyelashes are so long, I bet every woman in his vicinity is not only jealous of them but would also fall in love instantly. It's such a stark contrast with the rest of him. He's tall, all muscles under his simple white t-shirt. It's not even tight—he clearly doesn't try to get a small size just to show his muscles underneath—but it still feels like the material is forced to accommodate his large limbs. I'm afraid I will start drooling if I don't stop looking at his broad shoulders, so I snap my gaze back up.

His eyes are a light brown, almost a terracotta hue that makes them hard to stare at. How can such a thick color be so piercing? They narrow in the slightest, observing me with an intensity that makes me squirm. I realize I'm staring when they relax and light up with amusement. I feel a blush come over me, aware that my porcelain skin flushes easily. I bet his never does. He's a bronze tone that makes him look like a Spartan warrior.

I try to take a step back, the feeling of embarrassment slightly overwhelming, but I'm quickly reminded of my own body against the shelves. Sensing my need for space, he takes several steps back.

He raises the small package of the charger between us. "Is this what you wanted?"

I feel my eyes widen. Yes, of course, the charger. That's why I'm here. The sudden reminder of where I am and why is like a bucket of cold water being poured all over me. My lungs beg for a sharp inhale, and my mouth obeys. I nod, not finding my voice, and extend my arm to grab the small box. He's taken enough steps back that I can't quite reach it. If I want it, I have to move away from where I'm standing, but I feel strangely safe with my back against something.

He senses my hesitation and shakes his head. "You're not from around here."

It's not a question since it's probably written all over my face, but I nod anyway.

"Are you lost or something?"

He doesn't look like a threat, but my heart is going crazy from his captivating presence and the state of heightened anxiety I've been in. I'm hesitant to respond. If I say yes, he could take advantage of me. If I say no...I can't say no because it's evidently a lie.

"I'm not lost," I finally say with as much confidence as I can muster. "I was crossing town and my phone died. I'm just getting a charger and I'll be on my way."

He looks me up and down. "Ah," he nods. "The traffic diversion."

I feel my eyebrows rising before I get my facial expression under control. He sees my surprise anyway and adds, "You're not the first person who got lost on the North Shore today. I wouldn't hang around for longer than you need."

Is that a threat? A warning? Is he helping or taunting me?

"Can I have the charger?" I extend my hand again. This time I take a step toward him.

He lets me grab the box, but he doesn't let go.

He looks at me unimpressed. He doesn't seem like the kind of guy who ever has fun. "I didn't hear the magic word. I did grab it for you."

I take a deep breath, trying to calm the anxiety.

"Please." My voice is barely audible, and he looks at me with pity when he lets go of the box, and I pull it to me.

I push past him and hurry to the register.

He's right behind me, a pack of candy in his hand, however I decide to ignore him. The cashier eyes my black Amex, and I wonder if I should have paid cash. I mumble a thank you and look down as I hear the guy who helped me ask for a pack of cigarettes and a lighter.

The moment I exit, I stare at the empty parking lot in confusion. It only lasts until reality hits me.

My car is gone.

"What the hell?" I gasp as I walk around the lot. I don't know why I'm doing this. There are only two cars parked, and neither of them is mine. I stop at the spot I had parked earlier, and my sneakers crunch on broken glass.

"You have *got* to be kidding me."

My car is gone.

My phone's in it.

And I'm stuck on the North Shore.

A smooth voice rises behind me, enhancing the anger in me. "Welcome to the North Shore."

My teeth clench as I snap around. "Did you do this? Did you steal my car?"

He runs his tongue against his front teeth as he shakes his head. "I was in there with you."

"You were probably distracting me while your...your gang was breaking into my car," I rage, the fear of being stuck here growing in me and making me say stupid things.

His broody stare meets mine. "My gang, huh? Sounds scary." How can he keep such a straight face when uttering sarcasm?

"Stop making fun of me," I snap. "I didn't want to be here in the first place. Stupid diversion."

He takes a step forward, towering over me. "Want me to let you in on a secret, cupcake? No one on the North Shore *wants* to be here, but unlike you, we don't have a choice."

I struggle to swallow as I realize how unsympathetic my words were. "I..."

"I can lend you my phone if you want. Then you can call Mommy and Daddy to come save you from my scary gang. There's traffic because of the diversion, so make sure they take the helicopter."

My heart is out of control from the fear and embarrassment. He hands me his phone and I shake my head.

My shoulders drop. "I don't know my parents' number." God, I feel so dumb. We don't have a house phone, because who has a house phone these days, and I never learned their cell numbers. I don't know my friends' either.

"Fucking hell," he huffs like I'm a responsibility he doesn't need right now. "Alright, get in my car."

My eyes widen as I shake my head repeatedly. "No...no, no. It's okay." I look around, knowing it's anything but.

"You don't even know your parents' phone number.

You're like a baby chick just coming out of their little shell. Leaving you here on your own would essentially be murder. Come on."

I'm pretty sure he can read the terror on my face. "I'm not gonna hurt you, cupcake. Where do you need to go?"

Time stops as I try to read his eyes. This could be a trap. Once I'm in his car, he could take me anywhere. The brown swirling in his stare is unreadable, apart from a big *you're fucking annoying* written all over his face.

Out of nowhere, I smell smoke. There's no smoke. I know there's no smoke.

I'm the only one smelling it, aren't I?

I take another step back, knowing a panic attack is coming. For a second, I'm back in that burning house. I shake my head and glance around me. I'm all alone; the only chance someone will find me is if my dad checks my location. He only does it when I don't pick up his calls or ignore his texts, and he would have left me alone for the day. He'll probably check on me tonight.

Tonight is in a long time.

I don't want to be here by the time the night comes.

"Hey, are you okay?"

It's only when his voice reaches me that I realize I've been hyperventilating. I've fisted my hand and put it against my diaphragm, trying to push air out of my lungs.

I'm so close to a panic attack...and then what? Anything could happen. I lose sense of reality when I fall into the darkness. I disassociate, and my body isn't mine anymore.

I can't do this here.

"P-please," I pant.

No, no. Stay in the present, Alex.

"I want to go home..." My pleas from that night resonate in my voice and I wonder if I say them out loud.

A hand comes to the back of my neck and another to my chest. "Deep breaths." He presses on my sternum. "Push back against my hand."

The voice is smooth, deep.

"I got you."

Out of nowhere, the smell of bergamot and spices hit me; it's mixed with something earthy and warm. Something I don't recognize yet I love. The hand on my neck tightens. "Hey, hey, come back."

I take in some deep breaths, following the pressure of the hand on my chest. My vision clears again, and I twitch when I understand the man is holding me.

I gulp some much-needed air and shrug him off me.

"Wh-why are you touching me?" I say as I step to the side and turn to him.

He blinks at me. "Are you okay? You were...gone."

I struggle to find my words as I look around again. There's only one car left in the parking lot, so it must be his. A black Ford Ranger. He follows my gaze to it before peering back at me.

"Where do you need to go?" he asks calmly.

"SFU," I huff.

His lips curl, a silent '*of course the rich girl was on her way to the rich, private college*'.

"Come on." He puts a hand at the small of my back and guides me toward his truck. "Let's get you there."

I let him open the door for me. There's a step to get inside the car and he helps me up. He grabs my seatbelt, but I put my hand on his.

"I can fasten my own seatbelt," I murmur. My mouth still feels a little like cotton, but it's not what's been keeping me speechless. It's the fact that he just stopped my panic attack from getting bad. He just...*stopped it*. He just pulled me back to reality before I truly lost myself, and I don't even understand how.

He slaps my hand away and clicks the seatbelt into place. "I don't know. You're still giving me baby chick vibes right now."

A small chuckle escapes me. "Baby chick is a pleonasm. Did you know?"

He cocks an eyebrow at me, so I keep going. "Using more words than necessary to say the same thing. A chick is already a baby bird. You don't need to specify it."

"You're fucking annoying." There he finally said it.

I give him a small, knowing smile and stare ahead. I should say thank you for all of this, but something is stopping me. I'm still not convinced he wasn't involved in my car's disappearance. I'm still not sure I'm safe in his presence.

He gets into the driver's side, and in less than twenty minutes, we're leaving the North Shore by the other side of town.

"Are you feeling better?" he asks after long minutes of silence. We're on the highway now, going back toward the south of Silver Falls.

"Yes," I nod. "Um, thanks for driving me back." I look his way, but he's looking at the road.

This man is so handsome.

He's got a tattoo on the side of his neck, a Fatma hand with an eye in the palm. His prominent jaw is enhanced now that I'm seeing his profile. His long eyelashes and plump lips are so obvious, and electricity shoots from my chest to my lower stomach. I look away, feeling my cheeks warm.

"It's no problem. After all, my gang did steal your car

while I was distracting you by grabbing a phone charger for you."

The heat in my cheeks starts burning from the embarrassment. Now that he says it out loud and the anxiety of being on the North Shore has abated, I can see how ridiculous my statement was. "I'm so sorry about that. It was out of line."

The lack of response makes me babble. "I was being ignorant. I know not everyone on the North Shore is part of a gang." God, I feel so stupid right now. I really acted like the typical Stoneview girl.

My eyes dart to him again, only to catch his tongue going over his front teeth before he shakes his head. "S'alright, cupcake. Don't fret about it." His eyes still don't come to me. I'm dying to see the thick, muddy browns on me, to catch some sort of interest, but there's nothing. He doesn't look my way.

He enters Silver Falls from the south bank and finds his way around easily—no need for GPS or signs. Before I know it, the streets of Silver Falls go from middle class to absolute elite. Beautiful mansions line the streets, their manicured lawn a perfect green. Some of them adorn Greek letters, showing which fraternity or sorority they belong to. We're getting closer to SFU's main campus, and the contrast with the North Shore of Silver Falls is stark. I wonder why this guy has been here before. He clearly knows his way around.

"Do you come here often?" I ask as he takes a left and the gigantic, gated campus makes an apparition. It's recognizable by the huge castle-like red brick building that dominates over every other of the college's buildings from the top of a high hill.

He shrugs. "Sometimes. Do you know which dorm you're staying in?"

"I'm in Iris Hall."

He only nods to acknowledge my answer and keeps driving.

I look around, seeing volunteers show freshmen with their parents around. Everyone is walking by with a box or a suitcase. Plastic bins are overloaded with things, and the students are looking excited and scared at the same time.

I watch as a bunch of girls walk past our slow-driving car. Their checkered burgundy and white skirt flies in the summer wind and their laughs are carried to my ears.

They look so happy. My stomach twists with excitement. My new life is about to start and everything that used to scare me can be left at the gates of Silver Falls University.

The car stops, and I look at him. Finally, he turns to me. "Iris Hall, huh? Were the shared dorms a bit too tight for you?"

I hide my face in my hands as an awkward laugh escapes me. "The apartments are for three people and my two best friends go to SFU, too, so we thought it'd be nicer to be together."

"I'm only fucking with you, cupcake," he says. "Do you often feel the need to justify every decision you make?"

I glance back up, feeling my eyes widen at the truth he's just pinpointed.

"Uh..." I hesitate.

He shakes his head. It seems *unimpressed* is his default setting around me, and yet his face still makes me melt at how handsome he is. This man should not exist.

"Come on. I'll walk you to your door."

He exits the car before I can react. I hurry out, meeting him in front of it. "It's okay." I put my hands in front of me.

"You've done so much for me already. I insist you go back to your day now."

"You're still giving me baby chick vibes. You're gonna fall down the stairs as soon as I turn my back. Come on."

He walks to the building, and I'm forced to follow. I'm the one who lives here, after all.

There's a student in uniform by the building door. Her crisp white shirt is ironed perfectly, and she has a massive smile on her face.

"Hi!" she beams. "I'm Carly, your student rep for Iris Hall. Welcome to SFU!"

She's directing her words at me, like it's so evident that the man with me can't possibly be the one moving to SFU.

"Hi." I offer her a small smile. I know this kind of girl. I bet she moved straight from Stoneview to SFU, overly nice and welcoming so she can stab you in the back later. Her focus is solely on me, the rich-looking girl who can potentially bring her something down the line.

"I'll just need your apartment and room number. You should have received a magnetic card by mail, it gives you access to the building. All the apartments have an electronic keypad to get in and you should have received the code in your welcome pack."

A gust of wind wafts her choking perfume in my face and my mouth twists.

"I had a problem with my car and my welcome pack was in there. I can't access it right now. Do you have a spare card, maybe?"

"Oh." She gives me a fake sorry smile and tilts her head. "I'm afraid I can't do that. We're very strict when it comes to security. Let me take your name, and I'll contact the administration."

She's already looking down at the sheet attached to her

clipboard, her eyebrows drawn together and waiting for me to say my name.

"Alexandra Delacroix," I mumble.

Her head snaps up. "Oh." She pauses. Then it truly sinks in. "*Oh.*" She looks at her sheet again. "Yes. Absolutely. I'm so sorry. I'll get you a card."

Her eyes finally go to the man standing right next to me. "You must be her security. We don't usually give people access to the building after moving day, but if I take your name down and register you, I can give you a card too."

"That won't—"

I don't get to say *be necessary* since he cuts me off. "That would be great." He barely offers her the shadow of a smile that she's already melting for him.

"Of course." Her tone is so much nicer to him now that she's actually taken a second to look at him and realized how gorgeous he is. She grabs the pen she was keeping behind her ear. "Go ahead."

"Ziad Benhaim," he says calmly.

"Zi-add," she repeats. "How do you spell that?"

"Z.I.A.D."

"and Ben-hime?"

"B.E.N.H.A.I.M."

I try to keep cool, to act like I'm not interested, even though I know what's happening in my mind. There's a special place that saves his first and last name, like a little gift to keep for myself. Ziad is never going to come back here after today, but I want to keep a memory of the man who helped me.

Once we've got a card each, we follow her inside the building. It's a brand-new condo with high ceilings and marble floors. There's a man at reception who welcomes us with a smile as we walk past. Everything looks perfect.

You can taste the luxury in the air as she takes us to an elevator.

"You're in the penthouse," Carly says as we all go in. "The elevator doesn't take you directly inside the apartment, but you're still the only ones on the floor." She presses the P on the elevator, and we go up.

"So," she explains, "I don't have access to your keycode for the front door." She's addressing me, but her eyes keep going to Ziad, her eyelashes fluttering every time he looks back at her.

"It's alright. My friends are in," I snap, getting her attention back to me.

God, the woman is obsessed. We get it, he's so beautiful it feels like an opportunity not to miss looking at him.

I'm the one who's acting obsessed right now.

We reach the top, and Ziad and I walk out of the elevator. I put a hand up when Carly starts to follow. "We got it from here. Thanks."

I'm only too aware of how cold I am to her, but she annoyed me. It's senseless to think that way, and yet here I am.

The doors close and she finally disappears.

I turn to Ziad and put my hands on my hips. "Security guard?"

"What have I been doing all day?" he chides. "Been saving you like it's my fucking job." Is he reprimanding me right now? And why do I feel hot from it?

My heart skips a beat, and I take a step back, shocked by my own reaction. This is not good. I need to be away from this man.

"Look, thanks for everything, but I need to get going now."

He cocks an eyebrow and moves toward me. "You look flustered," he points out honestly.

Taking another step back, I end up against the wall in the small hallway. "W-what? Not at all. I had a long day, that's it. Now leave." I extend my arm toward the elevator.

Another step from him. His eyes stay on mine, his body too close. "It must be nice to have a name that literally opens any door for you. I'm sure any order you give is executed right away."

I can't look back at him, his gaze too intense. I look at his chest instead, but then fingers come to grab my chin and tilt my head up. I gulp and notice the corner of his lips tilting up in the slightest.

"Don't ever order me around again, Alexandra. Delacroix or not, I'll put you on your knees and make you regret it."

My eyes widen as my throat dries up. Still, the worst is how my heart drops and my stomach tightens.

"Is that clear?"

I nod, the movement barely noticeable. My entire body is melting under his stare, and I can't seem to control my muscles.

"Tell me," he insists, his voice low.

My thighs tremble as I feel them squeeze and put pressure between my legs.

"Y-yes. It's clear." I want to look away from his captivating eyes, but I can't seem to be able to.

"Now, say thank you for getting you here."

"Thank you," I whisper, barely able to let go of the little air I'm holding.

His stern face doesn't soften one bit. His thumb comes to caress the outline of my lips. "Good girl," he says just as he lets go.

Oh, God. This man is so unyielding that hearing those words from him feels like earning a trophy.

He steps away from me and presses the elevator button. It comes in seconds. He steps in and turns around. "I'll see you around, Miss Delacroix."

I'm speechless, and I can only watch as he presses the button. His strong muscular body relaxes against the wall, milk chocolate eyes taking in my entire body. He runs a hand through his thick, brown hair just as the doors close, and he disappears.

I feel hazy, wondering if any of this happened. I'm unable to move, trying to process how my body just responded to his less-than-okay behavior.

The sound of a door opening resonates to my left and I blink back to reality.

"Alex!" someone exclaims. "Where the hell have you been, girl?"

I still can't breathe properly. Ziad's presence is lingering, his effect immortal. I'm having a real *I Knew You Were Trouble* moment.

"Is she in her head trying to match a Taylor Swift song to her imagination again?" Ella's voice rings somewhere to my left. It brings me back to reality, and I laugh. My friends know me too well.

3

XI

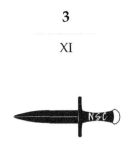

fuck this town – glaive, ericdoa

I park my car on the street, right in front of my mom's house, and cut the engine. Grabbing my phone, I text my friend Logan about today's sales before going in.

I walk in to find my stepsister, Emma, debating with her dad.

"Xi, where the fuck have you been all day? We need to talk," she snaps in my direction, pausing her current argument.

I nod a hello to her dad, Austin, before answering her. "Work." Instead of listening to what she has to say, I head to the kitchen and take in the smell of my mom's food. There's only one person in this world that can put me in a good mood: my mom.

"*Mama*," I call out to her. "It smells good." Turning away from the stove, her face brightens when she sees me.

"*Ziad, Assalamu alaikum*, I missed you. *Shalom.*" I take her in my arms before letting her return to her cooking.

Mom was born Muslim Algerian, and my dad—rest in

peace—was Jewish Moroccan. Since he passed, my mom has liked to greet us with both standards just to keep his soul alive.

"*Shalom. Wa alaikum as-salam, Mama,*" I greet her back. She gives me a big kiss on the cheek, pinching the other with her hand that smells of garlic, before tapping it.

"How's the house?" she asks right away.

A grunt is all she gets. After my dad died, we lived in our old house for a while. My mom, my brother Lik, and me. Then Mom met Austin, and we moved into his house. Although it wasn't much bigger than ours, just an extra room. Since Austin has two daughters, we still had to share a room here, and Billie and Emma shared the other.

I quickly moved out, taking over my dad's house since I could afford the rent. There's money in drugs. Dealing to Stoneview kids means I earn my share and can keep the place where I grew up. I can't keep it in a good state, but at least we still have it. It's important to my mom to keep Dad's spirit alive. It was the first house they lived in when they moved from Morocco, and it was also the house where he died.

I dip my finger in the sauce she's currently making, burning my finger but knowing it'll be worth it. As soon as I try to bring it to my mouth, she slaps the back of my hand. I still manage to get the goodness to my lips.

"Don't do that, *ya hmar,*" she calls me a donkey in Arabic like she always does when Lik or I do something stupid.

"Delicious." I smile brightly at her, and she shakes her head, glancing back at her pots.

"Go set the table," she mumbles, annoyed.

"Love you," I throw her way as I exit the small kitchen.

"Ziad!" she shouts after me. "The table!"

I close the door the best I can—the handle broke years ago, and we still need to replace it—pretending not to hear her and walk back to Emma and her dad in the living room. My stepsister is sitting on the sofa on her own, her dad in his old armchair. She doesn't seem like it, with her bleached blonde hair, extensions, and acrylic pink nails, but Emma is the head of NSC. Our crew is one of two fighting for control of the North Shore.

The North Shore Crew against the Kings of the North Shore, an ongoing war we'll never see the end of. Currently, they have the upper hand. Emma hates to hear it, but it's been just over three years since they've taken control of our town. To say I'm sick of it would be an understatement.

We're all suffering from it. Our territories get smaller every few months, and our own people are turning against us and joining their side, betraying us like never before.

Mainly? We've got no one supplying us.

A few years ago, Kayla King, the head of their gang, got herself a deal with the Bratva. The Wolves, to be exact. The ruthless organization has been supplying them with everything they need. Drugs, women, weapons. We're small gangs on the North Shore and rely on criminal organizations like the Wolves. We commit the crimes in their names. We go to prison for them. We make them more money, and we take a hefty cut while we're at it.

NSC used to have that kind of deal with the Bianco family from the Cosa Nostra. But Bianco went down and took us all down with him.

In the last three years, Emma has been doing her best to get us back on the Cosa Nostra's radar by having discussions with the Luciano family. They were the Bianco's enemies, and now that they're gone, the Lucianos are the most powerful family in the Italian criminal organization.

"Seriously," Emma tells me as I sit beside her. "Where have you been all day? Logan and Tamar said they were on a job for you but didn't see you all afternoon."

Logan works for me, stealing cars and dealing drugs, and Tamar is my closest friend. She's been for as long as I can remember. All the stupid shit I do, she's always in on it. Her and our other girl, Zara.

"Where's Zara?" I ask as I relax against my seat. I don't share a lot of things with my friends and family, and I'm reluctant to talk about who I was with today. It's not every day we see Stoneview princesses on the North Shore, especially one that had such an impact on me. Nothing could have surprised me more than to see Alexandra Delacroix on my side of town, and I want to keep the hazel-eyed girl to myself for now.

"She's with Racer at the shop. And you know what?" She gives me an expectant expression, and I know what comes next. "They were—"

"Looking for me too. Got the message. I was at SFU, checking out when the first parties are gonna be. Need to make myself some pennies, don't I, boss?"

I can read on her face that she doesn't like the sarcasm in my voice, but Emma has known me forever. She's used to the sulky bastard I am.

She grabs a strand of blonde extension and starts rolling and unrolling it around her index finger. "If you want to keep selling drugs to rich kids, you're gonna need supplies."

"This better come with some good news." I readjust myself on the sofa, sensing her excitement.

"I'm meeting with Vito Luciano tomorrow." She's excited but not smiling. Meeting with crime lords is good for us. It's also dangerous. "After getting my name to all the soldiers in his organization, he's finally happy to meet us. Patience pays. I told you."

My hand goes to the pocket of my hoodie, and I grab the lighter in there. I roll the spark wheel backward, liking the way the dents dig into the pad of my thumb. This is fucking great.

"You're one stubborn girl, and I love you for it."

"Love?" she snorts. "Not sure you know what that feels like. I can't even see the slightest excitement in you right now."

I guess I'm not very expressive, but if there's something that fucking excites me, it's power. The Lucianos can give us plenty of that.

"I'm more excited than a teenage girl getting her Taylor Swift concert ticket. Happy?"

She rolls her eyes and adds, "He wants to talk drug supplies, so you're coming with me."

Perfect. "Where are we meeting?"

"At a restaurant on the south bank. One p.m. and not one minute late. Vito Luciano isn't on Xi time."

I guess I can't blame her for the comment. Xi time has become a joke among us for how late I always am to events. Sometimes I'm too busy and something is holding me back. Handling small dealers who work for us isn't always easy. Sometimes I'm just selfish.

"I'll be there."

"If you're not, it'll be your problem when you have no drugs to sell to your Stoneview bitches."

"My Stoneview bitches pay my rent, you know?"

Ignoring my comment, she gets off the sofa. "Come on, let's eat. Your mom's waiting."

Dinner goes the same as it always does. Since Emma's younger sister, Billie, got into professional MMA and left our shit town, it's just the four of us most of the time. Once or twice a week, my younger brother Lik will have dinner with us.

We're not allowed to talk about business at the table. My mom complains about the violence on the North Shore getting worse. I try to convince her not to go on her nightly walks on her own anymore and she ignores me. The same way I pretend I don't hear when she tells us we're all part of the problem by perpetuating gang violence.

The Kings are vicious and ruthless. It's not even about not letting my guard down. It's about having to keep attacking. The moment we go into defense mode, they will eat us alive.

My phone rings as I help my mom clear off the table while Emma does the dishes.

"*Mama*," I say as I stare down at the screen to find that it's Zara calling. She shakes her head when she sees me approaching, her hand holding a cloth coming to rest on her large waist.

"You can't already leave," she complains. "You haven't even had tea with us, Ziad."

"I gotta go." I kiss her on the cheek and turn my back to her, walking out of the kitchen as I pick up the phone.

I wave Emma and her dad goodbye, and I'm out.

"Talk to me, baby girl," I say as I pick up. "Are you making me money?"

"*Hard to make any money when there's barely anything to sell. And don't call me baby girl.*"

I run a hand through my hair as I unlock my car. Just as I'm about to open the door, my eyes catch a green matte truck driving past my house.

"Text me everything you got," I tell Zara as I follow the

truck with my eyes. "All your stock. Emma and I might have a solution to the problem."

I hang up before she can say anything and immediately call another number.

"*What's up?*" Logan says on the other line.

"I'm pretty fucking sure I just saw the brothers drive past my mom's house."

I hear something fall to the ground. Probably Logan dropping the tool he was holding while working on a car. "*What the fuck? That's deep NSC territory.*"

"Yeah." I get in the car. "Elliot and Ethan are looking for trouble. And they might well fucking find it."

The two are stepbrothers, but everyone just calls them the brothers. They're high up in the Kings' hierarchy and very close to Kayla. They shouldn't be in NSC territory. It's a risky move. Bold. *Threatening.*

"*You got the info they want,*" Logan spells out the problem as if I didn't know.

"And they're not getting it. I gave them my conditions. I want a fight in the Death Cage with one of them."

"*That's never going to happen, and you know it. They're too scared to lose the North Shore. Or to die. This isn't even important, Xi. Just lower your conditions and give them the info. Get some territories back and be happy with that.*"

Pulling away from my mom's house, I get on the road to drive back to mine. "No," I say categorically. "I want my fucking town back."

For the second time tonight, I hang up on one of my friends. Problems keep piling up on my plate, but the hunger to dominate the North Shore never falters.

Fuck.

Time flew by while I was checking stocks with Zara, and I'm now running late for the meeting with the Lucianos. I look at the last text from Emma asking where I am. I need to be there in twenty minutes.

It takes me half an hour to make it to the restaurant and I hurry inside the family-owned Italian place on the nice side of Silver Falls. There aren't many people here. Two men are eating by the window; their old suits stretched to the limit as they shove pasta into their mouths. There's a woman behind the bar, using a cloth to dry some glasses. It smells like garlic here, and it's making me hungry.

Emma is sitting on her own at a small table at the back. She cocks an eyebrow at me as I approach her, totally unimpressed at my ten-minute lateness.

"You are so predictable, Xi. It's actually ridiculous."

"What?" I shrug as I sit down next to her. "They're not even here."

"No, of course, they're not because we are meeting them at one thirty. I had to add an extra thirty minutes for you to show up on time."

I pick a piece of bread on the table and bite into it. "That's smart. See, that's why you're our leader. That and because your dad was our old leader, I guess."

Her piercing blue eyes are on me the next second, attempting to annihilate me. She really hates when anyone takes away her hard work and mentions her dad being the reason she's our boss.

"Fucking hell, I'm joking. Relax, will you?"

"For things to sound like a joke, you must put humor in it. Not talk like a robot. And I'll fucking relax when the Lucianos offer us protection. I'm sick of the Kings ruling our town, and it's time to take them down."

"Amen to that," I mumble as I take another piece of bread.

Just before one-thirty, two people walk into the restaurant. One is a tall, broad man with dark hair and olive skin, the other a woman with long red hair and no life in her emerald eyes.

"Is that him?" I ask Emma as he stops by the bar to chat with the bartender.

Emma nods, her eyes on the woman with Vito.

"And that is?" I insist. She's apparently only got eyes for her. Knowing how much my stepsister loves women, I'm not surprised one as beautiful as that redhead caught her attention.

"That must be Lucky." Emma takes a deep breath and stretches her neck to the left and then to the right. "Vito's psychopath of an enforcer."

"Awesome," I huff. "If this ends in a bloodbath, we're fucked."

"Are you carrying?" Emma's head snaps to me.

"Of course, I'm carrying. Do you know a lot of NSC people who *don't*?" I pause, reading the answer in her eyes. "Wait, are you not?"

"Of course I'm not, you fucking idiot. We're meeting with the Cosa Nostra, and they will think you don't trust them."

"I *don't* trust them," I admit calmly. There is nothing in our world of violence that scares me anymore. Eat or get eaten, that's how I've always lived. I've been shot and stabbed before. I've faced death as many times as I've killed people. It's them or me.

My pulse doesn't rise anymore. It used to when I was a teenager, but I've built a thick skin and seen things so horrifying that nothing gets to me.

I wasn't born fucked up, but the North Shore surely made an unhinged man out of me.

Vito and Lucky start walking toward us, their gazes on the both of us. Emma fakes a smile, and she elbows me in the ribs.

"Smile motherfucker," she mumbles, keeping the fake cheeriness on her face. "Get us killed, and I will find you in hell, Xi. You've got my word."

"Can't wait," I murmur back, forcing my lips into a smile as well.

My stepsister knows me too well. She knows I don't take shit from anyone and that my violence often gets the best of me. But I'll make an effort for her. We have the same goal in mind, after all. To win back the North Shore.

Vito stops by our table, and Lucky takes a few steps back in true boss and enforcer style.

"You must be Emma Scott," Vito says as he extends his hands. "Vito Luciano."

There's a smoothness and elegance in his movements and the way he carries himself that doesn't shout *violence!* the way I do.

Vito Luciano has mastered the art of underground crime.

Whereas my appearance and behavior show I'm part of a gang from miles away, Vito lives like a wolf among sheep. And yet I bet he does more damage than I do.

"Nice to meet you," Emma says seriously as she shakes his hand. "This is Xi."

He shakes my hand and nods before sharing a look with Lucky.

"Stand up," she tells the both of us.

Emma's eyes are on me as she stands up. A hard gaze that silently tells me to listen to Lucky. She knows I hate being ordered around, but my stepsister worked hard for this, and I'm not about to fuck it all up for her.

Lucky is already patting down Emma, checking for weapons, when I finally decide to do what she said. She nods when she doesn't find anything, then turns to me. It takes her only seconds to find the gun at the back of my jeans. She pulls it away and cocks an eyebrow at me.

"You can have it for now," I grunt. "But don't forget to give it back."

Unimpressed, she tucks it at the back of her midnight blue slacks and turns to nod at her boss.

They both take a seat opposite us, and Vito doesn't waste any time. He is the definition of *straight-to-business*.

"Look, Emma." He shifts his hips on his chair and leans back, his eyes on her. "Your name has been on the lips of the men who work for me for months, if not years. Your prowess in helping them whenever they need has been noticed. You can be sure of that. I agreed to meet you because I recognize an important player when I see one."

He pauses, as if expecting her to thank him for the compliments, but he's going to wait a while if he is. Emma is not exactly known for being the most grateful person, especially when she feels something is due. She is a fantastic businesswoman and a ruthless being. She didn't wait in her life for Vito Luciano to point it out to believe it.

Realizing she's not going to say anything, he keeps going. "I don't trust small gangs," he admits. "You're hungry for power. It makes you volatile."

Isn't that the fucking truth.

"I'm not Mateo Bianco. I don't rush to conquer territories for the sake of having an army behind me. He was delusional, insatiable, and ultimately, that was his downfall. I understand you had a deal with him, however you won't have that with me right away. I only invest in what makes me money."

Sliding my hands in the pocket of my hoodie, I play with the cheap plastic lighter in there, rolling the spark wheel backward.

I don't like this guy. I can feel he's going to give us a deal that's bound to have all the risk falling back on us. Something to fuck us over.

I keep silent, waiting for him to get to his point.

"Tell me," he says as he stares at Emma. "What is it you need?"

"Supplies," she answers coolly. "Drugs." She puts her hands in front of her on the table. "We've been the number one dealers in Stoneview for years. This is the one last thing we still have over the Kings. If we lose that, we lose everything."

His gaze comes to me. He doesn't like me; it's evident in the way his face drops. "Are you the one in charge of that?"

I nod, not giving him a single word.

"How have you been supplying yourselves after Bianco?"

Emma gives me a look, encouraging me to share our information. "Small-scale suppliers. They only sell small, cut amounts. We have to cut it again on top of that, and our merchandise is becoming of lesser and lesser quality. They're expensive, meaning we only make a small margin, and they will sell to anyone who offers the most money." I shrug. "We can't afford to offer the *most money* anymore."

"How many dealers do you have?"

"I have five on the North Shore, two in Stoneview, and three on the south bank. I personally take care of Silver Falls University."

"Eleven in total, including yourself? That's a modest

amount, to say the least." He leans back against his chair. "I have to give you a minimum amount to make it worth my time. You wouldn't be able to push what I supply you with."

"I've had to cut half my men on the North Shore since we lost most of its territories. Give us what we need to take them back and there won't be a problem. In fact," this time, I'm the one who leans forward. "I can assure you we'll move twice your minimum. I know my dealers. They've been wanting to get back out there. People are hungry for money, and so are you. Every time we make a dollar, you make ten. Why waste time wanting us to court you when all that matters is money?"

He throws his head back, a throaty laugh resonating around us as he slams the table. "You're one ballsy motherfucker. I'll give you that." He turns to Lucky. "Court me? I love this guy."

Her lips curl, clearly not sharing the sentiment. I give her the equivalent of a middle finger with a simple stare.

"So, territories, huh?" he continues, asking Emma this time. "You want me to go to war for you?"

She shakes her head. "Give us protection from the police. We'll take care of the rest."

"I give you drugs, and you make me money. I give you police protection...and what do I get?"

"What do you want?" Emma says a little too quickly, her patience running thin. I catch the mocking smile on Lucky's lips when she notices my stepsister's struggle to stay still.

"You mentioned Stoneview," Vito says seriously. "It's rare to have access to such a protected town."

I nod my agreement. "The rich kids love their drugs and debauchery."

"A lot of politicians live there."

I can see where this is going, and so does Emma. "You want dirt," she states without question.

Vito smiles at her. "I prefer to call it useful information, but yes."

"Anyone in particular?" I ask, my right hand playing with the lighter as I sense the exact name he's going to tell us.

"Senator Delacroix will do."

A short chuckle escapes me. Isn't fate so fucking perfect sometimes? For me, at least.

I doubt Alexandra Delacroix will agree.

The second we leave our meeting, I call Logan. I texted him as soon as Luciano mentioned Delacroix, but it lasted another hour while we discussed the minor details of our agreement.

"*What's that about not touching the Porsche?*" Logan rages.

"Exactly what I said." I open my car and get in. "I'm on my way to your garage. Just don't fucking touch the car."

"*That's a whole lot of money you're asking me not to touch.*"

I pull out onto the street and accelerate through South Bank until I'm by the bridge leading to the North Shore. "No touchy, Logan. Last warning."

My friend and I share a strange relationship. We're both so stubborn it becomes unbearable sometimes. We end up in fistfights more often than we care to admit.

He hangs up on me and I shake my head. What a dick.

The moment I pull into his garage and get out of my car, he's on me. Black oil stains contrast with his pale skin. His dark hair falls into his eyes, and he wipes them out of the way. He strides toward me in a simple white tank top and dirty jeans.

"You better have a real good explanation," he tells me. "I was about to go to town on this baby."

Behind him, in the workshop, I notice Alexandra Delacroix's Porsche Cayman. The one Zara and Tamar stole yesterday while I was distracting the Stoneview beauty in the shop.

It was kind of fun to see her lose her mind with guilt after she accused me of being part of a gang and stealing her car, then going back on her words.

Little did she know that was exactly what I'd done.

But then she started acting weird. She was here, and suddenly she wasn't anymore. I don't exactly have the biggest conscience when it comes to this shit, but something in her called out to me.

Alexandra Delacroix has been through hell, and something inside her is trying to get her back there.

She's a fighter. I know it.

Or maybe I'm telling myself that to feel better knowing I'm about to use the fuck out of her.

I'm already in her good books for driving her home after her horrible experience on the North Shore. Imagine what kind of hero I'll be for bringing back her car.

I walk to Alexandra's car and look at the window Logan broke to steal it. "I need you to fix that for me."

"What?" he chokes. "Not only are you stopping us from making money, but you also want me to lose some? Did you hit your head?"

"It's a window, Logan."

"It's a *Porsche* window."

"I'll pay for it." I slide my hand inside and open the door.

Just like I expected, her phone and college welcome pack are on the passenger seat.

"Who leaves their car unattended with their phone in it?" I mumble to myself.

Logan is right by me a second later. "Someone who doesn't care about paying for a new one. Now just let me tear this baby apart."

I push him to the side before getting in the car and grabbing the two items I've been looking for. I pocket her dead phone first. A loud huff comes from my friend, but I ignore it. I'm too focused on opening the large envelope. Inside, I find exactly what that annoying student rep said I would; the keycode to her apartment.

Fucking penthouse.

I take a picture of the document and smile to myself. I have a key to her building and the code to her door. The moment I had her against the wall in her hallway yesterday comes back to the forefront of my mind. She felt so breakable under my stare. So obedient when I corrected her attitude.

I adjust myself in my jeans before putting everything back in the envelope. I've always liked the Stoneview girls. The bitchy, catty, rich girls who fall to their knees for the bad boy from the North Shore who is only good for one thing; supplying them with their weekly dose of cocaine.

It's always been my own personal form of revenge to fuck them into oblivion and turn them into the sluttiest girls for me. I'm the exact man their stuck-up parents always warned them about. The kind they look down upon until they're on their knees begging to suck my cock.

Alexandra Delacroix is different.

Of course, there was that haughty presence about her. She was too good to be stuck on the North Shore. Too scared we'd all come for her gold bracelet and pretty car.

But there's a real vulnerability in her that I want to explore.

Something that I know belongs to me.

"Tamar, come on. I'm in a hurry."

My computer genius of a best friend is our specialist when it comes to unlocking stolen goods and turning them brand new so we can resell them. She turns around from gazing at her computer and throws me a deadly look. "First of all, stop ordering me around. I don't care about your lack of patience and shitty moods. Secondly, do you want it done well or quickly?"

"Quickly," I snap. "I've got a meeting with Zara in twenty minutes."

I'm meeting with my other best friend to get the first shipment of supplies from the Lucianos, and I can't fucking be late again.

Tamar, Zara, and I became best friends in preschool. Our parents were from Maghreb and if they were friends, we had to be too. Tamar lost both her parents to the Kings. They were in the wrong place at the wrong time in a town where there was no right place and time.

They were in Kings' territory on a day they wanted to make examples out of people. Riddled with bullets. That's how they were found. Tamar was fifteen, and she's been on her own ever since. Just like me, she never went to high school, and when her parents died, she managed to escape the system through her computer skills. To the government, she was eighteen. Of course, she wasn't, and now she's twenty-four, just like me, but her papers say twenty-seven.

"Alright, it's all unlocked for you." She unplugs Alexandra's phone from her laptop and hands it back to me. "Any reason you wanted me to hack into a senator's daughter's phone? A dying need to end up in prison, maybe?"

I come to stand right in front of her, looking down at the tiny woman she is. "You're funny," I say without an ounce of humor in my voice. I mess with her dark curls, and she shrugs me off. "I owe you."

"You owe me so much already," she shouts at my retreating back. "You can start with a thank you, asshole!" I jog out of her house, not caring one bit what she has to say.

I'm late to meet with Zara, but there's only one thing on my mind as I drive across the North Shore.

Alexandra Delacroix is about to get so much more of me than she ever imagined.

4

ALEXANDRA

Get Stüpid – bülow

"Welcome to our castle," Ella exclaims as she opens the door to Chester. I hear his shy laugh before he walks in, followed by our other friend Wren.

Chester's smile radiates as his gaze falls on me. I'm sitting at the kitchen counter, a plate of chopped fruits in front of me, finishing my snack and reading a book my dad sent me yesterday. I must read a different book every three to five days. Doesn't matter the length or topic. I have to finish it. The two men hug Ella before coming into the open-plan kitchen.

"Where's Peach?" Wren asks as he gives me a quick hug.

I pop a strawberry in my mouth and nod toward the hallway. "Napping," I answer while chewing. "We're all so dead from rush week." I point at a plate on the counter. "I made cookies for everyone. Help yourself."

"Sweet."

We've spent the last five days going through each round for the sororities we were interested in. I went through all of it for the sake of it, but I know the one that was my number one all along. Thankfully it went perfectly well on preference day yesterday, and I'm almost certain I will get a bid today. There is still the stress of everything going wrong and not being picked. My mom would lose her mind.

Chester comes to me, giving me a tight hug and a kiss on the cheek. "I heard you got invited to your top two choices yesterday."

"Yup," I beam as I grab my last strawberry. Then I get off the stool and bring my plate to the sink.

Ella opens the fridge and grabs a couple of beers, giving it to the guys before taking one for herself. "Do you want anything, Alex?"

"I'm alright, thanks." I've always been the boring friend who doesn't touch alcohol, although they're used to it. They know how my dad is and that there's no point insisting. Instead, I grab the can of Coke Zero I've already opened.

"Peach!" Wren screams from the kitchen. "It's bid day for you. Get out of bed!"

"I'm so jealous you guys both got into the same frat house. If the girls and I end up in different sororities, I might die," Ella pouts.

"Zeta Nu, baby." Chester taps his beer bottle against my can of Coke as he winks at me. "I'm excited about it," he adds.

"Remind me the sorority you want," Wren inquires before taking a swig.

"Xi Epsilon. Oh my God, guys, we've told you a million times," Ella whines.

"Of course," Chester chuckles. "Miss Legacy has a spot waiting for her in that house."

"Peach and I have been kissing asses all week while Alex

was just making appearances and waiting for every single sorority to go on their knees and beg her to join them."

They all burst into laughs at Ella's words.

"Except Xi Epsilon," I defend. "My mom said they're harder on legacies. They don't want them to take things for granted." A band of stress wraps around my stomach. If I don't get in, I'll never hear the end of it.

Wren snorts. "I'm sure that's true for anyone whose name isn't Delacroix."

My gaze lowers to the can in my hands. I play with the pull tab, my nail pressing on it repeatedly. They might take me, but once in, who knows how they treat the girls they feel threatened by.

"Don't worry, Alex," Ella reassures me as if she can read my mind. "If the bitches go hard on you, Peach will kick their asses."

"She's going to do a backflip right into their faces," Chester adds. "Same with Ella."

Ella nods. "Gotta put those cheerleading skills to good use, babe."

Chester wraps an arm around my shoulders. "We'd protect our favorite girl at all costs."

A thankful smile spreads on my face as I gaze at all of them. "I love you, guys."

"Alright." Peach's groggy voice resonates in the room as she appears from the hallway. "Time to find out who our sisters are going to be for the next four years."

"You girls are my sisters," Ella adds in a cheery voice.

"So cheesy. You're killing me." Wren messes Ella's hair, and she pushes him away.

"Stop it, we're cute," she fights back as we gather all our stuff and start making our way out. We have to join everyone on the football field. That's where they will give us our letters so we can find out where we've been invited.

Weirdly, I thought being accepted into Xi Ep would make me feel happier than I do right now. I feel great, relieved knowing my mom will be proud of me for getting into the same sorority house as her. But the day was long, and my mind seems to be wandering back to one person and one person only.

They've shown us which of the bedrooms in the house will be ours once they start initiation. We'll be staying in our dorms till then. Of course, the sorority houses at SFU are like nothing I've heard of before in my life. We all get a private bedroom with an ensuite. One for each of the fifty girls living here. The house is practically a castle, and I got lost in there around five times today. That should have kept me busy, but all I could think about was Ziad.

I met my big sister, Harper, who will be guiding me in the next few weeks. And while I was smiling and talking to her, my brain kept going back to the last time I saw the man who helped me. To how close his body was, how he was holding me against the wall, his fingertips on my chin.

By six p.m. I'm ready to go to bed. This whole day was exhausting, and I'm not as social as I used to be. Peach is on me the second she sees my gaze getting lost in nothingness.

"No. Alex," she whispers as she snaps her fingers at me. We're all sitting in the gigantic living room, listening to the president's end-of-day speech. "You are not acting like a grandma and going to bed at eight p.m. tonight."

"Ladies," our president calls out to all of us. Camila Diaz is a beautiful woman with the most gorgeous curves I've ever seen. I can see Peach practically devouring her from the corner of my eyes. "We're going to leave it here for today so you can go home, get rest, and get ready for our bid party tonight. The party will start here at eight p.m., and eventually we'll join the Zeta Nu guys during the night. Please, remember to behave yourselves at frat parties. You represent Xi Epsilon now, and we are respectable ladies. I'll see you girls later."

There's a round of applause for her before we all make our way out of the house.

"I'm exhausted," I groan as we start walking back to the main campus. "Do we have to go to that party?"

"Here she goes." Ella rolls her eyes as she nudges Peach. "Our little antisocial worm is back."

"We're going to find her wrapped under the covers if we don't keep an eye on her."

"Alex, you're not allowed to nap when we get home. We'll never get you out of bed if you do," Ella scolds me.

"Let's just get ready and drink at our place. We'll invite the guys," Peach suggests as she gets between Ella and me, wrapping an arm over each of our shoulders.

"Fuck yeah. That's what I wanted to hear," Ella jumps in, encouraging Peach's idea of fun.

"You know what," I smile. A party and drinking could take my mind off Ziad and the countless thoughts I've had for him in the last few days. "Let's do it. I might even have a drink. We ought to celebrate being Xi Ep girls."

"Oh my God, girls. I love you."

"Ella is getting emotional again," Peach laughs. "Let's get her a beer."

"Oh, oh. Wait!" I grab my Polaroid camera from my bag and extend my arm in front of me. "Get in. This is this month's picture."

Click.

I stop by the entrance mirror as Peach opens the front door. "Come on, Alex. We're late."

I finish putting on my lipstick and dab it with the tip of my forefinger. It's a fuchsia color that perfectly contrasts with my porcelain skin, which I used to love wearing. I haven't worn it since that fateful night, but I'm feeling a little more like myself today after all our fun, and I want to keep the mood going.

The moment we step back into Xi Ep, my big sister, Harper, finds me. "I love your dress," she squeals as she grabs both my hands and takes a step back to admire me. I'm wearing a black bodycon dress with spaghetti straps that embraces my curves perfectly—especially my boobs.

"Thank you," I smile. "I'm so excited to be here."

"Come. Let's get you a drink. I've been waiting for you to do some tequila shots. We're joining the Zeta Nu guys in an hour, and then we can get onto the hard stuff there."

The hard stuff? Aren't shots of tequila hard enough?

I'm not sure how I feel about downing shots. I've practically never had a drink in my life apart from the occasional glass of wine my dad would share with me to teach me how to taste them. I follow her to the long table with all the drinks anyway. Peach and Ella are with me, so I know I'm safe.

By the time we make our way to the frat party, I'm drunk and having so much fun. I'm screaming the Xi Epsilon chants down the street with my sisters, holding Peach and Ella's hands like there's no tomorrow, and when we finally get inside the house, happiness is adding to my euphoric state.

"Chester," I shout as I see him up the stairs. "We made it!" He's just as drunk as us. He's got Zeta Nu written in black marker on his forehead and a tie tied around his head, the long bit hanging to the side.

"Yes, baby." He runs down the stairs and wraps an arm around my waist before he lifts me and spins, making me feel like I'm flying. He drops a kiss on my cheek as he puts me back down. "How's bid night going?" he slurs.

"So good. So, so good. I'm happy."

His eyes cross with mine and an honest smile spreads on his handsome face, his light eyes lighting up. "I like when you're happy, Alex. You deserve it."

I slap his chest and shove him away. "Shut up, you big softie. I love you."

"Same. Come, let's find Peach and Ella."

I turn around, so sure they were behind me. "I don't know when I lost them."

"S'alright." He takes my hand and drags me through the house.

"Hey, do you know what antipode means?" Without waiting a second, I tell him the answer. "It's a point on earth that's diametrically opposite to another. Did you know Bermuda is antipodal to parts of Australia, mate?"

He bursts out laughing at my failed Australian accent. "I missed your definitions over the summer, Alex."

Crowds of different Greek houses are mixing in all the rooms and the heat is almost unbearable. It's so hot in here that I feel my hairline dampening. It smells of alcohol, sweat, and fun. *Pursuit of Happiness* by Kid Cudi rings from the speakers, and everyone starts cheering and singing to the song.

As soon as we find my two best friends with Wren, Chester and I start dancing with them. Our drunk bodies all hit against each other, and I can't stop wrapping my arms around them and telling them how much I love them. We were a tight group at Stoneview Prep. Those four people were with me when I recovered from the kidnapping. They held my hand through police inquiries, panic attacks, and sleepless nights, and I couldn't ask for a better start to college for the four of us.

A couple of songs later, the girls and I decide to head outside for some fresh air. We've had a few drinks, so we all stumble into the backyard together.

"Guys, guys, guys," I pant as we all sit on a bench. "I have to tell you something."

"This better be juicy. You've got your spilling tea voice on." Ella holds her hands out as if holding a cup of tea and a saucer, and Peach pretends to pour some in before Ella mimes tasting it. "Yum."

I burst into laughter, needing a few seconds to calm myself. "I know I'm only saying this because I'm drunk. But remember how I told you that guy from the North Shore basically rescued me and brought me back here on moving day?"

"Uh-huh," Peach nods. "You said he was hot."

"So hot," I nod. "I can't stop thinking about him. I keep dreaming of when we met, replaying the moment in my head. And last night...last night I dreamed we had sex."

"What?" Ella shrieks. "Is this baby girl dreaming naughty things with a bad boy from the North Shore?"

Peach takes my hand and kisses the back of it. "This cutie is going to lose her virginity this year."

"Stop it," I laugh. "He's just so...rough."

"Rough?" Ella giggles.

"Yes," I nod. "I think I like rough. Like, holding you by the neck and fucking you hard, kind of rough."

"Oh my God," Peach cries out in laughter. "Who are you, and what have you done to Alex? Girl, you used to date Chester. *Chester.* He's like a little Easter chocolate bunny. That's how fucking sweet he is. You've never done anything with him, or anyone, and you're now telling us you think you like it rough because some guy from the North Shore drove you back here on the day your car got stolen. I can't...I fucking love you. You're the best."

"I get it," Ella nods repeatedly. So much so that her face becomes blurry to my drunken eyes. "I like it rough too. I like a man who can take control. I like it even better when he's older and knows what he wants."

"Please, kill me now." Peach pretends to bring a gun to her temple and shoots. She even pops her tongue out and fakes to be dead.

"Oh, shut up, Miss Badass," I fight back. "Wren basically has you on a leash."

"Wren and I aren't even dating," she snaps back. "And we will never date. He's a controlling little shit, and I would fight him every step of the way."

"He's hot, though."

"So hot," I agree with Ella.

"He treats women like shit. Wake the fuck up."

"I'd let Wren treat me like shit," I admit.

"Sadly, he only has eyes for Peach," Ella sighs dramatically.

"He does *not*," she chuckles, but I can see the slight tint on her cheeks, illuminated by the yard's fairy lights.

A group of people spill out from the house into the backyard and I shake my head, my eyes betraying me.

"What the hell?" I sit up and glance at the patio where

97

he sits down with two girls and another guy. One of the girls is Harper.

"What's up?" Peach says, her head resting on the back of the bench we're sitting on as she looks at the stars.

"Here's here. Th-the guy who rescued me."

Peach snorts. "The *North Shore* guy is at our SFU party? No more drinking for you."

"I swear." I gasp as the realization hits me. "I'm not being a drunk idiot. I recognize the tattoo on his neck."

It's the tattoo of a Fatma hand that I saw when he was driving me, and I couldn't stop looking at him. It's big enough that I can see it from where we're sitting.

"What?" Ella yelps at the same time as Peach's head snaps back up. "Where?"

"Right there, on the patio. The guy with the dark hair and the black hoodie who's lighting up a cigarette. That's him," I say with excitement.

What are the chances? What is he even doing at an SFU frat party, and how did he get in?

"Xi?" Ella chokes, shock ringing in her voice. "Your North Shore savior that you can't stop dreaming of is *Xi*?"

5

ALEXANDRA

No Romeo - Dylan

"Xi?" I repeat.

"Yeah, it's pronounced *Zi,* and he spells it X. I."

I guess that must be his nickname. He said his name was Ziad.

"Alex, how have you never heard of Xi?" Peach facepalms herself.

"I feel like you're going to tell me something bad about him, and I'm not sure I'm ready to hear it, honestly." I pout and look at Peach then Ella. "Please don't crush my dream."

"He's a fuckboy, Alex," Peach says without mercy. "He's the fucking worst, and no one gives him shit for it because he always fucks the catty bitches from Stoneview who want to try a bad boy before they go back to their rich boyfriends. They deserve him, and he deserves them."

"And he's so rude and moody," Ella adds. "It's impossible to have a conversation with him unless he wants to fuck you. Even then, I'm pretty sure he puts the minimum effort into getting girls in his bed."

My heart drops in my stomach, disappointment weighing heavy on my shoulders. "He was really nice to me," I murmur. I guess he wasn't *nice*, but he did rescue me.

"Of course he was nice. Have you seen yourself? He one hundred percent wanted to fuck you," Peach keeps going with her typical bluntness.

"How do you guys even know him?"

"I met him at a North Shore party," Ella shrugs. My eyes widen and she hurries to add, "I didn't sleep with him. I think I was a little too nice for him. He's into the *real* Stoneview girls, you know? Like Camila Diaz and her clique."

Camila was a senior when we were freshmen. She was the queen of Stoneview Prep and perpetuated the culture of only one queen bee and everyone else must love her or have a dreadful time through high school. She indeed was a bitch, though she seems to have changed since then. She's the president of Xi Epsilon now, and she was kind and welcoming during rush week.

"Or like Harper," Peach agrees as we all stare at the way Harper settles on Xi's lap.

"Harper is not a Stoneview bitch," I say.

I gaze at my friends, their pointed looks saying it all. "She's super nice," I defend.

"Alex," Peach huffs. "You are too naïve for this world. Everyone is nice during rush week. Wait for initiations and see how she really is."

Her words twist my stomach, but I ignore them. Peach is a pessimist. It makes her strong and prepared for anything, but she also lacks dreams and passion.

"Well, she's been polite to me, and I'll keep believing she's a good person until she proves me wrong. Like Xi. Oh my God," I beam. "This is my *Sparks Fly* moment, girls.

Taylor would be so proud." I flatter my lashes at them before singing some of the lyrics. *"You're the kind of reckless..."*

"And that's exactly your problem," Peach cuts me off. "You're a dreamer and only see the good in people. It's exactly why everyone always walks all over you. This is not a fucking Taylor Swift song, Alex."

"Sparks fly whenever you smiiiile," I sing drunkenly.

"Peach," Ella scolds her as she comes to the rescue. "Leave her alone."

"Come on," she groans. "We're telling her right here and now that Xi is a shit guy and Harper is a bitch. But watch her not listen to us in the slightest and get heartbroken when she realizes she was being too nice again."

"There's nothing wrong with seeing the good in people, Alex," Ella tells me as she pats my thigh. "Just be careful. And Xi really is shit."

"He's a fucking drug dealer," Peach snaps. "That's how I met him. Is that bad enough to keep you away?"

My throat tightens. "God, I get it. Stop being so annoying."

"One tear because of that guy. *One*, and I will lose my shit," she warns me.

"Stop it," I bark back at her. "You just don't know when to stop being a bitch, do you?"

I stand up, my head spinning from the alcohol, and remember why we're all being extreme. Peach gets meaner when she's drunk and, apparently, I get...messier. I should have known I'd be the ugly cry kind of girl. I'm emotional and always think I've done something wrong, and it gets so much worse with alcohol.

I know we're all a little too drunk, but I'm hurt now and want to be on my own. "I'll see you guys at home."

"No, Alex, don't leave," Ella pleads. "Peach, say sorry."

"I'm not saying sorry. She needs to toughen up."

"You're so goddamn stubborn," Ella hisses at her. She stands up and grabs my hand. "I'll walk you home and come back. I don't want you to walk home alone at night."

"This is dumb, I'm going back inside," Peach says casually as if she hadn't just worked all of us up.

"Peach, wait," Ella calls out. She turns back to me. "I hate when you girls do this."

I shake my head and slip my hand out of hers. "Go with her. Don't ruin your night for us. I'll be fine walking home on my own, I promise."

"I don't like leaving you alone. I know how you feel about it, especially since—"

"It's okay," I cut her off, not wanting to get into it. "I'm tired anyway, and I need the walk to sober up. You go after Peach since she loves being a drama queen."

A soft laugh escapes Ella and she nods. "We won't stay out late."

"It's okay if you do. Enjoy yourselves." She gives me a big kiss on the cheek and jogs back inside to find Peach.

I let out a long huff, letting my head fall backward to look at the sky. Time to be a big girl and walk home on my own, I guess. Maybe I don't actually fit in at these parties. It's the first time I tried, and while the beginning was fun, I'm starting to feel like Taylor in *Antihero*.

I let my feet guide my drunk body back to the patio so I can walk back inside, but the moment I walk past the group of people sitting there, a dark voice calls for me.

"Alexandra."

My stomach twists. My name sounds so delicious on his lips. My head snaps to the side without my being able to control it, and I'm surprised I don't melt on the spot.

His disheveled deep brown hair moves with the night breeze, and his eyes narrow as he takes a drag of his cigarette. There are tattoos on his fingers I noticed when he was holding the steering wheel. The skeleton of a hand covering his flesh and around his wrist, writings in Arabic.

I freeze the moment our eyes lock. His are the color of tiger's eye crystals—different shades of brown mixing and glistening from the light over his head.

"H-hi," I manage to squeak. My entire body feels on alert. My knees are shaking a little from his strong presence and the fact that three other people are observing our interaction.

His eyes light with amusement, clearly aware of the effect he has on me, yet there's no smile on his face. Almost like he won't allow it to spread.

"You guys know each other?" I startle when Harper's voice cuts through our intense staring.

I look at her, my heartbeat accelerating. "Erm," I hesitate.

"Yeah, we do," Xi answers casually. "Come sit with us," he orders more than offers me. "I didn't know you were Xi girl."

My heart stops, my body suddenly hot, not understanding the meaning until I realize he means Xi Epsilon, the sorority. Not...one of his girls. Of course not.

My eyes dart to Harper as hers harden. "Actually," she says as she readjusts herself on his lap and wraps an arm around his neck. "Alex is a pledge, so she's not *really* part of the sisterhood yet. Not until she passes her initiation. Right, Alex?"

I nod stiffly. "Yes, of course."

Xi drags another puff out of his cigarette and turns his

head to exhale. "You're gonna go easy on her, Harper, right? Would be a shame to damage her."

Xi's words say one thing, but his eyes tell a different story when he talks about damaging me.

Almost like he would love to do that himself.

The way Harper's jaw tightens tells me Xi is going to get me in trouble, and yet I can't seem to find my voice to put a stop to it.

"She's going to get no special treatment," Harper says, anger simmering in her voice. "Not because she's a legacy, and not because her last name is Delacroix. Everyone is treated equally at Xi Ep."

"I wouldn't want—"

"Alex," she cuts me off. "Be a dear and get your big sister a drink." Silver bracelets jingle around her wrist as she extends her arm, offering me her red solo cup. "White claw."

I nod again, hurrying her way and grabbing her cup. "Sure." My eyes dart to Xi as he watches me walk away.

My heart is still racing by the time I make it to the kitchen fridge. I grab a can of White Claw and pour it into Harper's cup. Putting it on the counter, I then grab the edge and take a deep breath.

I need to bring Harper the drink and go home. Obviously, she doesn't want me in her way, and I refuse to compromise my four years at a sorority for one man. Especially one my friends warned me about.

Determined to end this night and wholly ignore Xi in the process, I bring the drink back to Harper. A wave of disappointment washes over me when I notice he and his friend are gone. Instead, they've been replaced by two other girls from our house, and they brought ten shots of tequila with them. Except that's not what shocks me the most. No, it's the white powder they're currently gathering in a line on the table using a black Amex.

I approach carefully and hand Harper her drink. "Here you go."

"Aw, thanks, sweetie. You're the best. Come on," she taps the seat next to hers, "sit with us."

"I'm okay." I put my hands in front of me. "I was going to go home. It was a long day of—"

"Don't be ridiculous." She grabs me by the wrist and pulls me until I fall on the seat next to her. "You're our sister. You've got to party with us."

Taking a deep breath, I nod. "Sure."

The girl to my right bends down and takes the line of coke she's just finished cutting. My eyes widen, but I try to control my reaction. I've barely been to a party in my life, let alone done drugs.

Harper grabs a shot of tequila and her friends cheer as she downs it. She looks at me, grabs two on the table and gives them to me.

"No, thanks. I've had enough." I smile shyly. My face is still warm from all the alcohol I've had. Any more, and I'll black out.

"You gotta do double what your big sister does. That's the rules tonight," she reminds me. Her perfect fake smile is bright even at night. My stomach twists as I eye the shot glasses in my hands. It was easier to do that earlier at the house when I was sober.

"I really don't think this is a good idea."

"Come on, Alex," one of them insists. "It's bid night. We shouldn't be telling you this, but we like you, so we will. We use tonight to check on all the weak girls in the sorority and see who we should go hard on during initiations. Honestly, you better take the shots because it'll be worse at initiations if you don't."

I turn to Harper, checking if that's true with a silent stare. She nods. "We really want you to be part of our circle, Alex. Don't get left behind."

Without further thought, I drink the two shots. I cough, some of the tequila spilling down my chin, before wiping my mouth with my forearm. They all explode in laughter as Harper tilts her head to the side. She's the only one not laughing. No, she's just observing me.

"Nice," she says, tapping my back to help with the coughing fit.

She takes a small packet out of her purse and pours some more cocaine on the glass table in front of us. She cuts it with her card, makes a neat line, and one of her friends hands her a rolled hundred-dollar bill. Harper lowers her head and inhales half of it in a split second.

"Damn," she giggles. "The new stuff Xi brings is fire. The bastard is good."

Peach was right. Xi *is* a drug dealer, and it's clear. The proof is right in front of my eyes. It's disappointing to know I was going crazy over someone who clearly isn't for me.

They all agree with Harper before she moves to give me the rolled bill. "Your turn."

I shake my head. "I don't do drugs."

Harper cocks an eyebrow at me. "Really? Then how do you know Xi?"

"Um..." My head is spinning, and her voice is hard to understand through my drunk brain. Words tumble from my lips without me being able to think if I should lie or not. "He sort of...sort of rescued me from the North Shore when my car got stolen."

"Rescued you?" one of the girls snorts. "Are we talking about the same asshole?"

Harper cackles a mocking laugh. "Xi is no hero, believe me."

I nod, showing I don't wish to contradict her. "No, I don't think he is."

She grabs a tequila shot and downs it before turning to me. "Your turn."

"I can't. I'm so drunk already. I'll be sick."

"God, Alex," she snorts. "Are you always so boring?"

I gulp and shake my head. Instead of standing up for myself, I grab the two shots and down them.

The others clap. "Well done," one of them says.

My stomach churns, and I have to swallow back bile. I really don't want to be sick right now. It would be so embarrassing.

"Alex," another calls my name. "What do you think about Xi?"

"He's so hot." The words just escaped me, and I put a hand in front of my mouth. They all giggle except Harper.

"Look," Harper says as she puts a hand on my knee. I look at her with heavy eyelids. "I hate being that kind of girl because my sisters always come first. But Xi and I have sort of had a thing going on for a while."

My brows furrow, and she smiles at me. She's so satisfied right now. "We've never been official or anything, but everyone in our sorority knows he's off limits. In other words, he's mine, and I really don't want you to get in the way."

"O-okay," I slur. My head falls forward when I try to nod, and they all laugh at me.

"You're one of us, Alex. Right?" Harper insists. "You don't

want to go against your sisters. I would hate for your life to get difficult at Xi Ep."

"I w-won't get in the way. I promise." I try to turn to her, but she grabs the back of my neck.

"Show me you can do what you're told." She shoves the hundred-dollar bill in my hand and grabs my wrist to put my hand on the table. Before I know it, she's shoving my face down.

I whimper, sure I'm going to hit the glass, but she holds me back.

"You'll see. It feels really good," she whispers in my ear. She presses her finger to my left nostril, her manicured nail practically cutting my skin as I bring the note to my right. With a trembling hand, I line the bill with the white powder and inhale. Harper is the one guiding me as I breathe it all in.

She pulls my head back up and I drop the bill. My nose hurts, like I need to sneeze even though I can't. I feel like I'm going to get a nosebleed as I start coughing and rubbing my nostrils.

They all start laughing. "You're amazing," Harper claps. "I'm going to make the best little sister out of you."

A rush goes to my head, and everything starts spinning.

"I don't feel very well," I squeak.

"Then maybe you should just go home," Harper suggests with a wry smile.

"I don't think I can walk home like this," I slur. "Can you...can you help me?"

Tears spring to my eyes when they all go quiet. "You'll be fine," are the only words Harper offers me before she hushes me with a hand gesture.

They all stare at me, clearly waiting for me to leave. I get up, and the whole world tilts. Swaying to the side, I hit the patio barrier. Laughter resonates around me, but I keep going, holding the barrier to keep myself upright.

It takes me God knows how long to make it out of the house. The party is still raging, and I have to cross too many rooms to count. I want to call Chester or the girls and look for my phone in my pink purse for a few minutes before remembering I don't have a phone.

I ordered one to be delivered the day after it got stolen with my car, but it still hasn't arrived. Running my hands across my face, the rush I'm getting from the cocaine is accelerating my heart rate and making me panic.

I take a deep, shaky breath. I'm high and completely drunk. My vision is blurry, my body shaking, and I've basically been kicked out of this party.

All this because I admitted to knowing Xi and finding him attractive.

Peach was right. Harper is a Stoneview bitch, and Xi is nothing but trouble.

Struggling to put one foot in front of the other, I cross the lawn and take forever to get back to the street. The SFU area and its surroundings are perfectly safe; I have no reason to worry. But I'm a woman in a vulnerable state, and I don't trust anything right now.

I'm swaying as I walk, sometimes almost sprinting, sometimes feeling too sick to even keep going. The back of my throat tastes disgusting, like some of the white powder is still stuck there.

Two cars have driven past me; one was clearly full of drunk students. They shouted how hot I was, but none of them offered to help. It's a good thing, anyway. I just want to get home and not talk to anybody.

But the universe seems to have a different idea.

I hear a car slowing down behind me. Too scared to turn

around, I accelerate and cross my arms over my chest. I feel like I'm going to have a heart attack. Everything is so intense right now, and my eyes keep blinking. The car keeps at my pace and fear wraps all around me. I start jogging, and I hear the car accelerating.

My mind spirals into panic as I prepare to sprint, but I hear. "Alexandra."

That voice. The way he says my name.

6

ALEXANDRA

Sparks Fly - Taylor Swift

I stop right away, turning around to find not only Xi, but Xi driving *my* car. The one that was stolen.

Are the drugs messing with my brain?

"I'm so confused," I admit in drunken honesty.

In his typical *I'm an unhappy man and I am annoyed* behavior, he leans over to open the passenger door. "Get in."

I don't think twice. After the scare I just gave myself, I'm happy to see a familiar face. I hop into the passenger seat of *my* car and turn to him as he starts driving.

"How...?"

His tongue grazes his front teeth. "I asked around and made sure to get it back." He turns to me and despite the haze, I can't miss his square jaw. He's dazzling with the trimmed five o'clock shadow he sports.

"You're so beautiful." I squeeze my eyes shut as soon as the words slip out. "Sorry."

"Don't apologize for complimenting me." His order is rough, undoubtedly scolding me.

"Of course. That was dumb. Sorry."

He cocks an eyebrow. "And don't apologize for having apologized."

I nod, biting my lower lip to ensure nothing else comes out.

"You're drunk," he says matter-of-factly.

"And high," I add.

He brakes so suddenly my head hits the board. "Ow!"

"Seatbelt. Now."

"God," I moan as I put it on. "Are you always so bossy?"

He grabs me by the chin and forces me to face him. "What did you take?" he says, leaning toward me. His eyes flick from one of mine to the other, probably trying to check my pupils.

"The cocaine *you* provided."

He shakes his head. "Don't do that fucking shit. It's disgusting, and you're better than that."

"Better than that?" I snort. "You don't know me."

His fingers dig into my skin, making me hiss. "Don't fight me, Alexandra."

The silent *or...* sends goosebumps down my neck.

"I got drunk and took drugs. I'm a college student, that's what we do." I don't mention that I was forced into doing it, because that's just too embarrassing. I can't admit to the man I've been dreaming of that I have no backbone or have never done drugs in my life. I'm from Stoneview; he probably assumes I do it on a weekly basis.

"You shouldn't even be drinking," he says as he lets me go. "You're not twenty-one."

"How old are you?"

"Twenty-four," he says as if to prove a point.

"You're a drug dealer. How old do you have to be for *that* to be okay?"

He ignores me and my head falls against the seat. "I feel sick," I admit in a huff.

"That's what happens to college girls who can't pace themselves. You've got the biggest baby chick energy I've ever seen. At least try to be safe."

"Chick," I huff. "Baby chick is the same thing."

I wouldn't know he was joking if I had to judge from his tone alone. But he looks at me and that tiny smile is back at the corner of his lips. The slightest pull. That's his entire smile, and I'm only realizing it now. I bet the whole thing must be dazzling.

"You're so mean." I turn to him and give him a pout.

He looks back at the road, not taking the bait of my baby face. "We're almost home. Don't get sick in your car, you just got it back."

I swallow back bile and open the window when something hits me. "Did they break a window to steal it?"

"That's how people tend to steal cars, yes," he deadpans.

"But...I have windows." My sentence-building isn't the best right now. My brain is a little too busy dealing with the coke.

"I got it fixed for you." His simple words make my heart want to explode out of my chest.

It's the drugs. Please, let it be the drugs.

"Why?"

He shrugs. "We're not all bad on the North Shore, cupcake."

That stupid nickname makes me want to melt. He must never use it again.

Before I know it, we're parking by my building. I open the passenger door, but the moment I stand up, I stumble on my feet and watch the ground head my way helplessly. A shriek escapes me just before two arms catch me.

"White girl wasted really doesn't look good on you. Come on. I'm taking you to your room."

He goes to grab me in what I like to call *delicate princess style*. Chester used to carry me like that all the time after his lacrosse games. I would cheer for him on the side, and at the end, he'd put his jacket on me and carry me to his car.

But for some reason, my drunk ass refuses to be a princess as I fall into Xi's arms, wrapping mine around his neck and my legs around his waist. I guess I'll be a delicate koala instead.

"Delicate koala," I cheer.

"What the fuck," he groans as he adjusts from the surprise and takes on all my weight. "Comfortable?"

"Yep," I say as I bury my face against his neck. "You smell so good."

"Thanks."

"What's your cologne?" I ask as he taps the card to get inside the building.

"I don't know. My brother gifts it to me every birthday."

"You have a brother? What's his name?"

"Malik." His short responses tell me he's not exactly enjoying the conversation. Yet, at the same time, he's not ignoring me.

"Ziad and Malik," I test the names on my tongue. "I love your names. Any other siblings?"

He gets us in the elevator and presses the button to the penthouse. "Two stepsisters."

"Really?" I ask way too excitedly. "I wish I had sisters. But I'm an only child. I guess Peach and Ella are like my sisters. I think my parents should divorce. There's no love whatsoever in their relationship. How old were you when your parents divorced?"

"They didn't. My dad died. And I was thirteen." I don't think he realizes, but his arms tighten around my waist.

Lead drops in my stomach. "Oh my God, I'm so sorry."

"Don't be. It was a long time ago," he murmurs as he taps the keycode to enter the penthouse. He doesn't sound sad, but then again, he doesn't sound *anything.*

He enters and walks straight to the open-plan living room. "Which way to your room?"

I point at the hallway behind him. "I'm the last room—wait. How do you know the keycode?" I try to pull my head away from his shoulder to look into his eyes, but he presses a hand at the back of my head, keeping me tight against him.

"I'm your security guard, remember? I know everything, cupcake."

I giggle into his neck as he enters my bedroom and finally puts me down on the bed. I can't seem to stop talking. "I feel sick, and there's a horrible taste at the back of my throat. Is that the drugs? Am I dying?"

He cocks an eyebrow at me. "You've never done coke before, have you?"

I shake my head and let myself fall back on my pillows. "I don't think I ever will again."

"Coke drip. That's what it is. It'll go away by morning. I'll get you a glass of water to help with it."

Time becomes meaningless. He's out of the room and back in before I even understand he's gone. He sits on the edge of my bed and helps me sit up before giving me the glass of water.

I drink a few sips and put it on my bedside table. "You keep saving me," I murmur.

He looks into my eyes but doesn't respond. I'm noticing

that when this man doesn't want to talk about something, he simply doesn't.

My drunk brain doesn't seem to care.

"I dreamed of you last night. It was...interesting." I wiggle my eyebrows at him, but his unimpressed stare doesn't falter.

"Don't tell me you had a sex dream about me, cupcake."

I feel the rush of warmth going from my neck to my cheeks. I can imagine the way my porcelain skin blushes in the low yellow light of the room.

He moves closer to me, his thigh now touching my hip. My bodycon dress is a few inches from uncovering my underwear, and I gulp when his eyes dart to the space between my legs.

"Tell me." His eyes come back to mine with a glint in them. "What was your dream about?"

I shake my head, making the room tilt and my vision blur. "I can't."

He leans toward me, our lips practically touching.

"I could make your dream come true," he murmurs.

Where is that glass of water again? My throat is suddenly dry.

Your friends warned you, Alex. Don't let him do a fuck-and-forget on you.

I break eye contact and turn my head to the side. "No," I finally say as a wave of clarity washes over me. "Really, I can't. I know you and Harper are a thing. I don't want to be the kind of person who gets in the way of a relationship."

As I look back at him, I see him run a hand against his face. "Harper and I aren't in a relationship."

"You know what I mean." I roll my eyes. "Regular fucks or whatever it is you two have." I completely fail to hide the jealousy in my voice. "You have a thing."

He licks his lips, watching me with a knowing stare. I guess he heard the jealousy too. "No relationship, no regular fucks, no *thing*. Only her imagination."

Biting my inner cheek, I blink at him. "Are you sure about that?"

"Happened once. Last year. Nothing else."

I purse my lips, not even liking the idea of that. This man owes me nothing, yet I'm making him reassure me that he's not into Harper just because I need to hear it.

What am I doing?

With a small shake of my head, I give him a sorry smile. "Doesn't matter. She's into you; we're part of the same sisterhood now. Sisters come before anything else. Sorry."

Apparently, the concept of sisterhood is also on the list of things that don't impress him.

"You say sorry way too much. It's annoying."

His left hand comes to wrap around my naked thigh, just under the hem of my dress. "Why did you mention your dream if you didn't want to tell me about it?" he asks with genuine curiosity.

"I don't know," I huff. "I'm drunk and high and...I feel safe with you."

His grip tightens and his hand comes higher. It's one slight movement, and it brings the hem of my dress up before he stops.

"See, that's your mistake, Alexandra."

Just like that, I sober up.

I force a chuckle out of my mouth. "That's not funny."

His hand moves higher again, and I shift, pressing myself deeper against the headboard. "Xi..."

"What kind of naïve girl are you? Getting yourself in uncontrollable inebriated states and letting a man like me into your bedroom?" Is he...scolding me?

I feel my eyes round, a small whimper escaping me as he raises his hand again. Another one of these movements, and he'll be touching my underwear. I feel my breathing accelerate as a tight band starts pulling at my lower stomach. It twists every time his low voice resonates and his warm skin presses against mine.

I imagine the kind of things he could do to me. The ones I dream of sometimes. If I say no, will he hold me down and force me?

A wave of pleasure crashes through me, making my clit tingle.

What the hell is wrong with me?

"You wouldn't hurt me," I whisper, now scared of him finding out how I'm really feeling.

I must get this man out of here.

"Is it really hurting you if you enjoy yourself? Don't be so scared to admit you want me even after Harper said to stay away."

And just like that, his hand leaves my body as he stands up. "Do *not* let strangers in your house, Alexandra. It will get you killed. Sleep off the drugs and alcohol. I'll see you around."

I watch with wide eyes as he leaves my bedroom.

The moment he's gone, I breathe out. My body crashes, and I'm shaking, my teeth rattling. I grab the first thing in my bed to cover myself with.

I put a piece of clothing on, shocked when I smell him on it. This isn't mine.

I look down, recognizing the black hoodie he was wearing earlier. He must have taken it off at some point.

I struggle to swallow. The mere memory of him mixed with his smell makes my thighs tighten. I roll under the covers and put my hands in the front pocket of the hoodie.

There's something in there, and I can feel the shape of a plastic lighter.

I close my eyes, pressing my thumb against the spark wheel and loving the roughness against my skin. It helps with the stress that's suddenly engulfing me.

Xi is no savior. No hero. How could I believe for one second that I was safe with him?

My last experience of the North Shore should have taught me better than that.

7

ALEXANDRA

sex scenes and video games – Grady

I grab a bottle of water in the fridge and make my way back to the kitchen counter. We need to empty the fridge at some point tomorrow, or everything is going to go bad. No one is in our penthouse tonight. We moved all our stuff to Xi Ep today, and that's where the girls are, but I decided to spend one last night here to catch up on work before the craziness of initiations begins. My dad has been keeping an eye on all my homework and has deemed that I didn't have enough essays in my Introduction to international relations class, so he had a private tutor send me some essay questions to answer.

I huff as I sit back down at the kitchen counter, facing my laptop. Instead of turning on the main lights, I've only lit up the fairy lights hanging above the kitchen island. I lit up some candles around me, and I'm wearing my short silk pajamas with the black hoodie Xi had left behind. It still smells like him after three days.

I look at the fully furnished room around me, the

kitchen opening into a large living room with a floor-to-ceiling window that has a view of the campus. It doesn't look like we've moved out. This penthouse will stay empty of tenants the whole year while we live in Xi Ep because our families don't care about paying two extortionate rents.

I gather my hair into a bun, some strands still damp from my earlier shower and open the email I received from my private tutor. Just then, my phone rings, and I roll my eyes at the name on the screen.

"Hi, Dad."

"*Did you receive it? Leo said he sent three questions. He suggested you only pick one, but I think you could do two. One tonight, one tomorrow, maybe.*"

"The girls at Xi Epsilon are organizing a movie night tomorrow night. I was hoping to do that rather than do extra work. I think one is enough."

I hear the disappointment in his huff and the anger behind it. "*Alex,*" he scolds me. "*It's while people have movie nights that you should work. How do you expect to be ahead of the curve if you lounge around doing nothing. Is that really the best I can expect from you?*"

"No, but—"

"*But?*" There's a silence as I hear his breathing harshening. "*Did you just say* but *to me?*"

My stomach twists with fear. One he instilled far too long ago for me to control today.

"I'm sorry," I say in a hurry. "I just meant that it would be nice to get to know my sisters," I run my index finger against the hairline on my forehead, "but I understand there are more important things. Of course."

"*You know I hate the word* things. *There's always something it should be defining.*"

God, I'm exhausted. This man takes everything out of me, and I can never catch a break from him.

"Yes," I agree. "I should have said, I understand there are more important *matters.*"

"Better. Alright, get working, then. Don't go to bed too late."

"Okay, Dad. Bye—" The sound of the line cutting tells me he's already gone.

I pinch my lips, putting my phone on the table and pressing my thumb and index finger on my tear ducts.

He's not here. He can't hurt you. Just do your work and send it back tonight to keep him happy.

Collecting myself, I take a deep breath and read the essay questions Leo sent me.

I've been reading articles and planning my essay for hours when a knock on the front door startles me.

Who could possibly be coming here now that we've moved out? Sighing to myself, I jump off the kitchen stool. I bet it's one of Ella's men who left something behind after a one-night stand.

I open the door, ready to tell him she's not here, when my eyes meet cinnamon ones. Fall colors swirl around his pupils, and my mouth falls agape, brain stalling.

"Peach here?"

A slight fissure cracks in my chest and the knowledge that it's disappointment annoys me. I can't hope for this man to bring me any sense of happiness. That's not who he is.

All probabilities run through my head.

Did she sleep with him? Is he so hooked he's coming back for more?

Did the man I can't stop thinking and dreaming of fall for my best friend?

If someone can make a fuckboy forget all about his sick ways, it's Peach. She's gorgeous, funny, badass. And that unbelievable, round ass that got her her nickname is to die for, truly. Everyone falls for Peach.

Xi fell for Peach.

I must stay silent for too long because he leans down ever so slightly, like an adult about to explain something to a child. "Peach. Is she here?" His emotionless voice brings me back down, like a bucket of cold water splashing over me.

"Um...no."

His annoyed look deepens. Like I'm wasting his time. He checks his phone and back at me. "She said to meet her at her place."

My disappointment shifts into sadness, and I give my best fake smile. "There was a misunderstanding. This isn't our place anymore. We moved into Xi Ep today, so...yeah. That's where she is. Sorry."

He's wearing a black baseball cap, the bill at the front and hiding his face slightly, but his annoyed stare is unmistakable.

I go to close the door in his face, feeling like the most stupid girl for ever thinking the fact that he retrieved my car for me and took care of me when I was vulnerable could have meant that broody Xi liked me.

My movement is stopped, the door stuck in place just before slamming, and I look up to see his hand wrapped around the edge.

"How many times do I have to tell you to stop saying sorry."

He pushes the door back open, and I'm forced to take a few steps back as he enters uninvited.

He closes the door behind him and walks the hallway into the living area without even a look back.

What the hell is going on?

He pauses when he notices the laptop and notepads next to it. The kitchen island is a mess of crumpled papers, pens, highlighters, and political science books.

"Wild Monday night, I see," he says deadpan.

I roll my eyes behind his back and move to the side of the island perpendicular to his. I wouldn't want to be too close. His smell drives me crazy. His energy does nothing but attract me to him.

Sitting back down on my stool, I insist. "As I said, Peach isn't here. Is there anything else I can help you with?"

He digs inside the pocket of his black cargo pants and throws a small plastic seal bag on the counter. "Just bring this to her when you see her. She already paid for it."

I lean over the island, taking a closer look and realizing it's a white powder.

"Oh." Peach and Xi didn't sleep together. He's selling her drugs. "No, no, no. I'm not touching that."

He wipes his hand against his mouth, like hiding a mocking smile. I'm dying to grab his wrist and reveal what it would look like.

"Are you that much of a good girl you can't carry a bit of coke to your friend?"

I shake my head, looking down at my laptop and pretending to focus on my essay. "I'm the daughter of a senator. Do you even understand the repercussions if I got caught with this? I'm sorry, but I can't. You're going to have to bring it to her to Xi Ep. Sorry."

A short growl resonates in his chest as I feel him get

closer. I see my screen move, giving me barely enough time to pull my hands away as he slams my laptop shut.

"That's enough fucking apologizing for one conversation."

I can feel him standing behind me, his breath in my ear and his hand now flat on top of my laptop. His other hand slides between my legs, grabbing the stool. He spins me around, making me gasp. He's now towering over me, my breathing accelerating and shortening at the knowledge that his hand is so close to my core.

I look up, *sorry* at the tip of my tongue, but I stop myself just in time. I lick my dry lips.

"You have to bring it to her," I repeat. "She'll be spending the night at Xi Ep. I-I just came here to work in peace."

His eyes dart around my face, that crease between his brows ever so present. Both of us are now silent, as I watch him drag his enchanting eyes down my body, noticing how the muscles at the base of his neck tense when he stares at my bare thighs.

"Will you?"

His eyes snap back up, looking directly at me and making my entire body tense from his silent strength.

"Bring it to her," I insist when I realize he's lost track of our conversation.

If possible, his face falls, looking even more annoyed than usual.

"No," he finally says.

"But I told you...I won't."

"She can wait."

"Okay," I whisper, the conversation becoming incredibly quiet.

"Alexandra," he murmurs. The syllables of my name

become waves slowly coming to caress the shore with their impenetrable presence.

Whenever this man talks to me, digging far into my mind to grab a piece of my soul, I hear Taylor's *Wildest Dream* resonating in my head.

"Yes?"

He pulls the stool closer so my nose practically touches his stomach. He's so incredibly tall I struggle to take him all in. His other hand leaves my laptop to grab my hair at the back of my head, forcing me to tilt my head up.

His head lowers, his lips brushing mine. This close, I can feel everything he is. The anger within him, constant, like a burning fire. The danger he represents, tempting and daring me.

And his delicate soul.

Reaching out to mine in the search of something as simple as faith.

Falling Slowly - Vwillz

What the fuck am I doing?

I'm dying to kiss her. Just a taste of her soft lips, and I'm pretty sure everything would change.

I've never had a problem doing whatever needs to be done to achieve my goals. Stab someone who threatened one of my dealers? Done.

Set the Kings' house on fire to protect my family? Done.

Kill members of the King's crew who tried to take over one of our territories and only leave one alive so they can warn the others not to try again? Done.

Getting into Alexandra Delacroix's head to find info about her father should be as easy as taking candy from a baby.

Except that's the fucking problem.

It *is* as easy as taking candy from a baby.

She's annoyingly naïve and gullible. Getting herself into situations I need to protect her from.

Fuck...I want to protect her.

"Alexandra."

I should kiss her. Kiss her, fuck her, get her weak for me, and then extract all the info I need. Then I can break her fucking heart in peace, and we will get all the protection we need from Vito. Once we're safe from the police, the reign of the Kings will be over.

But here I am, barely an inch away from her lips, feeling her breath on my face and inhaling her scent of jasmine.

"Yes?"

And I can't fucking do it.

Because who has a voice this soft. Like silk on your cheek. A Sunday morning.

Winter at the door, rain on the window. Alexandra is the kind of person you hug in bed, then.

She's the breeze on a hot summer day, caressing your back and bringing goosebumps of relief to your skin.

I can't hurt this girl, because my fucking conscience is holding me back.

"It's a quarter to midnight," I say low. "What the hell are you doing up and working?"

I want to slap myself in the fucking face. I've known myself for twenty-four years, and I've come to learn that despite hating everyone, I know what it means when I want to protect someone. I know what it means when I uncontrollably want them safe. It happened once before, and it won't happen twice. I learned my fucking lesson.

So why do I care if she's sleeping or exhausting herself with work?

Fuck.

I should have left her on that lot outside of the convenience store.

I should have let her walk home alone, drunk and high off her fucking face.

I should have gone to Xi Ep the second she told me Peach was there.

Alex doesn't do cocaine. Alex doesn't even want to get near it.

She's too sweet for that. Too innocent.

Her eyes widen slightly like they always do when she's confused, when she doesn't know what to respond with.

Why is she so confused that someone might care about her?

"I..." her voice trails, her eyes darting around my face before they drop to her lap. My hand is still between her legs, holding the wooden stool and making sure she's not going anywhere. "...have homework?"

Is that a question?

"My...my dad gave me an essay to write."

"Your dad gave you..." What fucking world does her dad live in? Who holds their child to these standards? "You're going to exhaust your brain staying up doing shit like this. When was the last time you had a break?"

She looks above her shoulder at the clock on the oven. "I think I started around eight?"

I feel my eyes narrow. She's been going at it for almost four hours without a break.

You don't care.

I can see the eyebags weighing heavy on her beautiful skin.

You don't care.

And her lips are a bit dry, probably because she's been forgetting to hydrate while she was focused on working.

You don't care!

"Take a break." I finally step away, taking my cap off and running my hand through my hair. I turn my back to her and hear her release a breath. I walk around the island before opening the fridge and grabbing a small bottle of water. I crack it open, take a swig and walk back to hand it to her.

She eyes the end of the bottle, her eyes going from it to me and then back. "Thank you," she murmurs as she grabs it. I watch her lips wrap around the plastic and observe her drink, her throat working as she swallows, her chest moving slightly.

Holy shit. I'm getting worked up over a girl drinking water.

"Alright, enough," I grab the bottle back, some water spilling over her, and seal it shut again.

"What..." She gapes up at me again, wiping her mouth. "What are you doing?"

"Your belly is going to ache if you drink too quickly." A shit excuse for *I was starting to get hard watching you do something as simple as drinking.*

Her brows furrow in the slightest, and her lips part as she breathes in. I'm hyper-aware of everything about her. I feel my heartbeat accelerate every time her eyes shift.

"Um," she hesitates, licking her lips before she talks again. "What are you doing?"

"I *was* working, but I now need to make sure you don't kill yourself before returning to what I was doing."

"I can take care of myself," she snorts.

"Really? When were you planning on taking a break?"

"I don't know, I—"

"What time do you start tomorrow? How many hours of sleep were you going to get?"

"I don't know, five—"

"When was the last time you ate?"

She pinches her lips.

"Alex." I try to act like this isn't pissing me off, though

my scolding voice is the only thing that keeps coming out. "When was the last time you ate?"

She mumbles something, peering away from me.

"Look at me and answer clearly." Her eyes flick back to mine fast. Something new in her gaze following my order. She shifts in her seat, and I watch her thighs press together.

"Last night," she says a little louder.

I blink slowly, take a deep breath, and clench my jaw. This is the best I can do not to snap at her right now. I'm annoyed that it annoys me. Fuck, if she took care of herself, I wouldn't have to.

"Sounds about as baby chick as it gets," I say low.

My favorite thing to watch on Alex is the way her lips press into a thin line when someone says something grammatically incorrect. The way she stops herself from being an annoying know-it-all and how she practically bites her tongue so she doesn't correct them by accident. Sometimes, she still can't stop herself, though, and it's the cutest thing to watch. Everyone has their flaws, yet somehow hers make me want to smile.

"I just haven't had time. I had early classes this morning, and we spent the whole rest of the day moving our stuff."

"Put your homework away. You're going to eat."

"I was going to eat when I went back to Xi Ep. Look, I appreciate the...whatever this is, but I have to finish my essay. I hate to be a burden, and I can take care of myself and..."

She stops the moment my arms cross over my chest and my face hardens.

She takes a deep breath and lets it out on a long sigh. "I don't understand you."

Me neither.

She stands up in a sudden movement, her hands going

to her face before letting out a sarcastic laugh. "Oh my God." Her fingers rake through her hair. "You're hitting on me. You're...you think you're going to have sex with me!"

Fuck, what I would do to have sex with her right now. The fact she thinks I'm seducing her while I'm actually making an effort to hold back is fucking ludicrous.

"I'm not trying to have sex with you. Just trying to get you to eat so I don't have to pick your fainting body off the floor before I leave."

"Sounds to me like an excuse to stay." Her eyes narrow so innocently, she could kill someone with that cuteness. "Sounds like the guy who loves having sex with Stoneview girls found someone new."

The little girl thinks she can actually tease me.

"You can call it fucking, Alex. I assure you that's what it is." Her mouth parts, and I relish in the shocked expression on her face. Shocked but curious. "And no. That's not what I'm trying to do. I'm going to feed you, and then I will leave."

"Is that the part where you say you're going to feed me your cock? My friend warned me against you." Holy shit, this girl knows nothing. She's discovering life one situation at a time and it's killing me.

"You're not getting my cock. I wouldn't want you to choke on your meal."

"Xi!" she gasps. I roll my eyes. She wants to play, but we're nowhere near the same levels of the game.

"Clear the fucking table, will you," I tell her, hearing the harsh tone in my voice. I want to repeat myself in a better way. But then she moves and starts packing up her stuff, listening like the good girl she is.

I check her fridge again and grab the packet of fresh gnocchi and the mozzarella. Moving to the cupboard, I find some tomato sauce and herbs.

I'm already cooking the gnocchi in the sauce, adding some onions and herbs, when she comes to stand next to me.

"Are you cooking for me right now?"

"Seems like it."

"It smells so good. What are you making?"

"Mozzarella gnocchi bake."

"It's always such a pleasure to converse with you, Xi." The sarcasm in her voice forces me to stare at her. I stop stirring the sauce so I can focus on scowling at her.

"I thought I told you to rest. Judging my conversation skills isn't taking a break, is it? Do something else. What do you do for fun? Count the dollars in your bank account? Video call your pony?"

She brings a book she's holding in her right hand just below her eyes, hiding the lower half of her face as she flutters her eyelashes.

"I read."

"An introduction to political philosophy," I read on the cover. "That's not a fucking break. Give me this." I snatch the book from her hand, pointing at the sofa at the other end of the room with the wooden spoon. "Go watch something stupid on TV."

"I don't want to watch something stupid on TV," she moans. "Can't I just talk with you?"

"No."

The light in her beautiful hazel eyes dims slightly. "Do you hate me or something? Why are you cooking for me if you don't like me?"

"I don't hate you," I mumble under my breath. "I fucking hate everyone. It's not just you." I turn back to the kitchen counter and grab the glass dish, pouring the sauce and gnocchi.

"You truly know how to make a woman feel special. I understand now how you *fucked* so many girls."

She spins around and heads for the sofa as I angrily slice the mozzarella and add it on top of everything in the dish.

What the fuck am I still doing here...and making her food on top of that.

It pisses me off to know that I lied. I don't hate Alex. Not even a little bit, which annoys me the most. Why can't she just be like all the other Stoneview girls? Rich and bitchy. Infuriating and selfish.

No, she has to be sweet *and* pleasing *and* selfless *and* make everyone around her love her.

I put the dish in the oven and turn around, leaning against the counter. She's on the sofa, her back against the armrest and her knees up. Apparently, she grabbed another book from somewhere because she's now reading *The Rise and Fall of The Great Powers.*

I huff to myself, cross my arms over my chest, and do something I will most certainly regret. I get to know her. "So what's that essay about?"

Her head lifts from the book, and she looks at me. "International relations. Geopolitics, to be precise. I'm writing about the place of immigrants in Western countries when they escape a war the West funds."

"Is that your major? Politics?"

"Political science, yes. What did you study?"

A small chuckle escapes me. "I didn't even set foot in high school."

"Oh. Sorry, I didn't know."

"Did you just say sorry to me again?"

The corner of her mouth twitches. She's been caught.

"Well, I..."

"You're not responsible for my school attendance. That's all me. You worry about yourself, like the fact that you say sorry way too often. Fuck, who taught you that everything is your fault?"

She looks down at her book and back up at me. "No one," she mumbles. She knows exactly who, and I wish she'd tell me. I want to have a word with them.

Quickly changing topics, she shifts on the sofa, facing me entirely. "I don't know why you're here. I mean, I know why you're here, but I don't understand why you're *still* here. Cooking me food."

I shrug, staying silent. I like the way Alexandra talks. It's light, eloquent, easy on the ears. She's like a lady talking to her court. Polite, discreet. Everything she does is light as air.

"I like that you are, but surely there must be a reason for you to always take care of me."

Yes, there is.

"Perhaps..." She plays with the corner of her book, bending the page with her nail "...you're attracted to me."

Good God. I won't only hurt her if I go ahead with Vito's task. I will completely crush her. She is too naïve for this world. She belongs in a fucking Disney movie.

The oven timer beeps, saving me from telling her that I am, in fact, attracted to her.

I grab oven gloves and take the dish out.

"Mm," I hear as she approaches. "It smells delicious." I grab a plate and help her to a serving of baked gnocchi. "Do you often cook?" she asks as we settle down.

"I live on my own, so yes."

"Are you not eating?"

"I've had food in the last twenty-four hours. Unlike you."

I pull the chair and look at her pointedly until she sits down.

I sit down on the perpendicular side to hers, watching her as she sets a napkin on her lap and grabs the fork and knife like we're eating in Stoneview's best restaurant. She delicately cuts a piece of the bake and blows on her food, before swallowing it like it's caviar. Her mouth is firmly closed, her back straight. She puts her cutlery back down and dabs the corner of her mouth.

"It's delicious," she finally says once she's swallowed her first bite.

"That's the most Stoneview way I've ever seen someone eat dinner. No one is watching you, you know?"

"You are." She smiles, her lips closed. "You're always watching, aren't you?" My heart skips a beat. "Otherwise, how would you know I'm walking home drunk and high in the middle of the night on my own. How would you know where to bring my car back to me." She leans forward, both her palms on the table. "How would you know the code to enter this apartment?"

Her eyes shine with pride before she goes back to her plate.

"You're annoying," I lie.

"So are you. I'm not exactly a huge fan of the 'I hate everyone' personality, but I'd like to believe it's a front. I'm sure you'd be passable if I get to know you."

"Passable?" I mutter. "Are you aware of the kind of person you're alone with right now, Alex? I wouldn't anger me if I were you."

"You're always angry. Life frustrates you, and it's written all over your face. You must do something about it, or it'll swallow you whole. It seems fucking your way around town isn't helping either."

Being that perceptive can't be good for her, surely.

There's a short pause before she changes the topic, like a

girl well-trained in not letting a sensitive conversation last for too long.

"So, no high school. What did your parents think about that?"

"My dad was already gone, and my mom couldn't stop me."

"Why did you choose not to go?"

"I needed money and fast. The streets offered that, and high school didn't."

"What did you need money for?"

I feel my jaw tighten and narrow my eyes at her when I realize what's happening. "We're not doing this, Alex."

"Doing what?" she asks innocently.

"Getting into my past."

"Why not?" She starts playing with the gnocchi on her plate. "After all, you're here at almost one in the morning, feeding me and making sure I take care of myself. Why not get to know each other?"

Ignoring how she tries to get me to admit I like her again, I lean forward. "If you don't stop playing with your food, I'll tell your mommy and daddy you're up so late. Now eat."

She chuckles to herself and starts eating again. "Do you want to fuck me? Is that why you're here so late?"

I absolutely, one hundred percent want to fuck you.

I ignore her question again, my back settling against the chair as I cross my arms. I feel my biceps clench when her eyes graze over them.

"How do you do it, tell me. You cook them dinner, and then what?"

"You don't want to get into this."

"I do," she says. "I want to be warned."

"Your friends already warned you. You're the one who

keeps mentioning fucking. Do you want me to fuck you, Alex?"

"That's not what I said," she fights back, her cheeks reddening. "You're always where I am. Only you don't want to get to know me. I can safely assume that's how you get the girl, isn't it? You make her feel a bit special, and before she knows it, she's in your bed. But you wouldn't want to talk about each other, that's a little too deep."

"I can go deep, don't you worry."

She gulps, her throat working hard as she puts her cutlery back on her plate. "I'm done," she says hastily, getting up and bringing her plate to the sink. She turns it on, grabs a sponge and soaks it in dish soap, then rubs the plate, quick and hard. I know she's just working to keep busy now.

I get up slowly and walk to her, stopping at her back. My hands grab her waist, and I lower my lips to her ear.

"I can tell you one thing." My thumbs caress her above the hoodie she's wearing, and for the first time tonight, I realize it's mine. She's wearing my fucking hoodie. Wearing my scent on her skin. *Fuck.* "I don't cook them dinner, I don't make sure they take a break from work, and I don't tell them about not having been to high school. I don't ask them about their studies, either."

"Why not?" she whispers.

"Because I don't care."

I give her a second to take a ragged breath.

"Do you want me to fuck you, Alex?" I repeat my question, unable to control myself. What I'd give to fuck her without any repercussions. Just because I want to. Just to hold her afterward, watch her sleep, and then do it all over again.

She shivers under my touch, washing the now clean plate.

"Could you take it?" I insist. "The way I fuck?"

I slide my hands to her front, one of them cupping her pussy through her shorts. "It's rough, and sometimes I like to make it hurt."

I feel her breathing accelerate as my hand lowers. I touch her naked thigh. Her skin is softer than the silk she's wearing. I slip my fingers underneath, my heart accelerating when I realize she isn't wearing anything else. My breath hitches when I feel her wetness.

"I like punishing my girl when she does something bad. How much do you like being degraded, Alex? Do you like being treated like a little slut, being made to wait and beg before I give you the satisfaction of touching my cock?"

A small whimper escapes her, more wetness pooling between her legs.

"Could you handle me?"

My hard-on is painful in my jeans, and I grind against her perfectly round ass before letting the tip of my finger press between her lips and at her wet entrance.

She jumps and spins around to face me, as if my touch brought her out of a trance. Her movement forces me to retrieve my hand, both of them ending up on her hips. "I'm a virgin," she gasps. "I—oh my god." Her eyes widen when she realizes what she just said.

I reel back. Why am I surprised? Of course, she's a virgin.

Her phone rings, startling both of us, and she glances at the island behind me.

"It's my dad," she says knowingly without even looking. She walks around me, making sure not to touch me, and grabs her phone.

"Dad." She eyes me, blanching as she disappears in the hallway. "No, I'm almost done, I promise. What about..." Her voice slowly fades before I hear a door closing.

Alexandra Delacroix is the sort of girl who does extra essays until midnight. She dabs the corners of her mouth after each bite. She's a pretty angel, glowing from all the riches she was born into. She's sweet, innocent...and a fucking virgin. *Still* a virgin. I can't fucking destroy that.

Except I told Emma and Vito Luciano, I would.

9

ALEXANDRA

Ghost (dark version) - Confetti

I pack my stuff into my bag and look up to see Chester waiting for me by the amphitheater door. I smile at him and jog to meet him.

"No one, and I truly mean no one, brings as much shit to class as you do, Alex," he laughs as we exit the room.

"Oh shush, I like to have all my colored pens and my notebooks."

"We like to take notes on these things called laptops now, or iPads. Why don't you just use your iPad as a notebook?"

"Because, Chester," I pull out my favorite notebook, place it next to my face, and point at it, "that's why."

"*Get it off my desk*," he reads. "I don't get it."

"That's because you're not a Swiftie. Peach and Ella got me this notebook, so who am I not to use it?"

"Please, tell me you don't have a notebook that refers to a Taylor Swift song. You're not thirteen anymore, Alex." His voice resonates with the laugh he's holding back while he tries to scold me.

I stop and pin him with my stare. "There is no age to be a Swiftie. Don't even fight me on this."

We exit the Political Science building and go down the marble steps leading to the manicured lawn. It's a beautiful day, the sun shining bright despite being early September, and I smile as I close my eyes and tilt my head back, taking in the warm sun rays.

"I love that we have Introduction to American Politics together," I sigh happily. "That man is so boring, I'm glad I'm not suffering alone."

"It could have been because you love me, because I'm your best friend, or because you enjoy spending time with me, but no. It's because you want us to suffer together."

I cackle a laugh, looking back at him. "Suffering together is beautiful. True love."

He smiles back at me, but his eyes tell me what he doesn't. He's still hurting that we're not together anymore. Pretending I don't notice it, I change the topic of conversation.

"Didn't you say you had to go to the store? Let's go together. Should I buy us some Hubba Bubba? We haven't had those in ages."

He nods, starts walking again, and drags me along with him. "Yes! I love you when you think of that. Have you got your fake I.D. with you? I've been tasked to buy the alcohol for tonight's party."

My mouth twists, and I recoil slightly. "I do, but I'm scared to use it. If I get caught, my dad will never let me hear the end of it."

"Don't worry." His bright smile is reassuring. "We're in Silver Falls now. Not everyone knows who you are."

Nodding to myself, I smile at him. "Okay, let's go." A gust of wind goes through my skirt as we hurry to his car. The uniform we're made to wear at SFU is just as bad as the Stoneview Prep's one. The burgundy and white tartan skirts match the color of the ties, and our white button-downs are as dull as they come.

I throw my bag at the back of his G Wagon and hop in the passenger seat. "What do you think will happen on your first night of initiation?" Chester asks as he starts the car. "Ours have been horrible. I puked in class yesterday because they made us drink until seven a.m. And it was the first night."

I huff and let my head fall back against the seat. "I don't want to go through initiations. Harper has been so fake to me since the bid party, and I just know she's going to be horrible."

I don't add that I've been avoiding her, given that I'm too scared she's going to find out what happened with Xi.

I want to laugh. Why do I even care? The man ran away as soon as I told him I was a virgin. Girls who don't have experience don't excite him. He went as far as making me dinner and pretending he cared just to get me in his bed. But a virgin? God, no.

A few days have passed since we moved into our sorority house. I haven't seen or heard from him since, and I don't think I will. He was obviously being a typical fuckboy, which means I can put all of this behind me. As long as we stay out of each other's way, I don't have to worry about anything.

I shake my head and look at Chester while he drives, explaining that if I feel unsafe with the Xi Ep girls at any point, I should call him, and he'd come get me.

Chester is such a prince. The kind from the fairy tales.

His blond hair always shines in the sun, and his blue eyes make all the girls melt under his kind stare.

He is everything I would never want again. Not after getting a taste of what it'd be like with a more rugged man —someone who would take the choice away from me and couldn't hold himself from having me.

If you were mine, I couldn't keep my hands off you, no matter what you said.

The words from my kidnapper have always stayed with me. It's what I've always been ashamed of wanting. My dirty secret no one will ever know. It's the same reason for which I came under my kidnapper's hand.

I want someone to not leave me a choice.

Xi felt like that. His left hand holding my waist, his right beneath my shorts. His body blocking me while he described how he would degrade me.

Sighing, I nod and smile at Chester. "You're the best."

He parks in front of the liquor store on the south bank of Silver Falls and we both get out of the cars. He buys so much alcohol we spend around forty minutes putting it all in the car.

"My arms are dead," I huff as I sit back down inside the car.

"You're the best for helping me out. And thanks for the Hubba Bubba." He puts half of the roll of bubblegum in his mouth. He puts a hand on my thigh and shakes it playfully. "You're so much stronger than you let out."

I dramatically bend my arm like a bodybuilder and flex my biceps. "Years of cheerleading and swimming, baby."

He explodes in a laugh before wrapping a hand around my biceps. "Damn, girl." He lets me go and runs a hand through his hair before giving me a sorry smile. "You were such a good cheerleader, Alex." His mouth twists.

"No. Dude, we're not going all 'poor Alex' right now."

I can live a relatively normal life now, considering my forearm had been broken in two, and the rehab was long and painful. Although I can't cheer or swim anymore, the sports are too hard on the arms. The doctor said I could slowly get back into it in a year, and compete again in two. But competitions don't wait for the injured. The two athletics are pretty much over for me.

"I'm not. I promise." He hesitates, then admits, "Okay, maybe I felt a bit sorry. I just feel bad that you had to quit because some bastard broke your arm and dislocated your shoulder. It's not fucking fair."

My heart beats a little faster when I recall my night on the North Shore. "Well, it wasn't him. I broke my arm and dislocated my shoulder by throwing myself against a boarded window." I shrug. "Survival mode makes you do stupid things."

"It's still his fault," he says, his tone now frustrated. "I wish they had caught him. Him and all his friends. Then maybe we..." He shakes his head. "Never mind."

My friends don't know *exactly* what happened. They know I was kidnapped, held for ransom, and that they tried to leave me in a burning house. That's enough to justify my panic attacks to them. They don't know what happened when I was in that house. No one does.

I put a reassuring hand on his shoulder. "We're better as friends. We both know that."

He licks his lips and gives me his best fake smile. I know him too well to know it's not real. "Yeah."

His phone ringing in the car cuts our conversation short. He presses the button on the car screen.

"*Heyoooo*," a loud voice calls out. "*What's up, pledge?*"

Chester rolls his eyes before answering. "I got all the

alcohol like you asked. I'm going to make my way back now."

"*Good, good. Just one last thing. You're gonna pick up the pills too. Our guy will meet you in the parking lot, so don't leave yet. See you later.*"

The call drops and Chester turns to me. "I can drive you to Xi Ep and come back."

"Don't be silly." I mess up his silky hair that falls to his ears. "So, what are you guys doing tonight?"

"We're hosting a huge party, and I'm sure there'll be plenty of dares for the pledges. I think you girls will be coming over."

"Are we? I wish I knew what Harper and Camila have in mind for us. It's scary to be kept in the dark. I heard one of Harper's friends talk about making the pledges run around the yard completely topless last year."

"Fuck," Chester huffs. "I wish I'd seen that."

"Shut up," I laugh as I slap his arm. "I just hope they don't go full-on hazing. At least I have Peach and Ella with me."

Chester's phone pings, and he peers up at a car parking right in front of us. I follow his gaze and my heart drops when I see the black Ford Ranger.

Xi.

Of course, Xi is the one dealing him the drugs. How could I not think of that?

My heart squeezes when I notice the beautiful girl sitting next to him in the car.

Don't be sad. You know that's what he's like.

The girl has beautiful black hair falling to her shoulders and robust features that obviously show she's someone not to be fucked with. I bite my inner cheek, thinking this is probably the kind of girl Xi likes. The strong ones that stand up for themselves.

I slap myself mentally, hating the way I blame myself for not keeping an unreliable man around. I should be thankful I pushed him away.

My phone vibrates in my lap, my body stilling when I see the message.

> Xi: Tell me you're not alone in a car with your ex.

How the hell did he get my number? Why is his saved on my phone? And how does he know about my past with Chester?

I gaze back up at him through the windshield and watch his hard eyes on me. He can be so damn scary.

Well, screw him. I refuse to allow Xi to drag me back to him when all I've done this week is attempt to keep him off my mind. I failed. But the point is I tried.

> Alex: What's the name of your new conquest?

I watch his eyebrows shoot up and his eyes glance to mine before he texts back.

> Xi: Worry about yourself and not getting in trouble with me.

Huffing, I narrow my eyes at him and type.

> Alex: I can do whatever I want with Chester. That's none of your business.

> Xi: I'll get rid of him, then punish you. Do you truly think being stubborn is a good idea?

I barely stifle a gasp. I know he's not serious. He can't be serious. On the other hand, Xi is a criminal, and I can't help thinking he could easily get rid of someone. Plus he told me he liked to punish his girls...

When I don't reply, he texts again.

> Xi: I'm not enjoying seeing you alone with another man, Alexandra. So, get out of the car.

"What the hell is he doing?"

I startle in my seat when Chester talks. Turning to him, I open my mouth even as no clear words come out. "I-uh...I don't..."

"I thought he was going to come to me, but maybe I should go to him? I've never picked up drugs before."

"I'm not sure," I say weakly.

I look back down at my vibrating phone.

> Xi: This is my last warning. Get out of the car, or I'll tell Harper what happened between us.

My heart freezes. Without thinking, I undo my seatbelt and turn to Chester again. "I'll go get it." I grab the stack of bills he had put on the middle console before getting out quickly.

I stride to Xi's window and extend my hand when he opens it, showing I'm expecting the pills he was meant to bring.

"Get in," he orders before closing the window.

I bite my inner cheek so I don't throw insults at him and get in the back of the car.

"Are you done playing games?" I snap. "Just give me the damn pills."

"So rude," he says low.

"Yeah? Well, you're an asshole. I guess we both have our flaws." It seems I'm a little angrier about him leaving my apartment without saying bye than I thought.

He doesn't seem to like my retort, but the girl next to him laughs as she brings her hand to her bra and grabs something from inside the cup. I watch with my mouth agape as she pulls out a large bag of pills. How many did Zeta Nu order? There must be at least thirty tiny pills in there.

The girl silently passes them to Xi and he turns around. "Come closer, cupcake."

"Stop calling me that," I mumble.

Xi huffs and gives the girl a quick look. Without a need for words, she opens the glove box and pulls out a gun that she puts on her lap, her hand on the handle.

"Whoa," I gasp as I press myself against the seat.

"You just love getting me to repeat myself, don't you?" Xi says coldly. "I said *come. Closer.*"

My heart beating harshly, I bring myself closer. I watch his hand slowly grab my tie and push it to the side.

"You're hot in your uniform." My gaze darts to the girl, watching her brows narrow. Must he really say this when his current girlfriend is right next to him?

He unbuttons the first button, and my breath catches in my throat. He undoes the second one even quicker and my eyes go up to his. "Wh-what are you doing?"

The third pops and I bring my hand to his, but he pushes it away. "Tsk, tsk," he tuts me. "We got a gun. You got nothing. If I was you, I'd just stay still."

"*Were*," I murmur on a trembling breath. "If I *were* you."

What is wrong with you? Is now really the time to correct someone on their grammar?

I'm so mad at myself, but these sorts of things are a coping mechanism. When I can't think straight, automatisms take place. I've been corrected all my life, so I do the same. *Annoyingly.*

"Little miss know-it-all." His gravelly voice penetrates my chest in the most perfect way.

"Xi," I panic as the fourth button goes.

He brings the bag of pills to my chest just as he pulls one cup of my bra down, revealing my taut nipple.

"Calm down, cupcake. I'm just hiding these. You're not leaving my car with a bag of pills in your hand. Now listen to me. You give these to your friend only, yeah? Because I swear to God, if I hear you've taken one of these, my hand will come down on your ass so fucking hard you're not gonna remember your own name."

I try to ignore the tightness inside me and the wetness now coating my panties. I can feel it so clearly between my legs. His brown eyes dig into mine and I nod slowly. "They're not for me."

"Atta girl."

He puts the pills in my bra before putting it back in place, not without making sure he's squeezed my boob in the process.

"How do you have my phone number?" I murmur. "And why do I have yours?"

His expression doesn't change as he buttons the last part of my shirt. "I'm your security guard. It's only normal we have each other's numbers."

This is the second time he uses this excuse and I'm not liking it one bit.

"I don't think I should feel so *unsafe* with my security guard."

"Fire me, then," he tells me matter-of-factly as his hand

caresses mine. He takes the money and gives it to the other girl.

I'm about to say something else when he cuts me off. "Bring him his pills. Then you're leaving with me."

"With you?" I ask, confused.

"I'm not letting a baby chick back into her ex's car. Boys have bad intentions, Alex. Don't you know that?" His sarcasm isn't lost on me.

It's not written on his face or in his voice; it's just the words he says with that deadpan voice of his. He loves acting like I'm a kid who doesn't know anything. However, everything tells me he's the last boy I should be in a car with.

I gulp before nodding and hurrying out of the car, rushing back to Chester.

"Alex," he hisses as soon as I get in. "Why did you do that? You don't even know the guy."

"Don't worry," I smile. My heart is beating, the adrenaline rushing through my body, and I kind of like it. I like what I'm about to do next even more. "Start the car."

He starts without hesitation and drives away just as Xi realizes I'm not coming back to him. The moment we're on the main road again, I receive another text.

> Xi: Why play games when we both know you're going to lose?

Feeling the excitement coursing through my body, I type back quickly.

> Alex: I won't be another girl on your list. But nice try.

> Xi: Alright. We'll see next time you're having a baby chick moment if I'll take care of you.

> Alex: Why don't you just take care of the brunette with you in the car.

> Xi: I guess if I don't have you...she'll have to do.

I try to ignore the disappointment that makes my heart heavy. It's annoyingly making me realize how much I like Xi taking care of me.

That's what he does, isn't it? He chases, he fucks, he moves on. The guy isn't waiting for me.

I try my hardest to be disgusted by him. His behavior should make me feel the way it makes Peach and Ella feel. Repulsed and appalled.

So why do I just feel jealous? Why do I crave him and his attention?

It's because he touched me.

There.

I've been craving someone's touch for so long that my body just dug claws of desire onto the first man who almost gave me pleasure since someone who shouldn't have did.

I take a deep breath, feeling my thighs tightening as I think back to the night of my birthday.

Why did it feel so good? Why can't I forget about it? Why did it have to be me whose life he ruined?

A small whimper escapes me, and I feel my body becoming heavy.

No. Not now. Please, not now.

"Chester," I try to call out as I smell non-existing smoke, but it's too late.

I hear him saying my name, panic resonating in the car. I take a deep breath, only there's no point. My muscles start spasming as my throat closes up and my head falls back.

Ringing in my ears.

Darkness at the edge of my vision.

And I'm gone.

I can feel him, right there, him and the smell of burning smoke. He touches me, and he makes me feel good. Too good. I disgust myself.

I feel my chest heaving and my head going from side to side as my body convulses, but I'm not aware for more than a split second, losing consciousness quickly.

I can't even think of trying to fight it. All I know is that it's a big one.

When I come back to, I'm in a recovery position on my left side. I'm against the grass, my head heavy and feeling like I just woke up from an exhausting nightmare.

Two voices are arguing.

"Dude, get the fuck away from her," I hear Chester. His voice is serious.

"Don't call me *dude*, I'll break your fucking legs."

Xi.

The fog around my brain starts to dissipate as I hear the two.

"I let her leave in your car, and that's what fucking happens. Now get out of the way—"

"She needs space while she's having a seizure. She could really hurt herself, now *back. Off.*" I've never heard Chester talk with such a strong voice.

Unsure of what else happens, the next thing I know, the smell of bergamot and something else I love reaches me. One hand comes to the back of my neck, holding my head up a bit, and the other loosens my tie and pops the first button of my shirt to press against my chest with a strong touch. They're rough. His hands, I mean. They feel so good on my damp skin.

I take in a sharp breath as I feel myself take control over my body.

"Welcome back to earth, baby chick." His gravelly voice has a certain softness that I didn't expect from him. I blink up at Xi's face right above mine. He places my head on his lap and caresses my hair away from my sweaty forehead.

The sun is shining too brightly, and I'm forced to put my hand in front of my eyes. I feel lethargic, like someone's just put me into a washing machine and I've been tumbling for hours.

"You're okay," he says softly, more like an order than anything else.

I blink up at him, struggling to form any word.

"Do you remember what happened?"

I nod. I want to sit up, except I don't have the strength.

"Alex." Chester's worried voice contrasts with the calm strength that is Xi right now. My eyes flip to him, standing right next to us. "I'm going to get water from the car. Don't move, we're on the side of the road and I don't want you to get hurt."

I look around to see he's pulled over near the entrance of a park, hence the lush grass.

Chester comes jogging back with a bottle of water in his hands.

"Let her sit up," he snarls at Xi. "She needs to drink."

Xi helps me into a sitting position, then grabs my waist and pulls me between his legs so my back is against his.

"I told you to leave," Chester growls as he lowers himself next to me. He brings the bottle to my lips, and I drink, struggling to swallow. "I called Ella," he explains. "You said not to call 911 last time, so I didn't. Is that right?"

I nod as he pulls the bottle away from me. "Thanks." It's a low whisper without much strength behind it. There's no point calling 911 because the attacks always pass. As long as I haven't hurt myself falling or hitting something, there's nothing to do but wait.

"I took you out of the car and laid you down in a lateral safety position so you wouldn't hurt yourself. Is...is that okay?"

Bless his heart. The last time I had a seizure from panic in front of him, Ella and Peach were there. They know exactly what to do. I can't imagine the fear of dealing with me on his own.

I blink, trying to find the strength to answer him. "Thank you." I take a deep breath. "Can you take me home, please?"

He stares at Xi behind me and repeats, "She wants me to take her home. Now let her go."

Xi's hold on my waist tightens before he lets go. He stands up and helps me to my feet. My knees suddenly buckle, and he catches me at the waist again.

"I'm going to carry you." His matter-of-fact tone makes me shake my trembling head multiple times.

"It's okay. I don't want to be carried right now."

I'm exhausted, completely lifeless, but it's always this way after an attack. And I'm used to it.

The two men help me to the car and sit me inside, Xi buckling my belt. "I can come home with you."

"She doesn't need you to come home with her," Chester snaps.

I watch Xi's features go from his constantly unimpressed expression to a harsh scowl. For a second, I'm afraid he will turn around and punch Chester in the face, so I intervene. "I'm okay. Really. I just need to rest. Chester will drive me."

His upper lip curls, but he doesn't say anything as he steps back and heads to his car. The slam of his door startles me. Why does he care so much about what happens to me?

The drive is quick and silent. Chester's eyes keep darting to me, and I force a reassuring smile on my face. I hate making myself his responsibility. I'm not. Not anymore.

He parks in front of the Xi Ep house and calls Ella. She's out in a split second, opening my side of the car.

"Hey, baby," she says as she smiles softly. "Are you alright?"

I nod, my eyes blinking heavily. "Exhausted," I rasp.

"Let's get you to bed."

Chester exits the car and helps Ella get me to the front door.

"Do you want me to come in?" he murmurs as he caresses my hair.

I shake my head but smile at him. "No boys in the house."

"I got it, don't worry," Ella intervenes as she wraps me in her arms. "You go back to the frat before getting in trouble. Wren said they're waiting for you."

"I don't care."

"I got it, Chester. Go."

Ella helps me to my bedroom. Peach is waiting there already, a mug in her hands.

"Hi, pretty girl," she smiles. "I made you a hot chocolate and drew you a bath."

I nod, tears welling up in my eyes.

"No, no," Ella says in a hurry. "We're doing it because we love you. Not to make you cry."

"I don't deserve you guys," I sob. Tears fall freely from my eyes as my two best friends come to hug me.

"We all don't deserve each other," Peach chuckles. "That's why we deserve each other."

I laugh through the tears, sobbing some more as I hug them tighter.

The bath really helps, and the hot chocolate even more. I wash my hair and relax in the bubbles, making sure to respond every time one of the girls knocks to make sure I haven't fallen asleep. I rinse, wrap myself in a robe and my hair in a warm towel, and announce that I'm going for a nap. The girls both give me a kiss and leave my bedroom. I take a breath, crawl into my bed, and let it go. I fall asleep before I even realize it, exhausted from the attack.

Even so, in my dreams, the only person who comes back is the one that I shouldn't be thinking of. Xi is there, touching me and kissing me. He brought me back from my panic attack. I remember when he stopped it when we were on the North Shore. I remember the way he touched me and made it all better.

And for some reason, my sleep is unlike any before.

10

ALEXANDRA

Bad Ones – Call Me Karizma

"Girls." Camila claps her hands as she raises her voice. "You will all be asked one question about Xi Epsilon, one by one. If you get it right, you get to come to Zeta Nu with us. If not, you're going back to your room for the night."

Initiations have officially begun and, so far, we've already done three shots, knelt next to our big sisters, and been told that they've put cameras in our bedroom for the night. Every time we fail to obey the rules, we're sent back and have to go on all fours in our bedroom. With our uniform skirt up and our sorority paddle on the floor next to us. Our sisters are allowed to come to the room and spank us. Peach has already been sent back to her room. Of course, the girl can't stand being told what to do.

Camila keeps going, "Let's test your knowledge, slaves."

One by one, we're called by Camila to answer a question about the sorority. When it's my turn, I walk to her and bring my hands in front of me, looking at them as she asks, "What does Xi Epsilon stand for, slave?"

Relaxing at the thought that it's an easy one, I keep looking down as I answer. "It stands for *Xeinobake Eimi*, mistress Camila," I try to pronounce. Yes, we have to call our sisters *'mistresses'* this week.

She nods and adds, "Bonus point. What does it mean?"

"It means to be mad for the love of a stranger, mistress Camila," I answer. My heart accelerates, knowing exactly which stranger I am going mad for and finding the irony intense.

"Very good, slave. You may come with us to Zeta Nu."

The party at Zeta Nu is rowdier than I expected. The frat boys are drunk out of their minds, especially the pledges who have a bottle of liquor taped to each hand. Rap music is playing loudly, and I can barely hear when Harper gives me orders.

Wren stumbles toward me, a massive smile on his face. "Alex!" he shouts in my ear, making me recoil slightly. "You girls are here finally."

He's topless and sweaty, his abs prominent and undoubtedly making every other girl stare at him the way I am. Wren is the definition of a hot guy. He's ridiculously tall, probably the tallest man in this room. His chestnut hair contrasts with his blue eyes, but what we all drool over are his firm muscles he couldn't hide if he wanted to. Especially his shoulders. We would all fall head over heels for our best lacrosse attacker when we were at Stoneview Prep, but my friend has only ever had eyes for one girl, and she didn't make it here tonight.

"Is Peach here?" he asks without wasting time.

I shake my head, opening my mouth to explain what

happened when someone pulls my hair, dragging me backward from the force.

"Ow," I gasp, surprised.

"Sorry," Harper taunts me. "Slaves aren't allowed to talk at this party."

I blink at her, confused, until she points at another one of the Xi Ep pledges. She's got gray duct tape stuck to her mouth. The same kind that's been used to tape the bottles of liquors to Wren's hands.

"She talked," Harper explains.

I look back at Wren, mouth agape, and he explodes into a loud, drunken laugh. "You Xi Ep girls are fucking ruthless. Sorry, Alex. I'll talk to you tomorrow, I guess."

Harper nudges me on the shoulder. "Go get me a drink from the kitchen. Pick something I like. If I don't, you'll be licking it off the floor."

I hurry to the kitchen, ignoring the people attempting to talk to me. I can see a couple of other girls from Xi Ep with tape on their mouths and my stomach twists. Initiations are so stupid, but then I think of all the memories my mom told me she had with her sisters at Xi Ep, and I remember once the initiations are done, the fun begins.

It's just a stupid tradition.

I look at the White Claws on the table, hesitating between raspberry and black cherry, trying to remember which one Harper likes. If she tries to make me lick the drink she spills on the floor, I'm going to have to refuse. She'll send me home, leading me to spend the rest of the night on my hands and knees, but I don't care.

I grab the black cherry, observe it, and put it back. I grab the raspberry, hesitating.

"This is ridiculous," I mumble to myself.

"Black cherry," a voice says behind me. I startle, looking

around to find Xi leaning on the door frame, arms crossed over his firm chest. He's wearing an oversized white tee that somehow still shows his solid muscles underneath—a beautiful contrast with his bronze skin. The black cargo pants he's sporting make me wonder how many drugs he's got in the multiple pockets.

I open my mouth but clamp it back shut. I can't say anything to him.

"Come on." He starts walking toward me. One slow step at a time. "Don't tell me you're taking this initiation thing seriously and not talking to anyone tonight."

I avoid his gaze as he stops right in front of me, staring down at me.

His eyebrows scrunch with disappointment. "It really is some privilege shit to be able to create your own problems and force yourself to listen to a bunch of girls on a power trip."

He touches my cheek, but I turn around, facing the kitchen island again. He's not wrong, although I won't stop prevailing just because Xi calls me *privileged*. Of course I am. I'm from Stoneview. It doesn't get more privileged than that. Yet while we might live different lives, I'm not going to stop living mine because he disagrees with it.

Yes, initiation is a stupid problem we make up for ourselves, but I want to become a Xi Ep girl, and I refuse to let him make me feel stupid for it.

Just as I grab the black cherry White Claw, I feel two arms on either side of me as he bends forward, blocking me between the counter and him. "You know," he whispers in my ear, "I followed you in here to check how you were feeling after what I saw earlier. I was worried for you." I feel his breath on my neck when he asks, "Are you okay?"

I nod, not answering anything. We might be alone in the

kitchen, but I want to play by the rules.

I always play by the rules.

"I'm not sure I like this game," he says low. "But I do have to admit I would love to see your mouth taped. I'd play with you and watch the way it holds your moans down."

A shiver I can't control courses through my body, and I bite my lower lip to stop myself from saying anything.

"I'm gonna need you to pass on a message to your ex-boyfriend from me." He pauses for a split second, pressing himself closer to me. He lifts one of his hands from the kitchen marble and slides it against my waist, my stomach, and keeps going lower until it touches my thigh. He stops then, going back up but under my skirt this time.

"If he ever puts himself between you and me again, I will set him on fire."

I gasp when his fingers brush my panties. The slightest touch, right where my clit is.

"I really hate privileged Stoneview girls, Alex. Did you know that?"

From what I've heard from everyone around me, he hates *everything*, so I'm not surprised I'm on the list.

"I hate how you all behave as if all things belong to you, like you're more important than everyone, like you're better than us."

His lips are right by my ear, his breath bringing goosebumps to my skin. Then he's tracing a line down my neck, barely even grazing my skin with his. His smell envelops me, and my hands come to grip the counter. I want to lean back against him and lose myself in his embrace. I want to grab his hand and press it again between my legs.

"I don't fucking understand why I don't feel that way toward you," he growls against my skin. I feel his teeth grazing my neck and a ragged breath escapes me. "You're a little miss know-it-all who constantly needs rescuing and lives in a fairy tale." Gently, he pushes my panties to the side and presses two fingers against my clit. "You're so fucking innocent." He slowly starts circling.

A moan escapes me, and I buck my hips forward, wanting more pressure.

"So why is it that all I want to do is wrap you in my arms and protect the fuck out of you, so the only person who can hurt you is me."

Another slow circle melts everything inside me.

"I'll hurt you so fucking good, cupcake. Would you like that?"

"Yes," I moan.

There's a low chuckle in my ear, the sound surprising from him even though it has no humor in it.

"You lost your game, Alex. Don't you care anymore?"

I shake my head. "I don't care," I pant. "Just keep go—"

My pleasure is cut short by the door slamming open. I jump away from Xi as Harper walks in.

"Where's my drink, sl—"

Her smile drops.

I open my mouth to say something, before remembering I'm not meant to talk. I shake my head instead, as if saying this is not what she thinks.

There's no point. Her eyes dart to what I'm assuming are my flushed cheeks and disheveled state and then to Xi's tented cargo pants.

Instead of a furious shriek, telling me off, or slapping me in the face, she smiles at me. That sickly, dangerous smile Stoneview girls like her can give before stabbing someone.

"Xi," she says before flipping her hair back. "Can I talk to you for a second?"

11

XI

I GUESS IT'S LOVE? – The Kid LAROI

Harper drags me through yet another hallway of the frat house, holding my hand tightly in her perfectly manicured one. She pushes a door open, walks in, and brings me in with her before slamming it shut.

She turns to me, her smile straining at the same time as one of her eyes twitches angrily.

"Xi," she pouts as she sits on the edge of a large bathtub. "You didn't even talk to me tonight."

I lean back against the double sink and cross my arms, barely able to pretend I'm listening to whatever rant she's about to go on.

I genuinely don't give a shit. I've met clingy girls in my life, but no one quite compares to her. I don't know what the fuck she still wants with me, but moving on doesn't seem to be in her vocabulary. Who even needs to move on from one. Single. Fuck.

I'm going to listen anyway, because if there's something I

know for sure, it's that the more Harper is here with me, the less likely she is to make life hell for Alexandra downstairs.

"...are you listening?"

Running my tongue against my teeth, I nod. "'Course."

She rolls her eyes. "Anyway. As I was saying, maybe we can ditch the initiations and just head to yours."

Mine? As if I would ever invite this girl to my house. No one ever goes there except me. It's the family home I grew up in and the last place I ever saw my dad. I'm not going to bring some random girl there.

"You know, we can party with the rest of your crew. Is Logan there? Maybe you, me, and him should have a few drinks together or something."

I see. She thinks my house is the one she's come to party at before. My stepdad's house, where we host our NSC parties. She also thinks Logan and I are up for a threesome with her. Funny enough, I couldn't pay Logan to fuck a Stoneview bitch.

Standing up, she presses herself against me, running her hands along my biceps before trying to uncross my arms.

"Why don't you want to invite us to the North Shore tonight? You have before. You love having us Stoneview girls at your disposal."

I let her push my arms down to my sides before she presses her tits against my chest. I'm about a few seconds away from slamming her head into the sink. "Come on," she purrs. "You know I want you."

She has a real problem ahead of her then, because since I saw Alex in the car with her ex-prince charming, and since he tried to push me away when I wanted to get to her...all I want is, well, *Alex*.

There's absolutely no way in hell she's going to someone

else. I've done my best to try and hold myself back, because that means I won't hurt her. But what if that means she falls for someone else? What if he gets to touch her, and all I get to do is watch from the side?

Yeah, that's not happening.

Pretty little cupcake is mine. Only *I* get to taste and take a bite.

"It's initiations. Don't you have to stay with your pledges?"

She snorts. "I can make these little bitches do whatever I want. If I tell them to wait on their knees while I go party on the North Shore, they'll do exactly that. And I'll return here to sobbing messes because their joints hurt so much."

"That's fucked," I say, my lips curling when I remember *these little bitches* include Alex.

Fucking Alexandra Delacroix.

She couldn't just be some bitch I can use for my own benefit. No, the girl has to be a calamity who keeps on putting herself in vulnerable positions and triggering the protector in me. Fuck, I shouldn't care in the slightest about her. I'm not a man of remorse.

It's her innocent hazel eyes and the way she looks at everything with her wide-eyed gaze like she's never been allowed out of her house before. She's a butterfly right out of her cocoon, and if I'm not here to keep an eye on her, she will get caught by the first net. Her pretty wings will get pinned to a fucking board.

I want to catch her.

I want to pin her wings.

Just me.

"Oh please, you're part of NSC. You've done worse."

I cock an eyebrow at Harper, trying to remind myself what we're talking about. Right, doing fucked up shit.

"Out of survival. Not because I was on some sorority power trip."

She shrugs. "That's how the rich play survival of the fittest." Her eyes light up with a playful gleam and she licks her lips. "Have you ever killed someone?"

I look down at her. This bitch has only one goal in mind tonight. To get on my fucking nerves. Lucky for her, that's pretty easy to do. Everyone gets on my nerves.

Slowly, I wrap my hands around her tiny waist and make her sit on the edge of the tub again. I grip her jaw tightly with one hand, enough to see her slightly wince.

"I have," I say low.

Her eyes widen, lust and fear mixing in them.

"I've stabbed people and shot some others. I've tortured some and choked them to death."

I lean over, bringing my lips to her ear. "I drowned someone in a bathtub when I was seventeen."

Her sharp intake of breath joins her trembling limbs.

"Harper," I whisper.

"Y-yes?"

"You gonna buy something from me, or what?"

She shakes her head, now visibly struggling to breathe.

"Then stop wasting my fucking time," I growl as I push her back.

She falls backward into the empty tub with a shriek. I straighten up and leave the bathroom. What a bitch.

I try to find Alex downstairs, but she's not around. There are so many people at this party I never see two faces twice. Someone tugs at my arm, and I turn around to find some frat boy. "Bro," he slurs. "We ran out of pills. More people than we thought." He hands me three one-hundred-dollar bills. "Can I get another 12?"

I fold the bills and put them in my pocket before grabbing a few small packets. I check the amounts and hand them to him.

"Thank you, bro. You're the best."

He goes to slap my shoulder in a thank you gesture, but my glare stops him right away.

I'm stopped twice more, and just like every party, just like every day of my life...I just want people to leave me the fuck alone.

Except for one person who I can't help but scan the room for again.

"Man," someone says as they grab my arm. I turn around, ready to punch them in the face when I recognize Zara. My best friend. The girl who was in the car with me earlier today when Chester and Alex came to pick up a bag of pills.

She's started helping me distribute in SFU since we now have a ton of supplies we have to get rid of for the Lucianos to take us seriously.

Zara is everything I need in a friend and a dealer; discreet, good at math, street smart. And she's not fearless, which is the problem I have with most of my male dealers. They think they're above everything and unbeatable. Zara knows her own limits and strengths. She knows when it's time to go home and not push your luck.

"All out, boss." She spreads her arms. "Wanna give me some of yours?"

I nod, passing her a few bags of cocaine and weed. "They're either gonna start asking for cocaine to keep the night going, or some weed to calm their high and slowly turn this into an after-party. Whoever is too off their faces to know what they're spending, give them a one-and-a-half higher price."

"Noted." She points at a sofa. "Good spot?"

"Very good spot," I confirm. "I'll sit with you."

And that's my first mistake. The moment I sit down, one of Harper's friends comes right next to me, sandwiching me between Zara and her. My broad shoulders are touching both of theirs, making me feel fucking trapped.

"Xi," she yells in my face so I can hear her over the music. That and she's entirely off her face, which doesn't help with the level of her voice.

I wait for her to ask me what she needs, except nothing comes out. Instead, she puts a hand on my thigh. "Harper is in the backyard," she attempts to say with a sultry voice. "Do you want to take me upstairs?"

I hear Zara trying to hold back a laugh.

"Do me a favor..." I pause, realizing I've fucked this girl behind her friend's back and yet can't remember the first letter of her name.

"Tilly," she smiles brightly.

"Get me a beer," I huff.

She leaves in a hurry and Zara bursts into a laugh.

"You're the worst man-whore in all the history of hoeing around. Every time I see you talk to girls, it makes me like you a little less."

"Shut up," I growl as I let my head fall back. "I think I'm getting too old for that shit."

She takes on the voice of a sports commentator, "Xi, our big fuckboy, wants to retire from the game. It's great news for the rest of the male population, but what are the Stoneview girls gonna do?"

Just as I bring my head up for Zara to see I'm not finding her shit funny, Harper and Alex walk back into the room, the latter holding a platter of drinks as she walks one step behind the former.

My gaze follows Alex, unable to look at anyone but her. Her dirty blonde hair falls delicately to her hips and I follow it to the curve of her ass.

She looks beautiful. She's wearing her SFU uniform and simple black stilettos that make me want to bury my head between her legs and have her dig the heels into my back while I eat her out.

"Fucking hell, Xi," Zara says as she follows my gaze. "You're making your 'I've found a new prey' face. Don't tell me you've got it bad for that little Bambi thing over there?"

"She looks nothing like Bambi," I defend myself.

No, Alex is everything I love physically in a woman. The curves, the generous boobs, and the sort of hips I can easily hold on to while I fuck her from behind. She looks tall tonight in her heels, but she's average height. My favorite thing about her is her expressive hazel eyes. There is absolutely nothing she can hide from me when I look at them. She tries to make her small, soft voice sound tough sometimes when she fights me, but her eyes say it all. They're the window to her beautiful soul.

"Doormat has never been your kind of girl. You would annihilate her with your personality."

I drag my eyes off Alex to stare daggers at Zara. "What the fuck do you mean by that?"

She smiles smugly, like she just proved her point. "You've got a shitty, extra tough-ass personality, and you're always in a fucking mood."

Everyone always pisses me off about my attitude. Especially in the last two years. Of course, I've been in a constant shit mood; the Kings are reigning over the North

Shore. No one's gonna see a smile on my fucking face until I get my town back.

"You're a volatile, violent criminal who has domination of the North Shore in mind. That girl," Zara points at Alex discreetly, "is a fragile butterfly who's grown up in luxury her entire life and probably never had a single confrontation for as long as she's been alive. She's clearly a people pleaser who wouldn't know how to handle a man like you. You're a dick who will demand everything from her, and when she gives it all, when she listens like a good girl—which you hate, by the way—what are you gonna do?"

I feel my brows furrowing as I look back at Alex. Harper is ordering her on her knees, and she's doing it without even a second thought, struggling to hold the platter of drinks as she does so.

"Vito wants dirt on her dad. Emma insists on me *seducing* her and getting close to her."

"That's her? Oh thank God. For a second, I thought you really liked the girl."

My jaw tightens, forcing me to not throw back that I do, in fact, like the girl.

"She's a fucking kid. She...looks so innocent," my friend observes.

I huff, running my hand through my hair. She's not got one fighting bone in her body. I'm supposed to hate girls like that. They're boring and scared of everything. They do anything you tell them. They're not fun in bed, and it's the exact reason I've always gone for stubborn, bitchy girls like Harper. The kind who think they rule the world and whom I can prove wrong.

"Yeah," I agree again. "It should make it easy."

"She's the softest fucking thing I've ever seen in my

whole life. I'm pretty sure my kitten at home is badder than her."

Worse. That's what Alex would say right now. She'd correct Zara for saying badder, and we'd make fun of her for doing it.

"Probably," I huff.

I take a deep breath as I close my eyes. Alex really is as sweet as sugar, or cupcake wouldn't have been the first nickname that came to mind when I talked to her. The issue is that I turn anything sweet into poison.

"I haven't been doing what Emma wants," I admit.

"What like..." I sense her hesitating, deciding to keep my eyes closed so I don't see the disappointment on her face. "Like you're falling for her or something?"

I decide to ignore her. She can't ask me questions I don't have the answer to.

When I open my eyes again, Harper is looking right at me. She's got a scheming face on.

"What is the bitch up to now," Zara says lazily. She relaxes in her seat. "This is going to be fun, isn't it?"

"I like Alex because she's different." My answer is delayed, my thoughts running a million miles a minute.

Did I just admit to liking her?

"Man, NSC always comes first. You're about to break the fucking thing. Don't catch feelings."

"Stop calling her a thing," I snap, irritated. "She's a nice girl."

"She lets everyone walk all over her. I can see that from here. *Right now.*"

My hands turn into fists when I see another sorority girl shouting at her, and one by one, they pour their drinks on her, soaking her up in alcoholic beverages. Alex's eyes are full of tears, but I watch her throat work as she swallows them back.

"It's initiations," I add. "She's not allowed to defend herself."

"She wouldn't if she could, it's written all over her face." Zara glances down at my closed fists, up at my angry eyes, and shakes her head. "Are you for real? Are you going all savior on me right now?"

"These girls are pissing me off," I growl. "Why can't they just leave her the fuck alone? They're not that cruel with the other pledges."

"*Everything* pisses you off. Why can't *you* leave her the fuck alone? Focus on the fucking job. She's not your responsibility. Seriously, what is happening to you?"

I'm about to get up and grab Alex out of there when her eyes snap to me. She wipes a hand over her face to try and rid herself of the liquid. Her eyes widen, tears shining in them. She looks back at Harper and her friends, still on her knees, and shakes her head.

Harper stands up, grips Alex by the elbow and drags her up too. She walks her a few steps toward me and turns her around until she's facing my way. They're close enough that I can hear them now.

"Since you and him are so close, I'm sure he won't mind granting you that wish. Off you go, slave."

She shoves her my way and Alex stumbles on her stilettos before balancing herself. She doesn't look at me as she walks toward the sofa, her eyes on the wooden floor. I'm pretty sure the only thing that makes her stop is my black boots appearing in her field of vision.

All I can fucking see is the way her white shirt is turning transparent from being wet.

She scratches her throat, twisting her hands in front of

her before finally pushing her delicate voice to form the words she's been ordered to tell me.

"Um, Xi."

My eyes go to her neck, remembering the way her skin tasted earlier. So fucking sweet. I feel my dick waking up and internally roll my eyes. It seems I'm fourteen again.

I stay silent, and so does Zara. I don't even think Alex has noticed the girl she was jealous of earlier today is sitting right next to me. She's too preoccupied by the order she's been given.

"We want to come to a North Shore party tonight," she says in what she attempts to be a confident voice. "We want to go with you."

Zara's mocking laugh is cut short by my forearm slamming into her stomach.

"Look at me when you're talking to me," I order Alex. She is just proving Zara's whole point about her not being the kind of girl I should be with, and it's pissing me off. She needs to grow a fucking backbone.

Her eyes flick up and she looks away a few times before finally looking into my eyes.

"What were you saying?" I feign ignorance.

"Um, the Xi Ep girls. We want to come to your party. So, I'm here to ask you to take us."

"You want to come party on the North Shore?"

I'm dying to have Alex on my side of town. More specifically, in a bed where I can fuck the good girl out of her.

She nods, her eyes darting to the side where she knows her sorority friends are watching.

I lean forward, resting my elbows on my thighs and letting my dominating instincts get the best of me.

"I didn't hear the magic word, cupcake."

Those fucking hazel eyes. The way the gold and brown swirl in them when what I tell her turns her on drives me batshit crazy. I want to grab her by the neck and bend her over the closest table. No one should be that responsive from being talked down to.

And the fact she is...is going to be my fucking downfall.

She hesitates for a few seconds, although her resolve is short-lived. "Please, can we come to the North Shore with you?"

I don't think she likes the expression on my face because she shuffles back. My arm snaps toward her, and I wrap my hand around her naked mid-thigh, right where the hem of her skirt is.

She turns back, checking on her friends. "Don't worry about them," I order low. "Focus on me."

"Let me go," she panics in a whisper. "Please, don't get me into more trouble than I already am."

"What trouble could you possibly be in when none of these bitches have even the slightest chance with me. Not now that we've met."

She shakes her head, like she can't believe my words. Yeah, I can't believe they came out of my mouth, either.

"Harper—" she starts.

"You want my hand off you, cupcake? Why don't you fucking push me away, then?" Only now does she grab my wrist. She had to wait for my fucking authorization to fight back when she should have done it the moment I touched her skin. It's no use anyway because I tighten my hold. "But then I guess your chances of you and your friends being invited to the North Shore would get real fucking slim."

She tries to stifle her gasp and bites her lower lip, not understanding she's making it worse for herself. I shift, trying to give myself some relief from my ever-growing hard-on. Her hand leaves my wrist and I caress her inner thigh with my thumb as I bring my hand higher. It's under her skirt now, clear for everyone to see.

"Xi," she sighs. "Just invite us, please."

"I will. I just have two conditions."

"What? What do you want?" she asks in a rush, hope flashing in her eyes.

"I want a kiss. Right now, in front of all your friends." She tries to step back again, but I'm holding her too tightly. "And I want you to be mine for the rest of the night. The moment you get to the North Shore, you belong to me."

My hand goes up again, my thumb now rubbing between her legs. "We can finish what we started earlier, cupcake."

She shakes her head anxiously, glancing behind her again. "I c—I can't do that. You're going to get me kicked out of Xi Ep."

"Would that be so bad?" I snort. "This is obviously not where you belong."

Her features twist when I press her clit. "Xi," she sighs as her eyes flutter closed.

"Give me that kiss," I order sternly. "Then Harper and Co. can come party with us since they're so desperate for North Shore dick."

She opens her eyes, takes a deep breath, clearly weighing the pros and cons, and finally nods.

A stupid thing to do, really. She's getting herself into even more trouble, but I think her pussy is talking right now. Her brain shut off the moment my thumb touched her silky panties.

I can't give her a second to think. Not a second to change her mind.

I let go of her only to grab her hips and pull her to me in

a harsh movement. She falls onto my lap, forced to straddle me, and I put a hand at the back of her neck, forcing her to crash against my mouth.

Our lips meet in a harsh movement, and panic takes hold of me.

This is the exact moment I know I'm fucked.

The moment my heart explodes in my chest, and everything around me disappears.

The moment I understand I want this girl to myself.

The moment I know without a doubt that she's mine.

She smells of all kinds of alcohol. Her clothes are wet, her skin sticky. But her lips...they taste like the most delicious thing I've ever had the pleasure to devour.

Tightening my hold against the back of her neck, I press her harder against me. I lick the seam of her lips, demanding entry into heaven. She gasps, letting me in, and I force my tongue against hers. Her jasmine perfume mixes with the stickiness in her hair, and I want to bury myself in her smell, but I also don't want to let go of her mouth.

I feel both her hands wrapping around my biceps, my arms flexing in reaction to her skin touching mine.

Our kiss doesn't stop abruptly. We slow down gradually before separating in the slightest, our eyes fluttering open. I see the moment she realizes what she's done. Her hazel eyes have that sudden shade of worry in them. I lick my lips, addicted to her taste, and smirk at her.

She gasps ever so slightly when she notices something other than a scowl on my face.

"That's one of your conditions met, Alexandra. Ready for the second one?"

Coming back down to earth from the high we both just experienced, she scurries off me in a rush.

"Xi," she scolds me. "You can't..." She looks back and watches helplessly as Harper comes our way with a pretend smile on her face. Her left eye twitches like a crazy person and her cheeks tremble, the muscles strained from being so fake.

"Alex," she says in a voice trembling from hidden fury.

"Ready for that party, Harper?" I say casually. As if that life-changing kiss never happened.

"We're coming?" she asks, surprised.

"Sure," I shrug. "Bring all your friends. You know we appreciate the view."

Her smile turns real before she twists around and excitedly hops back to her friends. I don't think I'll ever understand why they all want to attend our parties. These people have everything they want here.

Except danger, I guess. They want the thrill of being with the gang members of the North Shore. They don't understand danger is part of our everyday life. They get to leave it behind. We don't.

I get up and slide my hand to the back of Alex's neck. I grip her tightly and pull her closer to me, lowering myself so I can talk directly in her ear.

"Don't forget the second half of our deal."

I feel her trembling under me, but she doesn't say anything, and I have no way of knowing if it's fear or something else entirely.

Harper and her posse come back to us. She takes Alex's hand. "Come. My chauffeur will drive us."

I hear Zara snort behind me. A fucking chauffeur to come to our shit part of town. The hypocrisy isn't lost on my friend and me.

They drag Alex away from me, surrounding her as they walk out of the house.

"Let's get the fuck out of here," I grunt as I turn to Zara again.

"Can I just ask that next time you want to practice a soft porn scene with *cupcake*, you wait till I'm not around to do it?"

I shove her out of my way, back to not being in the fucking mood now that Alex is out of my sight. "Shut up."

As soon as we reach my car, I grab my gray hoodie and put on my black cap. I'm done with the rich kids talking to me tonight.

"You coming to Emma's?" I ask Zara as I start the car.

She shakes her head. "Drop me home, please. You know I'm not really into parties."

I nod, driving out of the frat house's driveway.

"I like this," she yawns, pointing at a sketch I made and that I had left on the dashboard.

"Thanks, I drew it."

"What is it?" She squints her eyes to try and get a better look in the darkness of the car. "For fuck's sake," she huffs. "It's her, isn't it?"

Ignoring her, I keep my eyes focused on the road.

"At least it's beautifully drawn."

I shrug. "I'm good at doing things with my hands." I was going to stop there but decide to annoy her instead. "I thought you knew that."

She rolls her eyes. "One-time thing. I thought that was the deal with guys like you. No need to mention something that happened last year."

"My lips are sealed."

After a minute of silence, I feel her inhale deeply,

knowing she's about to talk to me again. "Are you going to be able to make it a one-time thing with cupcake?"

I run my tongue against my front teeth. "Of course. So I drew her. I was inspired. It'll be fine. We're gonna get the info we need."

But deep down, I know the truth. My fixation on Alexandra Delacroix is growing bigger every day. She's not seeing it coming because, for her, why would someone she just met suddenly be obsessed with her. If only she fucking knew.

That obsession.

Every hour, it becomes more intense. Every minute, it turns more dangerous.

I walk into Emma's house after dropping Zara off at hers. The party is still going strong despite the late hour. Logan catches me as soon as I'm in the living room.

"I fucking hate you," he growls as he hugs me with a hand grabbing my neck and a slap on the back. "You invite those bitches here and don't even warn Tamar and me. You know we hate them. At least Racer seems to be enjoying himself."

"Good for him," I say as I separate from him and look around. I grab a cigarette from the pocket of my hoodie and the tiny new plastic lighter I bought yesterday. I keep losing these things, or people borrow them and never bring them back.

I light up a cigarette, scanning the room. I can't fucking wait to get my hands on Alex. Once I do, she's not going anywhere.

"Is Alex here?"

"Which one's that?" Logan grinds another complaint.

"The one with the *I'm better than you attitude*, the one with the *oopsie, my skirt keeps rising up* attitude, or the one who literally told Tamar to get lost while trying to sit on my lap?"

I look at him blankly as I blow smoke to the side. He's so fucking dramatic. "None. The fourth one with the SFU uniform who's actually a decent person."

"Yeah, you must have made that one up, brother, because she's not here."

Looking around the room again, I notice Harper talking to my brother, Lik. I'm shocked enough that he's come to a party now that he's settled and happy in his relationship, but that he's actually making conversation with Harper makes me feel like I'm hallucinating.

"Yeah," Logan nods toward my brother. "He's here. Don't ask me why."

I tap Logan's shoulder, indicating I'm walking away from our conversation, and head over to Lik instead.

"Trouble in paradise, *khoya*?" I ask as I slam my hand between his shoulder blades.

He turns to me, a bright smile on his face. My brother and I look the same in the sense that it is written on our faces that we share the same blood, but we couldn't be more different. I'm a big guy, tall and bulky, and he's strong but skinnier and shorter than me. Where my jaw is square and my face hard, his is softer and more feminine. I'm rough. He's beautiful. That's what sets us apart.

Lik takes care of himself, even more so since two women got added to the relationship with his boyfriend. Long. Fucking. Story.

His nose is pierced with a ring on his nostril, and he wears pearls and a padlock around his neck. He takes care of his tight curls, which makes them look silky smooth. And he is always dressed in a fashionable manner.

I wear monochrome cargo pants, hoodies, and boots most of the time, and my hair is often hidden under a cap. Mine is softer, anyway. It's thick, but I don't have the curls he does. He got his hair from our dad and mine from my mom. I always find it ironic since he's closer to my mom. Because he's younger than me, he's always been her little baby. Lik can get away with murder, and I'll be the one shouted at for showing up one minute late to dinner.

I was closer to my dad. In his traditional ways, I was the eldest and would take over the family when he died, so we spent long hours together while he taught me how to take care of the people I love.

Now, the main difference between Lik and me is that he's a fucking ray of sunshine, and I'm a bastard that can't seem to enjoy anything. I'm aware of it. I just don't give a shit.

"All good. Just wanted to see my friends. *Labass*?" he asks how I'm doing.

"You guys," Harper says with a fake giggle. "It's so cute that you speak foreign to each other. What does *jo-ya* mean?"

There's a beat as Lik flicks his annoyed stare at me.

"Means 'my brother'," he answers, keeping his polite front. He's better at it than I am, that's for sure.

"That's cute." Her lips pinch, and she tilts her head to the side. "Was that Arabic?"

He nods. "Darija."

Her brows furrow, and she looks at me, confused. "Moroccan Arabic," I explain.

"*Is she annoying on purpose?*" Lik tells me in Arabic as he smiles at her.

"*She knows exactly what she's doing,*" I reply with a straight face so she doesn't get we're insulting her.

"Are you guys talking about me?" She bites her lower lip, and it takes everything not to roll my eyes.

"We're saying you're cute."

Lik's words make her flip her hair back. "Thanks."

"Where's Alex?" I jump in before I'm forced to have a lengthier exchange with her than needed.

"Oh." She digs her stare into mine, the bright blue eaten by her large pupils. She's high. She smirks and puts a hand on her hip. "She's at the house waiting for one of us to come back to be allowed to move."

"Be allowed to move?" Lik asks, surprised.

"Yeah, they have to wait on all fours until their big sister comes home and tells them they can move."

"I'm sorry...*what*?" Lik chokes. He looks at me, completely confused.

"Rich people shit."

"Don't worry," she waves her hand dismissively. "They'll be fine. We've had worse. During my initiations, I had to stand outside my big sister's window all night. Completely naked. One of the pledges even caught pneumonia that night."

"You didn't allow her to come here?" I say slowly, trying to get my head around what happened before I lose my cool.

"Actually, she's the one who said she didn't want to. Can't say I'm surprised."

She waits for me to say something, but my deadpan face tells her I want more, so she continues. "Alex *hates* the North Shore. Believe me, she would never set foot here on her own accord."

"Stoneview girls are so strange," Lik shares his thoughts.

He then proceeds to go into a long rant about sororities being totally fucked. My brother can talk to himself for hours, so I don't need to answer him. Instead, I silently seethe about Alex not holding her end of the deal.

"Are you alright, Xi?" Harper asks.

I feel my jaw tightening as I nod. My tongue caresses my front teeth as I scratch the five o'clock shadow I keep neatly trimmed.

"Yeah," I say simply. I take one last drag of my cigarette before turning around and pressing it against the ashtray on the table behind me. I grab a bottle of vodka from there too.

Then I disappear into the crowd, finding my way back to the front door and leaving my stepsister's house.

I don't want to be at this party if Alex isn't. I also don't want Harper to go back to her house anytime soon. Not while I'll be busy putting Alex in her place.

I grab my lighter and another cigarette and walk to the only expensive-looking car parked on the street. A chauffeur is sleeping in there. I knock on the window and smile at him. He lowers it, and I grab him by the tie, dragging him out of the car through the window.

"What the hell," he screams.

I let him settle on his two feet and take a step back to not appear too threatening. I know the image I give. "Go for a walk," I tell him. "I don't want to hurt an honest working man, but I'm also going to fuck up your car."

His eyes widen as he shakes his head in panic. "I can't...I can't..."

"I can fuck you up with it if you want," I add casually.

He takes a step back, putting his hands in front of him.

"How does that walk sound now?"

He turns around and sprints away from me. I guess he really needed the exercise.

Sliding my hand through the open window, I open the car from the inside. I spill the vodka all over the front and

187

back seats and leave the bottle in there. Taking a step back onto the street, I reach for my lighter and light my cigarette. I take a drag before I throw it inside the car. It takes a few seconds for the first spark to come, and I feel myself relax when a flame comes to life.

Zara and Tamar say I have a fire issue. That I'm dangerous. My friend Logan calls me a pyromaniac.

I find it soothing. Watching flames lick at something and turn it into dust makes me feel like the freest motherfucker alive.

I might not be able to leave this town behind, but there's nothing in it that stays if I decide it must go. Like Harper's car.

I watch with a sick smile as the flames grow more prominent, melting everything in the car, and a certain peace comes over me.

Time to find my little cupcake now.

12

ALEXANDRA

Manipulate – Mxze, Clarei

My knees and wrists are killing me. The moment Harper got me away from Xi, she had a go at me for talking. She's the one who asked me to get us into that North Shore party, yet she punished me for opening my mouth. Apparently, it was against the rules, and I should have known not to talk.

I didn't do much talking. No, I mainly did some kissing.

Just thinking of Xi's lips against mine makes me tremble. That kiss was so controlling I could have drowned in it all night.

Harper made sure to punish me the same way she had everyone else, resulting in her putting tape all over my mouth for talking to someone. She said I could still come to the North Shore party.

I couldn't. Especially not in the humiliating position I was in.

I didn't want to go anyway. I don't want to be on the North Shore and be plagued with memories of that night. Who knows how many people at that party are part of a gang. Who knows if the men who kidnapped me that night are there, roaming free.

Xi's promise almost made me change my mind. He has a way of making me want to do things I shouldn't. There's that controlling part of him that pushes me to submit to every single one of his orders. The promise of being his for one night makes my insides twist with pleasure.

The sound of my bedroom door opening brings me back to reality. Harper must be back from the party. I've been on my hands and knees beside the paddle for hours. My skirt is flipped up as she had requested, and the tape is still on my mouth. I'm exhausted. My joints are killing me, and I'm incredibly thirsty. However, I won't let the sisters of Xi Ep find another excuse to punish me. This is all part of the initiation process, and I will put up with it just like anyone else.

Her steps resonate behind me, heavy in the dark room. I don't dare turn around when I feel her stop right by me. I expect her to taunt me about the punishment, but she doesn't say anything.

A hand skims along my spine until it wraps at the back of my neck.

My brain understands who it is a split second before Xi pushes my head to the floor. My tired arms give up easily and I follow.

The smell of bergamot hits me. There's that pine-like earthy scent too. That's why I know it's him.

His hand feels large and powerful. That's why I know it's him.

And my heart...my heart is becoming crazy. It did the second he walked into the room. *That's* why I know it's him.

When his gravelly, whispered words reach my ears, I feel myself melting for him.

"Did you forget about our deal, Alexandra?"

I reach up with my left hand to peel off the tape from my mouth, but he grabs my wrist violently.

He tuts me, his admonishing tone making me want to curl into myself. "Your word is everything. Not keeping it gives me the right to punish you however I want."

I try to shake my head, but his hand at the back of my neck tightens. "I did say I'd love to see that pretty mouth taped. Now none of your *sisters* can hear the noises you'll make while I have my way with you."

I take a deep breath through my nose, trying to relax my body. I'm not scared. I don't feel the panic I usually do when I know I can't defend myself. There's a part of me that's aware Xi could hurt me, but there's also another that wants him to.

"I'm going to let go of you, and you're going to settle back on all fours. Can you do that for me?"

Now is the time to make a decision. I'm being given the free will to finally decide what I want in my life. It never happened with my upbringing. It didn't happen when I was kidnaped. I enjoyed what that man did to me, but I didn't have a choice in it.

Tonight, I can choose.

I can say no to Xi, and he will move on to the next girl. He'll leave me alone. Or I could say yes and finally enjoy the humiliating things I know I like—my darkest desires.

I don't hesitate one more second.

I nod, my heart beating in my ears and my head spinning from the lust. I can already feel myself getting wet, and he's barely touched me yet. He doesn't need to, though. His commanding voice and overwhelming presence already have an irrevocable effect on me.

He releases my wrist and my neck, and I settle back on

my hands and knees. He caresses my ass cheeks and I hear a low growl in his chest as he settles his hand between my legs.

He presses against me, and a long breath escapes through my nose. I push back against him and relish in his fingers sliding against the silk. He barely moves, yet I'm the one out of control. I roll my hips back and forth, knowing only Xi's touch can bring me what I need.

I've never had to share my disgusting secret with him; it's like he already knew. Like he can read in my eyes that I need him to force me to humiliate myself for him, to bring me the pleasure only he can. I need him to impose his rules on me and not give me a choice.

He takes his hand away from me and I choke on a whimper. I look back at him, but he grabs my jaw and forces me to look straight ahead again.

"Stay still. Your pleasure will come. You just have to take the punishment first."

I feel another wave of wetness soaking my underwear.

Punishment?

My thighs tighten and he chuckles behind me. God, that chuckle. It's only the barest glimpse of a laugh, but it's everything from the man who can never even spare a smile. "Punishments are not for you to enjoy. Spread your legs."

I feel something tap the inside of my thigh and then the other. I shift on my knees, spreading my legs and exposing myself to him a bit more.

"I think I finally found something I like about sororities." He caresses my ass cheeks with the object, and I finally realize what it is.

The first swat of the paddle makes me jump in surprise.

"Was I unclear when I said there were two parts in our deal, Alexandra?"

I shake my head, now worried about how much strength he's planning on putting in his hits. Xi is a big guy; his arms are strong, and I do not doubt he could cause some serious damage.

The paddle crashes against my left cheek, and I swallow back a scream that's not able to pass my lips anyway.

"I agreed to invite your friends to the North Shore and asked for something in exchange. A kiss."

Swat.

The violence in this one makes me fall forward. I whimper behind the tape as my chest hits the floor.

"Get back into place," he says calmly behind me. "Your punishment isn't over until I see some tears on a very sorry face."

I put myself back into position, my behind burning.

"I asked for a kiss and for you to belong to me for the rest of the night. I remember distinctly saying you were *mine.*"

Swat.

I shriek, the sound staying behind my lips. My thighs are starting to tremble, and my ass feels twice its normal size.

His voice is so lax compared to his hits, my brain can barely process what is happening. I want more of him, just less of the pain he's inflicting.

"You thought you'd escape me?" *Swat.* "You can fucking try, cupcake." *Swat.* "But you are never." *Swat.* "Ever." *Swat.* "Getting away from me." *Swat!*

A sob explodes from me, my chest shaking as I feel tears rolling down my cheeks. I don't know if my skin is getting increasingly sensitive or if he's getting angrier and more robust, considering the pain is becoming unbearable.

"Alexandra," he rumbles behind me, the anger now

fitting the violence of his gestures. "Do you have any idea how often I become obsessed with something?" He circles me until he's right by my head. His legs are in front of my eyes until he crouches and grabs my chin, pulling me up until I can look at his face.

Mine feel swollen from the tears, but I don't care. All I can think about on repeat, is that once he's done with the pain, he promised pleasure.

I shake my head to answer his question. I don't know, because I don't know him. I don't know Xi as a person, only as the man who brings my dirty fantasies to life without even knowing.

"Never," he finally says. "But once I do, no one can take it away from me. I've become obsessed twice in my life, and you are one of them."

I gulp, struggling to swallow with my neck in the awkward position.

"You won't deny me again." His thumb caresses my cheek, wiping away hot tears. The fact that he's touching them seems to calm him. Like he knows these tears are for him. The pain is his. "Do you understand?"

I feel high, worse than when I was forced to take cocaine. The pain, mixed with the lust, has pushed my body past what I can handle. My heavy eyelids close before I force them back open.

"Do you understand, Alexandra?" he repeats. "That when I say you're mine, I mean that every single inch of you belongs to me. So next time I expect you somewhere, you better fucking show up. Because if I have to come get you again, tonight will feel like a trip to Disneyland compared to what I'll do to you."

His face lights up when his words make me tremble, my

chest shaking to the rhythm of silent sobs. "Do you understand?"

There's a blend of fear and trepidation inside me. Something that tells me what he's saying can't be true. No one is that obsessed with someone else, not in such a short time. I nod anyway, my chin still in his hand, because I've always wished for someone to want me so badly he would demand everything from me.

"Are you sorry for being a bad girl, Alexandra?"

I nod again as I feel myself clench with need.

"Good."

Slowly, he peels off the tape, and I take a deep breath, making my entire body shake. He throws the piece of tape on the floor and slides his hand in my hair, grabbing a handful.

"Tell me you're sorry," he says low.

"I-I'm sorry," I splutter.

His other hand goes to his belt, unbuckling it, followed by the button of his pants before unzipping them.

"Show me."

I feel my eyes widen. "I don't..." *know how to do this.*

I feel the embarrassment flaming my cheeks. Xi has slept with countless girls. I can't imagine the number of women he's had on their knees pleasuring him. I don't compare, and I know it.

"Just get into position, baby. I'll show you how," he whispers as his grip tightens. "But don't make me wait."

I sit up on my knees the next second and watch his cinnamon eyes light up. He licks his lips before he talks. "Pull it out."

With trembling hands, I reach for his boxers, lowering them so I can grab his hard dick. I must refrain from gasping when I finally wrap my hand around it. He feels soft and thick, and my heart accelerates in my chest.

I pull it out, lowering the boxers some more. He's big, a large vein throbbing underneath and leading to the velvety head. His slit is wet, and I instinctively rub my thumb against it. Then I look up at the same time, watching his eyes flutter closed before staring into mine again.

"Show me your tongue," he says slowly, as if trying not to rush me into this.

I pull my tongue out as much as possible, my head tilting back slightly and pressing against his hand in my hair.

A low hum resonates in his throat, making me feel the effect I have on him.

He presses his tip against my tongue and a saltiness invades my taste buds. Slowly, he pushes in all the way into my wide-open mouth, rubbing the underneath of his cock against my wet tongue. He repeats the process a few times before pulling out.

"Lick me from my base to my tip, baby," he says in a ragged voice. A pull at my hair pushes me into action. With my hands on his thighs, I lick the entirety of his dick, repeating the gesture until I feel him groan above me.

It brings sensations all the way to my needy clit. I'm so wet I feel sticky between my legs. Being on my knees in front of Xi after a punishment seems like the epitome of erotism. I've never done any of this with a man, and I never thought of the pleasure it could bring me to satisfy him.

"Wrap your lips around me, Alexandra."

With a hunger I didn't know I had, I wrap my lips tightly around his head and push forward, sliding him into my mouth.

"Shit," he hisses. "Keep moving your tongue when you take me in."

I do exactly as he says. I lick him as I bob my head up and down and follow the movement he's forcing on me with his grip.

"I need you to take more of me, baby," he mutters. I feel the lust in his voice everywhere inside me. My thighs squeeze and I shift, placing the heel of my foot between my legs to press against my clit.

I moan around him just as he brings me closer, thrusting into my mouth. My moan is cut short when his tip hits the back of my throat and I choke around his length.

I squeeze my eyes shut when I realize I'm still not holding all of him.

"Breathe through your nose," he orders softly. An order, nonetheless.

I attempt to do as he says, tears falling from the corner of my eyes. I can't seem to be able to drag more air in, and he retreats slightly before pushing again.

"Swallow me, baby. Be a good little slut for me."

A good little slut.

I want to die and come back. I've never been so turned-on in my life.

He pushes again, and I gag as I attempt to swallow him. My lips are stretched from his girth, and my throat feels tight from how much of him I'm taking down.

"That's right," he says tightly. "You're such a good girl."

I moan again, and he inhales sharply. "Fuck, Alex." His movement accelerates, and within seconds he's fully thrusting into my mouth, face fucking me and driving me insane from need.

Saliva spills down my chin. The noises I'm making are

ridiculous, embarrassing, and yet they do nothing to calm my lust.

In a rushed change, he pulls out of my mouth, grabs his cock, and rubs himself before exploding onto my face. I gasp, cum now landing into my open mouth.

I don't know what I expected.

But I didn't expect this.

He pulls at my hair, forcing me to get up, and pushes me onto the bed. "You deserve your pleasure," he rumbles. "And I deserve to taste you."

I grab the sheet, wanting to wipe him off me, but he rips it out of my hands.

"Don't you fucking dare. I want my cum on your face when you come apart for me. Put your hands above your head and don't move."

I hurry into position, placing my hands right above my head on the mattress.

He grabs my hips, bringing my ass to the edge of the bed and kneeling on the floor. "I'm going to make you come, hard, Alexandra. Try not to wake up the whole house."

I gasp when his mouth presses between my legs. He's not taken my panties off yet, but I can feel his warm tongue lapping at my wetness through the silky material.

He focuses on my clit, dropping heavy, wet kisses against it.

"Take it off," I pant out. "Take...take my underwear off."

He pulls away, and I lift my head to look at what he's doing. "You're gorgeous when you're desperate for me," he whispers in a gravelly voice. "But I'm going to need that magic word."

My heart lurches in my chest. For a second, I fear I'm dead from the emotions that overwhelm me. I've never felt this before, and it scares me.

"Please," I whimper, writhing from need.

As if he was the one who couldn't wait a second longer, he rids me of my underwear and presses his mouth against my burning core. There's an untamable fire inside me. I can't control my reactions anymore. I grind against him as his tongue laps up all my wetness. He pushes it inside me, and I cry out for him.

"Xi," I moan. I lose all sense when two fingers push inside me, and his tongue comes to focus on my clit.

The slow strokes of his tongue drive me desperate with need. My chest is heaving, my entire body lighting up. He takes his time devouring and tasting me like a fine meal. He drags the pleasure on and on, until I'm so taut with need I cry out in desperation.

"Please," I breathe. My lungs are burning with lust. "I need to come." There are tears in my eyes from the tension in my body. I'm on the precipice and I need to fall, or I fear I might burst into flames.

Without relenting, he tips me over with his tongue, making me fall, crash, and burn in an explosion of sensations.

I curl onto myself, my muscles draining the last remnants of pleasure before I fall back on the bed, panting.

Xi stands up and drops onto the bed next to me, sliding an arm under my body and bringing me closer.

"Next time I see you, I'm going to fuck you," he says without an ounce of hesitation.

"So, there's going to be a next time?" I whisper, my head resting against his shoulder.

"Do you want there to be a next time?"

My heart doesn't only skip a beat. It pirouettes like a ballet dancer and kicks against my chest.

"Yes," I murmur.

He twists and positions himself above me. His hands are on each side of my head, and he glances down at me. "Today was just a taste. I want to do more to you. Things that will hurt you and degrade you but that will bring you much more pleasure." His eyes dart around my face, staring at my lips before they meet my gaze again. "Can you handle my wicked side, Alex?"

Sometimes, it feels like Xi has direct access to what I've always hidden from everyone. He says things that make me want to get on my knees and beg him to be true to his word. I want it more than anything else I've ever wanted.

"I can handle anything. As long as you promise not to break my heart."

The tip of his tongue darts to his two front teeth before the corner of his mouth tips up into what I've come to understand is his full smile.

"I'm not going to break your heart, Alexandra."

"That's exactly what someone who plans on breaking my heart would say."

Instead of answering, his lips crash on mine. He swallows all my doubt in a kiss from heaven. I moan into his mouth, letting him take an all-encompassing hold of my soul until he pulls away and kisses the tip of my nose. "No breaking your heart."

He slides off the bed and gathers himself. "Get some rest. I'll text you tomorrow."

I watch him walk out of my room like all of this is normal. Like I didn't just ask a man I barely know not to break my heart.

Actually, if there's one thing I do know about him, it's that he *is* a heartbreaker.

13

XI

I Chose Violence – iamjakehill

"These things just evaporate into thin air, don't they?" the shop owner tells me as he turns around to grab a plastic lighter for me.

"Sure do," I mumble, checking the text from Logan telling me Tamar, Zara, and him are at his garage.

"Any specific color you want?"

"No." But then I look up. "Actually, can I get that pink one?" I point to the one I mean.

Fucking shit. I'm a lovesick puppy desperate to be as close as possible to his owner.

The owner being Alexandra Delacroix and her obsession for *pink*.

"Sure thing. Dollar fifty."

I put two dollars on the counter and leave.

An hour later, I've officially spent too long with my friends and have neglected the texts Emma has been sending me.

"Oh fuck no!" Zara screams just before throwing herself to the side, holding the PlayStation remote close to her.

"Moving your own body won't save you," I say. "Why don't you learn how to play instead?"

Tamar laughs behind us before putting a bottle of beer in front of Zara.

We're playing video games at the back of Logan's garage while he works at the front. My phone beeps on his desk for the millionth time, and Tamar grabs it.

"Emma isn't happy," she tells me, dropping the phone on my lap. I look down at the countless texts and back up at the game.

"What does she want?" Zara asks before going back to biting her tongue, refocusing on the game.

"Updates on the Delacroix situation," I say calmly, overtaking her on the circuit. I drop a banana just in front of her.

"Motherfucker!" she screams. "I fucking hate you."

I win the fifth race in a row and throw the remote away. "I think we've established who owns your ass," I chuckle.

"I have a gun on me right now," she throws back. "Say that again," Zara grunts.

"Oh, she's tough," I mock her, deadpan. "*Gangster*."

"Remember when we were kids, and you were a decent person?" Zara pushes my shoulder. "I miss that guy."

"Can't say I remember him," Tamar jumps in. "Are we talking about the same Xi?"

"Yeah, he went by Ziad back then." She enunciates my name correctly, like my mom does. *Zee-ad*. "When people used to pronounce it well and shit."

"Zi-ad is so American," Tamar laughs. "Do you remember how to pronounce your own name?"

"Holy shit, I forgot you two together are *unbearable*." I

stand up and grab my phone before running my hand across my face. "Fuck sake," I mutter to myself.

"What's up?" Zara asks with genuine worry this time.

"I don't know what to tell Emma."

"Well, what's the update?" Tamar insists.

I shrug. "Got nowhere yet."

"What about the NSC party?" Zara asks.

"Alex wasn't there."

"You said you went to her house," Tamar adds.

Shit. I forgot I said that. "Yeah," I run my tongue against my front teeth. "Nothing happened. She's a good girl." Except for me.

"Oh shit," Zara huffs. They exchange a look.

"What?"

Zara takes a sip of her beer and puts it back on the table. "You're lying."

"I'm not—" They both give me a look that silently tells me to not even try lying anymore. "Look. Before Alexandra Delacroix invites me to her family house so I can get some dirt, there will be a lot more to do than a little bit of flirting and first base at her Sorority house."

"First base, my ass," Tamar cackles as she exits the backroom into the workshop with a beer for Logan.

"Man," Zara sighs.

"Don't say it." I run a hand through my hair and turn my back to her, pretending to be on my phone.

"Don't lose sight of the end goal, please."

"I won't." I already have.

She's about to talk again when a scream breaks our peaceful afternoon.

"Xi!"

Tamar.

We're both in the workshop in a split second. Logan is on the floor, groaning and rubbing the back of his head.

Unwell, but alive.

This might not be the case for my best friend in a few seconds since Ethan Torres is pointing his gun at her.

"Don't you fucking dare," I growl.

"Xi, how funny. You were the exact person we were looking for," his stepbrother Elliot says, casually sitting on the hood of a car, holding a heavy-duty wrench. He must have used it to hit Logan on the back of the head.

"If you want to talk to me, you find *me*. Don't impede on a man's business and don't point your gun at my friends."

Elliot jumps off the hood and my eyes go to Tamar again. She's shaking like a leaf. The girl rarely leaves her house. Maybe a party now and then, sometimes hanging out with us. She left the safety of hiding behind her computer to spend time with us today, and this town is throwing it back in her face.

I'm not worried about Ethan and Elliot. They want something from me, and they can be sure they won't get it if they kill me or my friends.

Next to me, Zara slides her hand behind her back.

"No, no, pretty girl." Elliot's smile is creepy. "There's only space for one gun in this garage, and I believe that's the one pointed at your friend."

I place a placating hand on Zara's shoulder, encouraging her to let go of the gun tucked in the back of her jeans.

"We just want to talk, really." I wouldn't believe him even if he wasn't playing with the wrench right now, rolling his wrist and tracing circles with it in the air.

"Grab Logan and go to the back," I tell Zara. If I can spare at least two of my friends from this, I will.

"Xi," she complains.

"*Now.*"

She huffs and helps Logan up. He's still dizzy from the hit, understandably. The brothers don't seem to have a problem with them going to the back. Maybe they know there's no way out and they can't get help. Maybe they don't plan on staying long enough for our crew to get here.

It's terrifying to see how much this town broke me. My heartbeat doesn't rise. The fear for my best friend's life is manageable, overridden by the need for survival.

"Let's talk outside," I say with a cool voice.

Ethan shifts on his feet, his unreadable black eyes darting to me.

"If we go outside, how can my brother threaten sweet Tamar's life while I do this?" He brings the wrench down on the windshield of the car he was sitting on.

Tamar gasps, her hands coming to her mouth. "Don't!"

I take a step toward Elliot, ready to end him, but Ethan takes one toward my friend. "Tsk, tsk," he tuts me, pressing the gun against her forehead this time.

"Please, this garage is Logan's whole life," Tamar whimpers. "It's the only way to feed his family!"

"Aw," Elliot pouts, tilting his head to the side. "Hear that, Xi? It's his *whole. Life.*" He brings the wrench down on the mirror, detaching it from the car.

"Where the fuck is she?" He hits another car.

"You want to know where she is?" I say calmly. "I'll tell you."

He stops and looks at me with surprise on his face. This man is so emotive; he's an open book.

"After a fight in the Death Cage."

Elliot snorts. "Once I get you in there and kill you, how are you gonna give me what I want?"

"See it my way." I take another step toward him. "Once I

205

kill you, I'll give the info you want to Ethan. He'll happily join her once the North Shore is mine."

All I have to do is win *one* fight in the Death Cage for NSC to take over. The rules are the rules, and I'm a beast. It's the only reason the Kings don't want to set it up. I've been winning fight after fight at the warehouse. They're terrified to put me in the Death Cage with one of theirs.

"Deal?" I insist, stopping right in front of him. A slow smile spreads on his lips, the total opposite of my unmoving face.

As a response, he lifts his arm again. This time I'm close enough to grab his wrist, take the crowbar from him, and before he can react, I hit him across the body with it.

One. Powerful. Hit.

He falls to the ground, grunting as he holds his side.

But my move is useless.

"Xi!" Tamar's whimper grabs my attention. Ethan is behind her now, holding the gun to her temple.

"I don't think you understand how the game goes," Ethan grits. "Step back."

I press my lips together, exhaling through my nose like a fucking raging bull.

And I take a step back.

Only to watch as Elliot gets back up, laughing at me. "This is going to be fun."

And all I can do at this point to save my best friend's life is stand there, helplessly, as Elliot Pearson destroys Logan's garage.

It takes so long. Every hit is a blow to my chest. Every blow makes it harder to withhold information from them.

On the North Shore, sacrifices have to be made all the time. NSC's ultimate goal is to take back our town, and as long as I have something on the brothers, I have an advantage worth more than this garage.

Elliot is panting when he's done, clearly enraged that I still haven't opened my mouth. He hates that there wasn't even the shadow of a wince on my face. He and Ethan look at each other, understanding the cause is lost, and slowly retreat.

"Take your time," Elliot says before he's entirely out of the repair shop. "There's more we can do."

The second they're gone, I run to my car.

"Xi, don't!" Tamar shouts after me. "Zara!"

They'll try to stop me, and there's no fucking way. Zara sprints to me, pressing a hand on my door as I try to open it.

"Don't waste my fucking time," I growl.

"Don't. Let's talk to Emma."

"*Fuck Emma.*"

I push her away and climb inside, speeding out of the small parking lot outside of Logan's garage.

I speed through the streets of the North Shore, not hesitating one second before going into Kings' territory. Fucking shoot me for all I care. *Try.*

The brothers' house is deep into Kings' turf. There's no way I could have taken a wrong turn. I make it there before they do. I park on another road so they don't find my car the moment they arrive and check everything is clear before I get out.

Feeling for the pink lighter I bought earlier in the pocket of my hoodie, I put my cap on, then the hood on top of it. I take the crowbar I keep in the bed of my truck and run to their backyard. Then I slide between the two garbage cans they use as a delimitation of their property and make my way across the yellow grass. I try the bedroom window in case it's unlocked, but it's not. In one swift movement, the glass is broken, and I undo the lock before pushing it up. I slide into their house like a thief in the middle of the night. Except I'm a raging brute in the middle of the day.

I don't waste time destroying the house. I go straight to the kitchen and kick open the door leading to their basement. I run downstairs and immediately find what I want—a nice big canister of gasoline. I run back up the stairs, knowing my time is limited.

I'm done in less than a minute, anyway.

And when I hear their car park in front of their house, my body finally wakes up. I think it's excitement. The door unlocks, and they both stop in the hallway the second they walk in.

Elliot's eyes look down at the oily liquid covering the floor between them and me.

"How was the drive?" I ask with a composure Elliot could never even dream of.

I grab my pack of cigarettes and the pink lighter, taking my time to put a stick between my lips. I light it up and look at both of them, exhilaration feeding my heart.

"You shouldn't come for my friends." My voice is low and a clear threat they can't miss. "Ever."

I pinch the cigarette between my thumb and forefinger. I take my time removing it from between my lips, tempting him to come to me.

And it works.

"Motherfucker!" Elliot is about to jump toward me, except level-headed Ethan holds him back by the t-shirt, dragging him to him a second before I throw my cigarette on the floor.

We all take a step back as the heat blazes us in the face.

If only he'd let him throw himself at me. I would have

watched Elliot burn alive and finally smiled at the fucking world.

I'll settle for their house burning to the ground. The smoke starts prickling my eyes, but I still keep them on the brothers.

"Come at me again," I tell them. "See what happens."

And I'm out, back through the bedroom window, and running back to my car as they run out through their front door.

I take a deep breath the second I drive back to NSC streets. I park in front of my house and let my head fall back against the seat.

There's only one person I want to see right now. One woman I want to hold in my arms and calm me down.

14

ALEXANDRA

Falling – Trevor Daniel

"Alex." I startle when someone grabs my arm.

Looking up from my phone, I notice how close I am to falling off the stairs in our house.

"Girl," Ella sighs. "You've been living in the clouds in the last week, and I'm worried you'll get yourself killed."

Of course, I've been living in the clouds. I'm dating a man who is dying to know my body and soul by heart for the sole purpose of giving me pleasure.

Xi has been sneaking in and out of my bedroom every night for an entire week. While he had promised to fuck me the night of initiations, he's been respectful to take things slow since he knows I'm a virgin.

So instead of fucking me, he spends nights worshipping my body and bringing me so much pleasure I feel like I'm constantly floating, even when he's not here.

"I'm so sorry," I mutter, putting my phone away. "What were you saying?"

She gives me an annoyed look, and I offer her my most

apologetic smile. My friends have not been the biggest fan of me seeing Xi. Peach is wholly against it, although Ella at least hears me out when I want to talk about him.

"I was saying Camila and Harper have been asking everyone to help prepare for the Halloween party, and you're the only one who hasn't signed up for anything. That girl will eat you alive if you don't start pulling your weight."

"It's in a month," I groan. "Why does everything have to be so strict?"

"I bet the parties on the North Shore are going to be more exciting." Ella wiggles her eyebrows at me, making me laugh.

"Too bad we'll both be stuck here. You said you wanted to go as a dead bunny, right?"

"Yes, baby." She joins her hands in front of her and hops on the spot.

"I can sew that for you. It's honestly so easy. I'll get a short bodysuit, sew a little bunny tail, and make the ears..."

"Alex," Ella sighs. "Why are you like this? I'll buy it. I don't need you to sew it for me. Our friendship doesn't rely on the favors you do for me. You are *too* nice, babe."

Maybe having my dad on the phone earlier messed with me slightly. I wanted to know if I could use the lake house for the weekend without mentioning wanting to bring Xi, and he asked what I would give in return for the privilege. Since I couldn't offer anything, he said no.

"Of course," I smile at my friend. "It was in case you didn't have time or—"

"I have time. And you take care of yourself, okay? I love you. Goodnight."

I say goodnight to her at her door and walk all the way to my room. Then I undress out of my uniform and get in the shower. There is not a second of the day I'm not thinking of Xi, and I want to spend all of them with him.

I sit down at my desk after my shower and open my laptop. I need to catch up on some essays. It's all good and well to have a boyfriend again, but I can't let it affect my SFU work.

I open an email from my English professor and click on the link to my latest grade. I will have to send an update to my dad to ensure he doesn't show up asking to see every single essay I've written.

It's been a strange experience to be away from home and without his constant reminders of how I should act. I smile to myself, realizing the second I moved away from the house, I started doing everything he ever forbade me to. Drinking, parties...seeing someone from the North Shore.

There's a certain excitement burgeoning in my belly when I think of the independence I could develop far from my dad. There's a weight off my shoulders at knowing I can be my own woman without anyone telling me how.

The link loads, I follow the line next to my name...and everything comes crashing down.

"What?" I gasp. I press my index finger to the screen and trace the line from my name to the C minus. There must be an error. I handed this in on Tuesday, and it's Thursday. He corrected them way too quickly. I spent hours on this essay...how?

The happiness that was in me seconds ago turns heavy. I've been working on this essay in between seeing Xi and doing all sorts of stupid tasks for the Xi Ep initiations.

My phone ringing practically makes me jump out of my chair. I look down at Xi's name and answer right away.

"I'm in front of your window, cupcake." It's always strange to hear a sweet nickname in such a flat tone. Xi has this weird way of making everything sound like it's nothing to him, even though I know I get more human emotions from him than anyone else. A cute nickname is probably his best effort.

My eyes are still on the catastrophic grade I just got, my brain anticipating the disappointment from my dad when he learns about it. I can't tell him.

"Hello?"

"Uh, yeah, sorry."

"I'm not coming in tonight. You're coming out." His calm order is everything that defines him, and it pulls at something inside me. Wouldn't everything be so much simpler if all I had to do was listen to Xi? But that's not how life is. Life is college and money. It's pressure from my dad, the Stoneview world, and the girls I surround myself with.

Life is more complicated than falling for the heartless boy from the wrong side of town.

"It's a Thursday," I tell him without much fight in my voice.

"Oh no, please don't tell my mom."

I roll my eyes even though he can't see me. "You know sarcasm is meant to have at least an undertone of mockery. You can't make jokes with a flat tone."

"I seem to be getting away with it just fine. Come out."

I head over to my window and glance down at him on the front lawn. He's wearing a black hoodie with a black baseball cap and black jeans.

"How many black hoodies do you have? I already have one of yours."

"Keeping it for when you miss me, cupcake? Give it back. You can have me whenever you want."

"It's mine now, sorry," I say playfully. "I own it."

"And I own you. Full circle."

I have to refrain myself from sighing with pleasure. I feel like the main character in the song *Style*, knowing there is this man who has the strangest effect on me, and there's no way I can control it. Knowing that he could be so bad for me, yet only wanting more of him. He taps into some unexplored desires I want to show him.

Being owned? By Xi? Yes, please.

"Are you going to come down, or do I have to come up and get you?"

"Romeo, Romeo. Wherefore art thou Romeo?"

"Romeo is going to spank your ass if you keep quoting Shakespeare instead of coming down."

"Big fan of British literature, too, huh?"

"Alex," he growls. "Why are you diverting the conversation?"

I huff, aware I've been completely caught. "I received a bad grade."

There's a moment of silence as I watch his unmoving shadow on the lawn. I imagine him blinking at me and not understanding why I'm so upset. I expect Xi to mock me. Wouldn't even take it the wrong way if he did. I know how ridiculous I sound. He's twenty-four and didn't go to high school. Worrying about grades has never been an issue for him. Even my friends don't understand why I make such a big deal out of it. They don't know the pressure I'm handling at home.

"Okay," he says slowly, as if thinking twice about what to say. "You're upset. Do you want to talk to me about it?"

Oh, God. I expected anything, but I did not expect *that*.

Talk about it? Like he cares? How can he do this to me when I'm trying so hard not to fall for him even more?

Following my silence, he continues. "I've had a bit of a shit day too, and I wanted to take you somewhere special where I go to clear my mind. I think you'll like it. You can rant to me there."

My head falls forward, my forehead hitting the window. "Stop making me like you," I groan.

"I'll wait for you in my car." Knowing perfectly well I'll follow, I watch him disappear from the lawn.

The moment he's out of sight, I run to my bed and grab his hoodie. I put on my long fuchsia trench coat and a black baseball cap and run to the mirror. I'm wearing my black leggings, my face completely bare of makeup. I hesitate momentarily, wondering if I should put on some mascara and blush, then decide otherwise. He's not going to run away, is he?

I go down the wooden stairs two at a time, my Gucci crossbody bag hitting my lower back and excitement bubbling in my chest now that I know Xi doesn't think I'm an idiot for being upset about grades.

I'm rushing through the entrance hall when someone calls my name. Harper is standing in the doorway leading to the living room.

"Going somewhere special, pledge?" Her eyes narrow on me and I offer her my best fake smile.

"Late night ice cream."

She cocks an eyebrow before walking toward me. Women like Harper are so aware of their feminine power. I don't like her, but I'd give anything to walk around with the assurance she has. To cross my arms over my chest and cock my hips in a threatening and confident way like she does.

And how I wish I had her balls.

"You remember the first night of initiations, Alex. Right?"

Feeling myself shrinking under her intense stare, I nod.

"Do you remember when we said we had *cameras* in the rooms that night?"

My chest tightens, remembering what I did with Xi then. How could I forget about the cameras?

"It looks like you *really*," she drags on the word, twisting the knife, "enjoyed yourself. Didn't you?"

"Harper—"

"I asked you one thing. *One.* To stay away from him. Only you couldn't keep your slutty ass in check, could you? Are you that stupid? Don't you think we all fall for his tactics?"

"I'm so sorry," I squeak.

"Sisters over anything else, Alex."

A lump blocks my throat when I try to apologize again. Tears fill my eyes, making her scoff. "Oh, please. Don't act like a sweet, innocent girl." She crosses the boundary of my personal space, talking in my face now. "You're a little slut who went behind her sister for a guy who will throw you to the side the first chance he gets. Think about what you did before crying to anyone."

The conversation is over. Not giving me a chance to defend myself, she turns on her heels and goes back to the living room. I can hear a few of them watching a movie in there.

I wipe my tears and head for the door.

Fuck.

Fuck this girl and this sorority. All Harper's been doing is taking pride in bullying the pledges and dragging out initiations.

I find Xi's car down the road and jump in. Slamming the door, I look out through the window, attempting to collect myself before I turn to him.

"If I don't get a kiss in the next two seconds, I'm going to start getting mean."

My heart thunders at his words. Everything seems to take second place when Xi is around.

It should be worrying, though I could use the distraction right now.

His hand wraps around the back of my neck, and he pulls me to him. I turn around from the pressure, only for his lips to meet mine in a devouring kiss.

"Don't make me wait next time," he growls as he pulls away. He observes my face just as I sniffle and I watch as his thick, dark eyebrows draw together in the slightest. The faintest line appears between them, and I bring my thumb to it, rubbing between his brows.

"You're crying," he states without an ounce of worry in his voice. Nevertheless, I see it in the way he scoots closer to me. I feel it under my thumb. It makes my skin tingle.

"Harper is a bitch, but I'll be okay."

"What did she do?" He's clearly as done with her as I am.

"She watched a video of us on the first night of initiations. There were cameras in the room that night, stupid initiation stuff. I...I had forgotten about it until she so kindly reminded me."

There's a brief pause before he pulls away. "For fuck's sake," he huffs in that way he has of letting the world know it's pissing him off.

He opens his door, and I throw myself over him, grabbing his arm. "What are you doing?" I gasp.

"I'm gonna talk to her. She needs to know her fucking place."

"No, no, no. You're not talking to her. I can handle this."

"*This* baby chick," he says, looking me up and down. "Don't make me laugh."

"Laugh? Oh no, don't worry, we all know that's too much to ask."

His eyebrows shoot up. "So you *do* have retorts."

"Yes, when I want to. I can handle my problems, Xi. You don't need to save me all the time."

He licks his lips, his gaze lost, his mind running. "Maybe I like saving you."

I feel my cheeks heat, unable to stop the smile from spreading on my lips.

All my life, I've been wanting someone to save me. From home, from the kidnappers, from my own mind. I've grown up swallowing back whatever fight I had in me and learning to do anything I was told to. I would dream of someone coming to my rescue, of someone realizing what was happening inside the beautiful mansion of Senator Delacroix.

I lost my voice. My will to fight. Xi telling me he *likes saving me* means more to me than anything else I could have heard at this moment.

My throat is dry when I try to reply, having to clear it. "I shouldn't rely on you like that."

He looks deep into my eyes, his hand moving to rest against my cheek. "You are more than capable of handling yourself, Alex. Just know that you will always be safe with me. No matter what."

I let the moment stretch, enjoying that someone is making me feel safe for the first time in forever. He was the least likely candidate. In my life, I imagined someone from Stoneview, a wealthy man taking over his parents' company and whisking me away to New York City. I imagined us working in the city every day and coming home to each other. I imagined the vacations we would take, and that by keeping me away from my father and Stoneview, he would be saving me.

I did not imagine drug-dealing Xi from the North Shore to be the man to save me.

"Thank you," I rasp through my tight throat.

He pulls away and starts the car, my face feeling cold now that his warm breath is no longer fanning my cheeks. I take a deep breath, inhaling his scent.

"Where are you taking us?" I ask as he drives away from campus.

"Somewhere special."

My body tingles everywhere with the knowledge Xi thinks I deserve a special place.

"A special place for a special girl?" I joke, the undertone of hope clear in my words.

"You have no idea." His eyes stay focused on the road as I look at his handsome form. The baseball cap hides what I know is thick, brown hair. His hoodie is up, giving him an ominous image. In all black, he could disappear into the night without a trace.

"Why do you always wear baseball caps?"

His eyes dart to me. "Are you wearing one to match me?"

"Yeah." I smile proudly. A silly kid wanting to match their parents. "The Xi style."

"I do it because I like the anonymity. Moving around the North Shore is easier when people aren't sure who you are. Not sure you fit the Xi style with that coat."

My fuchsia coat is indeed not making me blend with the night as his attire does.

I open the window, letting the cool night wind flick my hair. The nights are getting much colder. I'm a summer girl.

Camping at Stoneview Lake with my friends, stargazing from our small town. Boating activities.

My favorite thing, however?

My parents are usually away on vacation. Washington D.C. is a mere forty-minute drive from Stoneview, hence why we have so many politicians in our town. My father can easily drive back and forth. Well, his driver does. So he's home a lot. Except during summer, when they're away. That time used to be my favorite occasion of the year.

I'm not a winter person. I don't like the cold, the rain, or sometimes the snow we get. It hasn't been too bad lately, even though evenings are starting to smell like Fall. The light noise of leaves falling, the bite of cold in the air.

I stay silent as Xi guides us out of town and through some cliff roads. My eyes tear up from the wind, but I like it. With his presence by my side and the taste of freedom on my lips, I feel light.

We park on the edge of a cliff, with nothing around us but sandy, dusty ground and tall trees.

"Where are we?" I ask as I inhale the fresh air. He turns to me and puts a strand of my hair behind my shoulder.

"We're at the falls."

"That's not the falls," I chuckle. "I know what it looks like around the falls, and that's definitely not it."

He shakes his head. "You know what it looks like from the south bank. This is what it looks like on the North Shore."

The words are delivered with a coolness I've come to enjoy.

"Come on." He takes my hand and helps me out of the car.

The faint noise of the waterfalls that gave the name to this city can be heard in the background. There's gravel and dust where we're parked, but only space for one car. Everything else is forest. It's a very small viewpoint without any infrastructure.

I walk closer to the edge of the cliff and watch the horizon. The falls aren't actually here. All I can see is Stoneview Lake. It's a vast lake that looks like a black hole of nothingness at night. There are no lights around here. The only thing shining are a few of the Stoneview Lake houses far away in the distance from us. Just dots in a midnight blue background. Fireflies in the darkness.

I can faintly see my small hometown on the other side. Here, the water is barely accessible. The cliffs haven't been structured to access the lake like it is on our side. I guess one could jump in and quickly climb back out, but there are no wood platforms and human-made pebble beaches like we have. And there are certainly no lake houses. Yet, there's something special about this place. A calmness that grounds me. It's not pretentious, it's just nature.

Xi's hand grabs mine, and he pulls me to the side. "Come, I want to show you something."

I follow him, my white, expensive sneakers already turning gray from all the dust.

He takes me through what barely looks like a path. It's not something official, but that's formed over the years of people walking here. He jumps down a few rocks, then turns around and holds me by the waist. My heart lurches in my chest, and my hands fly to the top of his shoulders as he picks me up to bring me down to his level.

The lack of light makes it all feel forbidden and a little scary. Like something could jump on us at any time. Like someone is hiding and watching us. It makes my heart accelerate in the best way.

I'm not really scared, though. I trust Xi. It's more like

watching a horror film, being aware of fear, but nothing can happen to us.

"Are we even allowed to be here?"

He lets go of my waist to grab my hand again. "Try living a little, cupcake. Don't worry if things are allowed."

"So, no."

He lights up a path with his phone, and we walk for around ten minutes, the noise of the Silver Falls getting louder and louder. He pushes through some thick wild bushes, and I follow him despite the small branches scratching my arm.

And I'm glad I do.

"Oh my God," I gasp above the now loud noise of water going down and hitting the river many feet below.

"You like the view?" Xi sits down in front of me and taps the ground next to him. His feet dangle into emptiness, and my belly flutters looking at the falls crashing down. It's not easy to see, only lit up by the moon, but my eyes adjust quickly like a predator of the night. The falls are gigantic. The other side of them is where the south bank trail leads to. It's a nice hike to do on the weekend and leads to a spectacular view. But not this close.

I've never felt so alive.

"Be careful," Xi says as I sit beside him. "No barriers here."

When I'm finally sitting on the edge, I realize there's something under us. Another layer of cliff that would catch us if we slipped. It's not as dangerous as I thought it would be and I feel myself relaxing.

I play with some pebbles next to me, both of us listening to the falls for a few minutes.

"You said you had a bad day." My voice is a little raspy,

but he hears me even over the sound of crashing water because he's listening.

That's the thing with this man. He listens. It's beautiful and dangerous, as I must constantly be careful what I wish for.

"Yeah," he huffs. He removes his hat to rake his fingers through his hair before settling it back on.

"Would you like to talk about it?" In the dark of the evening and the noise of the fall, I hope he will allow himself to open up to me. He thinks that I can't handle it. He thinks I probably wouldn't last a minute in his world, with his problems. He's right, but I can still be here for him.

His hand grabs mine on the dusty ground, his fingers threading through my own. "Bad things are happening on the North Shore. Things that put everyone in danger."

There's always something *thing* should define, and Xi is avoiding that on purpose.

For a minute here, I had forgotten that this beautiful piece of paradise is on the North Shore of the falls. His reminder twists my stomach.

"Are you involved in them?" I ask in a whisper.

I know what Xi does. I know he's a dealer. Ultimately, it's not the end of the world. Illegal, yes, but surely just a pawn in a big game. He's not part of any of the gangs that plague the North Shore with dangerous activities.

Or I would know...right?

His lack of response makes me doubt. "Xi," I ask with a tone that betrays my fear. "You're not...you're not involved, right? In the...*stuff* that is dangerous." For lack of a better word, and considering I'm too ignorant to know, that's as thorough as my question can be.

We hear all sorts of sordid stories in Stoneview, and it's hard to always differentiate stupid rumors from what truly happens in this town. All we really know is that there are two gangs, and they're both as bad as the other.

Ignoring my question, he stares at the silver water below us. "Are you really that scared of the North Shore?"

Deciding that if one of us starts being honest it would help us move forward, I go for the truth. "Yes. I have bad memories here."

He doesn't ask me what. He simply takes it in silently.

"Sometimes," he says low. "It scares me too."

I feel my muscles tense at the admission. "Because of what could happen to you?"

He shakes his head. "Because of the man it's turning me into."

I put a hand on his cheek, forcing him to look at me. "One place doesn't define you. It's who you are inside, your hopes and dreams, that do."

He snorts, his eyes darting away. "They've all been crushed, Alex. All that's left is bitterness."

"Good thing I'm as sweet as a cupcake, then, isn't it?" I smile, giving him the kindness he so desperately needs.

Without warning, Xi grabs my waist and pulls me onto his lap.

This conversation is over, just because he decided so. A glimpse of how he truly feels inside, and he's done opening up to me.

"You're wearing leggings," he whispers as his hand slides under my trench coat and his thumb goes under the elastic waistband of my leggings. "I prefer skirts."

"I can't wear skirts all the time. Leggings are more comfortable, and I look fine in them."

"You look perfect in anything, baby." His hand slides under my leggings and my underwear. "I'm talking about access to your beautiful pussy."

Two fingers come to press against my clit and I gasp. "Do you understand now?" he insists, starting to circle my clit.

"Yeah," I sigh.

"But it's okay. Nothing can stop me."

His movement is languid, taking his time as he drags pleasure out of me. "I'm sorry about your grade."

"It-It's okay." My hips jerk forward uncontrollably, trying to force him to accelerate.

"These things are important to you. Grades. College. Sorority. I get it."

"Uh huh..." I can barely hear him. The air is suddenly stuffy, and my body is on fire.

"I shouldn't take so much of your time. Coming over every night, making you feel good..."

"Yes," I moan. "Do it."

He keeps going, rubbing my clit as I relish in his warmth. His voice lulls me into a different universe where all that matters is reaching the nirvana I know is so close.

"Oh God," I cry out. "Xi..."

I feel his other hand move my hair away from my neck as he kisses my shoulder, making his way up the sensitive skin and sucking right below my ear.

"Come for me, baby," he whispers softly. "You're so gorgeous when you explode on my fingers."

"Fuck!" I scream as I do exactly what I'm told. I rub myself against him, pushing harshly to enjoy every single second of my orgasm. "Fuck," I pant again.

"So beautiful."

I'm so wet. My pussy feels swollen and so evidently in need of more. I'm wracked from the orgasm, but I want to feel so much more of him.

"Come," he says as he taps my thighs. "Let's walk down to the river."

I feel his hard-on against my ass cheeks, and I make sure to rub myself against him before standing up.

"Don't tease me." A command more than a playful remark.

He jumps to the flat layer of rock just below us and twists around. He grabs my waist, taking me down.

"I like when you do that," I admit, clearly orgasm drunk.

"When I carry you?"

I shrug my shoulders. "Yes, when you guide me and carry me and take me special places."

He grabs my hand, guiding me along a descending path. "You're fucking cute, you know that?"

"Yeah," I say playfully. "I'm like a cute princess, and you're my rugged villain. Whisking me away from the castle." I imitate his flat voice. "I'm never happy. I have real problems, Alex. Not fairytale issues."

He stops, turns around, and there it is. That pull at the corner of his mouth. It's so subtle.

"I can see you find me hilarious, Xi. No need to hide it."

"Annoying would be more accurate."

"I don't think so." I jut my chin and nudge him so he keeps walking. We trail down toward the river. And the moment we reach the running water, Xi lies down on the humid bank. Rocks the size of my head, wet and visibly uncomfortable. Yet, I don't hesitate one second before joining him. He settles comfortably with his arms behind his head, and I lie down beside him.

My mouth drops open as I look at the sky above us. A veil of diamonds covers the midnight blue, illuminating us and turning this moment magical.

"Wonderland," I murmur to myself.

"What?"

"Nothing." I shake my head, pushing the Taylor Swift song away from my thoughts.

I grab my Polaroid camera out of my bag and take a selfie of us. It prints and I shake it before looking at it. The flash illuminates my pale skin in the night. My cap isn't low enough to hide my face and the happiness is distinct on it. My coat is flashy, too. The combination of everything makes me the more prominent shadow on the picture. And next to me is my broody man, his face is hidden by the hood and hat combination. He's barely recognizable, but I know.

Putting my camera and the picture back in my bag, I lie back down again. My eyes are on the stars once more. It's the first time since I started the tradition that I take two memory pictures for a single month. One with my best friends. One with the man I'm unmistakably falling for.

"This is the most beautiful thing I've ever seen."

"So is this."

I tilt my face toward him only to find him staring right at me. My mouth opens to say something. I want to laugh, to call him cheesy. Something. *Anything.*

I can't, because the stars are reflecting in his captivating irises, and all I see in them is the truth in his words.

My chest heats, the blush running to my face and all the way to my ears.

"This is the best night of my life," I whisper.

"It's just..." He stops himself.

It's just stars.

We're just lying down by the riverbank.

Just a midnight walk with the man who is changing my life for the better.

I watch his throat work as he swallows thickly. "Alex, I have to tell you something."

A truth is on the tip of his tongue. Something heavy. A revelation I don't want to hear.

Please, don't ruin the moment.

I shake my head no. *Don't.*

I move closer to him, shifting and placing a hand on his hoodie before my mouth captures his. I lick his lips before he parts them, and I push into his mouth. My hands fist his hoodie and I feel his muscular chest flexing.

Sliding his hand under my trench coat, he grabs the waistband of my leggings and pulls me closer to him. Our kiss heats up and his dominating personality returns. He growls against my mouth as he lowers my leggings and panties at the same time, pulling hard to get it past my ass.

"Tonight," he murmurs against my lips. "I'm going to give you tonight, Alexandra. I will make love to you and worship you like the queen you are."

He kisses me again, ridding me of my leggings entirely. He pushes my hoodie above my head, freeing me of my hat and coat too, ensuring I'm completely naked.

"Tonight, we live in your fairy tale."

His mouth descends on my tits, licking one after the other. He nibbles at my nipple, making me writhe under him. "But after that, you are back to being my slut, got it?"

"Yes," I moan as he kisses his way down my belly and settles between my legs. He kisses my inner thighs, devouring and teasing me until his mouth finally touches my clit.

He spreads my lower lips and licks me from my entrance to my clit.

"You've my favorite taste," he shares his secret to the night.

He buries his face between my legs, bringing me close to

an explosion just like he knows how. His tongue plays with my entrance before replacing it with a finger. Then two.

The sensation I got earlier comes back. That *need* to be filled by something thick and hard.

"Xi," I whimper. "Do it."

He undoes his jeans, pulling out his throbbing cock. His hand goes up and down slowly as he strokes himself sensually, his eyes on my pussy.

"Beautiful," he murmurs to himself.

He aligns himself with my soaking entrance and I rub myself against his tip. He presses inside me in the slightest, crowning me.

"You're everything I want to keep close. You're my safe place, Alex."

And he pushes in. Slowly, with an erotism that I would never think possible outside of violence and humiliation. He destroys my dirty secret, showing me that I can get pleasure from more than what I believe I love.

He pushes until I feel myself open for him. A tension presses inside me, but the pleasure is too intense for me to care. I feel him groan once he makes it past it, and he sits inside me, unmoving.

"Baby, you're so tight," he growls as his head falls against my neck. "It's done. This beautiful pussy is all mine now."

He pulls away and pushes back in. Small movements first, making me pant with need, until he starts pushing harder. His hips roll, making me scream to the rhythm he chooses. My body doesn't belong to me anymore. My breath is his to command and his movements control my pleasure.

His thumb comes to my clit again, and I can swear I see another million stars joining the ones in the sky.

Everything around us disappears. The running river, the

shining sky. The sound of the falls crashing not far from us, the harshness of the rocks under my back.

All that is left is Xi and me. The way he moves, the sound of his breath in my ear, and the feeling of him inside me.

I explode around him, reaching heaven, touching the stars, and coming back down slowly as he comes inside me.

I can feel his crazy heartbeat through his hoodie and against my chest. His cap's fallen next to us. His body is heavy on mine, and I shiver from the sudden breeze. Maybe it was already there, but I was too busy losing my virginity to the man of my dreams.

"Let's get you back to the car," he says raggedly. Like this has taken everything out of him. Restraining himself, I mean. He pulls out of me and gives me space to move.

I sit up and my eyes widen.

"Oh," I let out.

"Are you okay?" he asks as he buttons his jeans and grabs his cap.

"I...it's..." My eyes go down to my legs as I feel wetness leaking out of me. "I need a bathroom."

He runs a hand across his face. "You are the most innocent girl I've ever met."

"I'm not," I fight back. "You...I didn't know..."

"You didn't know it comes back out?"

My cheeks light on fire. "Stop looking at me like I'm so inexperienced. I just...never thought about it."

"You're inexperienced. It's okay. Just means I can teach you everything." He grabs my hand, helping me back up. "You're all mine to mold however I want, baby."

He picks up my clothes. First, he kneels before me, and I use his shoulders to hold myself as he helps me slip back into my leggings. He kisses my clit before pulling the leggings over my ass again. He stands up, dropping a kiss on my cheek as he slides the hoodie back over my head and then helps me into my coat. He grabs the pink belt and ties it around my waist before leaving a kiss on the top of my head.

I grab my shoes and look around. Standing back up, I cock an eyebrow at him. "My underwear, Xi."

"Fuck the girl, keep the underwear."

"Xi," I burst into an uncontrollable laugh.

"It's my underwear now." Said in such an even tone as well.

"Oh yeah? I can't wait to see you in them."

"You just wait and see." A joke. Not evident, though a joke nevertheless. And I love when he jokes.

I walk back into Xi Ep through the front door before running upstairs and unlocking my window for Xi. I watch him climb the trellis panel up to me, and I help him get in before sliding the window back down.

"Oh Romeo," I smile as I flutter my eyelashes at him.

"Go shower," he orders softly as he falls onto my bed.

"Did you know that Shakespeare wasn't the first to write about the Capulets and Montagues? They're mentioned in Dante's poem *Divine Comedy*, two hundred and fifty years before Shakespeare wrote his play."

He looks at me from the bed. "How many random facts like this do you know?"

"Many." I smile proudly. "Did you know from the time Juliet and Romeo meet to the time they get married, only twenty-four hours have passed? Talk about love at first sight."

He crawls to the end of the bed, stands on his knees, and

pulls me to him by the waist. "Okay, my little know-it-all. I promise I'll listen to more Romeo and Juliet facts after you shower and are ready for bed. Or any facts, really."

He kisses me, and I smile against his lips.

He refuses to join me, but I don't care. He's here. We've had sex, and he's here. There's something that keeps pulling at my guts. A heaviness that steadily reminds me Xi is the kind of man who disappears. He's the kind who fucks and leaves.

Not this time, right?

He's still here.

Nonetheless, I shower quickly and grab a silk, fuchsia cami pajama top and matching shorts before running back to my bed.

"I'm back," I exclaim, jumping on the bed next to him. My heart is beating hard. I'm ashamed to admit out loud that I was scared he wouldn't be here when I came out of the bathroom.

There's a delicious ache inside me, a sting at my entrance, and I love it so much, knowing it's coming from him.

"There was no blood," I whisper, looking up at him.

He presses his lips against my forehead and kisses his way to my ear. "I'm not one of your college frat boys, Alexandra. I know how to fuck a woman and make it all about pleasure."

"We didn't use a condom. You're lucky I'm on the pill."

He must sense the other sentence I'm holding back.

"I got tested last week, and it was all good. I always use protection."

"But not with me."

"Not with you."

"Because I'm a special girl."

233

What I consider his smile returns and it basks my entire world in his light. "Yeah," he agrees. "You're my special girl." He puts a strand of dirty-blonde hair behind my ear, and I watch his eyes darken as he licks his lips. "My special girl and my beautiful slut. I made love to you, Alex. Now I want to show you what it's like when I fuck you."

My heart lurches in my chest just as my stomach tightens, a sudden dryness taking over my throat as anticipation makes my thighs tremble.

"Now?" I rasp.

"Now," he murmurs. "Lay back."

"I'm scared someone will hear," I admit in a whisper. "Tomorrow. Maybe we can go to your house?"

Am I planning when to get fucked? Is that really how I want to play this? *Let me put you in my calendar for five thirty p.m.*

I feel ridiculous, but at the same time, we're surrounded by Xi Ep girls in the other rooms, and this really won't help my case.

But Xi is done playing by my rules. I gave myself to him, so now the game has changed. He's in charge. Completely.

His hand flies to my throat, pushing me back until my back hits the mattress.

"When I say something, Alexandra, you listen. When I give an order, you obey." He releases my neck. "Don't move."

Going on his knees, he settles next to me. Still in shock from what he just did and said, I stay unmoving, my stomach twisted and pleasure pooling between my legs. His hand goes to my chest, before slowly grazing my nipples with his knuckles. One after the other, descending until he's cupping my pussy through the silk of my shorts.

He presses hard against me, practically shoving the material inside me and making me hiss.

"Spread your legs," he orders.

"Xi," I whimper as he pushes again. I squeeze my eyes shut, feeling myself getting wetter. "I don't want to get in trouble with the other girls. Harper..."

"Mention Harper one more time, and I'll put you on your stomach and fuck that pussy so hard you won't be able to walk tomorrow."

I try to take in a breath despite the pleasure coursing through me, squeezing my lungs.

"It's not just about her." It's so hard to force the words past my throat. My muscles are tense, and my stomach is twisted. "I—if the other girls hear..."

"I'm going to ask nicely one last time, Alexandra. Spread your legs."

With my heart beating harshly in my ears, I let my legs fall open.

"That's a good girl," he says, the gravel in his voice reflecting the lust in his body. "Look at you, you're soaking wet."

He pushes my shorts to the side and grazes my clit with the pad of his thumb. I shudder, a small moan escaping my mouth and making me bite my lower lip.

His other hand comes to my mouth, pulling my lip free before putting his finger into my mouth. "You sound beautiful," he murmurs. "Don't hide it from me." Hooking his thumb to my lower teeth, he pulls until my mouth is fully open before pressing the pad to my tongue.

I should turn my head to the side. I should push him away.

I feel a finger nudging against my entrance. Slowly, he enters me, one knuckle at a time. I shift, trying to push against him, as a throaty moan escapes me and resounds throughout the room.

"Stay still," he growls. "You'll get your pleasure, don't worry."

I whimper from need when he pushes further. It's just one finger, but my entire body is melting for him.

I feel my muscles turn into putty when another wave of pleasure traverses me. I moan against his thumb. He's keeping my mouth open and stopping me from hiding the ridiculous sounds I'm making.

His finger pulls away before he pushes two back in. I cry out, the stretch too much for me. Especially as I still feel the sting at my entrance.

"You're so fucking tight. I'm going to stretch you out real good. Would you like that, baby?"

I squeeze my eyes shut, unable to look him in the eyes when I nod.

His fingers disappear before he slaps my pussy harshly. I shriek in pain, even as electricity zaps through my nerves.

"Tell me. Say that you want me to stretch out this tight pussy."

He pushes inside me slowly again, teasing me before he stops. I can't talk with his thumb keeping my mouth wide open, but I try anyway because I need that pleasure.

"...esh...ee..." The humiliation of not being able to form a single consonant lights a fire inside me. My tongue keeps pushing against his thumb, but I can't move my jaw or make a clear sound.

How can this turn me on?

His fingers curl inside me and my eyes widen as a cry of pleasure leaves me. I roll my hips, pressing harder against him and chasing the bliss.

His hand stills, and he smirks at me. "Go on," he mocks. "Be a good little slut and make yourself come."

His crude talk is practically the end of me. I rub myself

against his palm, pressing my pussy to him so I can keep fucking myself on his fingers.

I'm seconds from exploding when I hear a door opening and closing in the hallway.

A whimper escapes me as my eyes dart to the door and back to Xi. I freeze, but he's the one who picks up the movements again.

"Please," I beg, even though he can barely make out the word between my wide-open mouth and the escaping moan.

He gazes down at me, malicious thoughts flooding his expression.

"You don't want your friends to hear you come, Alex?"

I shake my head, panic seeping through me.

"Stop," I gargle, knowing I'm close to screaming my release for everyone to hear.

He accelerates, and just as his thumb pulls out, he presses his entire palm on my mouth and nose. I let my whole body give in to the powerful orgasm. My legs shake, my thighs closing against his hand. My scream stays down my throat and it's impossible for me to inhale the air I suddenly need. I ride it all and then some, his fingers not stopping until tears well in my eyes.

I plead with him with my stare, overstimulated and feeling myself fading from the need for air.

"You're incredibly gorgeous when I hold your life in my hands."

Fear wraps around my heart as it starts beating crazily.

My eyes dart everywhere as my vision narrows. He pulls his fingers out of my pussy, but I realize he doesn't plan on letting me breathe.

I panic, now wishing I could call for help.

"You're going to be so fun to play with, cupcake. Every

time you think of refusing anything, remember this exact moment. Me, seconds away from killing you. I decide when you come. I decide when you live. I decide when you die."

He finally lets go, and I gulp the much-needed air. I cough over and over again, oxygen burning my lungs. I roll onto myself, seeing stars as I curl onto the mattress. Tears stream down my eyes when I understand how close I was to death. My head is swimming and my emotions are swirling in my brain. Why did he do this?

"You're scaring me," I choke.

A sob bursts from my chest and one of his hands comes to caress my hair. "Shh," he murmurs. "You're okay."

I barely have time to register the softness in his voice when he grabs my hips and rolls me onto my back. "Spread your legs."

My heart drops in my stomach just as I hear the sound of his belt unbuckling.

"No," I cry. "Xi, don't."

He grabs the top of my pajamas between my tits and brings it down in one harsh gesture. The spaghetti straps break as he pulls it off me. My shorts are next.

"I said spread."

More tears spill when I do. I feel myself turned-on despite the recent orgasm. I'm scared. I don't want it to hurt, but I'm somehow getting wetter every time he pushes me harder.

His hands slide to my tits, his fingers playing with my nipples. He rolls them between his thumbs and forefingers, making me gasp from pleasure. "Xi..." I try to press my thighs together, needing something pressing against my clit, except his body is between my legs now. I'm soaked and can feel the wetness on my inner thighs, and it makes my clit tingle from the need for touch.

I moan as his fingers start pinching me. "It hurts," I whimper.

"What do you prefer, baby? When I hurt you or when I degrade you like the little bitch you are?"

My entire body lights up. Something liquifies my stomach, and my heart drops into the pool of need.

The answer is so obvious from my body. Still, I lie. "I-I don't know."

"What makes you wetter, Alexandra? This." He pinches my tits again and I cry out, my mouth twisting in displeasure. "Or this?" He moves one of his hands to my face and grabs my cheeks. He presses his thumb harshly on one side and his other fingers on the other. My jaw hurts, my mouth opening. He leans over me, and before I understand what's happening, he spits in my mouth.

I panic, trying to get out of his hold as the taste of him reaches my tongue. I yelp, and a light slap to my cheek brings me back to the present. He keeps pressing on my cheeks, his dark gaze freezing me into position. "Swallow, little slut."

I do. The disgust and humiliation twist my insides in the best way. And when he barely caresses my nipple next, I moan loudly.

"I think you know what turns you on the most," he sneers above me. He runs the length of his dick against my slit, making me desperate for him. "Tell me." He rubs my clit with his tip. "Tell me you're a little whore who likes to be degraded."

I take a shallow breath that turns into a moan the moment he presses his dick against my entrance. "Say it, Alexandra."

"I-I," I pant. I feel dizzy from everything going on at the same time. My body is going through a million sensations a minute and I can't seem to pick which one I love the most.

"Do it."

"I'm a little wh-whore..." I gasp as his dick starts pushing in.

"Keep going," he growls. His hands grab my thighs to keep them tight against him. He's on his knees, my ass against his thighs, as he pushes into me a little more. "You're a little whore who likes what?"

"Who likes..." I moan when his thumb presses against my clit. "Who likes to be d-degraded."

"That's right." He pushes in and out a few times, barely inside me, until I cry out from need.

"Please, Xi," I moan.

"Want me to fuck that beautiful cunt, Alexandra?"

I nod. My hands move as I intend to grab him, but his hands on my thighs tighten. "Put your hands above your head. Right now."

I press my wrists against the mattress again. "Little sluts only take what they're given, don't they?"

He pushes deeper inside me and my mouth falls slack. "Y-yes."

"And you're a little slut, aren't you, Alex?"

"Yes," I gasp.

This time, he doesn't pull away.

"You going to come for me, cupcake?" I nod as my eyes squeeze shut. I throw my head back but feel a hand grabbing the top of my hair and pulling. Xi forces my head back up, and at this angle I can see his hips moving, see the place where we meet, and he disappears into me.

"Watch how good you're taking me. Such a fucking whore."

I explode from the mix of everything. Him moving

inside me, his thumb on my clit, the degrading way he's holding my body and talking to me.

I cry out my pleasure, riding the wave for a long minute before he pulls out of me suddenly. He gets off the bed and drags me by the hair, pulling until I'm forced to move to his side, and then lies me back down.

"Open."

With my head now falling off the end of the bed, he fists his dick and comes all over my open mouth. He uses his fingers to spread his cum all over my lips.

"Keep your mouth open, baby. Show me your tongue coated in my cum." He hums to himself when I do. "Don't move." He steps away and comes back above me. I hear a click. There's a flash, and a second later, something is being printed.

My Polaroid camera. He waves the printed picture above my head. "You look gorgeous."

He throws it on the bed and pulls up his jeans before pocketing the picture. He helps me up, but I feel dazed, completely confused. Too many things are going through my head right now. Sitting up in front of him, disheveled and breathless, I press my fingers to my sore pussy and look at them out of curiosity. I want to understand what this man does to my body. They're slick, wet.

After another shower, I lay down next to him in bed.

"Are you okay?" Xi asks in a whisper as I peer up at the ceiling. I still haven't said a word, and I can't seem to find my voice.

His hand comes to stroke my face. "I asked you a question, Alex."

Even now, his harsh voice does something to me I don't understand. I'm not mad, and I'm not scared. I'm confused.

I'm ashamed of what I like. I don't understand how my body works.

"Alex," he huffs. "Say something. I warned you about this. You told me you could take it. I need you to be honest with me."

"I can take it," I rasp before looking at him. "I'm just...ashamed."

"Don't be. There are as many kinks as there are people in the world, baby. What you love fits what I love. You're allowed to enjoy it. Just forget everything you think is wrong. Let me take care of it."

I close my eyes and breathe out. "I can take anything as long as you don't break my heart."

A dry chuckle escapes him, and he traces my lips with his thumb. "Rest, now."

I want to talk to him. To enjoy the moment as much as I can, because that little voice at the back of my head keeps telling me he'll be gone in the morning. The side of my brain that isn't high on him right now, my realistic side, can see it in the way he doesn't take his clothes off. It knows because he's not under the covers with me.

He caresses my hair as my eyelids grow heavy. Too heavy for me to keep them open.

"Please, don't leave," I murmur as I fall into the darkness.

15

ALEXANDRA

Better – Gracie Adams

"I'm loving this weather," Ella beams as we walk together across campus. "This is the best September we've ever had."

"It should not be this warm," Peach comments as she puts her sunglasses on.

"Please, don't ruin the mood. The sun is out, we've got food, and we're going to picnic on the lawn of SFU. I do not want to hear you complain."

We settle on the grass, and I put my paper bag containing a Philly cheesesteak I usually love next to me, but my stomach is too twisted to eat.

"I'm so hungover," Peach says as she lays down. "I fucking hate Xi Ep."

Ella shrugs. "We're probably over the worst of initiations. They won't make us do more than stand all night in our underwear while they throw wet paper towels at us."

"Fucking annoying," Peach groans. "But what pissed me

off the most was making us sleep on the floor of our rooms. There was a bed right there. I'm so tired."

"No one even came to my room to check. I went home at, like, four a.m. from Zeta Nu's party. It was only three hours of being on the floor. Horrible, but bearable." Ella's eyes light up as she unpacks her salad.

"We get it, your night was amazing. I didn't even get to go to the party." Peach grabs her bag and takes out her burger and fries. "I'm so ready for the grease right now."

For the third time since initiations started, Peach was not allowed to go to the party after snapping at her big sister. I went, but Xi wasn't there. I've not heard from him in four days, and he hasn't answered any of my texts or calls.

Ella shakes her salad box to mix it with the dressing.

"You're boring," Peach tells her. "No one eats salad when they're hungover."

"We've got cheer this afternoon. I'm not going to fly and tumble with a burger in my stomach."

"I certainly am," Peach snorts as she takes a bite.

Ella turns to me and pokes me in the arm with her manicured nail. "Hey, are you alright? You're super quiet."

I offer her a small smile. "I'm okay. Just hungover."

I check my phone for the tenth time today.

I checked my phone after breakfast and after my first class. I checked it multiple times during my morning classes instead of listening and focusing on the lesson. And when I check it again just now, there's still nothing from him.

The last text exchange we had was the day before the lake. When we had sex for the first time. His friend Zara is the girl who's been showing up to Zeta Nu's parties to deal drugs. Xi, he just...vanished into thin air. Exactly like Harper said he would. When I asked his best friend where he'd gone, she just ignored me and went back to work.

He slept with Harper. Probably countless other girls.

And now he slept with me.

You are my safe place, Alex.

Surely, he's not going to just...disappear, right?

I'm such a fucking idiot.

I lost my virginity to a playboy. It doesn't get stupider than that.

I gulp as I look at my paper bag again. There is no way I can eat anything.

"Guys," Ella groans as she peers behind me. She swallows a mouthful of salad and throws her head back. "Wren is currently playing lacrosse, shirtless, right in front of us. Why does he have to be so hot?"

Both mine and Peach's heads snap back, wanting to enjoy the view too.

"God," I sigh. Wren and Chester are standing a few feet apart, throwing a lacrosse ball to each other with their sticks. Under our end-of-September unusual heat, they both took off their uniform shirts.

"And when did Chester become so muscly? He was just a baby in high school." Ella nudges my leg with hers. "Did you know? Did you see him shirtless before? This is obviously the universe telling you to get back together with him. You know, after Xi."

Peach gives me the side-eye like she knows something, but I ignore her.

I shake my head. "Chester and I are friends." My voice is quiet today and I hate myself for it. I shouldn't care about Xi not giving me any explanation for disappearing. My heart sinks when I come to the understanding that us having sex was probably the last time he'd talk to me. The last time he'd chase me and compliment me.

He got what he wanted.

I put my hand in my bag and clutch the lighter he'd left the first time he was in my room. I play with it, my hand hidden. I like the feeling of the sparkwheel against my skin. It's rough, like him. It hurts a little, like him. And if I stroke it the wrong way, it's dangerous.

Like him.

"How do you know if a guy is ghosting you?" I ask unexpectedly.

My two friends stare at me, mouths full. Ella's eyes bulge as she swallows. "Is Xi not replying anymore?"

I shake my head, embarrassment creeping up my cheeks.

"You guys have been seeing each other for a couple of weeks now. You've been texting all the time. Maybe he's just busy?" she offers reassuringly.

Peach's eyes narrow, and she gives me that look again as if I need to admit something.

"Did something happen?" Ella insists.

Yes. I gave him what he wanted. I finally had sex with him. And now he's gone.

"How long has he been quiet?" she asks as she spears her salad with her fork.

"Four days."

"Four days? What the hell is wrong with this guy."

"It's over, then. Isn't it?" I ask, all hope fleeing my body.

"No," she waves her fork next to her face. "We don't know that. Some guys are just weird. Let's ask the boys. Hey guys!" Ella shouts as she waves at them. "Come sit with us."

"No, no, no, El's," I whine. Too late, they're already on their way.

"Ella," Peach scolds her. "What the fuck, we're enjoying a girls' lunch."

"Oh, shut up. You love Wren."

"He's a dick," Peach grits.

The boys join us, and we expand out our circle. Wren is already tanned, his olive skin easily darkening in the sun. Chester sits next to me, his thigh touching mine. I'm not wearing any tights with my uniform skirt today since it's so warm.

"Are you girls allowed to talk to us now?" Chester asks as he grabs my paper bag. "What's in here?"

At every single party we've been to, the pledges weren't allowed to talk to anyone. It's been driving us crazy.

"Yeah," Ella grins. "We'll see what else they come up with tonight."

"Philly Cheesesteak," Chester chuckles. "Is it still your favorite?"

I nod unenthusiastically. "You can have it. It's your favorite, too."

"Nice. Thanks, Alex." He grabs it, tearing the brown paper before biting into the sandwich.

"How long would you guys go without answering a text," Ella asks. "Like, if you're dating someone."

Wren shrugs. Of course, he doesn't date. He's just waiting for Peach to marry him.

"I don't know," Chester says with a full mouth. "If I'm busy with exams or something, and we're not *official,* then I might not reply for a few days."

"More than four days?" She cocks an eyebrow at him.

"I guess, yeah."

"See," she exclaims as she slaps my thigh. "He might just be really busy."

"Oh, come on," Peach groans. "He's ghosting you, and you know exactly why."

I do, though I refuse to accept it. It hurts too much. He was different with me.

"Our rooms are right next to each other. We share a wall, and I *heard* you."

Peach knows.

I gulp, and my eyes dart around to everyone. Peach's red hair is in a long ponytail today, the sun reflecting in it. She's a powerful woman. So tiny yet so damn powerful. She takes shit from no one, and I always feel like a stupid little girl next to her.

"I don't get it," Ella says. "What happened?" she asks Peach, then twists to me. "What happened, Alex?"

I bite my lower lip, looking down at my lap. In my bag, I press my thumb into the sparkwheel of the lighter.

My eyes dart to Peach, and she shakes her head at me, disappointed that I won't say anything. I don't have the courage to do so, but I know she will, so I just look at her and wait.

"God, you're a baby." Her eyes are on me when she says, "She had sex with Xi. He got what he wanted, then he disappeared as he does with every other girl. We warned her, and she didn't listen. Now she's sad."

"What?" Ella and Chester gasp simultaneously. "No, you didn't," Ella adds.

"What the hell?" The shock in Chester's voice makes me look down again. He's only too aware of the number of times I turned him down when we were together.

He wasn't the one. He wasn't rough enough. He didn't make me feel the things Xi does. He didn't take shamelessly like Xi did.

"I guess our baby girl is not a virgin anymore," Ella says in disbelief.

I stare directly at Peach. "You were right. Happy?"

Her brows furrow. "No. Of course I'm not happy. He hurt you. I'd have been happy if you'd listened to me and stayed away. Now I'm mad *for* you, and I want to kill the fucking guy."

My first smile of the day appears despite myself. "I love you, you crazy bitch."

"I love you too," she smiles back.

"Now you're going to have to sleep around to forget about him. Welcome to the club," Ella beams.

"No," Chester adds, annoyed. "You're not that kind of girl, Alex."

"*That kind of girl*?" Ella repeats.

"You know what I mean. Ella, you can do what you want, but Alex is just...different."

"Can we please stop talking about this," I mumble. "It's making me uncomfortable."

"I can't believe you just said that, Chester," Ella grits. "And to think I said you were hot."

As Ella and Chester continue arguing, I watch Wren's hand slide behind Peach, and he slowly wraps her ponytail around his fist. He pulls her head to the side and whispers something in her ear.

My insides twist solely from watching this. The deliberate roughness of his dominating gesture makes me want to have Xi's hands all over me again. Peach's porcelain skin dots pink and her jaw tightens. Wren lets her go, stands up, and waves us all goodbye.

Less than five minutes later, Peach gets up too. "I gotta go. Classes."

She disappears and Ella turns to me. "It's twelve thirty. What classes?"

I shrug, even though I've never felt closer to Peach in my life. I know what must be going on in her head right now. Complete madness.

"Alex, can I talk to you, please?" Chester finally drops in a serious voice. His eyes dart to Ella. "Alone."

I look at my friend, and she shakes her head to show she has no idea what's up with him either.

"Yeah, sure." I grab my bag, finally letting go of Xi's lighter. "I'll see you later, El's."

Chester and I walk together across the grass. He has a class that way this afternoon anyway, so I might as well walk him. We head onto a path that follows the main road and the silence starts to stretch slowly and painfully.

"What did you think of today's intro class?" I ask, unsure what else to say.

"Why was I not enough, Alex?"

My stomach drops. It takes me a second to realize Chester has stopped walking, and I'm a step ahead. I turn back, stress eating at me. I don't want to have this conversation with him because I'll never be honest about it.

"Chester," I sigh. "Please, none of this is about you. You're a great guy."

"A great guy," he snorts. He runs a hand through his blond hair and looks around us. We're all alone, most students still having lunch somewhere. "Is that what it is? Is it because I was too *nice*? Should I have been more of a dick like Xi? Fuck around with other girls so you'd want me."

His stern tone shocks me. Chester is a sweet boy. He would never raise his voice at me.

"Look," I try to placate him. I take a step forward and smile softly at him. "We're such good friends. So much better than when we were a couple. There's no point comparing or dwelling on the past."

"I was so patient with you."

"And I'm grateful for that because I wasn't ready."

"But you were for him?" A spark of violence tints his voice and forces me to take a step back.

He looks down at the spot from where I just moved and takes a step forward. "If I'd known all I had to do was be an asshole."

My brows shoot up to my hairline as my mouth falls open. I find the little retort I have in me and throw it back at him. "You're being an asshole now and it really isn't helping, is it? God, Chester, you're turning into such a frat boy."

He sneers, his lips curling into something I've never seen on him. "Your dad was right about you."

The mention of him makes me recoil. I go to take another step back, but he catches my wrist and pulls me back to him. Flushed against his chest, he talks right in my ear. "He said you were to be kept in check at all times. To make sure you were acting like a lady and keeping your family's reputation secure."

He puts a hand at the back of my neck, stopping my little attempts at moving away from him.

"Like a lady" He chuckles to himself. "If only he knew all you want is to be treated like a slut."

I manage to pull away, but he keeps a tight hold on my wrist. "Let go," I order in a wavering voice. I can feel my body starting to shake and my ears ringing. "I can't believe you and my dad talked about me like that." I attempt to take a deep breath, my lungs frozen. "Chester, let me g—" He's pulled away violently before I can even finish my sentence.

The man grabbing him is facing away from me as he drags Chester to the side, holding him by the neck of his shirt. He's wearing a gray hoodie and a black cap, but I recognize him. It's like I know his strong build and muscly back by heart.

Xi grabs Chester's right hand, the one that had been

holding my wrist seconds ago, and my ex-boyfriend's face scrunches up in pain as he rotates his wrist.

"Xi," I panic, going after them. I try grabbing him by the back of the hoodie, but he just shrugs me off.

I hear a cracking noise before Chester cries out. "Fuck!" he screams in agony.

"Oh my God." I attempt to walk around them, but Xi pushes him against a tree and Chester's head hits the huge trunk.

I stand next to them, gripping Xi's shoulder as he presses his forearm to Chester's throat so he doesn't move. His other hand is still holding his now limp wrist. "I'm pretty sure I heard her asking you to let go. Are you deaf, rich boy?"

"Alex," Chester calls out in terror.

I drop my bag and struggle to separate them again. "Xi, leave him alone."

He ignores me, focusing on the man in front of him. "I could break every single part of you that's ever touched her. I'd start with cutting off your fucking tongue. Maybe your lips." He smirks, looking down at Chester from his height. "Lucky for you, I won't have to cut off your dick."

"What the fuck, man!" Chester panics as his eyes go to me.

"Xi, that's enough." I glance around, running my hands through my hair. "Please, you're going to get yourself in trouble."

"Apologize to her."

"I don't care about apologies. Just let him go."

"*Apologize. To. Her.*"

"I'm sorry! Fuck...fuck, I'm sorry."

"That's a good boy," Xi keeps mocking him. "How's your wrist?" He squeezes it, making Chester whimper. "Sounds painful. I can do so much worse if you ever touch her, hurt her, or make her feel uncomfortable again. Fuck, I'll do it if she fucking feels like it. How does that sound? Clear?"

"Y-yeah. Yes!"

Xi presses his forearm harder against Chester's neck and the latter coughs, his face reddening. The darkness in Xi's eyes dilates his pupils, turning him demonic. He lets go of Chester's wrist to grab something in his back pocket. A lighter.

"Stop." I grab the back of his gray hoodie, yanking hard and yet not moving him one inch. He rolls the sparkwheel, lighting up the small, pink plastic object and bringing it to Chester's cheek, practically touching it. "Xi, you're going to kill him. Stop." My voice is a squeak, the alarm tightening it.

"Do you know what it's like to die by immolation?"

Chester is crying, but still unable to reply.

"Please," I rasp. "*Stop.*"

"Get in the car, Alex."

"What?" I pant, still trying to pull him off Chester.

"Get in the car, and I'll let him go."

Chester's wide eyes go from Xi to me, flitting back and forth. He's wheezing, clearly in need of air. Not able to think straight anymore, I stride to the car, open the passenger door, and get in.

The moment I close the door, Xi lets him go, calmly putting the lighter back in his pocket. Chester falls to the ground, coughing and heaving as Xi walks back over to his car. As soon as he's inside, I go to open my door again. My hand is barely on the handle when his dark voice reaches me.

"Don't even fucking think about it," he rumbles as he starts the car and pulls away.

16

ALEXANDRA

Hate The Way – G-Eazy, blackbear

"You've driven this road three times now." I wanted to say this the second time he did it, except I couldn't find my voice. I also wanted to call Ella for her to check on Chester, but my phone is in my bag, and my bag is on the grass at SFU.

Xi takes a left at an intersection and then another left. We've been going around blocks in a square for fifteen minutes. His hands are gripping the steering wheel so tightly the knuckles are white, which makes me notice they're also crusted with dry blood. He didn't hit Chester, so it must be from something else.

A few minutes later, he takes a left again and we're back on that road.

I scratch my throat. "If you're lost, I can direct you back to campus."

Staying silent, he keeps driving that same road, probably planning on turning left by the end of it again. "If you just—"

"I'm not lost, Alexandra," he seethes. His voice is low, slightly raspy from not having talked for a while now.

"Okay," I murmur. Doing my best to talk a little louder, I add, "It's just that we've been going around in circles for a while now, and I have classes this afternoon." I actually don't have classes this afternoon, but maybe that'll help convince him to bring me back to campus.

His jaw tightens but he doesn't say anything.

I stay silent for another minute before huffing. "Xi, how long is this going to last?"

"However long it takes."

"What is it you're trying to do exactly?"

"I'm trying to calm down so I don't hurt you."

My head snaps toward him just as my heart drops to my stomach.

"You want to hurt me?" I rasp.

"No. I don't *want* to hurt you." His nostrils flare as he inhales.

My heart drums against my ears; I feel it beating in my neck and my wrists.

"You don't like pain," he says, straining to control himself. "You only like to be humiliated, don't you?"

I gulp. Xi knows my body too well. I barely understand it myself, yet he seems to have it all figured out.

He finally changes his trajectory, going straight ahead and back into the main city of Silver Falls rather than the roads around the campus.

He casually changes gears, his strong hand choking the gearstick before it comes to grip my thigh. "What did I say about your ex, Alex?"

He's not looking at me, his sharp eyes are focused on the road.

My confusion keeps me silent. He overtakes a car in

front of us and squeezes my thigh. "When I ask questions, I expect answers."

"I-I don't know," I admit. He stops at a red light and turns to me.

"He put himself between you and me once. You were having an attack, and I pulled over to help. He tried to stop me."

"He was trying to help me. You're just a stranger to him."

"A stranger," he chuckles dryly. "A lot of strangers made you come before?"

I avoid his gaze. Yes. One other. In fact, one hundred percent of the men who have made me come were basically strangers.

I shake my head, sending the thoughts away. "I only meant he didn't know we were acquainted."

"And I had the decency to step away because I didn't want to make the situation worse. But I warned you, didn't I? I said next time he puts himself between us..." he raises an eyebrow at me, clearly expecting me to finish the sentence.

"That...that you'd set him on fire. Which, as I'm sure you can hear yourself, sounds utterly insane." I push his hand away from my thigh. "Xi, we were just having a discussion."

I'm not too sure why I'm defending Chester. I'm mad at him. About his chat with my dad and the words he threw in my face. I still don't think he deserved any of the violence Xi dished out, though.

"Sounded like a discussion you didn't want to have."

"It doesn't mean violence was necessary," I snap. "I don't like it. You *broke* his wrist, for heaven's sake."

"He's fucking lucky I broke his wrist," he growls. He grabs my forearm and pulls it in front of my face. My wrist is red, and bruises are starting to show from where Chester was holding me. "Looks to me like he should be six feet under."

I snatch my arm back. "That's enough." The light goes green, and he looks ahead again. "You hurt me more by ghosting me than Chester did just now."

He runs his tongue against his front teeth. "I didn't ghost you."

"Come on," I scoff. "We had sex, and then you disappeared. No news for four days. We both know your reputation precedes you. Ignoring me and then swooping in like a pretend hero makes no sense. Don't mess with my brain."

"Don't talk about my reputation. I was very clear about who you belong to. You can expect the same from me."

I open my mouth to say something, but I seem to be speechless.

"I was busy, Alex."

My eyes go to his knuckles at the same time as his dart to me.

I feel my brows furrow. "And you couldn't afford to respond to my texts. For *four* days. I don't want to play these games with you." I chuckle to myself. "God, you're good at this, aren't you? Such pretty words for someone who just evaporated into thin air."

He runs a hand through his hair as he turns right. "I didn't receive your texts because I change numbers often. I need to keep my phones untraceable. I'm trying to have a conversation with you here. Leave whatever you heard about me at the door, for fuck's sake."

"I don't *want* to have a conversation with you. Life is about choices, and you made yours. New phone? *You* text me then. How was I meant to know? You chose not to stay. You chose to fuck me and disappear. I don't care. I can move on. Go fuck your next girl for all I care. I'll do the same too. Fuck countless guys. It's about time I start enjoying myself."

He brakes so hard I grab the edges of the seat as the belt stops me from crashing forward. The band digs into my skin and cuts my breath short. He turns to me, stopped in the middle of the road, as someone honks at us and bypasses our car.

"Say that again. I dare you."

He's not touching me; the threat is all in his eyes and voice. It's all in the way his hands grip the wheel. My voice stays stuck in my throat. My vocal cords not daring to tremble. Someone else honks before overtaking us as well.

"Do it, Alexandra," he growls. This time his right hand comes to wrap around my jaw, and he brings me closer as he leans toward me. "Get anywhere near another guy, and I'll make you watch as I burn him alive."

His eyes look at both of mine, darting left and right. I feel my heart accelerating. I feel the way my body responds to his.

But for once in my life. I stand my ground. "You're so full of sh—"

His lips crash against mine as his hand slides to the back of my neck while the other pulls the handbrake. He presses me into him and demands access to my mouth. My lips part on their own accord as my eyes flutter close. I let his tongue come to stroke mine. It doesn't help that I know exactly the wonders it can do.

So much for standing my ground.

I moan into his mouth as one of his hands caresses my breast above my shirt. I pick up the pace, devouring him as his free hand unfastens my seatbelt. He pulls away only long enough to grab my hips and pull me over to him. In a quick gesture, he draws back his seat and drops me on his lap.

"Why is it that no matter what you do, I want to make you shut up by filling you with my cock?"

His mouth comes to my neck as he rips my shirt open. He keeps going down, dropping kisses of fire across my skin.

"I want you compliant and submissive..." Another dangerous kiss makes me squirm. "...but when you are, I want to push you until you can't take it anymore."

His hands slide up to my waist, crushing me in his possessive hold. I shudder, struggling to breathe.

"I want you to grow a fucking backbone and fight me..."

He bites my collarbone, my chest, and everything lights up in his path before he licks the wounds.

"...but every time you talk back, I want to shut you up by fucking you into oblivion."

He pulls my bra down and starts sucking on the swell of my breast, undoubtedly leaving a mark like he did on my neck last week.

"Oh," I gasp as he takes my nipple into his mouth. He starts sucking and nibbling at it and my head falls backward. My hands slip into his hair, relishing in the thick strands. I pull at them when he pulls away, attempting to move him back to me. He goes to my right breast this time, giving my nipple the same treatment all over again. My moans are loud and uncontrollable as he bucks his hips up, pressing against my burning core through his jeans.

He's so hard I'm dying to feel him against me. Skin to skin.

I feel his hand moving under my skirt and pushing my panties to the side. He gathers wetness from my entrance with his thumb before pressing it against my engorged clit.

As he starts circling it, I pant, "Oh God." My head comes to drop against his shoulder as my body tightens. I gasp for some air, my eyes closing from the pleasure.

"I think we need to lay down some rules, Alexandra," he rasps in my ear. "From now on, no more doubting me. Forget about the reputation and forget about the other girls. It's you and me."

Another moan escapes me.

"Say it. Tell me it's you and me."

"It's you and me," I cry out. "Fuck..." I gasp. "I'm getting close."

"Good," I feel his smile against my cheek as he drops a heavy kiss. "You're gonna come as soon as you agree to all my rules. You're going to give me access to your beautiful body whenever I want."

I nod, not caring what I'm agreeing to.

"Whenever I ask for you, I want you on your knees, waiting for my cock. I want that beautiful, wet pussy ready for me at all times. Clear?"

"Yes," I moan, rubbing myself against him.

"And Alex," his voice lowers as he grabs my hair and pulls harshly. I look at him, writhing with need. "No other men." He presses against my clit, making me wince. "I don't deal well with jealousy, baby. You don't want any deaths on your conscience. It weighs heavy."

His thumb leaves my clit just before two of his fingers push inside me.

"Xi," I squeak, the stretch intense despite how wet I am.

"Say it," he rasps against the skin of my neck. "No other men."

"No other men," I moan. "Just y-you."

"Good girl." His hand doesn't leave my hair as he pulls out his fingers to grab his dick. He slides the ridge against my wet seam, tapping the head against my clit and making me tremble. "Do you think you deserve to be fucked?"

"Yes," I pant. "Yes, please."

"Mm," he growls as his lips skim mine. "I'm going to ruin you, Alexandra." He presses the tip to my entrance. I can feel sweat coming down the back of my neck from desperation. "You're going to be my whore, baby. You'll live for nothing else but the pleasure I can give you."

He thrusts inside me, making me scream in the car. Not giving me time to take a breath, he pulls back and pushes in again. Letting go of my hair, he just grabs my hips, keeping me in place as he destroys my soul. I grind back, rubbing my clit against him. Everything inside me melts for him. I don't even think it's been minutes when I suddenly come apart. He puts a hand on my back before pushing my chest with his other until I fall back. Holding me there, he keeps fucking me until I can't breathe. Until my eyes can't stay open and all I see is stars from the intense pleasure.

"Look at me," he growls as he grabs my jaw. "Look at what you do to me."

He throws his head back just as his eyes close. He's beautiful. Breathtaking. I choke when he comes inside me. A slew of confusing emotions mixes with the pleasure, making my throat tighten.

He brings me back to him, kissing me as he slows down and we both come back down from the high.

Multiple honks make me jolt back up. I grab my shirt and wrap it around myself.

"Holy shit," I gasp. "I-I forgot we were in the middle of the road."

His face twists, and he hisses. "You're squeezing."

My eyes widen, understanding what he means since he's

still inside me. He helps me off him and settles me back in my seat.

Then, as if nothing happened, he puts the car in drive and moves us out of the way.

When he turns off the engine, I look around. I stopped paying attention to where we were going while I was coming down from the high.

"Where are we?"

We're parked on the street, and all the houses around us are rundown. I check the place right where we're parked. A small rectangle that looks like prefabricated housing. The magnolia painting on the front is flaked to an inch of its life, and one of the windows is covered with a wooden panel.

A heaviness settles in my stomach. "Xi, where are we?" I ask again. He turns to me and puts a strand of my hair behind my ear.

"We're at my home."

"You took me to the North Shore?" I sputter. My stomach twists and I glance around again. "I don't want to be here."

He ignores me, leaving the car and walking to my side. When he opens my door, I try again. "Take me home, please. I don't...I can't...I'm *scared*." The last word is whispered in shame.

His strangely fascinating eyes dig into mine. "Alexandra, look at me."

He doesn't pretend the place where he lives isn't dangerous. He doesn't act like I'm crazy for fearing being here. Still, what he says reassures me anyway. "When you're with me, you have nothing to worry about." His hand comes to caress my cheek. "I mean it."

And for just a second, the fact that Xi is a rough, violent man reassures me rather than anything else.

He grabs my hand and helps me out of the car before walking me to the front door. There are a few locks he must undo before we can walk in. We walk straight into what appears like the living room, a small area with a worn-out carpet. There's a sofa and a TV sitting on a plastic table that looks like it belongs outside. Multiple pots of paint are spread on a plastic sheet, and all the walls except one have been painted white. There's a small, round wooden dining table with two chairs around it, and a third chair missing a leg is turned upside down and resting on the table.

"Let's get you cleaned up," he says before dragging me across the room to a hallway. He takes me right and through a door frame without a door. There's a bathtub but no sink. It looks like it's been ripped off the wall. He turns the shower on, and I also notice the lack of shower curtain.

He must see the way I'm looking around because he runs a hand through his hair. "I'm redoing the bathroom. And repainting the living room. I'm...working on a lot of projects. It's taking time because I have to do it outside of work and—"

"Hey," I say, placing a hand on his cheek, "you don't have to justify yourself. I don't care about what your house looks like."

"I bet it doesn't look like yours," he murmurs.

I shrug. "At least you're independent. No one you have to ask for money from. No one who can tell you what to do. That's worth more than gold."

He peers deep into my eyes and nods. He lifts his hands to grab my shirt and take it off me. Slowly, he undresses me completely and helps me into the tub. I moan when I get into the warm shower. The heat is relaxing my tense muscles, and I smile at him. "Join me."

He shakes his head and runs his tongue against his front teeth. "Let me take care of you for now."

He grabs a loofah and pours soap on it. Holding my left wrist, he starts with my upper arm and slowly goes down. He slightly twists my arm and stops just as he's about to clean my inner forearm.

"That's a big scar," he says without taking his eyes off it. The blue loofah he's holding goes over it once then twice. It's like he's fascinated by it.

I feel like I need to say something, so I keep to the minimum of information. "I broke my arm."

"It doesn't look old."

"It was in February this year," I explain. "I don't..." I take my time swallowing the anxiety that threatens to choke me. "I don't like to talk about it."

His eyes come up to mine. He's frowning while he reads into my soul with his dilated pupils. "Does this have to do with your attack the other day? And the reason you're afraid of the North Shore?"

I have no control over my body when it attempts to step back. Xi is still holding my wrist and the tub is tiny, so there's nowhere for me to go when he easily pulls me back.

I shake my head. "You know me." I give him a dishonest smile. "I'm just a baby chick."

The corner of his lips curls up, but there's no humor in it. "I'm going to ask you something personal, and if you're not ready to open up to me, that's okay. But I promise you, you can do so safely if you wish."

My tongue darts out to lick my lower lip and I nod.

"Those seizures you have..." He lets his sentence hang to

incite me to finish his it, except my brain refuses to keep going. "Do you have epilepsy?" he asks.

I turn my head away. "No," I rasp. "It's called PNES."

"PNES?" It's so clear that he's fully invested in discovering me, in exploring the depth of my soul and my complicated mind.

I stare down at his hand still holding my forearm, the loofah just pressed softly against my skin. "Psychogenic Non-Epileptic Seizures. It's a...um...it happens to some people as a, as a," I feel my ears ringing as I stutter. "Sorry."

His hold tightens. "Hey, no need to apologize." He grabs my chin and makes me look up at him. "Take your time. If we don't talk about it tonight, we'll talk about it another time. Alright?"

I blink up at him. There's so much understanding in his eyes. "It's a response to intense trauma."

I watch the way his breathing stops for a few seconds, his gaze locked on mine. He nods to himself, before running a hand across his face. I notice he does that when he's in way over his head. "I see," he finally says.

"I've learned to live with them." I suddenly feel the need to reassure him. I want to wipe away the look of guilt on his face. He's done nothing wrong; it's all me. "They don't happen that often. I mean, they have lately because... everything in my life is changing, but I promise it's not something you'd ever have to deal with. Well, you have but—"

His lips on mine cut off my babbling. His tongue demands access, and I part my lips for him, letting him show me that he cares through a passionate kiss. When he pulls away, he runs his thumb against my lips again.

"I'm sorry." The depth of truth in his words makes me shiver.

My lips still graze his thumb when I answer. "What for?"

"For what happened to you. I truly am."

There's that thing between human beings. We're animals before anything else, and sometimes words aren't needed for someone else to understand what one has been through.

"If you've learned to live with your attacks, I'll learn to live with them, too."

My heart...it's doing incredibly strange things right now. An hour ago, I was furious at him for disappearing. Everything is telling me to run away from this man. And yet, when he slides his hands to the back of my head and drops another peck on my lips, I melt for him as I've never done for anyone prior.

He threads his fingers through mine, looking at my professionally manicured nails. And since he seems to understand me like no one ever has, he changes the topic. "Pink. You love that color."

"It's fuchsia," I correct him. "It's my favorite."

He cocks an eyebrow at me, showing he knows I can't help but correct the smallest of errors. "I like it on you."

He moves to the rest of my body, and I wince when he washes me between my legs. "Sore?" he rasps, undoubtedly turned-on by the idea.

"Y-yeah," I murmur as his movements become slightly harsher.

He puts a hand at my neck, pressing until I gaze up at him. "Good. Remember this next time your ex wants to have a conversation with you."

I gulp, feeling myself tingling all over again. Why do I feel so turned-on by this?

He finishes washing me and helps me out of the tub. While I dry myself, he grabs a clean hoodie and gives it to me. It's a simple black hoodie. Just as I'm putting my uniform skirt back on, his phone rings. He grabs it from his back pocket and his brows furrow.

"I have to take this. I'll just be one sec."

He leaves the room, and by the time I'm done putting all my clothes back on, he's still talking to someone on the phone in his living room. So I take the liberty to visit the rest of the house. It has two other bedrooms. One is empty bar tools and pots of paint, and the last must be his.

My mouth drops open as soon as I open the door and see what's on the same wall as the window. It's been painted in a way that makes it look like there is no wall at all but rather a night sky with thousands of stars. The optical illusion gives the impression that the person looking is sitting on the edge of a cliff and gazing into a clear night in the middle of nowhere.

There's a small, rectangular table just under the window with pots of acrylics and oil paint, a palette, spatulas, and more brushes than I can count. It's a mess, but it doesn't matter when I look at the art on the wall. The entirety of it is painted, and the window merely looks like a floating frame in the night sky.

"That's not where I left you," a voice whispers behind me. There's no humor in the tone, but that's just how Xi talks. I know he's teasing me.

"Did you paint this?"

He remains behind me, gathering my damp hair in one hand and pushing it to one side. "It's my midnight project."

"Midnight project?" I repeat.

"I paint it when I can't sleep."

"Wow," I sputter as I walk closer and let the tips of my fingers graze the paint. "The details are unbelievable."

My eyes catch on the bottle of clear liquid on the table

and I finally understand something. "Turpentine," I chuckle to myself. "That's what it is."

His body is close to mine again. He wraps his arms around me from behind and drops a kiss in the crook of my neck. "What about it?"

"I can always smell something apart from your cologne. A little woodsy and earthy. It's turpentine. What do you use it for?"

"Cleaning my brushes and thinning my oils mainly."

It makes so much sense now. That comforting feeling I get from him.

"My mom is an artist. She comes from a long line of famous painters. When I was a kid, she tried to paint with me, but I was so terrible that she quickly gave up."

"Alexandra Delacroix terrible at something? I don't believe you."

"Oh, *believe me*," I giggle. "The smell of turpentine reminds me of those moments in her workshop."

I take a step away from him, curious to see more. "Do you have other things you painted?" My mouth twists. I used the word *things*. My dad would have a fit. "Maybe I could talk to my mom about you." I move some papers and drawing books around on his desk. "She loves talented, passionate people. She could help you put your paintings out there—"

My heart stops when I uncover a small canvas. It's about the size of an A4 piece of paper. Next to it, there's the Polaroid picture he had taken of me in my bedroom. The one where I'm lying on the bed, my head hanging upside down and my mouth wide open. His cum is all over my tongue, running down my lips.

My thighs press together, remembering the night of our first time. On the small canvas, he painted me with oils. It's

269

beautiful, erotic. It's not exactly realistic, though it is incredibly artistic. He made my lips black and the cum a bright pink. My nipples are pink too, and he turned the rest of the room completely black. At the bottom right corner, he signed XI with two capital letters.

"*Shit*," he hisses, grabbing everything and pushing it to the floor. His fingers end up with paints on them from the palette that wasn't dry.

"That was me," I say with numb lips, barely believing it.

He runs a hand against his face, staining his cheek with some paint.

"Xi," I insist. "That was me."

"I didn't do it in a creepy way. I like painting...beautiful things." His eyes lock with mine.

"You're an extremely talented painter. It's breathtaking."

His brows rise in the slightest, showing me his surprise. He looks like a teenage boy who's just been told by his dad that he's proud of him. Maybe it's just the messy hair and the paint smudge on his cheek that give him that boyish look. Maybe it truly means something to him that I say his art is beautiful.

"Will you paint me some more?" I ask eagerly, wrapping my arms around his waist. "Like that?" I grab one of his hands and bring it under my skirt, pressing it against my damp underwear. "It makes me wet."

There's a low growl at the bottom of his chest, and it makes me tremble.

"Alex," he huffs. "You have no idea how much I want to fuck you right now."

"Then why don't you?" I smile up at him and kiss the hollow of his neck.

"Family dinner."

It's like a cold bucket over my burning skin. I take a step back. "Family dinner?"

"My mom called, and the whole family is at hers right now. It doesn't happen often anymore, so she wants me to come over."

"Of course. I completely understand. I'll head home."

He shakes his head. "Come with me."

I pause. Blinking up at him. "Come with you?"

"Yeah."

"To your family dinner."

"Yeah."

"With your mom."

He chuckles. "Yeah, Alex. I want you to meet her. She's a great woman. Like you."

"Isn't that...early? And for heaven's sake, if I'm going to meet your mom, can I at least get a smile?"

The corner of his lips tips up. Same as usual. Not a genuine smile. "No," he answers sternly. "And it's not early. We do things whenever we want, you and me. Just as long as it's that. You. And me."

I'm the one who breaks into a dumb smile. "Okay," I whisper, barely believing it. "I'll come with you."

I hug him again, pressing my ear against his chest and listening to his heartbeat. I need to know how fast it beats. I need to know if we're in sync because of the joy and excitement at this moment.

And we are.

I smile to myself as I close my eyes. "*Fearless.*"

17

XI

Flatline – 5 Seconds of Summer

"*Mama*," I call out as I open the door holding Alex's hand. I just spent a whole drive reassuring her that no one would care that she was wearing a hoodie and her uniform skirt and that she didn't have to bring a present.

Still, she made me drive down to a chocolate shop on the south bank and back to the North Shore so she could bring my family boxes of expensive chocolate. The kind none of us have ever seen in our lives.

"Ziad!" my mother's voice resonates from the kitchen, above everyone else's voices in the living room, and all the way to the doorway. "Come, *weldi*. Come to the kitchen!"

But before we can make it there, a small form jumps me, forcing me to let go of Alex.

"For fuck's sake," I grunt, taking a step back to balance myself as I wrap my arms around Billie. "You're so heavy."

"I missed you, too," she smiles brightly as we separate. Her eyes go to Alex, to her uniform, and she bursts into uncontrollable laughter.

"A Stoneview girl. Of course!" she hiccups.

"Shut the fuck up," I growl, ready to kick her. "Alex, this is my stepsister, Billie. Billie, meet my *girlfriend,* Alex." I feel the need to tell her that despite being from Stoneview, Alex is more than a quick fuck.

"Nice to meet you," Alex smiles politely, extending her hand. I can hear the shyness in her tone despite trying to keep a civil front. I push her hand back down. Taking it in mine. "Ignore her. She thinks she knows me."

"By heart," Billie says before wiping her eyes. "Nice to meet you, Alex. I hope you're one of the nice ones."

"Nice ones?" she asks me as I drag her away.

"Just ignore her," I say as I open our kitchen door. My mom is in there, by the stove. Austin is standing beside her, apparently saying something that just made her laugh like a schoolgirl with her first crush.

"*Mama, Assalamu alaikum. Shalom.*"

She turns around with a bright smile before pinching my left cheek and kissing my right. "*Shalom, Wa alaikum assalam.* I missed you, son. I missed you."

"I was here three days ago," I tell her softly. "*Mama,* this is Alexandra. My girlfriend."

"H-hello, Ms. Benhaim," Alex says as she extends a hand again. "It's so nice to meet you."

My mom waves her kitchen cloth in the air, ignoring it.

"You need to stop doing that," I chuckle. "We're not that formal. And, um, it's Mrs. Scott now." Her beautiful porcelain cheeks blush and her lips part.

"I'm so sorry," she blurts out.

"You couldn't have known," I reassure her with a hand at the small of her back.

My mother won't stop looking her up and down, of course. Since I'm her first son and this is important to her.

She stares Alex deep in the eyes and her mouth twists. "Skinny."

Completely lost, Alex turns her wide hazel eyes to me. "Wh-what?"

"She says this to everyone. Ignore it. She likes to feed people."

"I like to cook, too," Alex tells my mom excitedly. "What are you making?"

Ignoring her, she turns to me, unimpressed. "*She's skin on bones, Ziad,*" she tells me in Arabic. Alex is far from that. She's got hips and love handles, generous boobs, and thick thighs. But my mom doesn't necessarily care. She just wants to say something.

"*Mama,*" I scold her. "English." When she gives me a mocking smile, silently asking if I really want her to repeat that in English, I add in Arabic. "*Not that. Don't repeat it.*"

"I brought you these," Alex adds with a polite smile. On the outside, it's like nothing can shake her. But I sense the way she shifts closer to me, seeking reassurance.

My mom takes the chocolates with a forced smile. "These look expensive. Are you rich? From Stoneview?"

"*Mama,*" I snap.

Alex puts a calming hand on my shoulder. "Yes, I'm from Stoneview," she replies with a poised smile before pointing at the box and doing that ladylike trick of hers, changing the topic smoothly. "They're delicious. You should try the truffle ones. They're my favorite." Then she looks around. "Is there anything I can do to help?"

"I don't need help," my mom replies with toxic pride.

"The kitchen is her turf," I say lightly. "Let's go say hi to everyone else."

Introducing her to Austin is much easier. He wasn't that nice when his little girl introduced her boyfriend to him.

We then move to the living room, where my stepsisters are watching TV with my brother and his girlfriend.

They're clearly all waiting for me to introduce Alex. So I repeat for the third time today, "Everyone, this is Alex. Alex, this is Lik my brother, and Rose, his girlfriend. Emma, my stepsister, and you've met Billie already."

"Hi, everyone. It's nice to meet you." This time, she doesn't try to shake hands. I think she understood we're all a bit more casual than that. "Rose...White, right?" she asks. "We went to Stoneview Prep together."

"We did?" Rose's unimpressed croaky voice doesn't help make Alex feel any more welcome. She's lucky she's the prettiest woman on earth because her personality is shit.

"I was a freshman when you were a senior. My best friend's Ella Baker. Luke's sister."

Rose nods. "Yeah, I know El's."

Alex and Rose start talking, and I turn to Lik. "*Mama's being a fucking pain,*" I mutter. "She wasn't like this with you. With any of your partners."

"*No one's good enough for my son!*" she shouts in Arabic from the kitchen.

"Fucking hell," I huff. "Who has such good hearing at her age?"

"I hear you, *ya hmar!*"

Lik shrugs. "You're the oldest. I'm the *do-whatever-the-fuck-you-want-est.*"

Isn't that the truth.

I roll my eyes and turn back to my girl. "Here, take a seat."

Only when I find a space for Alex to sit do I notice the death stare Emma is throwing my way. Just like that, reality comes back to hit me in the face.

Spending time with Alex is like living in a bubble. A

pink bubble that smells like jasmine and where everything is soft and bright, and the only feeling that exists is the one of flying. She's warm, smooth, and light. She's a summer evening relieving my heart of the stress of life. My stomach gets that same feeling when an elevator goes down multiple stories. Except we never reach the ground. Alex and I...we just keep flying.

Seeing Emma today is a stark reminder of why I started going after Alex in the first place. Guilt replaces the peace my sweet girl brings me, and I feel the weight of everything falling back on my shoulders.

What a fucking mistake bringing her here.

Dinner goes kind of okay if we forget about my mother refilling Alex's plate three times and her having to dodge everyone's stare when she started eating like she was at the Queen of England's table. The stress makes her mutter random things to herself, and I can see Lik noticing. Every time, he gives me an inquisitive stare and I pretend to ignore him. Alex does that all the time, and I wish he would just fucking leave it.

"Where's your boyfriend?" Lik asks Billie as we settle in the living room again. We always play a game before everyone heads home.

"My fiancé, you mean?"

"Yeah, not in this lifetime," Emma snorts. It's the only thing she's said tonight. She's been in a fucking mood because of me, and I'm ready to give it right back to her.

Billie rolls her eyes at her sister and addresses Lik. "He's with his family."

Billie is dating a King. We might have accepted if she had started dating someone who was part of the Kings' crew, but the girl fell in love with not only our rival, but Caden King himself. His family built the Kings' crew.

They're the reason we all suffer on a daily basis. Caden and Billie have moved away from the North Shore, but we refuse to see them together every time they set foot in town.

I don't mention any of that. Not in front of Alex. I'm still trying to find the right moment to tell her I'm part of NSC. To come clean about everything. I tried last week before we had sex for the first time, but she cut me off. She wanted the moment to be perfect and I get it. I wanted that too.

To avoid explaining myself, and without leaving Alex out of the conversation, I simply tell her. "Billie and Caden had a bit of a Romeo and Juliet situation. But it's fine now."

"I see," Alex nods, her eyes full of hearts because she's a romantic. "*Love Story*," she murmurs to herself.

"What's those things you say to yourself?" my brother asks. Precisely what I wanted him *not* to do. The man has no concept of personal space or privacy.

Her cheeks redden and I can practically feel the heat of her embarrassment.

"Lik, shut up," I growl.

"It's okay." She puts strands of her beautiful locks behind her ears. "They're Taylor Swift songs. I know it's... stupid, but I started doing it when I was little. Mainly every time I was scared of something. So it kind of just became a habit whenever a situation fitted a song; I'd mutter it to myself. Like some sort of inside joke? But with only me, I guess."

Everyone gapes at her, blinking and lost for words. She gulps, the tips of her ears a bright red.

"It's silly," she chuckles awkwardly, rubbing the tip of her index finger against her hairline. "Just forget I said anything."

"I think it's really cute, cupcake," I say gruffly.

She looks at me, her hazel eyes brightening. "Really? But it's so...*stupid*."

I lean toward her so I can talk in her ear. "Say that what you do is stupid one more time and see what happens to your ass. Don't apologize for being yourself, baby."

"You know what," Lik chuckles. "I would expect nothing less from you. You're obviously a really sweet girl, and I think it's charming as fuck."

"It's the cutest fucking thing I've ever heard," Rose adds seriously. "Can we adopt you?" She turns to Lik, tapping his shoulder excitedly. "Can we adopt her?"

"She's not a puppy, Rose," I snarl, but Alex is laughing next to me.

"She sure as fuck gives me the same dopamine as one," Rose throws back, not even looking at me.

"No," Lik finally tells her. "We can't adopt her. Alright, what do we want to play? Monopoly or Trivial Pursuit?"

"Trivial Pursuit," Rose says right away, forgetting about the insane request she was making. That's what dating three people does to you. The woman is absolutely spoiled rotten.

Just like that, everyone has accepted Alex just the way she is. If there's something I expect from my family, it's putting up with people's weirdness. We've seen stranger things than that.

I shake my head. "Playing that game with you is a waste of time. You know all the answers. Takes all the fun out of it."

She snorts. "Sore loser. Why don't we let the guest decide? What would you like to play, Alex?" She's talking to her like she would a baby...or a fucking puppy.

"I quite like Trivial Pursuit," she answers with a polite smile. We're all sitting on the living room floor now, and everyone is staring at her. "Only if everyone agrees," she blurts.

"I wanna be on your team," I tell her before wrapping an arm around her waist and dragging her closer to me.

"I want to be on Rose's team!" Lik exclaims.

"Great, I'll be with Emma," Billie says unenthusiastically. "Is it even worth us playing?"

The answer is no. The next hour turns into a competitive game between Rose and Alex. The former is a freaking genius who never forgets anything, while the latter lives for studying.

Trivial Pursuit is meant to last forever since the questions can be so hard. But with Alex and Rose, the game is folded before we even have fun.

"That was extremely boring and entertaining all at the same time," Lik yawns.

"I like her," Rose tells me.

"I don't care if you like her or not," I say, deadpan. "It wouldn't change a thing."

Alex slaps my arm, laughing. "God, you're as grumpy as they come. Thank you, Rose."

Beside us, the sisters have started their own conversation, and it's getting heated, putting ours to rest.

"No," Emma snaps. "Just fucking leave it."

"It's nothing to me. Let me give you the money," Billie insists, not realizing we're all listening.

"Take the fucking money, Emma," Lik adds, not knowing what the hell this is about. "Always take the money first, ask questions later."

"*No.*"

"Fine. Be a stubborn fucking bitch and stay in your shitty situation."

Alex's eyes widen, clearly taken aback by the sudden

violence in Billie's words. If only she knew how much more violent she can get.

She shuffles closer to me, curling in on herself. "Are they okay?"

I stop listening to the argument for a minute, focusing on the way Alex's face is now twisted from anxiety.

"Hey, it's fine."

"It sounds violent. I don't...I don't like violence," she whispers, her eyes darting to the side.

"Don't worry, cupcake. It's just a stupid sibling fight—"

"Fucking *cunt!*" Emma's scream takes us out of our side conversation. More specifically, the moment she jumps on her sister.

"Now *that's* the kind of family night I'm about," Rose snickers.

"We have a guest," Lik grunts, annoyed.

When they roll over toward us, I'm forced to stand up and pull Alex with me, putting her behind me. I'm the only one who can hear her small whimper when Billie slaps Emma back.

"You two need to fucking calm down," I say calmly. With Alex trembling at my back, I grab Billie by the waist and pick her up off the floor while Lik does the same with Emma.

"How dare you hit me," Billie shouts. "That's my fucking career! Not everyone wants to die desperate and lonely in this fucking town like you."

"Too far," I snap at Billie. "Shut the fuck up now."

"I was just offering to help," she claps back at me as I release her and her feet touch the floor again. The girl's the tiniest thing that exists and still fights in the UFC.

"I don't want your money," Emma yells. "I don't need nobody's fucking money!"

"*Anybody's*," Alex whispers behind me. And even though it was barely audible, Emma's eyes flick to mine.

"What did she fucking say?" she seethes, ready to annihilate her next victim. I turn my head to Alex as she steps beside me, her hand on her mouth.

"I'm so sorry," she squeaks like a little mouse caught by a cat. "It just came out—"

"Drop it, Emma," I tell her sternly.

"I'm truly sorry," Alex repeats, panicking.

"No, you're not," I growl.

"She better fucking be," Emma hisses at me, ignoring Alex.

"I am," she whimpers, her eyes darting from me to my stepsister and back.

"Fuck that. It's a coping mechanism, and you were scaring her. So, no. She's not sorry. I forbid her to be when it's your fault."

Alex glances up at me, the surprise evident in her eyes. She didn't expect me to have figured that out, yet I did. When my girl is anxious, she becomes an unbearable know-it-all. If Emma can't deal with it, then she should have behaved in front of our guest.

Emma inhales through her nose, clearly trying to calm herself down. "Xi. A word. Outside."

I feel my jaw clenching, my teeth grinding as I try to not break everything in sight.

"I'll be back," I tell Alex softly, dropping a kiss on her forehead.

I walk to the back door that allows access to our small patio. It can barely hold two people, and the wood is so rotted that it threatens to break every time I step on it.

"What the fuck are you playing at?" Emma rages as soon as I close the door behind me. "Bringing her here?

Pretending you fucking care? You're meant to get info, not pretend you're going to marry her."

"I *do* care."

She pauses, looks me deep in the eyes, and shakes her head. "No. No, you don't. I'm not letting you."

"You're so dramatic today you should get a fucking Oscar."

"Xi," she seethes, her blue eyes spearing me on the spot. "We're at war, and we *need* the Lucianos' protection. Now get your head out of your fucking ass and get me the info I need on her dad. This isn't a romance film for teenage girls. This is our *lives.*"

"Keep it down," I hiss. My nostrils flare from the anger, my hands tightening into fists. I turn around, making sure the door is still closed and Alex can't hear us. "If she hears us—"

"What? She'll leave and break your heart? Don't make me laugh."

"That's enough, Emma. I'm done with your shit today. I was going to give you your info and make sure not to hurt Alex while I do so. But maybe I'll just drop the info part."

"Excuse me? What world do you live in that you thought you could get me info on the girl's dad without hurting her?" She takes a step toward me, the threat like knives in her eyes. Emma's not a big girl, but she's also not scared of anything. Not even me. "Vito Luciano asked for something. You don't say no to him. Not if you want to keep your head on your shoulders. Not if you truly care about getting the North Shore back from the Kings."

I could snap back at my stepsister. I could be the violent man she expects me to be. Instead, I shrug. "I like her. I played myself. What can I say?"

"I don't fucking care! Take your fucking Stoneview

princess, know-it-all, Taylor Swift superfan and get the fuck out of my house." Her eyes dart behind me, and she adds, "And remember you were in love with Billie and ready to kill for her yesterday, so don't expect me to believe you moved on so fast."

A gasp startles me. Only because I recognize it so well.

I spin around to find Alex with the door half open, and I know Emma intentionally added the part about Billie.

"Is that true?" she asks in a quiet voice.

What did she hear? Surely not the part about the dirt on her dad, or she would be already running for the hills away.

"It wasn't yesterday," I quickly answer. "It was more than a year ago. I have absolutely *zero* feelings for Billie, I promise you."

Her brows furrow, her eyes going down. "I think I should go." She looks up at me and gives me her best fake smile before turning around and leaving. "Thank you for having me."

"Alex," I call out, but Emma grabs my upper arm, attempting to pull me back to her. I let her, pushing and pressing her against the wooden railing. "You shot yourself in the fucking foot here. She breaks up with me, and you get nothing."

"I'm sure her prince charming will fix it all."

"Fuck you, Emma," I seethe. Grabbing her wrist and forcing her hand to let go of me. I hold tighter than I should, but she doesn't let it show.

"Your family needs you. NSC *needs* you. Don't turn your back on us, Xi."

"I'll do whatever the fuck I want."

"You're going to get me dirt on Senator Delacroix, and that's an order."

"An order?" I hiss in her face. "You're giving me an *order*?"

"Yes. As your fucking boss."

There's that stupid thing when you're part of a gang. It doesn't matter if it's NSC or the Kings...*loyalty* is everything. The Scotts, Emma's family, have been the leaders of NSC for as long as I can remember. Her dad is the one who gave me my first job. It doesn't matter what happened after, he recruited me, and I worked for him. I owed him my life.

When Emma took over, she became everyone's leader. It never felt like it because we're a true family, except tonight is a stark reminder. One I certainly didn't want to hear.

"Do it, Xi. Unless you want me to tell Alex who you *really* are. See how she reacts then. There's no forgiving *that*."

My heart drops to my stomach. She's got me, and she knows it. The fear of truly losing my girl paralyzes me until I find my anger again.

"Fuck you," I spit at Emma before letting go and striding back inside.

Alex is right by the front door, apologizing to Lik and Billie for leaving as she wipes away tears from her face.

"Alex, please don't leave." I don't take another step, too worried it'll scare her away. I feel like a hunter trying to make friends with his prey. One wrong move and she'll run off.

Emma is right behind me. "Don't worry, I'm sure Daddy will dry those tears with his stacks of bills," she mocks her.

"Emma!" Billie gasps. "Leave the girl alone."

But for once, I don't think Alex feels the need to be defended by someone else. Something shifts in her pretty eyes the moment Emma mentions her dad. Her face hardens, and her hand tightens around the door handle.

"You know what," she seethes, trembling from rage. "I *am* a Stoneview princess. God, we get it you hate us. I've never been in a fight. And I cry all the time. I'm not a badass like you and your friends. Hey, I even have bunnies as pets! But guess what, it doesn't make me weaker than you. You have no idea what I've been through. You don't know what someone does to survive in this messed-up world. So keep your judgement to yourself."

And with that, she's gone, slamming the door on her shocked audience.

"*Shake it off!*" she screams from behind the door. A last fuck you to Emma.

Lik whistles. "Damn. She hides that backbone pretty well."

A small smile pulls at my lips. I knew Alex wasn't a doormat. I knew the girl had a fire in her. I just had to bring it out of her over time. Light up some sparks like I always do.

18

ALEXANDRA

Mirrors on the Ceiling – mike.

How dare she? How dare she mention my dad? Telling me he'll dry my tears. If my dad knew I was here...I gulp. Anxiety is tearing at my chest. There's a block of ice in my lungs.

"Alex!" Xi's voice resonates as loud as his feet hitting the concrete when he runs after me. "Wait!" He catches me in no time since I'm only fast-walking.

"She hates me," I scowl the second he starts walking alongside me.

"She's a bitch."

"Your mom hates me too."

"My mom hates everyone who gets near her eldest son."

I stop in my tracks, turn to him, and we lock eyes. "You're in love with Billie."

He shakes his head. "I *was* in love with Billie." Then he snorts. "Scratch that, it wasn't even love. It was two people seeking refuge and peace. This town makes you feel claustrophobic. It was...weird. Stupid. Importantly, it's over."

"How do you know it wasn't love?" I ask. "How do you know you moved on?"

There's something that sparks between us. We're not touching. In fact, we're pretty far apart, considering we've spent the last few weeks pretty much glued to each other. Except the pull on the invisible string attaching me to him, is powerful. It tugs at my heart, and it's an authenticity I've never experienced before that forces me into clarity.

I know how I feel about this man.

And I think he knows it, too.

"Because," he hesitates, moistening his lips. "I know." His eyes are on mine, but he looks past them into my soul. "Believe me, I *know* I've never fallen for someone as hard as I've fallen for you."

There's something else he wants to tell me. I can see it right there, at the tip of his tongue.

"Alex, I..." In a split second, he changes his mind. "...I need you to trust me."

Everything inside me is screaming to end this now. My gut is warning me of an incoming heartbreak. Not now, but it will come eventually.

"Tonight was a harsh awakening, Xi," I whisper, looking down at my hands as my fingers twist together. "We should cut our losses while we can."

"Look at me, Alexandra." His low voice triggers something inside me, and I peer up. "It's already too late for that."

"Emma made me feel like none of this is right. *We're* not right."

"Well, for once, baby, why don't you do me the favor of not caring about right and wrong."

I inhale sharply as he takes the small stride separating us. Shouting back at Emma today is something I've never done. I didn't even know I had it in me. Xi has been awakening a dormant side of me. Every time he tells me not to apologize. Or every time he forces me to speak my mind, to put words to my frustration, to just be myself; it gives a pulse to the Alex I've never met before.

"Why don't you start worrying about what *Alex* wants, instead of what everyone else around her demands."

Everything is saying no.

He brings his hand to my cheek, his knuckles pushing blonde strands away from my face.

"Forget about being a good girl. *Misbehave.* Lean into what feels wrong."

Everything except my heart.

He leans down, his lips grazing mine. "Just for the taste of it."

That damn silly heart.

My lips crash into his as I push on my toes and wrap my arms around his neck. He grips my thighs, pulling me up, and then he carries me to his car while I forget what oxygen is.

Tonight I don't go home.

Because, fuck behaving.

Xi walks backward into his bedroom, our mouths glued together as he drags me with him, until he falls onto the end of the bed. I move to follow him, but he stops me with a hand on my chest.

"Look at me."

I do. My heart is beating harshly, my lips stinging from his rough kiss.

"How do you want me to fuck you tonight, Alexandra?"

I gulp. I didn't expect him to *ask*. I prefer when he *takes*. It's too embarrassing to say what I desperately want out loud, and from what I'm seeing in his eyes, I understand that it's precisely the point he's making.

"I want..." I inhale a sharp breath. "I want you to take control."

He licks his lips but doesn't seem happy with my answer.

"You want more than that, and you know it." He frowns when he sees that I'm not anywhere near saying anything. "Take a few paces back."

I take exactly three.

"More."

Four. Five. I'm practically against the wall now.

"Take your clothes off."

I do so with trembling hands. First goes his hoodie. My shoes. Then my skirt. My bra is next.

"All of them, baby."

I shimmy my panties over my fleshy hips and drag them down until I can step out of them.

He bites his lower lips and adjusts himself on the bed.

"Good," he says low.

Xi's voice is usually so flat it's undeniable when lust begins to color it. It becomes gravelly, dyed with a darkness he can barely control.

My boyfriend is what I've come to accept and call a sweet psycho. The discreet kind who moves in silence and who treats me like a queen. Sweet to the woman he wants to possess, deadly to anyone who gets in his way.

I want to taste Xi's danger.

I want to feel it on my skin. For it to lick me with burning flames.

I want Xi to feed my lust as hard as he obliterated my sanity.

I look deep into his eyes with the strength he's helped me awaken and allow him to observe me silently until I can feel the satisfaction boiling in him.

And when he deems me ready, he says with an unmatchable calm, "Now drop to your knees."

It only takes me a split second to do so, though the descent feels interminable. With our eyes locked, our breaths in tandem, I watch him eat me whole from a distance.

"Crawl to me."

I close my eyes and swallow the need inside me. It drops to my stomach and liquefies. The wetness between my leg is proof of everything I thought I hated about myself. Proof of everything I love now that it matches Xi's needs.

I crawl to him slowly, doing my best to make it look sensual. I curve my back, pushing my ass out. I aim to please.

When I'm finally at his feet, I look up at him and silently beg him with all I have.

Touch me.

Play with me.

I'm yours to use.

Just do it.

He hears it all. I know he does, being that he says, "Look at you." Just because he ordered so, my eyes dart down to my spread knees. To my position of utter submission.

"So desperate to be mine."

And isn't that the most truthful definition of me tonight?

He drops his elbows to his knees, his hands hanging between his legs, just before me. He lowers his face to mine and his lips come to whisper in my ear.

"Turn around, drop your face to the floor, and present your pussy to me. Let me see how eager she is for me."

It takes all of me not to moan at his words. I blink up at him when he pulls away from my ear and grazes his lips against mine.

He doesn't push me, and he doesn't insist. He simply waits for me to be so desperate for him I finally move. I turn around and spread my hands on either side of me. Then I lower myself until I press my cheek to his rough carpet and push my ass out.

"Spread wider."

My knees scrape against the floor as I spread my legs for him, giving him an unobstructed view of my dripping pussy.

He presses something to my inner thigh. I'm confused as to what it is. "You're wet all the way to here."

And it's oh so embarrassingly far down my inner thigh.

I whimper from need when he moves higher, and I finally understand what he's touching me with.

His boot.

The top of the leathered tip is sliding against my wetness, stopping short of touching my pussy lips. So, *so* short of grazing my swollen clit.

"That's me taking control, Alexandra. I can give you orders all night long and never give you what you truly need."

"Please." My breathy voice embarrasses me further. The man hasn't even truly touched me yet.

"Do you want me?" he challenges.

"Y-yes," I gasp. "I do."

"Tell me what you *truly* want."

"You. I want you," I blurt out. "I want...I want you to make me feel good. Please."

"How? Say it."

I take in a ragged breath, swallowing and accepting the woman I am. The one who decides what she wants her man to give to her.

"Degrade me," I squeak.

He heard me. I know he did, except he tortures me further. "What was that?"

"D-degrade me," I repeat. "Please."

"Louder." The tip of his shoe presses against my ass, almost where I need him the most.

"*Please,*" I cry out loudly. "Degrade me."

I hear him chuckle. There's a beat of silence that feels like an eternity. "If you want me so badly. Degrade yourself for me."

He presses the leather against my pussy, and I push back without hesitation, grinding my clit against it.

"Oh God," I moan.

"More," he orders low.

I press harder, my eyes rolling to the back of my head as I take my pleasure. My breathing accelerates at the same time as my harsh movements.

"That's it, baby, cover my boot in your wetness. You're going to be licking it clean in a minute."

His words add a pleasure I can't control. I rub myself like the wanton woman he's turning me into. I buck my hips, moving closer to him. I let out a long moan I couldn't control if I tried. But before I can bring myself to climax, he pulls away and I feel him stand up behind me.

"Turn around."

Back on all fours, I turn around before I can consciously tell myself to.

He looks down at me from his god-like position. "You

know what I want, Alex. The longer you make me wait, the longer you delay your reward."

His pants are tented, and I lick my lips, but he clicks his tongue. "Not yet."

I look down and see my glistening wetness on the leather of his right black boot.

"Tick tock," he presses me.

I lower my head, my hair falling on either side of my face, and instead of killing myself over something that is clearly what I want. Instead of torturing myself for what I like and who I am, I go for it.

I flatten my tongue against the leather and run it against his boot. I lick my sleekness over and over again.

"Fuck," I hear him hiss above. There's the telltale of a zipper and I feel him shift.

I don't glance up to see if he's taking his dick out. I know he is.

Because, just like me, he can't resist it. It eats him from the inside; it burns an unextinguishable fire in his veins.

I know there's nothing left on his boot, and I know I licked a bigger surface than I touched, but I don't care. It tastes like freedom. It tastes like I'm finally doing whatever the hell I want with someone I can trust.

There's a rumble above me when I moan against the leather and kiss the wet shoe. A second later, he's grabbing me by my shoulders and forcing me to stand up. He grabs my waist, pushing me back and lifting me to sit on his desk.

"Do *not* move." His dark voice makes me tremble, and so does the lust burning in his eyes.

He grabs a few things beside me, some that have fallen on the floor, but all I can focus on is his hard dick. His pants open, boxers slightly lowered, and his cock calling out to me.

"Don't," he growls, as if he knows the next thing I was going to do was grab him just so I could feel the silky skin between my fingers. So I could press the hardness against my needy pussy.

I look to the side and watch him mix colors on a paint tray. "What are you doing?" I rasp.

"Open your mouth." That's all I get.

I open it, and he puts two paintbrushes in my outstretched mouth, sideways. "Bite."

Closing my mouth, I hold the wooden brushes between my teeth. "Not too hard," he adds.

I nod to show him I understand.

He grabs a third one and dips it in the paint he just mixed. It's a bright pink, and my questioning eyes dart to his confident ones.

"Close your eyes," he whispers.

They flutter closed.

"Put your hands behind your back, push your tits out."

My shaky hands go behind my back, and I grab my wrists to hold them there. It forces me to push my breasts out, although I push them further anyway.

"Good girl. Don't move. And, Alex...do not drop those brushes in your mouth, or you can kiss your orgasms goodbye."

I inhale sharply through my nose.

Not orgasm. Orgasm*s*.

I startle when I feel the wet bristle of a brush on my right nipple. He strokes me once, twice, and that's it before he moves on to the other one. I squirm on his desk, moaning through the wood I'm biting.

It's rough and smooth. It's cold against my burning skin. It's the exact amount of friction I need against my hard buds.

I chase the feeling when he pulls the brush away. The paint is thick, wet.

"Relax your jaw." His lustful voice makes me press my thighs together. "And keep those legs spread."

He grabs a brush from my mouth, replacing it with another.

This time it's bigger. The bristles are thicker, and there are more of them. He proceeds to paint me with broad strokes.

The brush caresses my hips, kneading the flesh of my love handles before following the curve to my waist. He pauses, then he's back on my stomach, dripping more paint and creating goosebumps wherever he goes. He spreads the thick liquid all over me. My chest, the curves of my breasts, my legs, my arms. More, and more. The smell takes me by surprise. I'm coated in it everywhere except in two places.

My dripping pussy and my nipples.

The hard buds only have those two layers he painted that are slowly drying.

And the more they dry, the more the paint hardens and pinches them.

I moan when he flicks one of them with his fingers.

"How does that feel?" he whispers.

He pinches one.

"Sensitive," I whimper. I'm not sure he hears it with all the paintbrushes in my mouth.

"Mm, it looks like it." He strokes the thick brush just below my nipple, enhancing the difference between the thick, wet paint and the thin, drying coat.

"I have never had a muse before," I hear him murmur to himself. It feels forbidden to hear, like I shouldn't be privy to the artist's thoughts.

I'm just an object of art, sitting on his desk among the

others. A mixing palette, a brush, a bottle of turpentine, and Alexandra Delacroix's body. All of them are tools he uses as he chooses to create magic.

Silently, he paints some more. He's lost in the fine piece he's making, covering me in heavy paint and ignoring that underneath, my body is writhing, desperate for his touch. My pleasure has been forgotten, and his concentration is directed toward art.

It's everywhere.

Everywhere but my nipples, and the dry paint on them becomes unbearable compared to the thick wetness he's playing with all over my body.

"Xi," I whimper against the brushes in my mouth. "Please."

I need him to touch my tits. I need him to lick them better, to play with them. My body is hypersensitive, my pussy sodden.

"Shh," he reassures me. A hand comes to rest against my cheek. It's wet, and I feel him smear some paint over my jaw. "You wanted me to paint you again."

He takes the last brush from my mouth and puts back the thick one.

My eyes flutter open only to be met with the most beautiful man I've ever seen. His hair is disheveled, smudges of paint on his t-shirt and his face, his gaze focused on the pink color covering my body.

When his eyes flick up to mine, his lip curls up. "Bad girl," he sneers. He grabs something next to me, and before I know what's going on, he's pressing a cloth to my eyes and knotting it behind my head.

It smells of him. It smells of turpentine and paint.

And it feels like everything else is heightened. It's not the same as closing my eyes. It's *better*.

So much better.

This time, the brush has no paint when it comes to touch me. And it grazes the *only* place that hasn't been getting any attention this whole time.

"*Oh,*" I moan around the wooden sticks in my mouth. It was so delicate I barely felt it, even as it lit my entire body on fire.

I wait, unsure if I made it up or not.

But then it comes back.

Soft, delicate bristles going from just above my clit, descending on it, and ending at my wet entrance.

It's gone as fast as it came, and I push my hips forward, seeking the mind-blowing feeling.

"Settle down," he tells me.

I inhale a ragged breath through my nose, and it's back. Slower this time, making me moan low in my throat. My body electrifies, but it's gone too soon.

A whimper escapes me. I want to cry. This is pure torture.

My heavy breathing is turning loud, whiny. I'm trembling while I wait for the next indulgence that I know will only last a second.

"You're so wet," he rasps. "I can paint your little clit with your wetness over and over again while you tremble under my brush."

And he does it.

Over.

And over.

Again.

I writhe, I chase, I strain and tense, and finally, I break.

"Please," I sob. It's muffled by the brushes in my mouth, but my desperation is apparent anyway.

I can barely take another breath when he ignores my plea and drags the soft brush again.

"Why?" I cry out. I don't understand. Didn't he say he would give me orgasms if I was good? If I did what he said? If I let him gag me by doing something as simple as biting two paintbrushes between my teeth?

"You're going to come, baby. Be patient."

I shake my head, wanting to explode in tears. I want to see him. I want to let go of my arms so I can grab him. I want to spit the brushes on the floor.

But I want to come more.

"Relax. You will come slowly. Like this."

"*No,*" I mumble between two sobs. I need more pressure, more speed.

"Shh," he insists. He rubs his thumb against my nipple covered in dry paint, making me cry out some more. "It'll come."

One slow, torturing stroke after another, he keeps going. His pace slow and erotic. The pressure is so light I tremble every time. And just like he promised, my orgasm ripples over me gradually. It's sensual and gentle, but it breaks everything inside me.

I bite on the brushes. I shake.

And I cry.

Real tears fall down my eyes from the leisurely release. He doesn't stop because I'm not overstimulated. I keep chasing for more, and he gives it to me at the same speed.

A deliberate slow stroke.

A long beat.

The sound of his soft movement.

Another gradual stroke.

And the whole time, I feel it all exploding inside me. A rush of adrenaline like never before.

I wonder how long it lasts and how many times I come. Time is a concept of the past. It's weak and ineffective. My life is not measured by the ticks of a clock anymore. It's measured by the strokes of a brush against the most intimate part of me.

When I'm so weak my entire body is shaking, the brush he was using is added to the two in my mouth, and he rips the blindfold off me.

His lips crash against mine, and I moan into his mouth. "You're so beautiful," he growls against me. "You're so perfect."

He grabs his dick and lines it with my swollen entrance. He rubs the tip in the wetness and groans, "You're so mine, baby. It's you and me, right? Just you and me."

I nod.

"*Say. It.*"

"It's you and me," I gargle around brushes.

"That's right."

He pushes into me so intensely I cry out and everything falls out of my mouth. But it's good, so freaking good I don't dare stop any of the noises that come out of me.

I moan and sob and call out his name like the god he is.

I pray at his damn altar while he pounds into me and curves his hips to hit the perfect spot. I grab his shirt, then his neck and his hair. I beg him to make me come again.

He flips me around and presses my upper body to a canvas next to me, the paint smearing on there.

And he makes me come again. Enough times that when everything has ultimately detonated inside me and set fire to my soul, all he has to do is pick up the ashes and attempt to put me back together.

He showers me and puts me to bed, whispering the sweetest things I've ever heard.

I'm his special girl.

I'm his muse.

I'm the woman he doesn't deserve.

And he's *never* letting me go.

"Alex," he murmurs in my ear as my eyes close, feeling heavy from the need to sleep. I'm wrapped in his strong arms, my head resting on his chest. I'm listening to his calm words and unsteady heartbeat at the same time. "Whenever someone makes you feel like who you are is not who you should be, or that us being together isn't the *right* thing, I want you to remember this moment. When I hold you in my arms, it's exactly where you belong, and the moments we share are yours to own. I want you to know that I belong to you. I will *always* keep you safe."

"*I Know Places,*" I yawn, my heart swelling with happiness.

I've never felt so safe in my life.

His chuckle is the last thing I hear before I fall asleep with a smile on my face—the kind no one can take away from me.

I wake up again when I feel him get up. And, while pretending to be sleeping, I watch him work on what he keeps murmuring is his *masterpiece.*

Me, simple Alexandra Delacroix—who's always been told there's nothing she can do right, who's always felt threatened, who's always been terrified of being a disappointment—I am a *masterpiece.*

19

ALEXANDRA

Hazel Eyes – Ollie

I think my mind is so accustomed to anxiety, that my body immediately senses when something horrible is coming my way.

I spent the next day with Xi since I didn't have any classes. When I return later in the evening and open the door to Xi Ep, I hear voices I recognize in the living room. Reluctantly, I make my way there, not wanting to face my mother. Being an old Xi Ep girl and a primary contributor to the sorority, she can come by whenever she wants. She's also good friends with the house mother as well, although I was hoping I wouldn't have to see her so early during the year. Initiations aren't even over yet. I still hold out hope I misheard as I walk into our common area.

I don't only end up disappointed that she's here. I end up utterly petrified that my dad is with her.

"Alex!" My mother beams as she stands up and comes to hug me, but I feel like a ragdoll as she does so, incapable of hugging her back.

Fathers aren't allowed in the house. Men, in general, aren't allowed in the house. We know many girls sneak them in after parties anyways, but my dad definitely shouldn't be here.

"What are you guys doing here?" I ask with more vehemence than I wanted to.

"Well, is that a way to greet your mother? We came to see how you were doing. It was your dad's idea, actually. You know how he is, always worrying."

Always worrying that I'll be doing things I'm not allowed and actually start building my own personality.

"Dad isn't allowed in the house," I add, pretending I'm concerned about my place at Xi Ep. "Initiations are still ongoing. You guys are going to get me in trouble."

"Oh, please," she waves a hand in the air, dismissing my words. "Cassandra said it was absolutely fine. Right, Cass?"

"Of course," our house mother nods. "We're so happy to see you here."

Rather than accepting defeat, I take a different approach. "People are going to freak out if they see Dad. It's not every day a senator walks into your house. You should have thought of that. It's hard enough making genuine friends with the Delacroix name."

My mother scoffs. "Alex, you have plenty of friends. Stop being silly, now. Plus, we won't stay long. We want to take you out to dinner tonight." She scans me up and down. "What are you wearing? Is that hoodie part of SFU's new uniform?"

I shake my head. "It's mine. I was just cold." I put my hands in the front pockets and, surprisingly, feel a lighter there. I press my thumb against the wheel, trying to control my anger.

"Okay, well, go get changed. We have a reservation in Stoneview at seven thirty."

I clench my jaw, doing my best not to scream that I don't want to go to dinner with them. I simply smile and nod, before heading to my room.

The moment I walk in, I grab the first thing and throw it against the wall. It's a box of candies I love. The little moon-shaped sugary treats spill all over the wooden floor, and yet it doesn't help with my frustration. I was finally starting to live a life without having my dad on my back constantly. Now, here he is, making sure I know he's always watching.

I take off Xi's sweater and throw it on my bed, ending up in my bra and skirt. I need to find a dress decent enough for a Stoneview dinner. Probably some heels too.

I'd give anything for another night at Xi's place rather than there. I shower and style my hair, find a designer dress in my closet and slide it on. A silk olive-colored dress that falls to my ankles. The bodice hugs my waist, and I'm attempting to tighten the corset at the back when my door opens behind me.

I flip around, "Hey, wrong r—" My voice dies in my throat when I see my dad walk in and close the door behind him. He rearranges the sleeves of his suit and looks up at me calmly.

"I-I'm almost ready," I stutter as I pull the strings at the back some more.

"I called you multiple times today. Where is your phone?"

I gulp, remembering my bag and phone I left on the grass at SFU yesterday. I'm sure I will find it in the lost and found, or one of the girls might have brought it home. The point is, it wasn't with me.

"I...left my bag on campus. With my phone in it."

He walks to me until he's so close I can feel his warmth. He grabs my shoulders, delicately spinning me until I'm facing the mirror, and settles behind me. He grabs the corset strings and looks at my eyes through the mirror. "Did you leave it behind when you left for the North Shore?"

My eyes widen as my heart drops. He yanks harshly on the two strings, cutting my airflow just as it all hits me.

The bracelet. How could I forget about the tracker in the cuff he gifted me. It's been so long since he started tracking me that it sometimes slips my mind. When I'm happy, for example, and enjoying myself.

"You forget I know where you are at all times, Alex. Now do you want to explain why you spent the night in a town you have no business to be in?"

My heart accelerates, and I feel my lungs constrict as he pulls some more.

My silence nudges him. "You weren't with a boy, were you?"

"No," I lie. "I wasn't."

"Made some new friends, perhaps? Some people who show you what it's like to be part of the ninety-nine percent?"

I shake my head, struggling to draw in a breath.

"Would you like me to give you more time to think of an excuse?"

"Dad, please," I beg, peering up at him. "I was just..." I come short of a viable lie.

He shifts on his feet and crushes a candy under his expensive leather shoe. His eyes dart to the floor and back up at me, sneering. "Did you make this mess?"

I nod, not knowing what else to do.

He tightens the strings at my back and steps away.

"You are damn lucky no one saw you. That is not how a

lady behaves, Alexandra. You keep it in. You don't throw things on the floor like a degenerate."

"I know, but—"

"But?" he seethes. He hates when I contradict him.

"That's not what I meant," I panic as I put my hands in front of me to placate him.

"Do you not apologize for irrational behaviors anymore, Alex?" His voice is terrifying, warning me to do as I'm told. Xi spends hours forcing me to apologize less and be more myself. And my dad just swoops in and destroys it all.

"I'm sorr—ah!"

The slap is so hard I fall to the floor, my hand shooting to my cheek. His signet ring caught the corner of my mouth, and I can taste blood on my tongue.

"I'm sorry," I squeak as I crawl back. "Dad, please..." My back hits the drawers of my dresser, the handles digging into me as I press myself firm against it. My eyes fill with tears when I watch him move closer and unbuckle his belt. "No, no, no. Please...Dad."

"Don't you dare be so loud it brings attention to this room," he seethes. He slides the belt out of his suit pants and wraps it around his wrist.

"I'm sorry," I cry. "I'm sorry I went...I went..." The fear makes me stutter.

"Can you not form sentences anymore? Are you so stupid that you can't put two words together? Who made you that dumb, poor girl?"

A whimper escapes me. I hate when he calls me stupid; I hate everything about him.

I attempt to take a deep breath before I can talk again. "I was just with some friends. We went to the falls on the North side. Please...don't hurt me."

Whoosh.

The sound of the belt slicing through the air makes me squeeze my eyes shut. I pinch my lips when it hits my left upper arm. Falling onto my side, I curl into a ball, protecting my head with my arms.

"And what about that house? Who was it? Another *friend*?"

Crack!

I cry out this time, the belt slashing through my dress at my hip, and he hits me again for being too loud.

"Be quiet," he hisses.

He backs away, and I feel him lurking, preparing for his next move.

"What about the C minus? Was that because you hang out with your friends too much?"

Crack!

It's my outer thigh this time, making me whimper as I bite my lower lip.

"Please," I sob. "I'm sorry. It hurts…"

"It's supposed to hurt, stupid girl. You are going to get your act together, Alexandra. Because I will not have an embarrassing," *Crack!* My hip. "Idiot." *Crack!* My ribs. "For a daughter." *Crack!* My forearm. The one protecting my face.

He went for my face.

The beatings are not unusual, but he usually would never want anyone to know.

He retreats, panting and watching me sob. My entire body is on fire; I can feel the welts forming, thick and swollen. He puts his belt back on, rakes his fingers through his hair and rearranges his sleeves.

"Clean up the mess you made, shower, and put some makeup on. Don't make us wait forever."

My uncontrollable sobs don't stop, and he nudges me

with the tip of his Oxford. "Did you hear me, Alexandra?" he huffs.

"Y-yes..." I whimper.

"Then get to it."

I force myself to sit up and watch him leave. The shower burns this time, and I have to change my dress because he ripped the one I was wearing. My makeup needs to be heavy to hide the small bruise forming right next to my mouth. My lipstick is a bright fuchsia, hiding the red cut at the corner of my lips. I wear a shawl to hide the two bruises forming on my left arm and practice my fake smile in the mirror.

"Thank you." I smile at myself, rehearsing bits of conversation I might need at the restaurant. "Oh, how delicious," I say in a cheery voice. "Excuse me, I must go to the ladies' room." Tears shine bright in my eyes as I smile over and over again until it looks so real I almost believe it myself.

I gulp, grab a black faux-fur coat, and make my way downstairs. I'm ready to pretend we are a perfect family to the nosy population of Stoneview.

When I come home later that night, I lay in the dark, struggling to find a comfortable position. I bask in the pain while I stare up at the ceiling. And like most nights, before I fall asleep, I think of ways to kill my father. I imagine I would make it painful, and remind him of every single time he hurt me. It makes me feel better. But then I wake up in the morning and tell myself it's a shame I'm a coward.

20

ALEXANDRA

Without You – Lana Del Rey

I check my phone as I cross the grass, walking to my afternoon class.

Unknown: Look up, cupcake.

I've come to understand that every time I get a text from an unknown number, it's Xi's new phone. I guess these sorts of things come with dating someone who needs to be a shadow. He's untraceable. Nothing can be linked to him, and he's a terror to the environment with all these phones he throws away.

I glance up to see him leaning against a tree, a black baseball cap on and the hood from his hoodie drawn over his head. For once, I'm assuming he's not doing it to be invisible but more to protect himself from the terrible rain falling on us. I run to him, and he catches me in his arms, grabbing me by the waist and allowing me to wrap my legs around him as he lifts me.

His lips crash on mine, my arms curling around his neck, and we kiss as if we haven't seen each other in months. It's only been a few days, but after spending time with my parents last week, I feel complete and safe being back with him.

"What are you doing here?" I smile, catching my breath as I slide back down to my feet. "Coming to classes with me? Don't tell me it's because your work brought you here. I want to feel a little more special than that." I flutter my eyelashes at him, making him chuckle.

That's basically rolling on the floor from laughter on the 'Xi emotions chart'.

"Work didn't bring me here. I came because I missed you. You're *that* special."

"Oh, Ziad Benhaim." I pronounce his name Zee-ad, like I heard his mom say, slapping his chest. "You're making a girl blush."

"What did you just call me?"

My heart drops when I realize that might have been a mistake. "I'm sorry," I babble. "I heard your mom...I thought that's how you pronounce it."

It takes me a second to realize he's not angry. Just shocked. "Don't fucking apologize, Alex. That is how you say it."

"Why don't you correct people?"

He shrugs. "I used to when I was a kid. Then I got tired of it. It would annoy me when people struggled to say such a simple name under the pretense that they didn't hear it often since it's not American. So I just left it."

"I'm so—" I cut myself off. "That's unfortunate," I say instead. "I'm surprised you let people call you Xi."

"That was a weird misunderstanding," he explains as he grabs my hand. "In my last year of school, I barely followed anything in class. I used to draw instead and sign my art X. I." With his index finger, he writes it in the air between us. "My teacher thought it was a nickname I'd chosen. Xi. So everyone started going along with it. I did too."

I play with his fingertips, tapping them with mine. "It wasn't Xi you were signing?"

"No. It was eleven in Roman numerals."

A laugh leaves me when I get the misunderstanding. "Why would you sign your drawings eleven?"

"It was an artist name I wanted to give to myself. Eleven was a," he looks into my eyes while he searches for the right word, "defining age for me. It was the year before we learned about my dad's illness. Everything was so much simpler. So peaceful. No responsibility. After that, it all went to shit. Suddenly I was the man of the house. I started working. People relied on me. Childhood was over for good. Eleven was great."

I give him a small smile as I put a hand on his cheek. It's wet. We're both wet from standing under the rain like two hopeless lovers. "I know you don't think so, but you turned into a great man, Ziad."

He snorts. "I didn't."

He brings a hand to the back of my head, tangling his fingers in my damp hair. He pulls until I'm gazing up and into his eyes. "So I made you blush?" And I know our moment of talking about his past is over. "I've got many more ways to make you blush. Why don't I show you?"

I giggle, feeling my cheeks heat. The corner of his mouth tips up before he moistens his lips. "But first, I'm taking you to lunch." He lets go of my hair and grabs my hand instead.

"Oh, I can't." I shake my head, not following as he takes

his first step while I hold him back. "I've got another class in five minutes. I could do dinner?"

His hand on mine tightens. "No, I've got something tonight. I want to spend time with you now."

"I hear you, but I don't want to skip class."

His eyebrows shoot up before a glint of malice glitters in his gorgeous eyes. "Alexandra Delacroix. Don't tell me you've never skipped a single class."

I feel the embarrassment creeping up my neck. "I've had a severe upbringing."

"What about last week? When I took you to my house."

"I didn't have any classes that afternoon. Look, my dad would never let me skip."

"You're not meant to tell your daddy about it."

My heart squeezes from fear. The lesson from last week was bad enough. I don't want to bring his attention to me again.

"I know," I huff. "But he...he'd know."

The confusion on his face clears when it hits him. "Alex," he says seriously. "Does your dad track your phone?"

"Not my phone," I whisper in embarrassment. My eyes dart down to my wrist. I feel hot sweat pearling on my lower back as Xi grabs my hand and looks at the gold bracelet there.

He cocks an eyebrow. "Tell me you're joking." I pinch my lips and fearfully watch the bronze in his eyes turn black.

"I'm sorry," I panic as I try to drag my arm back.

His grip tightens, and his voice lowers. "Don't say sorry when there's nothing to be sorry about," he snaps. "When will you fucking learn?"

Biting my inner cheek, I swallow back the other apology trying to make its way out.

"How long has he been doing that?" He hauls me to his car and opens the truck bed.

"Since sophomore year," I admit shyly. "It used to be a locket my grandma had given me, but then..."

"Then?"

"Then I lost it. Well, it was stolen, and the tracker was broken when it happened." There's something profound in his eyes. Something serious and...apologetic.

Grabbing me by the waist, he lifts me up and sits me on the truck bed.

"Stay," he growls as I try to slide back down.

"That locket was so special to me. I hated that my dad put a tracker in it, but had it been working, I could have found it again. Now it's lost forever."

"I'm sorry to hear that, baby. I understand you were attached to it."

He grabs a duffel bag and searches through it, coming up with pliers.

"Oh god," I gasp in fear. "Don't." I shift away, but he puts a hand on my thigh, stopping me. "Xi, please," I whimper. "Don't take it off."

"Alex, you can beg all you want. You could get on your knees and offer me everything I want in the fucking world; this thing is still coming off."

"No. Listen, my dad...he's very strict."

"Yeah? Guess what, I'm strict too. I'm firm about you finding your independence and becoming a woman who doesn't live just to be a people pleaser. This fucking tracker is coming off, and you're coming to have lunch with me. And if your dad wants to take it out on someone, he can come to me. I'll happily have a talk with him. Although you know I'm not much of a talker, so forgive me if I use my fists instead."

He slides the small pliers between my skin and the metal. The bracelet is so tight that the cutting tool digs into my skin.

"Take a deep breath from me."

"Please tell me you've never chopped off someone's fingers with these."

"Don't ask questions you don't want the answer to. Now take a deep breath."

Instead of fighting some more, I hold on to the hope he's giving me and take a deep breath.

There's a barely audible click before I feel it fall off my wrist and onto my lap.

Xi takes it and shoves it into my hand. He helps me off the truck bed and back on my feet. Grabbing my shoulders, he spins me around and points at the grass closest to the building.

"Do yourself a favor and throw that shit over there. I don't want to see it no more; that way, he'll think you're still here while I take you for lunch."

"*Any*more," I correct him mindlessly. It helps me deal with the anxiety.

"Would you look at that," he says casually. "You might even get a spanking with that lunch."

"Sorry," I roll my lips. "I can't help it when I'm stressed."

"Come on, little miss know-it-all. Throw it."

I rear my arm back and throw the bracelet as far as I can. "Damn," I huff, centering myself. "That bracelet is forty thousand dollars."

"What?" Xi chokes as he spins me back around to face him again. "We're finding it when we come back. I can sell it."

"Well, it's broken now. And when we come back, I need

to keep it in my pocket. I can't have my dad thinking I'm in classes all day and night."

He gives me an unconvinced humph, and we get into his truck.

We eat at a diner on the North Shore. The food is greasy, the owner rude, and the entire place must have seen better days. I love it. It's everything my dad wouldn't want for me, yet I don't care about that. I love it because it's a place Xi knows and loves. Because there's an item on the menu named after his dad. A chicken sandwich he insisted they made for him every time he came here, apparently.

"Fried chicken, red cabbage, red and green bell peppers cooked in olive oil, and harissa," I read. "This sounds like heartburn waiting to happen," I chuckle.

"Try it," he says. "You won't regret it."

"I'm not very good with spice. Is harissa spicy?"

"Nah," he shrugs.

"I don't think I should trust you regarding spice levels," I add as I close the laminated menu and put it down. It's falling apart, and a page of it falls to the floor. I pick it up and look at him again. "You put hot sauce on everything you eat."

"You'll like it. Believe me."

The waiter stops by our table and chats with Xi before asking for our order. My boyfriend looks at me, expectant, and I smile at the waiter. "Two Moshe sandwiches, please."

When he puts the plates in front of us, I know I'm about to die. This thing looks like the kind of spice I could never handle. I take a deep breath and look at Xi.

"If I die, you'll deal with my family. Good luck."

He takes a huge bite, ignoring me. Cabbage and harissa

spill on his plate, and I take a second to admire his strong jaw working on the food in his mouth.

Does this man ever not look hot?

"Tell me about your dad," I demand before taking a small bite of the sandwich named after him.

"What do you want to know?" His voice lacks emotion, but I know this doesn't mean he's not feeling anything.

"You said he was Moroccan. Where exactly?"

"A city called Oujda, at the border with Algeria. He worked both in Algeria and Morocco; that's how he met my mom. She lived in Tlemcen, right on the border on the Algerian side."

I nod, taking another bite. His gaze keeps flicking from my eyes to my mouth as he licks his lips. He's already halfway through his sandwich, and I'm barely getting to the good part.

"What was his job there?"

"He was a chair maker. My mom's family had ordered a set from him, and he delivered it to their home. My mom was there to welcome him into the house. He fell in love right away. Came back the next day to ask her dad to take her out. He said no, of course. They weren't the same religion, which was a big deal back then. Mom didn't care. She kept sneaking out of her house for him. A month later, they were married."

I smile brightly at him. What a beautiful story. It makes me melt on the spot like butter in a pan. "That's so cute. I love love," I sigh. "When did they move to the U.S.?"

"In their late twenties. My mom was pregnant with me already. They moved to the house I live in now. We stayed there after he died. Then she met Emma's dad, and we had to move. I only lasted a few months before I told her I wanted my old house back. I missed my dad."

He must see the confusion on my face because he adds, "I know he was dead, but that house is...him. We were very close. Everything there reminds me of him. Especially since that's where we spent his last moments together. Where he asked me to take his place and take care of my mom and brother. I can't leave. It would be like leaving him behind."

"I understand." I nod. "You were fourteen when he passed, is that right?"

He nods, swallowing the last bite of his sandwich. "You remember?"

"Of course. It felt like important information."

He takes a drink from his cup, sucking on the straw.

"Was it his last wish?" I ask.

Putting the cup down, he cocks an eyebrow at me.

"To take care of your family. Was that his last wish?"

"How do you know?" he confirms with another question.

"Because I see the way you do it. Like the world would fall apart if you failed. You do the same with me."

His silence tells me I'm right.

"The world won't fall apart if you decide to care of yourself too. You don't have to protect everyone. You can't." My eyes start to burn.

"That's what he did." The seriousness in his voice breaks my heart.

"I would love to take care of you," I say softly. I cough and swallow past the swelling in my throat. "I think you're very brave, but you're allowed to rest too."

Tears well in my eyes, and I cough again.

"Are you crying?" he asks, confused as to the reason why.

"This sandwich is so spicy," I squeak. I really tried to

pretend I could eat it, but I've come to the end of what I can handle.

"Cupcake," he chuckles. "Were you eating this to make me happy?"

"You just love your dad so much," I choke as I put it down.

He gives me the smallest, closed-lip smile, and my heart thunders in my chest. I know how to tell when he's happy.

And God, I love seeing this man happy.

"Let's get you a milkshake."

21

XI

Eyes Off You – PRETTYMUCH

By the time we leave the diner, Alex is still on her milkshake. She's holding my hand as I close the door behind us. She begged me to pay for lunch, but I forbade her to, and she's too much of a good girl to insist. She did manage to convince me to take me for dessert in Stoneview so she could gift me something.

"Oh my god," she gasps. "How did I not see these earlier?" She drops my hand to run to the two vending machines next to the diner. They're the old kind from my childhood, with round storage at the top showing what they sell and a space for a quarter. One is a gumball machine that's not been used in God knows how long, and the other has capsules with little trinkets.

Alex splays her free hand on the round top of the capsule machine, her eyes shining with excitement. "I've not seen these in forever. I used to love them as a kid. Please, tell me you have a quarter?"

My heart flutters with happiness when I dig through my

pocket and pull out three quarters. She focuses on them, then back on the machine.

"Okay," she says with the seriousness of a CEO about to lead a merger meeting. "I really want some bubblegum, so we're keeping one for that. That means we have two chances to get this." She puts a demanding finger at the sticker on the machine that shows everything one could get. Her manicured nail is pointing at a little pink heart.

"A pink heart?" I ask, doing my best to hide the excitement at seeing her so eager.

"A pink heart," she scoffs. "That is a small box of *fuchsia* heart-shaped beads, my friend."

"Call me your friend again and see what happens."

She rolls her beautiful hazel eyes at me and keeps going. "I used to ask my mom for quarters when I was a kid and just kept turning the handle until that machine gave me these. Then I'd make my own little necklaces and bracelets with them. They're the *perfect* color."

"I don't even want to know how much of your mom's money you spent like that."

"Too much to admit. Give me a quarter."

"What's the magic word, baby?"

She fully turns to me, goes on her toes, and wraps her arms around my neck. I can feel the cold of her milkshake cup on my shoulder. The air around us is electric. The storm is over, but the rain is still drizzling, and it smells of wet concrete.

"Please," she breathes before giving me a soft kiss.

My heart fucking melts, and I hand her the coins as soon as she steps back. She starts with the gumball machine. She pops the massive ball in her mouth, wincing as she bites it. "That's much harder to chew than I remember."

She shifts to the right and puts a quarter in the other machine. She turns the handle, and a capsule falls. Grabbing it, I watch her shoulders deplete.

"It's a plastic ring." She turns to me and gives me the little ball. "I've got another chance. I want my fuchsia hearts." She puts the quarter in front of my lips. "Blow on it for good luck."

I harden my gaze, pretending this isn't the cutest fucking thing I've ever seen. Her cheeks are blowing from that giant gum she's biting, and I see the inside of her lips is starting to turn blue when she gives me a huge smile. I blow a breath on the coin.

She turns around, lowers herself, and goes through the same process to get a capsule.

"Aw," she pouts as she turns around. "It's stars stickers." She gives me that capsule too. "Oh, well. We tried."

Her little frown tugs at my heart. The way her smile has fallen off her face reminds me I'm way too fucking deep into this shit.

"Stay here," I murmur. I walk back to my car, open the back of the truck, grab my duffel bag, and pull out the crowbar.

Her eyes widen as I walk back. "Step aside."

"Xi," she says warily. "What are you—" Her voice cuts off the moment I hit the glass of the machine. "No!" she gasps.

The storage box shatters to pieces, and all the capsules fall out. I squat and search through them, finding the little hearts she wanted.

"Here," I say as I stand back up.

"You didn't have to do that." She looks around us, a panicked look taking over her beautiful face.

"Relax, cupcake. No one will arrest us for breaking a machine that hasn't been used in years."

"It's so wrong," she admits.

"You wanted the pink hearts. You got the pink hearts."

"They're fuchsia."

It's one of the strangest things; I love when she corrects me about colors. If there's one thing I know, it's motherfucking colors. I've painted since I was a child. Different shades of pigments are the only thing in the world I can't be corrected on. And yet, I insist on calling her favorite color *pink* just to hear her say fuchsia. Just to watch how her brain automatically throws the right color back at me because I know she can't help herself.

For a second, I don't reply. I bask in the pleasure of having Alex near me. In the fact that she knows nothing of who I really am and that she can love this version of me.

"Point is when you're with me, anything you want, you get. Clear?"

She nods, unable to stop a smile from spreading on her face. "You're crazy."

"You bet your ass I am. Now let's get dessert."

"Mine," she murmurs as we walk to the car.

"Taylor Swift song?" I ask casually as I open the door for her.

She nods excitedly.

"Wanna put it on in the car?"

Her huge grin fists my heart and makes it beat twice as fast.

Stupid fucking thing my heart is.

22

ALEXANDRA

5,6,7,8 – LØLØ, girlfriends

Xi Ep rented a bus to take us wherever we're volunteering today. A sleek, black kind with leather seats inside as if we're superstars. I go to the back with Peach, and Ella is in the seat right in front of us. My head falls against the window, and I close my eyes while my dad's words from last week come back to me.

I will not have an embarrassing idiot for a daughter.

I will never get out of my dad's clutches. He will always be there, barging into my life to remind me how much of a disappointment I am.

The bus starts and Peach puts a hand on my thigh. "Hey." She shakes it as I turn my face her way. "You look like someone who didn't sleep last night."

"Because I didn't," I grunt. I was too worried about my dad finding out that Xi took the bracelet off yesterday. We found it again afterward, and I keep it in my bag so he doesn't get suspicious.

"Did *not sleeping* involve a certain someone from the North Shore?"

When I don't answer, she hands me something. I glimpse down to see a text Chester sent to her, saying he saw me leave in Xi's car yesterday and that I hadn't shown up to classes after that. I bite the inside of my cheek and my eyes dart to hers. "How's Chester?"

"Well," she snorts. "According to him, you were kidnapped by a gangbanger from the North Shore for the second time yesterday?"

"God, he's dramatic," I roll my eyes.

"Xi did break his wrist last week."

My mouth twists. "Okay, that was completely out of line, but he isn't part of a gang."

Peach's eyebrows shoot to her hairline and her eyes harden. "Are you for real right now, Alex?"

"Don't assume things just because he lives on the North Shore."

"And because he's a drug dealer."

"That doesn't mean he's part of a gang, Peach," I grit. I don't have the strength or patience to argue with her today.

"Ella literally met him at an NSC party. Wake the fuck up," she snaps angrily. "Ella." She taps our friend's shoulder in front of us. She takes her earphones out and turns to us.

"Alex is being a naïve little girl again."

"I'm not being naïve. I assumed the same as you the day I met him, and it actually made him laugh. He's not, Peach. He just lives on the wrong side of town. It doesn't make him a gangbanger. You're the one coming in with prejudice because one of your friends once saw him at an NSC party. It means nothing. He takes care of me; he's a good man. He's the one who found my car, got it fixed, and brought it back to me."

"Yeah, probably because he's the one who stole it," she mumbles.

"Just shut up. I don't have the energy for this today." I cross my arms and lean against the window, looking ahead of me so I don't have to see her.

"I can't fucking stand how gullible she is," Peach tells Ella. "He's going to take advantage of her. You know that, right?"

"I'm right here," I snap. "Don't do that. I hate when you talk about me like I'm not right here hearing you."

"Alex," Ella intervenes. "Calm down, babe."

"Just because she can't figure out her relationship with Wren doesn't mean she has to come and ruin mine."

"You don't have a relationship," Peach retorts. "He just snaps his fingers when he wants to fuck you and you run to him. He does that with every girl."

"Okay, enough," Ella barks. "I have had it up to here," her hand comes above her head, "with you two not being able to have a civilized conversation for more than one minute."

We both stop talking, our mouths hanging open. Ella is in a bad mood, and that never happens.

"Sorry," I murmur like a scolded child. "Are you okay?"

Peach leans toward me, whispering, "Ghost from the past called her last night."

"Chris called you?" I squeak.

"No!" She shakes her head. "Well, yes, but it doesn't matter. It doesn't mean anything. Just..."

"He was drunk," Peach adds in my ear, but Ella can still hear everything.

"Enough," she warns.

"He told her he wanted to break up with his girlfriend for her."

"Peach, shut up," Ella snaps. "Oh my god, *shut up*."

"That's big," I say. "Ella, what are you going to do?"

There are a lot of things that got in the way of Ella's relationship with her ex. He was a senior when we were freshmen, but Ella retook a year, so he was only two years her elder. He also now goes to Harvard, which would make it complicated for them to be in a relationship again. But the main issue was and will always be that he is her brother's best friend. And Luke, her brother, has always been extra protective of her. She would never want to ruin their friendship for the sake of a man. No matter how in love with him she was in high school.

Ella runs a hand across her face. "She's right. You're so gullible."

"What? Why?"

"Because he was drunk, Alex. He's a man. He was a drunk man." Her annoyed, pale blue eyes dig into mine.

"Okay, he was a drunk man. So what?"

"So they do that," Ella tells me as if I'm a kid. "Guys will say they want to leave their girlfriend for you just to keep you close. So that you don't move on from them because they like having options. Chris doesn't care about me." She scratches her throat as her eyes dart away. "He never has."

"Plus, you've already moved on from him. Right?" Peach insists.

Ella licks her lips, and her eyes fall to her fingers playing with her earphones. "Yeah. Of course."

The lie is so evident on her face my heart aches for her.

"Men are fucking shit," Peach huffs. She points at me with her thumb, "and in case they weren't shit enough, she also decided to pick the playboy gangbanger from the North Shore. Just to make it worse for herself."

"He's not a gangbanger," I hiss at my friend.

"Alex." Ella gives me a pointed look. "He is. And if you would rather believe his lies than us, check his left shoulder. That's where his tattoo is. A dagger with the letters NSC on the hilt."

I press my lips together, not wanting to argue with both of my friends. We're a trio. Usually, if two have a point, the other is in the wrong. "Maybe you saw wrong..." I say tentatively.

Ella suddenly realizes something. "Wait. How have you not seen it yet? You guys had sex."

It's only now that I realize I have never seen Xi topless. Whenever we've had sex, he somehow stayed practically wholly dressed. Is that because he's hiding his tattoo?

"Well..." My ears heat up and my friends look at each other.

"Did you even ask him properly? With a clear question?" Peach says softly and sparing me having to explain myself.

He ignored me when I did. Another thing I can't tell them.

"He was annoyed when I assumed he was part of a gang and—"

"Ask him and see what he says. Ella knows he is. She saw his tattoo. So, just check if he's honest; that will tell you a lot about him."

I nod, not really happy with having to do that but knowing it's the right thing.

"Alex," Ella says as she slips her hands between the two seats separating us and touches my knee. "It's all fun and games to sleep with the bad boy, but you can't have a relationship with Xi."

"Please, don't tell me you think we're better than him because we're from Stoneview. That's not like you."

"Of course not," she snorts. "You know what I think of Stoneview."

"Then, what," I push.

"You don't want to be in the middle of the war between NSC and the Kings. People die, Alex. This is serious stuff. Xi *is* NSC. I don't know how involved he is, but it doesn't matter. He's part of their crew, and anything could happen to you if you're associated with them. Just stay out of this."

I try my best to not show that her words terrify me. Nodding, I gaze out of the window again, now noticing we've definitely left the luxury of the south bank. "Don't worry," I try to say as casually as possible. "I'll talk to him and straighten this out. It's not like we have feelings for each other or anything."

That lie slipped out way too easily.

Especially since Xi's been very clear about us.

And I know all too well how wild my heart gets when I'm around him.

"Alright, ladies," Camila exclaims at the front of the bus. I can see we're now parking in front of a rundown two-story building. "Today, we're volunteering at a boxing gym. We have decided to support *One Life, One Dream*, an organization that helps places that offer free classes and activities in low-income areas. We'll be separated into three groups and rotate so everyone will be doing each task eventually. Group one will start inside the gym. You'll be helping Dickie, the owner, to declutter some rooms at the back. Group two, you will be cleaning the main room. Group three, you will be given flyers to go and hand out around town."

There's a general agreement before Camila continues. "Girls, a gentle reminder that we're on the North Shore of Silver Falls and to be careful of your belongings and your surroundings, especially when you're handing out flyers. Make sure you stay in pairs. I'm not saying you're in any danger, just to keep an eye out. Alright?"

"Great," I mumble. My friends both eye me and I add, "I'm fine. Don't worry."

They look at each other without saying a word. They know not to when I don't want to talk about it. I'm fine being on the North Shore. In fact, I kind of like it. Purely because there's a chance to run into Xi.

We all file out of the bus, grabbing a random number from a bag Harper is holding outside so we know our groups. When I come out with group one, Harper smiles down at me. "You'll see, Dickie is a nice guy."

I nod, not really caring. I take a step away, but she grabs my elbow. "Alex." She scratches her throat. "Look, I know how you feel about being here. So, if you don't want to go hand out flyers, that's totally fine. You can do another task twice. It's no big deal. Also, erm, just so you know, I deleted the video of you in your room."

I narrow my eyes at her, trying to figure out the catch. "Why are you being so nice? It's still initiations."

She shuffles back, her eyes darting everywhere in panic. "I-I don't know what you're talking about."

She's scared. Why is she so scared?

"Oh my god. Did..." *It can't be.* "Did Xi..."

"I'm just trying to be nice, okay?" she snaps. "Make sure you tell your *boyfriend* that."

"Harper, I didn't ask him—I don't know what he said, but—"

"Alex. Move." Camila's clipped voice startles me, and I step away when I realize I'm holding up the line.

Peach and Ella are both in group three, and I wave at them as they leave the parking lot with flyers. I head inside with my group and meet Dickie. A giant of a man with a gruff voice. Harper was right. Despite his appearance, he's really sweet and offers us all a drink and snacks before we get to work.

We walk into the main gym and group three goes to the back room. Dickie's office is on a mezzanine floor, looking onto the training room we're in. He's added some thin walls with a plexiglass window to have a proper separation. From down here, we can't see what's going on in there.

A Xi Ep girl hands me a sponge and a bucket of water. "I'm going to mop, but there are some pretty strong stains, so you need to go after me wherever they are."

"Sure," I nod.

Half an hour later, I'm on my knees, two hands pressing on the harsh sponge as I violently attack a stain that's not going away. I put my whole body into it, scrubbing back and forth. My tights are soaked, and my knees are wet from being on the mopped floor. Strands of hair have come out of my ponytail, falling in front of my eyes.

"Ugh," I grunt out of frustration. My white Xi Ep t-shirt has wet patches, which causes my fuchsia bra to be visible underneath. I'm meant to be volunteering right now, not acting like I'm in a poorly scripted porno.

Two worn-out black boots step into my field of vision, right next to the stain I'm working on.

I peer up only to find Xi's tall, broad form looking down at me.

23

ALEXANDRA

Better With – Friday Pilots Club

I blow on the hair in front of my face and my heart explodes in my chest. He looks like a god right now. His hands are in the pockets of his black cargo pants, and he's wearing a khaki t-shirt that looks too small, hugging his solid shoulders and biceps so beautifully.

And a pink heart-beaded bracelet.

He's wearing the bracelet I made for him after he broke the vending machine for me yesterday. I spent the afternoon doing it while he was painting and gave it to him before I left. Now he's wearing it.

My heart threatens to explode out of my chest.

I wipe my sweaty forehead with my forearm, and the corner of his mouth tipping up tells me he's enjoying the view too.

"You're wearing my bracelet," I whisper.

Instead of acknowledging my shock, he says, "I'm pretty sure I dreamed about this last night." He bites his lower lip with his perfect teeth. "It started with you on your knees..."

I sit back on my haunches, eyes darting around. "What are you doing here? Wearing my bracelet."

My serious voice seems to do nothing to tame him. He steps forward, towering so close to me I'm straining my neck to look into his eyes.

"I was watching Billie's fight with Dickie in his office. He trained her. And yeah. I'm wearing *my* bracelet. That *my* girl made for me."

He shakes his wrist in front of my face, but I'm not really listening. This gang question has been weighing heavy on my mind since the talk on the bus and I want to clear the air before anxiety swallows me whole. Not very comfortable talking like this, I drop the sponge and stand up.

"I need to ask you some—"

"You're bleeding," he cuts me off. I follow his gaze to my left knee and notice the hole in my tights and the blood there.

"Oh." I grab a paper towel from the bucket of cleaning supplies next to me. "I can't even feel it. It's just a scratch from being on my knees."

I dab my knee before peering up.

"Anyway, I was just saying. I know this is coming randomly and I kind of hate that I'm asking that. I just... God, I hope you don't think I'm judging you or anything. I—"

"Alexandra," Xi says low, his eyes returning to my knee. "You're still bleeding. I can't fucking focus."

"It's just a graze," I snap back. "I'm trying to address something here."

A low growl rumbles in his chest as his eyes harden. His hand wraps around my wrist firmly and he starts walking, ultimately pulling me with him.

"Xi," I squeak as he strides across the room and to the

stairs. My eyes dart around, noticing how the Xi Ep girls are looking at me with wide eyes.

He walks us into Dickie's office and closes the door behind him. Dickie's not in here, but it doesn't help me relax in any way.

"Xi," I hiss as he releases my wrist only to grab me by the waist and sit me on Dickie's old-looking desk. It shakes when it takes my weight, and I'm worried it won't hold me.

Xi turns away, opening a metal locker. I press my hands to the desk, ready to jump off. His back is still to me when he calmly says, "Don't even think about it."

I stop short, not liking how easily I let him tell me what to do and yet still do it anyway. He finally walks back with a red pouch that has a white cross on it. I read the thick writing on it.

"First aid kit?" I wonder out loud. He puts it on the desk, opens it, and takes out a few supplies before kneeling before me. I watch with wide eyes as he wipes my knee with a disinfecting wipe. "What are you..."

But it's so clear what he's doing. He's losing his mind over a tiny cut.

One. Silly. Tiny. Cut.

His hands slide under my skirt, and he lowers my tights until they bunch around my ankles. He removes my sneakers, rids me of the tights completely, and grabs something else from the kit.

He tears open a band-aid and sticks it on my knee. It's the big, square, flesh-colored kind as if I'd truly injured myself.

He drops a kiss on the band-aid and finally looks up at me. Still on his knees, he finally says, "You were saying?"

I struggle to drag a breath in. His head is right between my thighs, and I'm wearing my uniform skirt. I have no doubt he has a nice view of the pink underwear that matches my bra. Despite that, I don't want to hide or pull away. If anything, I want to press against his lips and feed the insatiable hunger that takes over me when he's around.

"Alex?" he insists, deadpan, but I see the playfulness in his stare. He knows exactly what he's doing.

"Are you part of a gang?" I spill out, not trusting what else would come out. "Did you threaten Harper? She was nice to me. She's scared of you. What did you do?" My thoughts are mumbled, and my questions unclear, but I think I got my point across.

A chuckle escapes him. "Overthinking is your thing, isn't it?"

"And yours is avoiding topics you don't want to discuss."

"You're observant," he says softly as he drops a kiss on my inner thigh. "It's very annoying."

"Xi," I sigh. "Just answer my question. *Questions.* Just answer."

Slowly, he trails his mouth up my thigh, his head now practically under my skirt. My hands move to hold the edge of the desk, but I stand my ground. "Just answer me."

He brings his hand under my skirt and slowly pushes my panties to the side, holding it there. He looks up at me, and his tongue runs against his two front teeth. "I'm not part of a gang. Now lay back and put your feet on the edge."

"And Harper? Did you hurt her? Threaten her? I don't want you doing this for me."

"I didn't like her attitude toward you. I'm glad it's fixed."

"What did you do to her? She's terrified. You can't do this. That's not how it works." I struggle to breathe, my question a pant more than anything else.

"To her? Nothing. But God knows she has many cars I

can keep setting on fire if she makes you feel uncomfortable again. I'm on two."

"Xi," I sigh as his thumb grazes my clit. God, it's so hard to be stern when all I want right now is to feel his tongue against my skin. "You can't do this. It's..."

"Alexandra," he growls between my legs. His breath caresses me, lighting up my entire body. "I do whatever the fuck I want *for* you. And I do whatever the fuck I want *to* you. Now be a good girl, lay back, and put your feet on the edge of this desk."

"We...we can't do this. Dickie could—" A whimper cuts me off as he presses his thumb against my wet entrance.

"Do as I say, Alexandra."

My head swims with need as I let myself fall back against the desk and put my feet on the edge. Have I really got that little fight in me?

His tongue is on me the next second. It pushes inside me, licking my wetness before bringing it all the way to my clit. I'm spread open for him, and he eats me like a feast.

I must bring my hand to my mouth to muffle my moans as his tongue strokes me over and over again. He doesn't relent, doesn't slow down. I wonder if he even breathes at any point. I'm so wet I can feel it trickling down between my ass cheeks, and my face flames.

No matter how ashamed I feel, I don't stop it. I can't. It feels too good. I come for him so hard my legs shut, and I capture his face between my thighs. He presses hard against me before pulling my legs apart and standing up.

He seems utterly satisfied as he looks down at the mess I am. Splayed on the desk, panting. I must look ridiculous like this.

"You're beautiful," he whispers, his eyes darting everywhere on my body.

I bring my hands to my face, hiding how I feel myself blushing. He grabs my wrists, pulling them away. "Don't hide. I like you in pink."

I laugh, fighting and still trying to put my arms over my face. "I have to go back," I sigh. "I can't bail on volunteer day."

As the orgasm high starts to drop, my friends' words come back to me. Ella is sure she's seen a tattoo. Xi tells me he's not part of NSC.

Why would he lie to me?

I grab the hem of his t-shirt, ready to pull it off, but I stop short when I feel his grip tighten on my wrists. In a split second, he harshly pulls me back up, observing my left arm.

"What the fuck is that?" he hisses as he looks at the bruise on my upper arm and the other on my forearm.

It's been a week, but they're still slightly visible. A muddy shade of brown.

My brain stalls for a second, his eyes darting everywhere on my body. He catches the large welt on my thigh, still swollen and bruised. "Alex." There's a panic in his voice I have never heard from him before—emotions blending with the worry.

"Oh." I fake a smile and act unperturbed despite my heart kicking at my chest. "It's nothing, I—"

One hand releases my right wrist and grabs my t-shirt. He pulls me so hard I'm forced to get off the desk. Pushing my top up to my throat, he observes my chest, my boobs, and his eyes finally fall to the other welt on my ribs.

Only one word leaves his lips. One simple question.

"Who?" he growls.

"Me," I lie in a reassuring tone. "Will you stop worrying

so much? This is from a drunken fall. It's initiations. I still get drunk practically every night."

Wrapping a hand around my jaw, he drags me until my back hits a wall.

"Xi," I gasp. "Stop..."

"I'm going to ask one more time, and you're going to tell the truth." His harsh breath warms my face, his beautiful eyes intensely dark. "Who did this to you?"

"It was me." I blink up at him, the lie acidic on my tongue and burning my throat. "I promise it was just a drunken fall on my side when walking home from Zeta Nu. I fell into a bush."

His nostrils flare as I watch him trying to stay calm. I don't want him to lose it. I don't want him in the same state he was when Chester wouldn't let me go. Xi can't even hold a conversation when I've got a cut on my knee. What would happen if he knew what my dad does to me?

"You better be telling the truth, Alex. If I find out you lied, you'll watch me kill the person you lied for."

I gulp, nodding for lack of finding words.

"I have a lot of work tonight, but I want you to text me when you're home safe. I'll call you before bed."

I nod again.

"Tell me you're going to let me know when you're home safe," he adds in that annoyed voice of his.

"I-I'll let you know when I'm home safe."

He exhales as he closes his eyes, his long lashes fanning his cheeks. "Good girl," he murmurs.

He presses me against the wall, his hand still on my jaw, and plants his lips on mine.

Just like that, the fear disappears.

All it takes is a deep kiss that makes my heart somersault, and all my anxiety disappears.

I can't control the yawn that makes its way up my mouth. We've been hanging out in the parking lot in front of a convenience store for forty-five minutes. We hand out flyers inviting people to join boxing classes at Dickie's gym. The leaflets say *Get off the streets, it's free!* In bold letters and I cringe every time I see it. How to not address young people 101.

Cassie, the girl with me, huffs as she shifts from one foot to the other. "I really need the bathroom," she repeats for the fifth time.

I smile kindly at her. "There's a diner across the road. Just go and ask if you can use their bathroom."

"We're not meant to leave each other alone."

"It'll only be two minutes," I reassure her. I can't believe I'm the one reassuring someone on the North Shore. "I'm not worried about being left alone."

She nods and bites her lip as she thinks. "Okay. I'll be super quick." She hands me her flyers and runs to the crosswalk.

I sit on the metal bench outside the convenience store and force myself to appear relaxed. It's all fine. She'll be right back.

A dark matte green truck parks in the spot in front of me, and two men walk out. They're tall; one of them has wavy, ear-length blond hair that he flips as he gets out of the passenger seat while laughing. He walks around to join the other one. With black hair and a severe look on his face, he couldn't be more of a contrast from the first one if he tried.

They eye me as they walk past me, looking at me like we know each other but not sure where from. I'm confident that I don't know them.

They walk in and I let out a breath, my heart beating hard against my chest. I look across the road, but Cassie hasn't returned from the diner yet. I didn't even look if she got in. She's nowhere to be seen so she must have.

A few minutes later, the two guys from the matte green truck come back out. They walk my way again, and I discreetly put a hand on the flyers, covering them so they don't get curious. I pray they don't talk to me because I have a strange feeling about them.

No such luck.

The blond one stops right in front of me, hiding the sun still shining, and covering me in his shadow. "What's that you're handing out?" he says with a bright smile. His blue eyes shine with excitement.

"Oh, um," I grab a flyer and hand it to him. He eyes it and snorts as he passes it to his friend. As he does so, I catch a tattoo on his forearm. A crown.

My heart drops to my stomach. That's the tattoo of the Kings' crew. This guy is part of a gang and I have no doubt the other one is too.

The serious one looks down at the flyer and the corner of his lips barely lifts. I guess that's his amused face.

"How kind of you, rich people, to get us off the streets," he says sardonically.

I shrink on the bench, not knowing what to say. I want to join Cassie at the diner, except they crowd me so compactly that I can't even get up from where I'm sitting.

"I feel like I've seen you somewhere," the blond one jumps back in.

"I-I don't think so."

He snaps his fingers and points at me. "Xi. You're Xi's girl." He eyes my t-shirt.

Shaking my head, I say, "That's just the name of my sorority."

He laughs. "But I've seen you around town with him. The other day in his car in the middle of the road. You were having a pretty good time, if I remember right."

My cheeks flush as my eyes widen. I'm at a complete loss for words. Many cars overtook us while we brazenly had sex in the middle of the road. They must have been one of them.

"You guys looked close," he chuckles. "Are you going to his fight tonight?"

Time stills for a few seconds before I can repeat, "His fight?"

"Yeah, at the warehouse. You should come."

A fight at the warehouse.

What is that? He never told me about this. He said he had work.

Just like he never told me if he has a tattoo of NSC on his left shoulder or not.

Did my boyfriend really just lie to me when I asked him if he was part of a gang?

"Okay." My voice seems so foreign I barely believe I'm the one who just agreed to go to a fight on the North Shore tonight.

"Give me your phone number. I'll text you the address."

I do and watch, numb, as he puts my number in his phone. In my head, I remember Xi's busted knuckles and now know how he got them. The blond guy smiles brightly at me and adds, "I'm Elliot, by the way. And this is my brother, Ethan."

I nod mindlessly, my heart squeezing painfully. "Alex."

"We'll see you there, Alex."

24

ALEXANDRA

Traitor – Olivia Rodrigo

I take a deep breath as I get out of a taxi at the address Elliot sent me. I shouldn't be here. What I should have done was calmly talk to Xi about this. But he lied to me once, saying he had work things to do tonight. What's to stop him from lying again if I mention this to him? I have to see this for myself and confront him.

I have this bad feeling in my gut. This doom hanging over my head. I'm not a pessimist. I've always been a dreamer, but sometimes even I have to admit not everything in life can be fixed by singing lyrics to a Taylor Swift song. Sometimes your boyfriend turns out to be a liar and you're left with no choice but to follow him to a warehouse on the bad side of town.

I'm too focused on the feeling of dread to take in how far I've made it since meeting Xi. A month ago, I was on the verge of a panic attack because I had to drive through the North Shore. Tonight I bribed a taxi driver who was refusing to drive me here.

I pause at the edge of the lot. What will I do if I find out something horrible? I feel like I tripped while walking on the edge of a cliff and Xi caught me before I fell. He's the only thing between me and a deadly fate. What if he lets go and watches me fall?

I'm wearing a pair of black jeans and Xi's black hoodie he gave me last week. I want to make myself as discreet as possible.

Many people are hanging out in the parking lot. Car trunks are open, blasting music outside while people drink and hang out. I'm guessing the fight hasn't started yet. I make my way inside and settle at the back, waiting as the warehouse slowly fills up. The minutes pass, and I lose my unrestricted view of the broken-down ring in the middle of the room. It separates the space into two distinct sides, and I can also see people coming in from another entrance. I wonder what that's about.

The first couple of people get in the ring, and I watch with wide eyes as they go at each other. Blood is spurting everywhere, and I retreat back every time I hear the disgusting sound of flesh hitting flesh. For someone who despises violence, I'm in for a treat. I've been on the receiving end of my father's fists too often to support this behavior.

One of them is punched unconscious and brought off the ring.

That's when Xi comes in. He's topless, only in black shorts, and I squint my eyes to try and check his tattoos, but I can't see anything from here. I'm way too far.

The fight doesn't last long. In less than a minute, Xi has knocked the other guy out. Another one comes in, and while it takes him a bit longer, I watch with wide eyes as he wins again. A third one has the same fate.

My boyfriend, who treats me like a queen and can't stand seeing a scratch on my knee, beats people to within an inch of their life as a hobby.

The crowd on my side doesn't seem to be supporting him, and they throw insults at him every time he wins. On the other side of the room, the cheers resonate loudly.

After the fourth, the competition seems to end, and Xi walks off without even celebrating. As if this is nothing to him.

Like coming out from underwater, I gasp as reality hits me. Oxygen burns my lungs, and I face the truth I've been blindly avoiding all this time: Xi is dangerous. Xi is violent.

It doesn't matter what he is like to *me*. It doesn't take away who he really is.

I bump into some people as I go against the crowd, making my way to the ring. I want to follow where he's going. Watching his back disappear through a door, accompanied by another girl, I go after them.

I lose them once I'm in the hallway. There are multiple doors, though I decide to ignore them, following through to the end. I take a left and stop. There are two ways to go, and I have no idea where he went.

I lost him.

You never had him.

How true. Xi is not someone I can have. After today, he feels more like an idea I fell for.

I'm about to turn around and go home when I hear voices coming from a room.

"You can't tell her, Xi." The feminine voice brings me closer to the door. I press my ear against it.

"I don't care what you all think I can or can't do." It's his voice this time.

Are they talking about me?

"You're not getting out of it." I recognize her. It's his best friend, Zara. "Vito will want something soon, and he won't take no for an answer. If you fuck up now, we're never getting any info. We'd all be fucked because of you."

Vito? What info?

"You don't understand," he huffs, and I can imagine his hard face expressing how sick he is of the conversation. "I told her I wouldn't break her heart."

Said heart drops to my stomach. They *are* talking about me.

"The whole plan is to break her heart!" she snaps, and this time it fissures. The kind that runs deeply. Just one more hit, and it'll explode into a million pieces. "You kept telling us that you were taking your time so she would really trust you. So she'd invite you to her house."

My house? Why would Xi ever want to come to my house? He hates Stoneview.

I hear his sarcastic chuckle. "I told you that because I *want* to spend time with her. Not for Vito Luciano. For *me*. You all can't fucking stand that for once, I'm putting myself first instead protecting all of you. No one bats a fucking eyelid when I burn houses to the ground and kill for NSC. But, fuck, I tell you I don't want to break a sweet girl's heart, and you all lose your shit."

"It's too late to not break her heart, Xi. How do you think she'll react when you tell her you've been dating her to get dirt on her father."

For a second, time stops.

No.

Without mercy, Zara continues. "The girl's made of fucking glass. One hit, and she breaks." There's a beat before the hammer nails the coffin shut. "The worst is done. She likes you. Shit, she's probably in love with you at this point. Do it the way you planned it all along. Say you want to meet her parents, go to her house and break into her dad's office. There'll be plenty to find in there. Get the fucking info and end it."

No, no, no. This isn't real. He didn't...he couldn't.

He had a plan all along.

None of it was real.

The fissure cracks some more, and yet I'm still holding on.

I wait. I wait and wait for him to say something. To defend our relationship. To snap back that *he's* in love with me.

Say that you won't do it, I beg silently.

Tell them I'm more important than NSC.

Say something...anything.

Please.

It never comes. His silence is what kills us.

Happiness is such a feeble thing. If it doesn't come from within you, anything can take it away. If you give someone the power to make you happy, to make you feel loved... you're never in control.

I felt so safe that I chose to ignore every single sign that told me Xi would break my heart.

I'm the stupid, gullible girl he played with—the one he used to try and get dirt on my father.

I let it happen because I wanted to believe so badly that he would be the one to save me from my miserable life. With him, I didn't have to put on a fake smile. I didn't have to pretend everything was fine. I was just myself.

Simple Alex. Kind and naïve.

Sweet.

So. Fucking. Sweet.

I swallow the tears, letting anger take over instead.

I'm done letting everyone control and use me.

I'm done not fighting back.

It's not Xi that ends up breaking my heart. It implodes from the pressure the rage is putting on it. It doesn't break into pieces.

It turns to dust.

Without thinking, I barge into the room, ready to crush him. I come face to face with Xi and Zara. He's showered and dressed now. She's right in front of him, between his legs, dabbing a cut on his cheek with cotton while he's sitting on a bench.

God, the way my heart twists painfully. I want to die on the spot, and my words get stuck down my throat.

"Alex," he says in surprise. He's obviously confused, but then he pushes Zara away, getting up instantly.

I look around only to see they're not alone. No, there are two guys and another girl in here. I recognize Logan because he stopped by Xi's house when I was there before.

My lips curl. All of them were plotting against me the whole time. I bet none of them thought that they should have watched what they said in this warehouse. It's too far from my pretty life. Too dangerous for sweet Alex to ever set foot here.

The confusion doesn't stay long on Xi's face. It turns into anger as he strides toward me, grabbing my arm and looking down at me. "What the fuck are you doing here?" he hisses in my face.

"I could ask you the same question," I spit back. "I thought you were *working*. New job, I see?"

"Alexandra," he says in that voice of his that brings goosebumps to my skin. "You better go home right fucking now."

"You're an asshole. I'm really stupid, but *fuck*, you're an asshole, Xi."

With his right hand, he grabs the back of my head by the hair, forcing me on my toes as he leans down. "Go home, or I swear to God I'm going to have a field day spanking your ass later."

Rather than trying to escape him, I wrap my fingers around his left biceps and push up the short sleeve of his t-shirt.

I can barely refrain from gasping when I see the tattoo of a dagger on his otherwise bare arm. It's right there, on his left shoulder. Exactly as Ella described it, the letters NSC are tattooed on the hilt.

Xi is part of the North Shore Crew, just like my friends had warned me. And instead of listening to them, I listened to his lies.

"You fucking liar," I seethe, tears threatening to fall any second.

"Alex," he rasps. He looks around, clearly changing his mind about me needing to leave when he realizes how serious this is. "Let's talk."

"There's no need to talk." My tone is flat, my heart beating slowly as I feel a darkness overtake me. "I heard everything."

He pauses, the shock so evident in his eyes. He thought I hadn't heard their conversation.

The bastard was going to keep on lying.

"I can explain."

"It's unfortunate I don't want your explanation. Let me go."

I twist, but his grip doesn't relent.

"I wanted to tell you, Alex." He looks at his friends behind him again. "I can't do this here."

"Xi, let me go," I hiss. "We're done. We're over, we—"

His other hand grabs my jaw, his fingers digging into my skin. "You have every right to be angry, but you're going to take that shit back right now."

My brows furrow. "You *betrayed* me. There's no coming back from that!"

"You can always go back when you don't have a fucking choice," he hisses in my face. "I will make it up to you, but you're not getting away from me."

"You're insane," I whimper as his fingers dig deeper, pouting my lips.

"Yeah," he growls. "Say that again, so it truly sinks in."

"Xi," someone calls behind him. "Let her go." I recognize Zara's voice even though I can't see her. Xi's strong body is obstructing my view.

He doesn't let me go. His intense stare is on me, silently telling me this isn't over.

"Xi," Zara repeats as a hand grabs his shoulder. "We've got angry Kings all around the warehouse. Keep her safe and let her go."

Angry Kings all around the warehouse.

That's their life. Two gangs barely co-existing in their broken side of the city. Always teetering on the edge of a full-on battle. They fight in a ring, cheering from two sides of the same warehouse. They plot silently to take the other crew down.

They use innocent women to do their bidding.

This man is so, *so* deep into the war between the Kings and NSC that my chest constricts at the realization that I never stood a chance. If it's between me or his gang, Xi will always choose them.

He releases me, but just as I'm about to step to the side, his hand slams on the wall next to my face. "I'm letting you go," he says low. "But I'm not *letting. You. Go.* Do you understand?"

I feel myself trembling. It's the need to cry, the betrayal. His words are clear; I can't escape him. Except he's wrong. I'm not letting him back into my life.

"Move your hand," I say with a coldness that brings goosebumps to my skin. "*Now.*"

His arm drops, and I run through the hallways without looking back.

I don't take a breath until I'm back in the parking lot. I wipe the tears as they come and finally slow down my run. How could I be so stupid? The man I have been wholly falling for is part of a gang. He was using me.

Slowly, I lose the crowd gathering in the lot. It's only when I'm walking down the street that someone calls my name. I turn around to see Elliot and Ethan coming my way.

"Did you enjoy the fight?" Elliot asks as they both stop in front of me.

I wipe my tears and shake my head. "Why did you invite me here tonight?"

"What's wrong?" he says as his light brows draw together. "Did he not want you here?"

"He...no, he didn't want me here at all."

"Damn," Elliot runs a hand through his blond hair. "Do you know what that means?"

"No," I sniffle. "I don't."

"That means he cares about you." His voice is different now. Ominous.

"W-what?" I stutter, completely confused. My brain is foggy from tonight's revelations, my heart is broken, and I'm unsure what this is all about.

Then something strikes me just as Ethan moves to step

behind me. I'm too late, of course. Too late, too naïve, too credulous. As always.

If only I'd remembered a few seconds before now that Xi's tattoo showed he belongs to NSC, and I know for a fact that Elliot and Ethan are Kings' crew.

Meaning they're total enemies.

Elliot smiles brightly at me, like my realization is written on my face. I take a step back, only for Ethan to wrap a hand around my throat from behind.

"And do you know what it means if he cares about you?" Elliot sneers.

My heart knocks against my chest as my back stiffens from fear.

I shake my head, not finding my voice. Elliot leans down, his smile turning predatory. "It means that if we hurt you. We hurt him."

A whimper escapes me as he grabs a switchblade from his pocket, clicking it open.

"P-please," My hands go to Ethan's around my neck. "I don't want any trouble. I just..." *want to go home.*

My voice resonates loudly in my head. It sounds just like that night.

I want to go home.

I want to go home.

I squeeze my eyes shut, forcing myself to focus. "He was using me. He doesn't care about me. I p-promise you this will lead nowhere."

"You're going to deliver a message from us." Elliot's voice is so hard now. His face lost the soft features I saw earlier today. "Think you can do that? In exchange...we let you live."

I try to nod, but Ethan's hand prevents that. "Y-yes," I squeak.

"You're going to tell him that we want the information he's been withholding from us. And that if he doesn't give it," he brings his knife to my cheek, the deadly end pressing against my skin. He's not pushing. He's not cutting me, but the fear is enough to make me whimper, and the message is clear.

"Does that sound like an easy message to relay?" Elliot insists.

My *yes* is barely audible because I don't dare take another breath.

"Good. Because if you don't, I'm afraid we'll have to hurt you real bad. We don't want that, do we?"

"N-no, please."

Ethan lowers his mouth to my ear. "Don't fuck us over. We know where you live."

"Please, let me go home." I explode into a sob, feeling the ground tilt under me. Dragging in a breath, the echo of my voice resonates everywhere as they finally let me go.

I want to go home.

My ears ring, and I feel the way I lose control over my limbs. They're shaking uncontrollably, spasming. The two disappear. I can sense they're not around anymore.

It smells like smoke, like every time I'm thrown back to that night.

I fall to the asphalt, as I start to lose consciousness.

No. Not here, not now.

"Alex," a voice calls out. A hand presses to my chest. "Take deep breaths. Push against my hand." Another hand comes under my head. "Breathe, baby. I'm here."

But it's too late. Total blackout.

25

ALEXANDRA

I fucked up - convolk

My eyes flutter open. I turn around in bed, attempting to get more comfortable under the covers. My arm suddenly spasming makes everything that happened come back at once. I drag in a deep breath as I try to sit up, but my muscles refuse to cooperate.

"Don't," Xi's voice calls out softly. I startle when I notice him sitting on a chair next to me.

I'm not in my bed, that much is clear. I think I'm in his bed. In his room. The light is low, coming from the hallway, and I can't really see much. It smells of him, his delicious cologne and the drying paint. I hate that, despite knowing everything, it reassures me.

He gets up and sits on the edge of the bed. "Don't try to sit up," he repeats. "You were still shaking less than a minute ago."

"What?" I rasp. "How long have I been out?"

"Not long. I don't live far from the warehouse, so I drove you here quickly."

I bring my hands to my face, hiding in them before raking my fingers through my hair. "I need to go home."

"Alex," he scolds me. "You need to rest."

"I don't want to sleep next to you," I snap. A whimper escapes me as my stomach and thighs contract. "Ugh," I huff in pain. "Damn it."

"You're still unwell. You can't go anywhere right now."

Tears well in my eyes and I look away. "I want to leave." I don't know how realistic that demand is. I'm exhausted, my eyelids barely keeping open.

"No." He stands up. "You're not leaving, and that's final." A cool command indicating that he's essentially keeping me hostage. "I'm going to get you some water."

The moment he exits the room, I force my body to sit up. I throw the covers over myself and sit on the edge of the bed. My heart drops when I realize I'm wearing one of Xi's shirts and boxers.

"What the hell," I murmur to myself.

He wouldn't...right? He wouldn't take advantage of me like that. I told him PNES comes from trauma. He wouldn't...I pinch my lips, reliving the moment I pulled up his sleeve to uncover his tattoo.

He's NSC. He's part of a gang. He *used* me.

I still can't seem to process the news.

He walks back into the room at my third attempt to get up.

"What are you doing?" He strides to me, tucking me back in bed. "I told you to stay here."

"Why am I wearing your clothes?" I push the covers away as soon as he steps back.

He drags them back on me. "Because, I wanted you comfortable."

"Liar," I hiss, pushing the covers off me again. "You're a liar. Nothing you say can be trusted."

Pushing my hands away, he pulls the covers over me. "Stop the bratty behavior right now. I did this for *you*."

"Where are my clothes?" I try to push the covers away yet again, but he holds on to them this time, and I don't have the strength to pull.

"They're in the wash," he barks. Then it softens again, like he regrets raising his voice at me. "You wet yourself, okay? Now drop it."

My mouth hangs open, shame engulfing me.

This can't be real.

My ears heat with embarrassment as my gaze drops. I release the sheet, not knowing what else to do.

"Look, it's no big deal, but I wasn't going to put you to bed in those clothes. So, I showered you and put you in mine."

"Oh my God," I groan in embarrassment, letting myself slide down onto the mattress and hide under the covers.

It's rare, but it's not the first time this has happened. Peach and Ella have had to deal with me multiple times. It's not something I can control, and my friends have never made me feel uncomfortable about it. But Xi? Could this night have gone worse?

My throat constricts, and I can feel fat tears rolling down my cheeks.

"Alex," he says softly as he uncovers my face. "Don't worry about it. It's not the first time this has happened to someone close to me. There's no shame to have, I promise you."

I shake my head and bury myself deeper into the pillows. His hand comes to my hair, caressing me, and he sighs.

"My dad used to have seizures from his cancer treatment. I'm the one who would take care of him. This is not a big deal to me."

I take a deep breath and finally do what I should.

"Don't touch me," I hiss as I push his hand away. I sit up again, fighting the pain in my body.

This time I push the cover off me and get off the bed on the other side. "I mean it, Xi. Stay away from me."

I watch his jaw work as I round the bed to the door. One step to the side and he's blocking the doorway from me.

"No."

"No?" I sputter. "Have you gone completely crazy?"

He juts his chin, pointing at my naked legs. "Leaving half-naked?"

"I don't care how I'm leaving as long as I'm far away from your lying ass. I loathe you right now, do you understand?"

"I can live with that. You'll come around to understand that when I said I have two obsessions and you are one of them, there was no going back from it. You said it yourself; life is made of choices. You could have chosen prince charming, but you chose me." He leans down, making sure his face is right in front of mine, when he adds, "I guess you chose wrong."

I feel my nostrils flare as I try to calm myself. No such luck. I'm pissed. For the first time in my life, I'm fuming.

So I slap him in the face. I use his shock to try and push past him, charging him like an NFL player and ignoring the pain spreading all over my body.

He effortlessly catches me at the waist, my weight and height nothing to him, and lifts me off the floor. In one long stride, he's throwing me back on the bed. "You're going to regret that, cupcake."

"Don't fucking call me cupcake!" I screech.

I roll off as he tries to grab my ankle and kick him in the shoulder. "Don't touch me!"

"Alexandra," he growls. "You don't want to see me angry."

"I thought being angry was your default setting. Isn't that why you chose the sweet girl to date? So you could have some sunshine in your life. Oh, *wait*," I bring my knees to my chest when he tries to grab me again, "you were just using me to get to my dad."

He grabs hold of both my ankles and pulls me until I'm splayed on the bed. "Let go!" I twist and try to kick again but he doesn't relent.

When he lowers himself right above my face, I don't let him talk. I bite so hard into his shoulder I rip a hole into his t-shirt.

His grunt of pain gives me all the wrong feelings. Butterflies in my stomach, a band wrapping tightly in my lower belly, and tingles between my legs. Wrapping my hair around his fist, he pulls until I'm forced to let go, then he straightens up.

"You *chose* the bad guy, Alex." He drags me until his t-shirt bunches just below my boobs. "You *chose* the guy everyone warned you against." He grabs my hips and flips me on my front, making me shriek. "Do you know why?"

I grunt in response, refusing to give him an answer.

"Because you like the danger of someone who could take your choice away, baby," he rumbles as he grabs the boxers I'm wearing and pulls them down.

"Don't you dare!" I scream.

"You like that I treat you like the little slut you are. Always desperate for my cock..." He slaps my ass and I shriek.

"Fuck you!"

What the hell did I get myself into when I started dating him?

"You chose the man who degrades and humiliates you because you love it. It's too bad for you I came with a no-return policy."

He spreads my ass cheeks before slapping them again. I feel him kneel between my legs as I attempt to turn around, but he grabs the back of my head, twisting his fingers in my hair. "Stay still, I'll give you what you crave."

"Don't," I panic. He presses harder, pushing my face into the mattress.

"I have bad news for you, Alex," he sneers behind me. "You're so wet I can see it in the dark."

"No..." I deny, my words muffled by the mattress. I can feel the wetness between my legs, though I refuse to admit it.

"You're so mine, aren't you, baby? Your pussy knows it."

"Please," I whine. "I need to be away from you."

"And I need to be inside you."

I feel two fingers press against my entrance, pushing in and stretching me, and the moan escaping me doubles my anger. Of course, this feels delicious when I should be mad. Of course, everything is heightened from the fight.

"How many fingers do you think you can take?"

He fucks me with two until I'm panting against the bed, pushing my hips against his hand in chase of pleasure. And then, he adds another one.

"Oh God," I whimper. "Too much..."

"Be my good little whore, Alex. Show me I can play with you however I fucking want."

I squeeze my eyes shut, the pleasure intensifying as my body adapts to him.

"That's right, look at this beautiful pussy all stretched out for me."

I feel his thumb at my back entrance. "No!"

His hand at the back of my head tightens. "Stay still, I don't want to hurt you. I know you don't like pain."

"Xi, please," I whimper as I feel him spread some of my wetness to my tight hole. "Fuck," I gasp as his thumb presses. A moan escapes me and he chuckles behind me.

"Only dirty little sluts like being fucked in the ass. Are you a dirty slut, Alex?" His words come with his fingers curling in my pussy, his knuckles pressing against my G-spot.

"Yes," I cry out in pleasure. "Y-yes!"

"That's what I thought." His thumb presses harder, pushing past the ring of muscle and I clench around him, the pleasure taking over.

He starts fucking my ass, his thumb moving in tandem with the fingers in my pussy, and I feel myself getting close to the edge. This is overwhelmingly amazing, and I can't help pushing against him.

"That's a good girl. Fuck yourself on my fingers."

I push harder, spreading my legs wider and using my knees for momentum. I'm about to fall to the other side when he pulls out.

"No! Please...I'm so close."

"Yeah," he grunts. "Except little pets who forget who they belong to don't get to come."

"Please," I whimper. "I need this...I..." Everything is too much. My head heavy, my eyes full of tears. I just need to come so the fog disappears and I can see clearly again.

Then I'll be angry. Then I'll leave. I just...

A slap on my ass brings me back. "Stay with me." I hear

the click of a plastic bottle before cold liquid spills over my ass.

"No...not there...I need..."

"You need me to fuck your beautiful cunt?" His hand in my hair now caresses my cheek. "Too bad this is a punishment."

I feel the head of his cock against my tight hole and anxiety envelops me. "It's going to hurt." I lift my head up, trying to catch his eyes.

"Alexandra," he growls. "You're going to stay still and take me, now."

He pushes in, barely his tip entering me, and my head falls against the mattress again. "Fuck," I gasp as he keeps going. "You're too big."

His hand on my lower back startles me. A reassurance I hadn't realized was possible.

"I'm halfway, baby, you're taking me so good."

"I c-can't," I mumble into the sheets, feeling myself stretch around his girth. His other hand comes under me, and he slowly presses my clit, running a circle.

"Oh God," I pant. "Please, let me come..."

"Not yet."

He stops his motion and presses further into me. Every time he pushes some more, he retreats slightly and then does it again. "Almost there," he whispers behind me. "I wish you could fucking see how good you take me."

A strange sound escapes me; muffled, mewled words I can't control. He pulls away slightly and pushes in one last time. I can feel his pubis against my ass and his balls against my pussy. I'm so full of him right now I want to cry.

"Good girl," he says with a strained voice as he sits unmoving inside me. "You did it, baby. You're taking all of me. Now stay still while I fuck you senseless."

Moving away, he thrusts back in harshly, pushing me against the bed. I cry out at the pain, but it doesn't seem to stop him, probably because he can feel my pussy getting wetter. I tremble under the violence of his thrusts. He plunges in and out with no mercy and not a single thought for me.

"You're going to feel me for fucking days," he growls. "You want to leave? You'll limp out of this fucking house with the memory of my cock driving into you."

I gasp when his fingers come to flick my clit. He presses two to the sensitive bud. "Tell me you're sorry."

"You lied," I moan, the pleasure escaping me contrasting with my accusation.

"Fuck," he grunts in anger, taking it out on my body. His movements accelerate, his fingers unrelenting on my clit, and before I come, his threatening voice pierces my ears. "You're not leaving me, Alex."

I explode, choking his dick as I feel my muscles tighten around him. He grunts as he comes inside me and keeps thrusting until he loses all his energy.

It hurts just as much when he pulls out as when he pushed in. I whimper, splayed on the bed, and utterly exhausted.

He falls on top of me, his weight crushing me as he rests on my back.

"You have to let me go," I rasp.

"I don't have to do anything." I can feel his rapid heartbeat against my back, but his voice is even as always.

"You can't sequester me forever."

I'm sticky everywhere, sweaty, his cum dripping out of me, but I could have stayed like this for days had he not betrayed me. Now all I want is to be far away from him so I can think straight and mend my broken heart.

He rolls off me and stands up. "Don't move," he throws my way as he heads for the bedroom door. "Unless you want me to tie you to the bed."

I stay still, closing my eyes, knowing his threat is to be taken seriously. He's back a minute later and I startle when I feel a warm cloth between my legs. He takes his time cleaning me before throwing the cloth to the side and massaging my back.

"You're going to sleep here tonight," he says calmly. It's like none of tonight's events ever happened. "Tomorrow," his hands knead my shoulders, "we'll talk about it again."

He helps me under the covers and slides in with me. Grabbing me by the waist, he spoons me from the back and talks low in my ear. "I don't want to hurt you, Alex," he says matter-of-factly. "But if I have to cuff you to this bed, I will. Do you understand?"

I squeeze my eyes shut, feeling the tears threatening to burst.

I nod just as I wonder how I could ever have gotten myself into such a distressing situation. I blame myself for ever trusting a man from the North Shore. Someone everyone warned me about.

"Tell me you understand," he says low.

I just want to sleep and forget all about this.

"I understand," I sniffle.

He can't keep me here forever, I tell myself on repeat while I wait for him to fall asleep. I pretend to sleep too, until I feel his breathing evening out and his hold on me loosening.

Even after that, I wait and wait...and wait. I need to get out of here, but I'm so scared any movement will wake him. After what feels like hours, I shift. The slightest movement just to test the waters.

He doesn't react, so I do it again. A bigger movement. On the third try, I manage to get out of his loose hold. I stand by the bed, the door on the other side of it.

Making my way on the tips of my toes, I reach the ajar door. I push, biting my lower lip and wishing it doesn't make a noise. The slightest squeak resonates in the room, and I freeze, hearing him take a deep breath. He shifts in bed. I squeeze my eyes shut, expecting him to see me any second now.

Nothing.

I open my eyes and watch him sprawled out on his front. He took his t-shirt off at some point, though I'm not sure when. Maybe I fell asleep while I was waiting. The last thing I remember is him sliding under the covers with his t-shirt and boxers on. My stomach twists looking at his strong back, the muscles seem bulged even in his sleep. As if he's got never-ending tension in his body.

I hurry into the hallway and find my jeans drying in the bathroom. A wave of shame engulfs me at the knowledge he's the one who had to take care of me. The attack was awful, and he ensured I was home and safe. He washed me and put me to bed.

He protected me.

Stop it, Alex.

He lied to you.

He used you.

My jeans are still damp, but I put them on anyway. I find my purse on the top of the washing machine and check that my phone is in it before heading back to the hallway.

I have to walk past his room again, and I have a near heart attack when his voice comes out.

"Letting you leave this house doesn't mean I'm allowing you to break us up."

With a hand on my chest, I turn to face him. He's sitting on his bed. In the dark, I can barely make out his form. He seems to have calmed down some if he's willing to let me leave.

"You lied to me, Xi." I watch him run a hand through his hair, even though I still can't make out his features.

Uncaring, probably. Unimpressed. Apathetic.

"I didn't have a choice." His tone portrays no regret. It never relays anything.

Tears well in my eyes. "There's always a choice," I rasp.

"Alex, I fucked up." A beat. "I know you don't believe me, but I'm sorry. I am so deeply sorry. I tried..."

I wipe my eyes before the tears fall. "When did it start?" I squeeze my eyes shut and attempt to swallow the ball stuck in my throat. Heartbreak hurts. It really does. "When did you start using me? Was it all planned? The parking lot that day? Did you have someone steal my car so you could rescue me?"

He shakes his head. "My guys stole your car, but it had nothing to do with your dad. It was just an expensive car we could get a lot of money from."

I sniffle, the rest of his plan becoming clear to me as my chest seems intent on imploding. "But bringing it back to me was part of the plan. Seducing me was the plan."

"I tried to tell y—"

"Listening, caring, and protecting me...that was all part of the plan." Oh God, saying it out loud is so much worse.

It makes it so obvious that it was a lie, because why would someone care for me so profoundly.

I gasp a breath, my heart squeezing in my swollen chest. It feels too tight in there.

"Alex—"

"You made me feel *special*!" I wail desperately. Tears fall as a sob shakes my body. I drive past the pain inside me only to add a few more whispered words. "You said you wouldn't break my heart."

"Alex, please," he goes to stand up, but I put a hand in front of me.

"Don't...don't come near me."

"I did it for my family," he says in a restrained voice. "You don't know what it's like here," he rasps. "The Kings are taking everything from us. All we have left is the little help we found. And they want something on your dad. I did it for NSC. They're everything to me."

"And I was just the plan."

"No," he grits. "Fuck." He fists the sheet in frustration. I can see he wants to get up but is respecting my wish to stay back. "Yes, it started like that. But falling for you wasn't part of the plan. Developing a conscience. The ever-growing obsession...that wasn't part of the fucking plan!"

Something hits me now when it should have weeks ago. I want to slap myself for being so blinded by him to see it.

"You never become obsessed, do you, Xi?"

He shakes his head. "I promise you I don't."

"Only twice. That's what you said."

He nods slowly, probably understanding where I'm going.

"What's the other one?"

"Alex—"

"What's the other one?" I rage. "Me and what else?" I hiss through gritted teeth.

"Taking back the North Shore," he mutters. The regret is so apparent in his voice.

Who knew that would be the first real thing I would ever hear in his platonic tone. No more indifference, only regret. It could have been love, but it's guilt.

I feel my chin tremble. "That's the problem, Xi." I take in a ragged breath. "You can't have both."

I step back to turn around, but his harsh voice stops me. "You lied to me too." His explanation comes with accusation. "I've seen enough injuries in my life to know those bruises on your body aren't from a fall, Alex."

I feel my jaw moving from side to side, clenching as I look for something to say.

I have nothing.

"I guess we're both liars," he accuses me.

"I guess it's good we're breaking up, then," I retort spitefully. I can't deny I lied. I can't be that kind of hypocrite.

"We're *not* breaking up," he growls. "Get that idea out of your fucking head."

Instead of giving in to his nonsense, I ask one last question. "Was there anything else? That you lied about." He hesitates. "Tell me now, Xi. You owe me at least that."

I can barely see him, but I notice a flash of his bright white teeth and how his tongue grazes the front top ones. It's that thing he does all the time.

"No, baby. You know everything."

He slowly stands up and takes a step toward me. Finally illuminated by the light, he stands like a god in front of the mere human I am. His beautiful chest moves slowly, inhaling the oxygen that fuels his lies. My eyes watch his abs carved in bronze. Everything in his physicality slaps you in the face with its perfection.

"Stay with me, Alex." His voice is a pleading rasp.

And I know.

I know right at this moment that I can never trust this man again.

If he weren't the epitome of immorality, he would have been my savior.

I could have loved a broken hero, but I can't love a willful villain.

"Goodbye, Xi," I huff, disappointed.

He couldn't even give me the dignity of ending things with the truth.

The second I pass his front door, the tears are unstoppable. I hurry down the street, not even knowing which way to go. The sky is orange and gray, the sun barely lighting some clouds as it rises. I need to get home and I don't know how.

Panic grips my chest, icing my veins. I'm alone. All alone on the North Shore without Xi and his protection. He ruined us, and I'm left here on my own, knowing perfectly well the danger that puts me in.

A car parks a few yards from Xi's house and a girl I recognize steps out. His stepsister.

"Alex?" The surprise in Billie's voice comes with worry. "What the hell are you doing here on your own? Where's Xi?"

I shake my head, more tears falling. "We're over," I sob. "We...I need to get home."

Everything comes crashing down. My fingers rake my hair, gripping the roots as I drop into a squat. My legs can't hold me anymore, causing me to fall onto my ass on the pavement.

"I'll go get Xi."

"No!" I shout. "I don't want to see him. Please...I don't want to."

She nods. "Okay, okay. Breathe," she says softly, lowering herself next to me. She shifts strands of hair away from my sweaty forehead. "Calm down, it's gonna be okay."

"I want to go home, please," I sniffle.

"I'll take you home. Just take a breath."

It's not a simple breath I need. It's a deep breath against Xi's hand. He would know what to do. He'd put his hand on my chest and press hard, forcing me to slow down my breathing.

Billie helps me up, opening the car door and assisting me into the passenger seat.

The drive home is filled with a heavy silence. She isn't a big talker and doesn't ask anything she doesn't want to know about. She doesn't make me feel uncomfortable, either. I'm sure she'll get her version of the story from Xi. He's her family, after all.

"Thank you," I rasp as she parks in front of Xi Ep.

I open the door, but she stops me, her voice sympathetic. "Hey." She glances away and back at me. "He can be a real dick sometimes."

"He really can," I sniffle.

I see she's looking for reassuring words, but they won't come. Instead, she grabs my purse from my hands and then my phone, unlocking it and putting her number in it. "If you need anything. Call me."

"O-okay," I nod.

"Get some rest."

Then it finally comes. What she genuinely wants to say. "I'm guessing you learned the truth."

My chin trembles when I nod.

"Look, I know what he did isn't right, and you probably don't want to hear this from me. But he was going to tell you."

"Right," I snort. "And when was he going to tell me he is part of NSC?"

"He was protecting you."

"He's a liar, Billie, and I don't think even he understands

it. *If you tell a big enough lie and tell it frequently enough, it will be believed.*"

"That's...not it."

I shake my head. "It's a quote from Walter Langer. He was a psychoanalyst..." I pause and softly close my eyes. Even *I'm* annoying myself. I open them again and smile politely. "It doesn't matter. Thank you for driving me back."

"He was sheltering you from the dangers of our lives, Alex. That's how he loves. He becomes overprotective and worries all the time. He was scared for you because once you get involved with NSC, there's no peace in your life anymore."

And don't I know it. Ethan and Elliot's threat still resonates in my head. But I won't tell Xi. They'll soon see that I'm not part of his life anymore. If I've learned something from my father, it's that you don't negotiate with terrorists. You don't give them anything. I will not be pulled into their war with Xi.

"That's how he loves," Billie repeats. "It's annoying and confusing, but that's the only way he knows how."

A chuckle escapes me, turning into a small laugh before I start cackling like a crazy woman.

"Are you...okay?"

I shake my head because the truth is I'm less than okay. "I'm so dumb. Oh God, I'm so stupid. This is *White Horse*," I hiccup between two crazy giggles. "*White Horse* by Taylor Swift. This isn't a *fucking* fairytale. How..." my voice lowers to a desperate whisper as the brutal reality extinguishes my laugh. "How funny."

Her eyes widen as she tilts her head to the side. She undoubtedly thinks I'm crazy, that I've lost it. I think I have, too. "You're the only person I know who can go from quoting psychoanalysts to quoting Taylor Swift in less than a minute."

"Yeah, well, I'm *special*. Didn't Xi tell you?" I spit out, not believing one word of it. I'm not special. I'm nothing. I give her a pinched smile. "Bye, Billie."

I shut the door, and she's off the next second. I turn back to take in the grandeur of the Xi Epsilon mansion.

Nothing feels the same. I've come to realize that my new life wasn't great because of the classes and the parties. It wasn't because of the sorority, my sisters, or even living with my best friends. It was because of Xi. The man who used me made me feel like I was worth something. I was more than an image for my father, more than the failure he calls me, more than the hits from the belt. I was not an idiot, and I was not a *stupid, worthless girl*.

Now I don't know what I am, but I need to figure it out soon. I can't be living through the men around me, waiting for them to tell me whether I'm significant or not.

I will change that. It's a promise I make to myself. But it will have to start once I don't feel like someone grabbed my heart and stabbed through it a million times before stomping on it.

26

ALEXANDRA

NEVER BREAK – Ethan Ross, Luga, Lames

"Will you stop biting your nails?" Ella whispers in front of me. "I'm trying to focus here."

"Sorry," I mumble. My English literature notebook is open right before me, but my phone rests in the middle.

I shouldn't be so focused on my phone while I'm meant to be working in the library. Except how am I meant to focus when all I can think about is Xi?

He's been texting me nonstop over the last three weeks since I found out about him using me. None of the texts I've received are reassuring. He said he would give me some time but that we weren't over. He's been asking about my days. He's been checking that I'm eating well, staying hydrated, taking breaks. He's been wanting to know about the bruises.

I didn't reply to any of those texts. He needs to know we *are* over despite anything he might believe. He can't force me into a relationship with him. That's precisely what he thinks, but it needs willingness from both sides, and I'm not willing.

No, I've got another idea in mind.

My eyes go down to my phone again, and my stomach twists. The text he sent me last night is different. It scares me.

> Xi: With or without your agreement, I will be getting the info I need, Alex. You're better coming back to me while I'm still giving you a choice.

He's got no shame. He's blatantly telling me that he will keep going with his plan even though it's what broke us up in the first place. His threat feels real, and I've been looking over my shoulder all day.

He wouldn't hurt me...right?

My stomach twists, making me feel sick. Stress has been eating at me, and I still haven't told any of my friends that I broke up with the man they told me would break my heart. Xi is a dangerous man, and yet my body still won't let me get over him. I can't help but touch myself to the memories of the things he did to me. I imagine other scenarios of him degrading me and making me love him for it.

"I'm going to deserve a drink after this," Peach groans as she keeps typing a science essay on her laptop.

"I'm so excited for tonight's party. Ready for Halloween," Ella says excitedly.

Peach stops typing. "You know it's going to be the worst night, right?"

"We're pledging by midnight, and that's all I care about." Ella smiles as she picks up the book she's reading again. "No more kissing anyone's ass."

"I have to admit that'll be nice."

They both turn to me, expecting a reaction from me too. "Agreed." My eyes dart down to my phone. "I think I need a night out," I sigh.

"How's Don Juan?" Peach asks.

I haven't even told them that I learned the truth about Xi being part of NSC. I can't imagine admitting he's been using me to get to my dad. That I was just a means to an end. Peach loathes the guy, and I don't need to put oil on the fire. Ella would go into protection mode and not leave my side.

I just want things to become simpler.

A small smile pulls at the corner of my mouth. Things will be better soon. I know it.

Ella grabs her phone, reads a text, and lets out a long huff. "I am so confused as to why my dad insists on having his birthday party at your house," she tells me.

I shrug my shoulders. "What's wrong with our house?"

"I wanted some neutral grounds so I could invite anyone I want," she admits.

"Ella, ninety-five percent of Stoneview will be at that party. It's not a party anymore, it's a festival. Who could you possibly want to invite that's not already on the list?" Peach mocks her.

"I don't know!" she defends. "Some cool people and not just Stoneview's finest. This is going to be the most boring festival in history. I want to have fun. Sexy fun."

"It's your dad's birthday," I mumble, reading over Xi's last text again. This is too distracting. "You can't have sexy fun at your dad's birthday."

"Luke is inviting all his friends like it's *his* birthday," she groans. "Chris is going to be there."

Peach's eyes light up, and she sits straighter in her chair. "And Rose? Is Rose White going to be there?"

Ella rolls her eyes. "Yes, Peach. Rose is going to be there."

A dreamy smile spreads on our best friend's face. "God, she's so hot."

"And taken," Ella snorts. "*So* taken."

"I missed my chance when we were in high school. She was in her total hoe phase. *That's* when I should have shot my shot."

"Can we circle back to my problem for a second?" she huffs.

"Huh?" Peach seems to come back to reality. "Yeah, sorry. Chris."

"He's going to come with his girlfriend. I don't want to be the loser who's not seeing someone when my ex is coming to my dad's birthday with practically a top model."

"You know what she looks like?" I question in surprise.

"Yes, of course, I know what she looks like. Who doesn't check their ex's current girlfriend?"

Peach and I eye each other. "Everyone?" Peach says as she tilts her head.

"Chester doesn't have a girlfriend," she says as if accusing me. "And you don't have an ex, just countless one-night stands and a man at your feet."

"Wren and me are not a thing." Peach's eyes narrow into slits.

"Wren and *I*," I mumble to myself.

"No one likes it when you do that, Alex," Peach huffs.

"Speak properly, then," I say, still looking at my phone.

"Oh my God," Peach cheers. "My baby is finally growing a backbone."

Yeah, because of the man who broke my heart, I don't say.

"Anyway, Wren and I aren't a thing. Period."

"Or so you say," Ella jumps back in. "But if I learn that

you have seen his penis and not shared the juicy details with us, I'm going to be so mad, Peach. *So* mad. The man is a god, and we deserve to know what a god's penis looks like."

"Please stop saying penis," I groan.

"What's wrong with the word penis?"

"It's weird," Peach agrees with me. "Just stop saying it."

"Do you prefer cock?"

"Yeah," Peach answers casually.

My fingers come to press my temple. "Nope. I beg you two to just stop."

"Dick," Ella says in a fake sultry voice.

"Hard shaft," Peach adds, imitating her as they both stare at me from across the table.

"Ding-a-ling," the other squeaks as she tries to keep her giggles down.

"I hate you both," I whine as my head falls against my notebook.

"God, you're such a saint," Peach laughs. "Are you sure you've seen Xi's love plunger?"

"Love plunger?" I choke as my head snaps back up. "You guys are going to make me puke."

They both explode into laughter as I shake my head at them, unimpressed.

"Oh my God," Ella gasps. "I know what I'm going to do." She points at me. "You're going to invite Xi to the party..."

"What?"

"...and you're going to tell him to bring a friend. Set me up on a blind date or something."

I freeze, mouth open for a few seconds. "Oh, I'm sorry, El's. Xi...he, um, he can't come. I already offered."

"Aw," she pouts. "That's so unfortunate. I guess I'm going to be the single ex, then."

"I'll ask him again," I lie. "And see if he wants to bring a friend. But I really can't promise anything."

"Thank you. You're the best."

I feel sick lying to my friends, but I'm nursing a heartbreak, and I don't need their pity or life lessons right now. No, I need to take back control.

"Let's go home and get ready," Peach says excitedly. "I need a fucking drink."

My two friends start packing their stuff while I look at my untouched work. "You guys go. I barely did anything. I'll stay another hour."

In the end, I stay more than two hours before I'm finally caught up on my work. It's dark outside by the time I exit the library. I'm not worried. The campus is well-lit and always alive with many students. I can walk back to Xi Ep easily.

As soon as I pass the library door, I feel someone's gaze on me. In the shadow near the entrance, some girl is smoking and watching me. I don't recognize her until she steps into the light.

Zara walks toward me.

"Hi, Alex," she says before taking another drag of her cigarette. "That was a long time you spent in there. Very studious."

"Um, hi." I rack my brain, trying to understand what she's doing here. I don't like this woman. Not now that I know she was encouraging Xi to use me all along. Even the night he told them he wanted to stop it all, she insisted he went through with everything.

My narrowed gaze does nothing to deter her. She takes a

puff and turns her head to the side to blow out the smoke. "Xi asked me to keep an eye on you."

I feel my eyebrows lift to my hairline. "Keep an eye on me? What am I? A ward?"

Ignoring my sarcasm, she adds. "He also said he didn't want you to go to the Halloween party at the frat house tonight."

"Is this a joke? I don't need a babysitter. And if he doesn't want me to go to a party, he can damn well tell me himself. He's had no problem texting me threats."

I readjust my bag on my shoulder. "I'm sorry he wasted your time, but I don't need any of this. It's...it's ridiculous. Xi and I aren't together anymore."

"Look," she says more seriously. "Xi can't be here, and he knows how bad frat parties get on Halloween night. I can't make you do anything, and I can't hold you hostage at your house, but what I can do is strongly suggest you listen to him."

"Okay," I smile sweetly. "Well, tell Xi that I wasn't born yesterday, and I know how to take care of myself. For fuck's sake, how old does he think I am? Oh, and also tell him that if he doesn't stop harassing me, I'll block his number. In fact..." I grab my phone from my bag and go to Xi's number. He's really done it. He's pissed me off. I block his contact and look back at Zara. "Done."

"You know he changes phones so often that's totally useless."

"I don't care. I'll block all of them."

I stalk across the lawn in the direction I take to go home. What a joke.

"No, he didn't," Ella chokes on her drink. I just told her about the Zeta Nu pledge named Duncan, who told me his final dare was to get a picture of a girl sucking his dick and that he had kindly offered for that girl to be me.

I refused. Of course.

An hour ago, my two best friends and I finally pledged to Xi Epsilon, and we were invited to party with Zeta Nu to celebrate. It's a relief to finally be at a party and not have to worry about anything I say or do. We're all wearing Halloween costumes, and I went for a dead Barbie. I'm wearing a vinyl fuchsia skirt with a white t-shirt that has *Barbie* written across my boobs. I've tied my blonde hair up in a ponytail and I'm wearing my fuchsia-colored lipstick. My usual Gucci bag is hanging over my shoulder, perfecting the Barbie appearance.

"That *Barbie* writing stretches so far across your double D's it's hard to focus," Peach admits before taking a sip of her drink.

"Thank you," I laugh. I know it's a compliment from her.

"Hello girls," someone says behind us.

Chester and Wren come into view. My mouth flattens when I see Chester's splint. We haven't spoken since the whole Xi ordeal. He never reached out to me to apologize and there's absolutely no way I will make the first step.

Wren wraps an arm around Peach's shoulders, but she shrugs him away. It seems they have unresolved issues as well.

"Guys, you're looking at three official Xi Ep girls. Where's our congratulations," Ella cheers.

Chester puts his drink in the air, and we follow. "To the three hottest Xi Ep girls I've ever seen," he slurs. He downs his drink and looks around. "I think I need another one."

"Damn, you're *drunk* drunk," Peach says.

He shrugs his shoulders. "It's the last night of initiations. Gotta make the best of it."

"I heard every guy has a mission to accomplish tonight before you get to pledge. What's yours?" Ella eyes the guys as she takes another sip, her curious stare making me giggle.

It's Wren who answers. "Sorry, we can't tell you. It's a secret."

"No way." I give him a friendly slap on the shoulder. "You can tell us. It's *us*."

They both shake their heads. "We're not gonna compromise our initiations for your pretty eyes," Chester laughs.

He points at me, his finger touching my chest. "I'm talking about you. *Your* pretty eyes."

A hand comes to slap his away. "Do you want another broken wrist?" Peach scolds him. "You guys are *exes*. Stop hitting on her."

I smile at my friend, saying a silent thank you.

"I don't see her boyfriend anywhere," Chester shrugs.

My drink suddenly tastes bitter. My boyfriend isn't my boyfriend anymore.

"The guy already almost killed you. You don't want to know what he'll do if he sees your hands on her again," Ella teases.

"Killed me. *Right*," he snorts. "And what about my hands? What's he going to do if he's not here, huh? What if I put my hands like this?" He presses both his palms against my chest, and I roll my eyes.

I open my mouth to tell him to move them, except another voice comes from behind me.

"Then I break every single one of your fingers."

I startle when I feel a possessive hand at the back of my

neck. Looking up, I catch the daggers Xi is throwing at Chester.

"He's joking." I force a chuckle out of me and glance around at all my friends.

"No. I'm not. Alex, I need to talk to you, privately." His indifferent tone reminds me of everything I hate about him.

I force a smile, even as his tugging at the back of my neck doesn't leave me much choice anyway. "I'll be back in a minute," I tell everyone as he hauls me away.

"She won't," he throws as we leave.

Going through the entirety of the ground floor, he takes me down the stairs and into the basement. It's a gigantic game room that must be out of bounds tonight because no one is here. He closes the door and locks it behind him before turning to me.

I'm alone with Xi in a locked room.

Instantly, the temperature of my body rises. I've spent every single night this week touching myself to the thought of the depraved things this man does to me.

"What did I say about the party, Alexandra?" His voice takes that shade of darkness that makes my lower stomach flutter.

Standing my ground, I cross my arms over my chest. "Well, *you* didn't say anything. Apparently, you need a messenger to tell me not to go to a party. What the hell did you think? We're broken up, Xi. I have no reason to listen to you. I don't care what you want me to do or not."

"I told you to do something, and you refused. You know what happens after that."

"No." I stomp my foot. God, how old am I?

He chuckles and licks his lower lip. "Get on your knees."

"What?" Uncrossing my arms, I take a step away from him.

"I told you to make the right choice while you still had one. The clock has stopped ticking, Alex. Game over."

"I don't...I...we're *over*."

"I think I already told you how I felt about that. Now get on your knees and start thinking of how you're going to apologize for disobeying. I want to see some tears with your sorry's."

Shaking my head, I put my arms in front of me as he steps closer.

"Don't...Xi, we're at a party."

He's wearing black jeans and a black t-shirt today rather than his usual cargo pants. My eyes go to his belt as he unbuckles it. I notice he's still wearing the bracelet I made for him, which annoys me. "What-what are you doing?"

"I suggest cutting your losses and doing what you're told." He slides the belt out of its hoops and my eyes widen.

"Xi..." My hips hit the pool table behind me, my bag falling off my shoulder as I freeze. The last thing I want right now is to end up on the table while he's advancing toward me with his belt.

When he reaches me, his hand flies to my ponytail, wrapping it around his fist and forcing me to gaze up. His lips crash against mine and my hands go to grab his t-shirt. He ravages my mouth with passion as our tongues entangle and my body relaxes into his hold.

I feel his other hand around my neck, but I don't understand what he's doing until we separate, too taken by our embrace. I only realize what he did when he lets go of me, retreats back, and I'm forced to follow.

"What the—" I choke when something tightens around my neck. Looking at his hand, I notice the end of his belt in it and follow the leather to my... "Xi!" I shriek as my hands go to my neck.

He pulls again and, this time, I fall to my knees. "I'm going to kill you," I cough. It's too tight for me to slip my fingers underneath, and I panic when I see him take a step back again. "Stop!" I fall forward, catching myself with my palms.

"On your hands and knees for me again, baby. What a good girl."

I look up, squinting at him. "I hate you. God, I hate you right now."

"I love to finally see some fight in you. But don't think that's how you should be apologizing for disobeying. Try again." He pulls, walking backward, and I'm forced to crawl after him.

"Stop moving...it's tight," I cough again.

"Crawl quicker, then."

"Xi," I cry out, choking and in need of air. "Stop, I get it. I'm sorry!"

I hate myself for apologizing right now, but he's not giving me much of a choice.

"Not nearly enough."

He turns around, showing me the back of his legs as he pulls some more. The room is enormous. It's a game room with a pool table in the middle and multiple vintage arcade games. It's so gigantic it has its own bowling alley. Xi steps on it and I'm forced to crawl after him.

"Stop," I pant as I attempt to accelerate so I don't choke. "Please...I'm sorry. I'm sorry for coming to the party."

"That's right, you are. Keep going."

He's not even looking at me as he walks the length of the mini bowling alley. "I should have listened and stayed home."

"What about those texts you ignored for the past *three. Fucking. Weeks*?"

"We're broken up!"

A quick yank and I cough. "Fine! I'm sorry for that too. *Please, stop.*"

Getting to the end, he finally stops and turns around. His eyes are dark with anger and his jaw clenched. "I've been attending these parties for much longer than you have, Alex. I've been selling to rich kids for as long as I can remember. These parties aren't safe. I don't want you attending them when I'm not here. Is that clear?"

I nod as I try to sit back on my haunches, but he pulls harshly again, bringing me right back to my hands and knees.

"I *said*, is. That. Clear?"

"Yes!" I drag in some much-needed air.

"Tell me how sorry you are for putting yourself in danger."

"I'm sorry for putting myself in danger," I mumble.

Still holding the belt, he steps behind me and runs his hand against my tight, fuchsia vinyl skirt.

"Do you often dress so sexy for parties without me?" he growls as he pulls my skirt up and to my waist.

I wanted to flirt tonight. I wanted to get hit on by some guy who *isn't* Xi. But I can't tell him that.

"I-I...It's just a costume."

"Good," he approves, to my surprise. "I want everyone to see what they can't have." He grabs my thong and pulls it all the way to my knees. "Want to tell me why crawling for me on a leash makes you so wet?"

Squeezing my eyes closed, I bite my lower lip as I shake my head. He slaps my wet seam, making me moan in the process.

Walking back in front of my head, he smiles down at

me. "You're such a dirty slut, Alex," he chuckles. "Sit back on your knees. You're gonna give me some tears."

I sit back, looking up at him as my hands come to rest on my thighs. He undoes his jeans and pulls out his cock.

"You get wet when I treat you like a bitch in heat. I get hard degrading you. We're meant for each other, baby. Why would you want to take that away from us?" His tip comes to trace my lips, wet with precum. When he retreats slightly, I don't control my tongue as it licks my lips. My eyes flutter shut, and a short moan escapes me, as if I just tasted a gourmet meal. My eyes widen when I realize what I've just done, and I look up only to see the corner of his lips tipping up.

"Open."

I don't hesitate. My lips spread wide, and I push my tongue out as his cock slides inside my mouth. I wrap my lips around his shaft, my wetness doubling the second I taste him in my mouth.

Instead of grabbing me by the hair to control my pace, he wraps the belt multiple times around his fist, shortening the leash. With more control around my neck, he pulls and releases, helping me find the rhythm he wants.

"You've been a bad girl," he rasps. "Take me deep and show me how sorry you are."

I press harder against him and swallow him. I don't know where the eagerness comes from, but I feel his cock hitting the back of my throat, and more pleasure pools between my legs. I moan around him, only cut short by him tightening the belt around my neck.

He holds me tightly and pushes harder inside me. I wish I could say panic seizes me when he does so, but I'm only too happy to swallow him further. I relish in the spittle running down my mouth and onto my chin.

"I want that cute nose against my skin, baby."

I start to choke, needing to breathe. I try to move away, but he yanks on the leash. "More. Show me you want to be forgiven and take my dick deeper."

The moment my nose touches his stomach, I feel a sense of pride even though tears are running down my face, and I'm in dire need of air.

"Stay," he says the same way he would a dog.

Or a bitch.

"Good girl. Now tell me how sorry you are."

My eyes flicker up, but I can't really see him. He must sense my confusion and adds, "Say it, Alexandra. Say you're sorry with your mouth and throat full of my cock."

I moan from his words only. I shift, pressing my calf between my legs.

I say I'm sorry, not making any sense whatsoever since the sounds get stuck down my throat. He throws his head back, hissing as he feels the vibration through his cock.

"Again."

The tears are running down my face now. I feel clumps of mascara sticking to my lower eyelashes. I repeat that I'm sorry.

"Yes, baby. I can feel you are."

He pulls back suddenly and thrusts back in.

"Do you have any idea how worried I was? How desperate I am to keep you safe?"

Again and again, he fucks my face as I become increasingly desperate for him to touch me everywhere. Only he doesn't touch me. He just holds onto the belt until he finally explodes in my mouth. He pulls out, and I look around with wide eyes, needing somewhere to spit.

Understanding what I'm trying to do, he pulls me

toward him and slams his other against my mouth. "Swallow every single fucking drop, dirty bitch."

My eyes squeeze shut as I force myself to swallow the thickness in my mouth.

He finally lets me go and I fall back, lying on the polished floor of the bowling alley. I'm out of breath, dizzy from the face fucking, but all I can think about is feeling him between my legs.

"Xi," I whine as my hand comes to my pussy. I can't help but start rubbing my clit through the messy wetness. I watch desperately as he zips up his jeans, and I shake my head. "No, no, please."

Lowering himself, he comes on top of me, grabbing my hand away from my pussy and then the other before holding my wrists against the floor above my head. He brings a leg between mine and presses his knee against my pussy.

"Oh my God," I moan.

"Do you need to come, baby?"

"Yes...yes, please," I pant.

"Is my little slut desperate for my dick in her perfect pussy?"

"Yes," I groan as I shamelessly rub myself against his knee.

"You're making a big stain on my jeans, Alex," he mocks me. "Do you not care how fucking desperate you are right now?"

I shake my head, closing my eyes as I spread my legs wider to feel more of the harsh denim against my clit.

He lets me rub myself like a wanton bitch for several more seconds. I feel my breath shorten and my muscles tighten.

"Oh my God, Xi...Xi..." I moan.

Just as I'm about to explode, his knee disappears, making me shriek in frustration.

"What are you doing?" I scream at him. "I was about to come!"

He lets go of me and stands up. "You're being punished, remember? Bad girls don't get to come."

I scramble up, practically falling on my face as my thong slides to my ankles. I catch myself on Xi, holding his t-shirt tightly. "You can't leave me like this." The belt is dangling from my neck as I press myself against him. The very simple act of my hard nipples against his chest makes me melt. "Please..."

He puts a soft hand against my cheek, wiping my tears with his thumb. "Get back on your knees."

I do so at the speed of light, getting on my knees before him like he's my god.

"Open." He grabs the hanging belt and puts it flat between my teeth. "Bite." I execute without an ounce of hesitation.

He straightens up and takes a step back. "Now put your hands up by your shoulders like a begging puppy."

I squeeze my eyes shut as I follow the humiliating order. He truly is treating me like his pet, and instead of fighting back, I can feel my need to come doubling.

"Good girl," he says with pride. "Now stay." I open my eyes to find him grabbing my bag. He comes back with it and brings out my Polaroid camera.

"Don't move," he murmurs as he puts the camera to his right eye and takes a picture of me. It prints, and he starts shaking it. "Fuck, you're so hot," he sighs as he looks at the picture of me.

"Xi," I groan around the belt in my mouth. "Please..."

He puts the picture in the pocket of his jeans, the camera back in my bag, and comes to stroke my head.

"You'll come when I say you come, Alex. And that's not now. I want you to spend the evening with your thong soaking wet and the need to rub against my leg like the bitch you are. Then maybe you'll act like a good little pet next time I give you an order."

I whimper, pressing my head against his hand. "Don't do this to me." The belt falls from my mouth as I say this. "Please."

He lowers on his haunches. "This is what happens when you try to leave me, baby. I make you crawl back and beg. Try to say we're broken up again and watch me make you do this in front of everyone next time."

He wipes my hair away from my face. "If I catch you touching yourself before I allow it, this punishment will feel like nothing. Understood?"

I nod, squeezing my eyes as tears of desperation fall down my cheeks.

"Good girl." He undoes the belt from around my neck. "Sort yourself out. Your friends are waiting for you."

27

XI

Satin Black - iamjakehill

Watching Alex squirm the whole fucking night is the best thing this year so far. Every now and then, she throws me desperate looks that she alternates with a threatening gaze. She's got the most gorgeous eyes I've ever seen. It takes all of me not to give in and bend her over the kitchen counter right now. But I can't because I'm trying to teach her a fucking lesson. I can't believe she came to this party after I warned her not to. I've seen more crime going on the last day of frat initiations than on the North Shore.

Maybe not.

But I know they all get a fucked-up dare that defies imagination. I've seen them slipping drugs in women's drinks. I've seen someone come in a cup before mixing it with a drink and downing it just to be part of Zeta Nu.

I don't want Alex around uncontrollable men. I don't have the fucking time to murder someone at the moment.

Vito Luciano is on Emma's back constantly, meaning she's on mine. And, of course, the fact that I set the brothers' house on fire isn't helping with the tension. NSC is getting more money, slowly gaining back power, and the Kings are scared to death. The moment I bring something to Vito, we'll be free to finish the Kings once and for all without any repercussions. People are counting on me.

See, the thing is: I thought if Alex knew about the plan and broke up, that it would be it. It turns out I don't *have* to let her go. I don't have to do anything. I told her to be careful when I get obsessed. That it wasn't a good thing.

When someone belongs to you entirely, they can't escape.

She doesn't see it now, but she will.

My eyes go back to Alexandra. She's talking actively with her two best friends, throwing hands in the air and bending over in laughter.

She's so fucking beautiful when she laughs. The way her hazel eyes light up with gold and her perfect teeth all show. Her friend Ella adds something, making her laugh more, and she lets out the cutest snort before putting her hands on her mouth as they all cackle.

I grab the money the frat boy hands me and pocket it before going to my gorgeous girl. The fact that she thought she could get rid of me amuses me. Doesn't she understand that this thing between us doesn't end. Ever.

I put my hand on her lower back, slowly tracing her spine with my fingertips. I feel her tensing under me before I wrap my hand around the back of her neck.

"Hi, Xi," Ella says cheerily. "How are you? How's business?"

Ella talking to me in her usual welcoming voice tells me one thing for sure; Alex hasn't told her friends about the reason I dated her in the first place. And she hasn't told them she *broke up* with me. Or tried to.

"Booming," I answer deadpan.

In truth, I have no interest whatsoever in talking to Alex's friend. If it was up to me right now, I'd whisk her away from this party and straight to my house.

But I'm fucking working.

"Nice." Ella smiles brightly. That perfected Stoneview smile that she dons to not let any tension in the conversation.

Peach looks at my hand at the back of Alex's neck and throws me a dark look that I happily send back.

"I think you should know I don't agree with this bullshit relationship," she tells me sincerely.

"Peach!" Alex scolds her. "Please, not now," she groans. Alex tries to dislodge my hand, but I tighten my grip.

She doesn't say anything. She could push me away, tell her friends I'm an asshole, and tell everyone what I've done.

That's the problem with Alex. She hates confrontation. She would rather suffer and go through a horrible moment than raise her voice and protect herself. She's scared of repercussions. I don't know why, but I'll find out. And if it has anything to do with those bruises on her body, people will die. Slowly and painfully.

"When then?" Peach says, cocking an eyebrow at my girl. Her eyes snap back to me. "I swear to God if you hurt her...you're so fucking done, North Shore boy."

I feel the corner of my lips pulling up. If only she knew the things I've done to her friend. My obsession with Alex has been unhealthy for a very long time.

My phone vibrates in my pocket, and I check it to see a message from Sam. Technically, Sam is my brother's boyfriend. Before that, he was a hitman who chose no side on the North Shore. He completes his jobs and always stays quiet. I move bodies for him from time to time. Good money, plus I'm discreet. Our relationship is based on me making his victims disappear, and then us pretty much ignoring each other at family dinners. And so right now, he's definitely not texting me to talk about Friday's dinner with my mom.

"Anyway!" Alex changes topics, looking for something to say. "I'm excited for your dad's birthday party, Ella."

Ella fakes a pout. "Xi, it's a real shame you won't be able to come. You could have seen Alex's house as well! I would have loved to see you there. And one of your friends. But hey," she extends her hand to squeeze my biceps, then lets it fall back against her thigh, "next time." She twists her mouth, looking at my arm again, and mouths *sorry* to Alex as if now realizing her gesture was awkward.

But I don't believe Alex suddenly tensing up has anything to do with Ella touching me. No. She just realized she fucked up by bringing up the topic.

Alex has lied to her friends that she had invited me to a birthday party at her house and that I said I couldn't come. Fuck, this girl will never see the end of her punishment.

The little minx didn't want me to come to her house. Of course not, I betrayed her, and she now knows I want dirt on her dad.

What a perfect opening I have here. Poor Alex. She honestly thought she could keep me away, but I did warn her I would get what I wanted. I regret using and lying to her, but what needs to be done remains the same. It's understandable, though unfortunate, that she doesn't want to get on board.

"Didn't Alex tell you? I moved some stuff around and can come now." Alex freezes in my grasp and peers up at me.

"Y-you...you can?"

"Anything to spend time with you."

"You guys are just too cute," Ella beams.

"I'll bring a friend, Ella."

"You will?" Alex repeats.

"Yeah. I'll be there." I look at the two other girls. "I gotta go. I'll see you at that party. Can't. Fucking. Wait." I lower my mouth to Alex's ear, pretending to give her a kiss. "Isn't it just *so* hard to get rid of me?"

Letting go of her, I disappear into the crowd as I hear her call my name.

"Xi...Xi!" I make it to the front lawn before she catches up with me. "Xi, wait!"

I stop, turning around so quickly she bumps right into my chest. She takes a step back, catching her breath. "You can't come," she pants.

"Why not?" I ask as if the answer isn't pretty fucking obvious.

"We're done!" she rages at me. "Stop...*stop* this pretending that we're still together. You are not coming to my house." Her eyes go to my wrist. "And give me back my bracelet!"

I stride forward, our chests touching. "*I'm* pretending?" I snarl. "Who's the one who hasn't told her little friends? Who still gets wet like a little slut for me? Admit it, Alex, you don't *want* to break up. You're hurt. You feel betrayed. I get it, and I'm sorry. I will keep apologizing until you understand that I fell for you because of who you are, not because of what I needed from you. But we're not ending this. Don't you get it? No matter where you go, no matter what you do, no matter who you're with...you are *never* getting rid of me," I say through clenched teeth. "And it's *my* bracelet. You made it for *me*."

"I made it for the man who wasn't a liar. I know why you

want to come to that party, and there's no way I'm allowing you anywhere near my dad. All you want is to destroy him. You want to take my family down."

I run a hand across my face and close my eyes for a second, trying to keep my cool. Bringing a hand to her chin, I tilt her head up.

"All I *want* is to keep the people I love safe. I'm not the one who wants shit on your dad. That sort of info is held for blackmail by men much more powerful than North Shore petty gangs, believe me. It won't hurt your family, but it might save mine. I don't care about your dad and his politics. I care about the North Shore and who it belongs to."

"How can you say you care about your town when all you do is partake in destroying it? Instead of trying to take it back from the Kings just so you can instill more terror, try to make a change for once."

Her words hurt more than anything else she's thrown my way since she learned about everything.

Probably because they're true.

"You don't know shit about what goes on on our side of the river. Don't tell me what I should or shouldn't do about it. From where you stand, in your Stoneview castle, we're not even in your field of vision."

"Aurel Kolnai was a political theorist and philosopher..."

"Not now, Alex," I groan.

"He said..."

My tongue darts to the front of my teeth before I attempt to cut her off again. "I don't want to hear your random facts." A lie. I fucking love her random facts, but this is getting too much. There's only so long I can spend without going to my knees and begging her to take me back.

"*It is bad enough to persevere in barbarism; it is worse to relapse into it; but worst of all is consciously to seek it out.*"

My phone vibrates and I know Sam's getting impatient.

"I have to go," I tell her. "I'll be at that birthday party whether you want me there or not."

I turn around, but her sharp tone stops me. "And then what? You show up. You try your best to find something on my dad—which I'm sure won't be too hard, he *is* a politician after all—and then? Once you've destroyed my family, we elope into the sunset? Do you really think I will ever forgive you?"

"We're not breaking up," I repeat for the millionth time this week.

"Then I hope you enjoy having a girlfriend who hates you."

"I can change that."

"Not if you keep hurting me."

My tongue grazes my two front teeth as I try to collect myself. "I won't be hurting you again," I rasp. "Just have the tiniest faith in me, for fuck's sake."

She snorts and glances away. "Liar."

My phone vibrates again, clearly a call this time.

"I have to go," I murmur.

"Of course," she rasps. "Make sure you don't have a conversation with me for too long if you don't like what I say. And you're the one who tells me to confront my problems rather than retreat."

My phone rings again, and instead of fighting for us, I walk away.

"What?" I snap as I make my way to my car.

"*Can you write down an address?*" Sam's monotone voice asks me over the phone.

From where I'm parked, I can see Alex wiping tears and

turning around. She crosses the front lawn and disappears to the side of the house.

I'm a fucking coward. I leave her so I can go take care of other people's problems because I can't face mine. I'm so hellbent on giving Vito what he wants that I'm letting down the woman of my dreams and only apologizing about it.

Apologies are not enough. I should know that.

I have to make a choice—Alex or taking back the North Shore. I can't have one without the other. She will never forgive me if I manage to get something on her dad and bring it to Vito.

I run a hand across my face.

I'm a liar. I'm a con. I'm a bad person.

But the only way I can change is by starting with the person I love. Because for her, at least, it will be worth it.

I'm going to tell her the truth. Like I wanted that night by the river. I wanted to tell her everything before she gave me her virginity. I wanted to risk ruining it all so I could start fixing it.

It's a strange feeling to finally want to consciously change something. How many times does one *promise* themselves they'll stop doing something unhealthy?

I'll wake up early tomorrow.

I'll start exercising.

We do a disservice to ourselves when we betray our own will to change. We instill a pattern of failing our own thoughts.

I'll see my mom more often than once a week. Sorry, *Mama*, that I only show up when you ask me.

I'll stop fighting at the warehouse just to get the cheap satisfaction of kicking Kings' asses. But there I am, twice a week, just for the thrill of it. Just to keep the war going.

I'll show Alex I can be a good man. And yet I keep hurting her by choosing the North Shore over her.

"*Xi,*" Sam's British accent resonates from my phone. "*Can you write down an address?*" he repeats. Our code for *can you move that body away from the address I'm giving you.*

I'll tell Alex the truth.

I need to tell Alex the truth.

I take a deep breath. "No."

"*What's keeping you so busy?*"

"I have to win back the woman I love," I huff.

I hear his low chuckle on the other end of the line. "*I've been there. Good luck.*"

He hangs up, and I stare back at the lawn. Alexandra fucking Delacroix.

I walk back to the Xi Ep house in long strides. Ignoring the front door, I go to the side of the house, where I saw her walk. There are no lights at all there, and only the bass of the music can be heard.

Walking along the wall and through the darkness, I try to listen for anything. The door to access the backyard is locked, but I didn't see Alex walk back to the front lawn. She has to be here somewhere.

"Stop." It's a whimper, the sound coming from somewhere in the bushes. I would recognize Alex's voice among a million. I would recognize her whisper in a storm and her cries for help across the ocean.

No one hurts her. Not unless it's me.

"Just let me fucking do it," someone snarls.

"I told you no earlier—ow! *Stop*...let me g—"

"It's just a dare. Just fucking do it."

Shoving between two bushes, I find one of the frat boys with his jeans down and his cock peeking out of his boxers. He has a phone in his left hand, pointing it at Alex. He's holding her by her ponytail, keeping her on her knees in front of him. It's hard to see her face in the dark, but it's easy to hear her cries.

"Xi," she gasps.

Without needing me to say anything, the guy swiftly lets her go. She stumbles back, trying to stand on shaking legs and running my way.

"Let's go," she whimpers as she grabs my hand.

I don't move, of course. She grips me harder, but there's nothing she can do that would make me follow.

"What's your name?" I ask him, my tone depicting the storm to come.

He gulps as he hurries to pull his jeans back up. "Duncan."

I nod. "Well, Duncan." I walk toward him, watching him tremble as he attempts to widen his stance and make himself look bigger. "Why don't you start thinking of the words you want written on your headstone. I'll make sure to let your family know."

Before he can react, I jump him. Holding the back of his head, I grab the phone in his hand.

"Help!" he screams.

"Do you want to film my girl giving you a blowjob, Duncan?" I seethe.

"I didn't—It's just a dare," he cries out.

"Xi, stop!"

"Too fucking nice, Alex," I snarl. "You're *way* too fucking nice and that'll be the end of you."

"Please, I don't want you to get in trouble."

Of course, that's the only problem. Why would she care about being sexually assaulted when all that matters are others, not herself.

"Alex," I say as I reinforce my hold on Duncan when he

tries to shrug me off. "I don't know why you think you don't deserve to be protected. I don't know why you aim to make yourself small and pliable. To say yes with a big smile when you want to scream no...but no more." I look straight into her eyes, holding Duncan's phone with a deadly grip. "You matter, baby. Your feelings matter, your opinion matters. *Your. Happiness. Fucking. Matters.*"

Before she can answer anything, I crash Duncan's phone against his skull. Alex's shriek is really just a background noise through the anger pounding in my head. Once, twice, three times before the object splits in my hand and he starts to lose consciousness.

"Hey, hey," I slap him. "Stay awake." His head rolls from side to side as he uses me to try and stand up. "We're not done. You like playing games? Here's your dare: Pay the fucking consequences of touching my girl."

"Oh my God," I hear Alex gasp. "Xi, stop."

Grabbing Duncan by his t-shirt, I drag him through the bushes again while he gargles something that sounds like *please, leave me alone.* Alex runs after me and tries to grip my arm, but I shrug her off. She attempts to keep up with my pace as I drag the fucker to my car.

"What are you doing?" she panics. "Xi, please." Her breathing accelerates as she jogs after me, "Don't hurt him."

"Too late."

"Don't hurt him *any more*. He could sue you."

"Dead men can't sue, cupcake."

"What?" she squeaks. "No. No, no, no."

I open the bed of my truck and throw him inside. He groans and tries to sit back up just as I close the tailgate. Alex is looking around us, checking if anyone is witnessing my current kidnapping.

"Stop this," she hisses. "Taking matters into your own

hands could get you in a lot of trouble. Prison being one of them."

I flip around, grab her jaw tightly and bring her closer. "Listen to me," I seethe. "I didn't kill Chester because you said it was nothing. I don't know who gave you these bruises, so I'm being good about it. I think, all in all, I've been pretty fucking lenient." I take a deep breath, begging my brain not to flip a switch and kill everyone in my way. "But here and now, I'm swearing to God, Alex, that this piece of shit is not surviving the night."

"You can't do that!" she shouts at me. "You don't take justice in your own hands on the south bank, Xi. I mean it."

"Then I guess it's a good thing Duncan will be sentenced on the North Shore."

I let her go and walk back to the front of my truck. She's right next to me the moment I sit down, right in her place in the passenger seat.

"Don't do this. Please, please, I don't want blood on your hands. Not for me."

I start the car and turn to her, adrenaline and fury running through my veins. "Alexandra," I say softly.

In the dark of the night, her hazel eyes look black. All I can see is her fuchsia lipstick and her porcelain skin.

"I think I'm in love with you, baby," I say before pulling away.

28

ALEXANDRA

ARSON – Chri$tian Gate$

I think I'm in love with you, baby.

My heart is racing quicker than Xi on the streets of the North Shore. How can he do this to me? How can he tell me the words I've been dying to hear while at the same time kidnapping a man?

He could have told me when we were together instead of lying. He could have told me when I found out instead of keeping me hostage in his room. He could have told me he loved me instead of *forbidding* me to attend a party. God, I hate that he was right about this party, that he was right in trying to protect me.

"I wish you'd told me before," I rasp. "Before...all of this."

"I have."

"No, you've not," I fight back. "I've been waiting for those three words, Xi. I would have known if you'd said them. I would have remembered."

"I have, Alex. You just didn't listen." His eyes dart to me, then back to the road. "Every time I showed up because you weren't taking care of yourself, I was saying I love you. When I kept you away from NSC by not telling you I was part of it, I was telling you I love you. When I kicked you out of the warehouse so the Kings wouldn't find out you're my weakness, I said I *love* you. I told you not to go to a party that could be unsafe for you, that was me saying I. *Fucking*. Love. You." His teeth are clenched, his words strained, but I hear every single one of them.

My chest constricts as I remember Billie's words. *He's overprotective, that's how he loves. It's annoying and confusing, but that's the only way he knows how.*

"You just didn't listen," he repeats. "Because you're scared."

"That's not true," I argue back like a petulant child.

Roads around us turn into gravel, and gravel into forest soil as trees surround us. Are we on the North Shore already? When did we cross the bridge? I was too focused on his gorgeous face and how he described the many ways in which he loves me.

"You didn't hear me because you're scared of someone loving you unconditionally. You didn't want to see it because, for the first time in your fucking life, someone is ready to do anything for you. And you've never known how that feels."

He stops the car abruptly. Nothing around us but the darkness of the forest and thick trees attempting to hide the moonlight.

"You didn't listen because you can't take it. You can't take *me*."

He exits the truck, slamming the door. I follow, running after him as he opens the tailgate and drags out Duncan.

Tears are running down my cheeks. I'm distressed and awoken by the fact that he's right.

No one has ever loved me the way Xi does. My mother was always too busy to raise me. Her gallery, charity balls, and media apparitions were too important, rather than taking care of me. Nannies could do the job. My dad never loved me. He's too obsessed with how I make my family look. All he's ever taught me is to shut up and listen. That not being perfect is a mistake and mistakes should always be fixed. I've grown up to be a woman incapable of love. I've grown up into an object he could use for his reputation.

"I can take you," I sob. "You're the one who couldn't choose between the North Shore and me. You decided taking over the Kings was more important than telling me the truth."

"I made my choice," he growls as he pushes Duncan to the ground. "I choose you."

My eyes widen. Duncan is begging and wailing on the forest floor, but neither of us is looking at him. Xi has a foot on his chest, pressing with all his weight, stopping him from going anywhere.

"The question is can you handle it? Can you handle being my only obsession, Alex? It's just you and me, baby. I will be there every day. I will make sure you're okay. I will fucking love you with all I have. I will kill the men who hurt you."

I shake my head, tears running as I glance at Duncan.

Xi grabs something at the back of his jeans, and I retreat when he pulls out a gun.

"Xi," I whimper, taking another step back, my eyes on the weapon.

"Look at me," he growls. I gaze up at him.

"This is all of me," he spreads his arms. "I'm a crook. I'm a violent murderer. I am *not* a good man. I already am all those things, but I don't have to be NSC if that's what you want. I'll leave for you. Fuck, Alex, you don't understand. I will burn cities to the ground if it means it's just *you and me*."

For the second time tonight, my heart threatens to leap out of my chest. It's trying to reach Xi's.

"So answer me. Can. You. Take. It?"

I nod. That's all I give him.

He aims the weapon at Duncan and brings a finger to his lips. "Don't scream," he says calmly.

Bang!

He said not to scream, so a loud gasp leaves me, showing my body subconsciously listened. Everything comes together as I squeeze my eyes. I only open them again because I feel Xi's presence right in front of me. He brings his hand not holding the gun to my face, cupping the back of my head and forcing me to look up at him. "Just you and me," he murmurs. "Say it."

I'm enthralled. There's something about everything he's done tonight that seems to have put me in a trance.

After so many years of looking for it, I can't believe I finally understand the love I need.

The crazy kind.

The toxic kind that poisons your veins and makes you feel like your thoughts don't belong to you anymore.

The love that drives you insane in the most satisfying way possible.

"It's just you and me," I rasp.

"Good girl." His gravelly voice has barely reached my ears when his lips crash on mine.

He kisses me like there's no tomorrow.

His hand at the back of my head, the other at my back.

The threat of his warm gun against my skin. My toes push me closer to him, my heart melting.

Nothing else exists in a world where Xi kisses me like this. For someone who's always wanted to feel special, *wanted*, this kiss portrays everything I've ever dreamed of. The possession in it is one that promises he meant his words: just me and him.

Xi is never letting me go.

We're both out of breath when we pull away. It reminds me of our first kiss. Back then, too, it hadn't stopped abruptly. We had slowed down, taking our time to separate, never wanting to let the other one go.

He rests his forehead on mine and a short, relieved laugh escapes him.

"Stop laughing," I sniffle.

"I'm in love."

"You just killed someone."

"My most justified kill ever."

"No," I pinch my lips. "I don't want to hear that you killed other people."

His hand slides in my hair at the side of my head. I feel his warm palm against my cold ear. "I would kill another hundred for you, Alex."

He pulls away and goes to his truck. Coming back with a canister of gasoline, he pours some on Duncan's dead body.

Why am I not panicking anymore? There is a corpse lying less than twenty feet away from me. The man I'm desperately in love with is a murderer. He's crossed the line so far over that I'm forced to teeter on the edge of it myself.

Love.

Such a pure, simple feeling driving you to the most senseless actions.

Xi reaches into his jeans and comes up with a pack of

cigarettes. He pulls one with his lips only and shoves the rest of the pack back in his pocket. He searches his jeans again, front and back, his hoodie is next before his head falls back.

"Ah, fuck," he huffs around the cigarette before looking up again.

In the dark of the night, I can see the moonlight illuminating his beautiful bronze skin. His profile is one of a god. A square jaw covered with a five o'clock shadow. Plump, dark lips. His nostrils flare as he frowns his bushy eyebrows. His long lashes fan out on his cheeks when he closes his eyes and inhales deeply. I sense him trying to calm himself down, his shoulders rising to the rhythm of his deep breathing. His Adam's apple bobs up and down as he swallows with his cigarette between his lips.

He doesn't have a lighter—the one he meant to use to set the dead man on fire.

Reaching into the fuchsia Gucci purse strapped across my body, I unzip it and slide my hand inside. Feeling for the plastic little pink lighter I know belongs to Xi, I press the pad of my thumb against the sparkwheel and roll it backward. Just like him, I ground myself as I inhale cold air into my lungs, taking time to process the decision I'm about to make.

What says I love you more than sacrificing my life and freedom for you?

I would take the most significant risk and be an accomplice in your crimes.

I'll be the Bonnie to your Clyde for a simple taste of forever with you.

Taking the lighter out, I close the distance between us. His eyebrows rise as I lift the lighter to the end of his cigarette and light it. He takes a drag on the stick before pinching it between his thumb and forefinger. He pulls it out of his mouth, his hand coming to rest by his side, and blows the smoke to the side.

"Nice pink lighter."

There's a tension inside my belly like never before. The good kind. "It's fuchsia."

"Just say it." The calm in his tone is only betrayed by the impatience and hope shining in his eyes.

My lips twitch. For once, he's waiting on me, expectant.

"I'm in love with you, too," I murmur.

The corner of his lips tips up, and, for the first time ever, I watch a bright smile spread on Xi's face.

It's beautiful. Breathtaking. Everything I could have imagined and more. White teeth, sharp canines. And a single, tiny dimple on his left cheek. Terrifying and addictive. It's him in his purest form.

Without looking back, he throws his cigarette a few feet behind him, and I watch as it falls on Duncan's dead body, lighting him on fire.

I take in a sharp breath just as Xi grabs my hand and hauls me back to the truck. We watch from inside as the body disappears into dust, making sure the fire doesn't get out of control.

"What now?" I whisper.

"Now I take you to your room and fuck you like the bad girl I turned you into."

And as we drive back, he puts *I Did Something Bad* by Taylor Swift on.

"You like Taylor Swift now?" I chuckle.

"The woman I'm in love with associates every situation in her life with a Taylor Swift song. You can bet your ass I was going to listen to every single excruciating album."

"Why?"

"To understand you better, baby." His eyes dart to mine and he puts a hand on my thigh. It's as simple as that.

"Her albums aren't excruciating," I pout.

"Agonizing."

"Xi!" I gasp.

After a pause, he adds. "Okay, *1989* was my favorite."

"Oh my God, isn't it so good?" I shriek from excitement. My whole body shifts to face him.

"It was bearable."

I smile to myself as I rest back on the seat. A second later, my big, bad villain is butchering the lyrics to *Blank Space*, and my heart explodes in my chest.

I guess Xi has two ways to show me he loves me. Killing a man for me and listening to my favorite artist.

29

ALEXANDRA

From Hell With Love – Ryan Caraveo

I smile to myself, remembering the talk Xi and I had after we went back to Xi Ep. The way he opened up to me and explained exactly why he was looking for info on my dad. The Lucianos are a known crime family on the East Coast, and I'm not surprised by the kind of demand they made to small gangs for their protection.

That's not what makes me smile, though. It's that we finally talked about the future without including his illegal activities in it. Xi doesn't want to leave the North Shore, he's set on staying close to his mom and his family, and I understand that. What he does want is to make it a better place. He admitted that if he went for the Kings again, the war would never end, and he would rather work on making his town a better place. He said he would talk to Dickie about it, since he's the only man he knows doing his best to stay neutral and keep the kids who come to his gym out of trouble. Apparently, that's what he did with Billie.

The hardest, though, will be leaving NSC for good. He

said he started mentioning it to Emma, but it did not go well. Discussions are still in progress. It's been for two weeks.

"No, oh dear lord, do *not* walk into that room. Especially not with your filthy boots. There's a $1.5 million Persian rug in there, sir." My mom's stern voice brings me back to Stoneview.

The florist holding the vase of carnations and lilies twice the size of my head stops on the spot.

"I'm so sorry, ma'am. I thought this was the room."

My mother rolls her eyes to the far back of her head. "Why would we have a birthday party in our drawing room? Third door to the right. Reception room. That's where you're going."

She rolls her eyes again as he approaches the indicated room and turns to me. "Incompetent. That's what they are."

"It's okay, Mom. They didn't go in." I put a hand on her shoulder, before rubbing it against my black leggings when I realize how clammy it feels.

It's Ella's dad's birthday, and my anxiety has been eating at me. There are so many things I don't like about this day that I haven't been able to eat more than a slice of bread in the last forty-eight hours.

The main thing would be that Xi is coming, and I will have to introduce him to my parents as my boyfriend. I haven't even told them my boyfriend is coming. I want people around when I tell my dad, so he's forced to react in a decent manner. I already know what I'm going to hear from him privately. That I shouldn't be dating anyone and focusing on my studies. I don't even know at what point we're going to have the *what does he do* conversation and, even worse: what do his parents do.

"Stand up straight, Alex." My dad's voice startles me,

and my shoulders pull back automatically as I elongate my spine.

"Sorry," I murmur.

My mom smiles brightly at my dad. "I am so happy we can all be here for Gerald's birthday."

My dad nods, his eyes on his phone. "Wonderful," he mumbles.

I don't like Ella's father. Neither does Ella. He's a shady man who always makes me and my friends uncomfortable.

"You ladies should get ready," my dad says as he heads for his office. "Guests will be here in two hours."

My mother claps her hands, excited for another social event where she will be the center of attention. Everyone wants to be friends with the billionaire heiress of a renowned French artist.

"Alex," my dad says, still looking at his phone. "I had Lydia put your clothes on your bed. Don't go too heavy on the make-up. Some people from my party are going to be here."

Wonderful.

"None of that bright pink lipstick you wear. It makes you look like a cheap whore."

I recoil slightly when he says that and turn to my mom to check if she heard it. She pretends she didn't, like every time my dad insults me.

"It's fuchsia," I mumble as I head for the grand staircase and to my room.

When my dad walks into my room to check if I'm presentable for the party, I feel cold sweat running down my spine. I bought the same bracelet he had gotten me, minus the tracker. If he checked my credit card statement, he'd have seen it, but he still hasn't said anything. I'm wearing my new bracelet now since Xi cut off the other one.

I usually keep the one with the tracker in my bag and wear the fake one.

He observes me like a hawk does his prey, ready to pounce at any time. I try my hardest not to tremble under his stare, not to break and admit everything. My father can try to hurt me tonight, but it will be the last time he does so.

When he can't find anything to say about my outfit, my hair, or my makeup, he goes for my body. For things I can't control.

"You look a little pale."

Of course I do, I'm terrified he will discover what I did.

"I feel a little unwell," I admit. "The party will help, I'm sure."

"Your boobs are too big. We should think of a breast reduction before people start thinking they're all you're about."

I gulp. Would he really? He ignores my reaction and keeps going.

"One glass of champagne tonight and that's it. Show me how you smile."

I lick my dry lips. The pale pink lipstick tastes bitter. When I plaster my perfected Stoneview smile to my face, his falls.

"Dear God," he huffs. "You look like some trafficker is trying to get you through the border. What is wrong with you, Alexandra?"

"I'm sorry," I murmur meekly. "But I don't think people will be bothered about the way I smi–"

When he slaps me, I clench my teeth instead of crying out.

"You know how I feel about you saying 'but' to me. There are no but's. I say something, you listen, period."

I take a calming breath.

He can't mark you before the party. People would know.

"Of course. I'm sorry."

"You're always sorry, Alex." His threatening step makes me retreat. "Can't you just do *better*? Can't you at least try to make me proud? With the time, energy, and money I spend on you, can't you be thankful?"

"I do try." My throat is so taut I can barely hear my own voice.

"Try harder because it's exhausting to have a disappointment as a daughter."

He turns around to leave my bedroom, but before he crosses the doorway, I call out, "Dad."

"What now?" he sighs as he peers back at me.

My chin trembles, my voice thick with fear and hope.

"Do you love me?"

I need to know. Can someone be so cruel and still love you? Can that same person who breaks you on a daily basis feel something other than hatred? Is that behavior normal from a father?

What did I do? Why am I not enough? What mistakes have I made for him to think so little of me?

"Don't be ridiculous, Alexandra," he scoffs. "You're my daughter."

He leaves me with those words, managing to avoid answering my question.

I believe that...had he said those three simple words, I might have been stupid enough to forgive him for all the hurt. Except he didn't. And I think that's what seals our fates.

I just wanted to be enough.

．　．　．

Half an hour later, chauffeurs are dropping off guests in expensive dresses and suits as they round the fountain in our driveway. Some are driving their luxurious cars and handing them off to the valets we hired. Guests are filing inside our house, giving invitations to the security guards at the door. My dad, my mom, and I are standing by our front door, greeting everyone. My cheeks hurt from the fake smile on my face, and my ears ring from my mother's high-pitch voice every time she says *I'm so glad you could make it* while my dad gives firm handshakes.

I simply stand between them, my hands clasped at my front and nodding, smiling, saying thank you when I'm told how wonderful I look.

My dad has me wearing a dusty pink dress with a tight satin bodice and a mesh skirt that spans out all the way to my ankles. The spaghetti straps hold the sweetheart neckline close to my chest, so there is no chance of an accident like one of my boobs popping out. You know, so it calms his fear of people thinking that's all I'm about.

God, I hate him.

I hate my father, but I smile to myself. It'll all be over soon.

Ella hugs me while her parents say hello to mine and laughs in my ear. "I hadn't seen you dressed in a *daughter of a senator* outfit since we started at SFU, and it's so hilariously *not* you."

"I know," I snort in her ear.

"Alexandra Delacroix without any fuchsia just feels wrong."

"It *is* wrong," I giggle.

We separate, and I say a vague hello to her dad. His way of looking at women makes me deeply uncomfortable and makes me believe that the accusations against him might actually be true. That's not something we ever discuss with Ella. She prefers to brush it off and not even utter an opinion about it.

"Where's Lucas?" my mother asks Gerald's wife.

"His plane doesn't land until later," his dad explains.

"Has Baker's Café been keeping him busy in L.A.?" my dad inquires.

"Of course it has. It was about time he proved he has what it takes to handle a real business."

Ella gives me a look, annoyed at her dad's words and defensive of her older brother. If Luke comes later, he'll probably show up with his friends, and I'm slightly excited to see Jake White again. The king of Stoneview Prep will undoubtedly be as beautiful as ever, and I don't know one girl in our school who wasn't completely in love with him.

Peach looks gorgeous as always when she arrives in a long emerald satin dress, her red hair splayed around her shoulders and going all the way to her waist.

Both her dads are with her. One is much older, George Sanderson, and he was a local councilman for years. Now he's part of my dad's party because he wants to show he supposedly supports the LGBTQIA+ community. Her other dad is Georgio Menacci, a famous Italian actor who made it in Hollywood in the early 2000s. He retired when he married George, and they decided to have a child.

"Penelope," my mother beams at my friend as she takes her in her arms. "You look as wonderful as ever."

"Thank you, Mrs. Delacroix."

"Georgio," my dad says warmly as he shakes his hand. "I'm so glad you could come. We have much to talk about today."

"After a glass of champagne, if you don't mind, Senator," the other chuckles deeply.

We spend another half-hour at the door greeting everyone. Xi is not here yet, and my stomach twists. What is he doing? I don't have access to my phone right now so I can't check on any notifications. He better not be pulling a *Xi Time* kind of arrival. My dad hates people who show up late.

More guests will be showing up while we have drinks and hors d'oeuvres in the reception room, and I'm sure he will come then. I *need* him to come.

Chatter and clinking glasses fill the background noise of the room. Chester, Wren, Peach, Ella, and I are standing in a corner, my eyes trained on the door as they all laugh around me.

Wren puts a hand on my shoulder, jarring me a little. "He's coming, don't worry. Dinner hasn't even started."

"Is he coming with someone?" Ella asks right away, her excitement palpable. Luke and his friends haven't arrived yet, so we haven't seen Chris. Although I do know she's not exactly looking forward to seeing him and his girlfriend.

"He was meant to come with Logan, but Logan hates Stoneview, so I'm not sure he quite convinced him," I say.

"Oh." She looks around. "Well, then I better start flirting with some boys around here. Hey, Chester, is your dad still single?"

"Fuck off," Chester snorts as we all laugh.

Before I know it, we're saying hi to Luke and his friends. We've joked around and gotten Ella out of an awkward situation with Chris.

But someone is still missing.

The sound of cutlery hitting a glass cuts the conversation short. The noise in the room dies down as everyone focuses on my father, my mom standing right next to him.

"Ladies and gentlemen, if you'd like to make your way to the dining room. Dinner is served."

Everyone files out, following the servers to our guest dining room in another part of the house. I can't move though, because all I can think of is that Xi still isn't here.

30

XI

Sober – Josh A, NEFFEX

"Ow, Tamar, you're fucking strangling me."

I hear Zara snort behind me, sitting on Tamar's bed. I shoot her a look and her snort turns into a cackle.

"I'm trying my fucking best," Tamar mumbles, pulling on the tie again. "You're a dude, you should know how to put these on."

Her eyes dart back to her phone and the video playing called *Five easy ways to knot your tie.*

"That shit's too fucking small," I grunt, rolling my shoulders. Lik lent me a black suit and I can't breathe in it. "That's too tight, Tamar," I snap, pushing her hand away.

"That's how it's meant to be," she fights back, annoyed.

"I can't fucking breathe." I pull at the knot and undo all her hard work.

"I don't think that's got anything to do with the tie," Zara chuckles as she shoves a piece of gum in her mouth. I throw her another look, but she shrugs. "You're out of your comfort zone."

"I'm not."

"You're going to a birthday dinner in Stoneview with the daughter of a senator. You're more than out of your comfort zone," Tamar backs her up as she fiddles with the tie again.

"You're in the *anyone-could-arrest-you-at-any-time* zone." Zara's laugh is cut short when I fling the phone at her.

Tamar takes a deep breath and locks her brown eyes with mine. "Don't stress," she tells me calmly. "Remember who you're doing it for."

I have to wipe a hand against my mouth to hide the smile that's forcing its way onto my face.

I hate the suit. I hate the people I'm going to see. I've committed enough crimes in that town that anyone recognizing me could put me straight in jail.

But Alex is worth it.

Fuck, she's worth everything. Even the headache of leaving NSC.

"Is that a smile?" Tamar squeaks.

"No," I scowl.

"He smiles thinking of her," she adds, beaming. "Oh, we're fucked."

"Shut up."

"It's done, my big grumpy friend."

"Huh?"

"Your tie." She points at my neck. "Done. Can you breathe okay?"

I nod. My chest is warm, the tip of my fingers tingling, knowing I'll be touching Alex's soft skin soon.

"Alright, you should get going so you can be there right on time and not Xi time."

I glance in the mirror one last time. I don't look like myself. My hair is gelled, so there's no stray strand trying to get in the way of the perfect image I'm giving right now. The suit is a little too tight, but all it does is highlight my prominent shoulders and my strong arms. I shaved my five o'clock shadow and my jaw seems sharper.

Zara's face appears behind me. "I never thought I'd use this word to describe you, but you look handsome."

"Don't fall in love, I'm taken."

"Boohoo, the man-whore is taken."

"Xi, *go*," Tamar jumps back in.

We head to the front door and Zara leaves with me. "I'll walk with you. My car is parked near yours."

Tamar's street is the definition of overpopulated, and we both had to park down a nearby, quiet road.

"Have fun, Xi," Tamar smiles. "Use protection."

"Okay, I'm out." I close the door in her face and start walking with Zara.

"It's really fucking weird that you're going to a birthday party in Stoneview. Most of the people you'll see there buy from us."

I shrug. "I'm only going so Alex can tell her parents we're together. I'm never showing up at that house again after that."

She takes a deep breath as we turn onto another street. "So, you're really not gonna get us that police protection?"

The disappointment in her voice tugs at my protective nature. I would do anything for my family...just not that. I can't jeopardize my relationship with Alex anymore. I'm in love, and I don't care if it means it makes me a less ruthless man. It took the sweetest woman around for me to realize there are other ways to protect the North Shore, and I want to be part of the change.

"Emma will discuss with the Lucianos, and they'll figure out something else."

She nods to herself. "I trust you. I know things will turn

out fine. Plus, I'll be the boss when it comes to drugs now. Every single dealer will be eating from the palm of my hand. Especially Jack. He'll hate that I dominate him in bed *and* on the streets. I can't wait."

I try to give her a forced laugh, but a glint of anxiety weighs in my stomach. A lot of people relied on me. They trusted me to keep NSC safe and to keep the money running.

My truck comes into view, and we stop by it to finish our conversation. "Do me a favor." Zara smiles as she looks up at me, but I see the truth in her eyes. "Have fun tonight. Leave the North Shore problems on the North Shore. Okay?" She squeezes my biceps to reassure me, but it's right there. "I'll see you tomorrow. Get in, you'll be late." She's disappointed.

I watch her walk away and get into my truck. For once in my fucking life, I will be right on time if I leave now.

I start the car and send a quick text telling Alex I'm on my way as I pull onto the road. Looking around, I focus, knowing that this is a road that's adjacent to Kings' territory. They've been taking over our streets more and more, and I always have to keep an eye out.

I throw a quick glance at Zara's car as I drive past her, and my heart drops to my stomach.

"Fuck," I hiss, braking harshly. "*Motherfuckers!*"

Ethan and Elliot have cornered her by her car. She punches Elliot, and he doesn't hesitate to throw a hit back just as I grab my gun in the glove box and jump out of the car.

"Get the fuck away from her," I shout, sprinting to them.

"Ah, our little secret keeper gracing us with his presence," Elliot sneers. I point the gun straight between his eyes.

"Tsk, tsk," he smiles. "The cops aren't far. And only one gang has police protection on the North Shore."

His focus is on me now, and Zara uses the distraction to try and hit him again, but Ethan grabs her by the back of the head. Pulling her hair as he drags her away from me.

"Did you not get our warning, Xi?" Ethan says with the calm of a sky before the storm.

"What fucking warning?" I grit.

"Drop your gun," Elliot adds. "Then we can talk."

I lower it; the threat of the cops too real. "I will fucking end you with or without a gun." I keep my glare on him as I squat to put my gun on the ground.

He kicks it away and smiles brightly at me. "Didn't your girlfriend say we were coming for your loved ones?"

"You threatened Alex?" I seethe as I move toward him, our chests practically touching.

Zara's gasp forces me to look at her. Ethan's got a knife pointed at her stomach, and I find it hard to focus on the conversation anymore.

"Yeah," Elliot confirms. "We had a nice little chat. You know, told her she should let you know she's next on the list if you don't start telling us what we want to know."

"Next?" I ask, confused. These two love playing games, and I'm not in the mood for it.

"Yeah. We're ticking off the first one today."

A whimper drags my eyes away from him again and my heart stops altogether.

"No!" I scream as I push Elliot out of the way. I manage to catch Ethan in the nose just as he takes a step back. I'm on him the next second, red flooding my vision as I focus on him, refusing to look at Zara as I sense her body crashing to the ground.

"Fuck...you," I hiss between clenched teeth. My fist hits

425

his face on repeat. I only stop to grab his knife and throw it further down the road. I feel Elliot grabbing me from the back, but there's no stopping me as I rain punches on his brother.

"Xi..." A whimper drags me out of my trance and the second I lose focus, Elliot hits me at the back of the head.

I groan as I'm thrown off Ethan. His brother helps him up and he turns to me when they start walking away. "Next one is Alex," he shouts. "Give us what we want."

I'm on Zara right away, kneeling next to her. She's holding bloody hands to her stomach.

"Xi," she murmurs, her face draining of blood, her lips paling rapidly. Her eyes dart down to her stomach. "Shit..."

"No." I press one hand on top of hers as I grab my phone with the other. "Keep pressing. I'm calling Emma. It's gonna be okay." I sit behind her on the floor and drag her between my legs so I can sit her up and rest her against my chest.

She shakes her head. "I don't feel so good."

"Don't worry." Emma doesn't pick up, so I try again. "Don't worry," I repeat.

"Fuck...Xi," she rasps. "I think I'm fucking dying."

"You're not dying," I snap, refusing to listen to her. "Emma has stitched me up before, and I was in a worse situation than you. You're going to make it. It's gonna be okay." The more I say it, the more she'll believe it too.

Her eyelids start dropping just as Emma picks up. "Fuck," I growl. "Open your fucking eyes."

I can see her forcing her eyes open. "Xi..." A small smile tips at the corner of her mouth as she shakes her head. "I hide cash in P.O. Box 405 on the south bank. The keys are in the floorboard under my bed."

"Shut up," I hiss. "Shut up. You're not dying on me." I hold the phone between my ear and shoulder and press both my hands on hers to make sure we're pushing hard enough on the wound. "Emma!" I bark into the phone. "I need you to come to Maple Street right next to Tamar's. We're just after the junction with Twin Oaks."

"Please, give the money to my mom," Zara murmurs, her voice gone. "She'll need it."

"*What's going on?*" Emma asks as I hear her moving around.

"Zara," I start. "She's been stabbed...she..." Her eyes close again. "No. No, no, no. Emma hurry, she—"

I can feel the moment it's over. Her mouth opens slightly, and a rush of air comes out, like her soul is leaving her body.

A beat later, the lines of worry and pain painting her features disappear as her entire body relaxes.

"*Xi?*" Emma asks. I hear her car start.

But my phone falls to the ground in a clatter I barely hear as I grab my best friend and pull her to me. "No," I choke. I hold her in my arms as a tremble takes over me. "Zara...Zara, baby, talk to me."

I know she won't.

I know she's gone.

And I know the last memory I will ever have of her is the disappointment I heard in her voice when I told her I wouldn't protect NSC anymore.

I kiss the top of her head over and over again, her blood soaking my shirt and her body so heavy in my arms.

A scream rips through the air and my muscles tense. Emma must have called Tamar since we're so close to her house.

"Zara!" She falls on her knees next to us, her hands hovering over her body and not touching her as if scared to hurt her.

"I'm calling an ambulance," she panics. Something we never do on the North Shore. We can't afford it, and we don't want to answer for our crimes. We don't like adding to the gang-on-gang violence data they love to use against us.

Still holding Zara to my chest, I put a hand on Tamar's phone and shake my head. "It's too late," I rasp. My throat is so tight I can barely breathe.

Something presses on my chest as I hold her body close. The weight of guilt, the pain, the heartbreak... *something*. I realize I'm rocking back and forth, as if lulling her to sleep.

A wail explodes from Tamar, and she hugs us. I don't know how long we stay like this. The three childhood best friends who never spent a day without each other. The insufferable trio who always remained on the wrong side of the law.

By the time Emma gets here, Tamar and I are sitting a little further away. We laid Zara on the floor and covered her with my jacket. I'm holding my other friend in my arms as she cries on my shoulder. Her tears are never-ending, every single one of them adding to the weight on my shoulder.

The head of NSC looks around before her eyes fall on Zara's dead body. Blood is all around her, turning the sidewalk crimson. A stain that will linger for months to come.

Far away, the thunder roars, as if God heard our pain. It's not as loud as the scream that got stuck in my throat the moment I heard my best friend's last breath. I can still hear it echoing in my head, imprisoned in my body.

Emma lets herself be sad for a total of two seconds. I see her gaze go to Zara, her lip twitch, and her eyes harden again when she's looking back at us. This woman is ruthless.

"Who?"

"The brothers," I say low. Nudging Tamar, I get up and help her follow. She clings to me as I walk to Emma, avoiding looking at Zara.

"What did they want?" Emma asks, knowing there's always a reason for a murder.

"The same thing they keep asking."

Emma rolls a hair extension around her finger and unrolls it. "You're not giving it to them," she orders. "They hate you. Once they have that info from you, they'll kill you."

"I wasn't going to," I snap back.

Tamar's body trembles against me as another sob comes from her.

"Let's not discuss this here," Emma concludes. "Go home, both of you. I'll make an anonymous call to the cops."

"I can't leave her here!" Tamar cries out. "Not to be found by pigs. Are you insane?"

"Someone needs to tell her mom before the cops do," I add.

"I'll stay back and watch from afar to make sure she's taken care of." Emma huffs, thinking some more. "Tamar, you go tell her mom. Xi, go with her to rid her room of any drugs. Cops will want to check her place sometime this week so they can say it was a drug deal gone wrong. We don't want her mom in a situation."

"I want to find the brothers."

"Not now," Emma replies, her stern eyes on me. "Retaliation will have to wait. They know you. They know you're volatile and will expect you to strike back right away."

"I don't fucking care what they expect," I hiss as I shift

forward, leaving Tamar behind to cry on her own. "Kings are coming to *our* territories to kill *our* people. That's not how it fucking works."

"I thought you wanted out," she scoffs.

"I wanted to make this fucking town a better place. I wanted to end the ongoing bloody massacres."

She snorts and tilts her head to the side. "Those aren't your words, Xi. They aren't your thoughts. Those are the words of a little girl from Stoneview who has no idea how it works here and who put pretty dreams of unicorns and rainbows in your head."

My nostrils flare as the truth slaps me in the face.

"You don't change how the streets work. You adapt. And if you can't...people die. The Lucianos are a solution you threw back in my face." Her eyes dart to Zara. "Actions have consequences."

The weight of guilt practically makes my knees buckle. I failed my friends. My family. NSC.

All for Alexandra Delacroix's pretty eyes and her ability to see the good in everyone.

It was a mistake.

"I want to fight in the Death Cage. Against one of the brothers."

The Death Cage has determined the fate of the North Shore for years. One opponent from each crew, one cage, one comes out alive. Whoever wins that fight wins the North Shore. We had one about three years ago and lost our town to the Kings that night.

It's time for another fight in the Death Cage. I want to murder one of the brothers while their whole crew watches.

"There's no way I'm allowing you in the Death Cage. It's too risky." Her no is categorical. Like every time I've asked. The brothers always refuse anyway. They're too fucking scared. "Even if I convince Kayla King to accept a fight, I can't make her send Ethan or Elliot. She'll send her best fighter, and you might end up dead." She takes a deep breath. "No."

Not wanting to hear any more, I give Zara one last look, feeling my heart break into a million pieces. "We'll all help pay for her funeral. I don't want her mom to spend a single cent on it," I tell Emma. "I want every single fucking person from NSC to pitch in."

"You got it," she says softly. She looks at Zara again. "Take your jacket back. We don't want the cops to find it here."

I do. And then I wrap an arm around Tamar's shoulders and guide her to my truck.

We spend hours at Zara's house. The first one consists of me receiving insults from her mom. After screams of horror and heartbreak, she calls me all the names she can find in Arabic, but *murderer* is the one that breaks me the most. I take it all while Tamar tries to calm her down.

If you hadn't dragged her into this.

You made her a criminal. You made her a target.

For years I warned her against you.

Look at what you've done now.

All true.

Zara's mom is right, after all. Our moms were best friends, so we became friends too. The three Maghrebi kids in our community. Until I got roped into NSC and took the girls with me. Easy money, independence, freedom. That's what we were promised. That's what we sacrificed everything for.

I leave for Zara's room, checking everywhere for any

stash she would keep for me. But my best friend was smart and would never leave anything here if it put her mom in danger. I drop to the floor and slide under her bed, grabbing the key to her P.O. Box.

When I finally walk back into the living room, my mom is there, pouring Moroccan mint tea into a small glass for Jamila. She puts the teapot down on the table and slowly moves to me. Her slap is strong enough to make my head snap to the side. I look back at her, down at her tiny form, and her dark eyes say everything. She shakes her head slowly, disappointment seeping out of her.

"*Weldi*." My son. My eyes dart away, not able to take her in when I know she's about to say the words that will be the end of me. "*If your dad could see you,*" she says in Arabic. "*I hope God forgives your sins, Ziad.*"

I run my hand across my face and nod at her. There's nothing to say. Just pain to feel.

We stay with Jamila until the cops show up, and she's told for the second time tonight that her only child is dead. She has no husband anymore, either. I had to hide in the room since I was covered in Zara's blood.

By the end of the night, nothing is left of the good man Alex tried to make out of me. The fact that I missed that birthday dinner doesn't even cross my mind until I check my phone to see I missed calls from her and a message asking if I'm alright.

But I don't reply. The person she got to know isn't here anymore.

There's only anger and sadness. Rage and guilt. I feel it all.

It's time Alex meets the real me. Once and for all.

31

ALEXANDRA

i hope ur miserable until ur dead – Nessa Barrett

I twist and turn in bed, half asleep. I'm vaguely aware it's the middle of the night, yet I've been in that state for hours now. First, I couldn't sleep since I was worried about Xi. I couldn't stop thinking something terribly wrong happened. He hasn't answered any of my calls or texts, and there's nothing I can do. When I started accepting that I would just have to wait for tomorrow, my body was too anxious to fall asleep. I hadn't realized how much being back in my old room would affect me.

After my birthday, I spent countless nights, eyes wide open, expecting someone to break in at any point. I thought if my kidnapper hadn't been arrested, he would come back for me and finish the job. My only reassurance was that I hadn't seen his face or the faces of his accomplices and that they should believe I wasn't a threat to them, to begin with.

Still, I was terrified, kept awake by one seizure after the other. My parents even had a private nurse sleep in the room next to mine to care for me.

They would never do it themselves.

Dad confined me in my room for weeks, too afraid I would do something socially unacceptable if I were to be let outside, ultimately making things worse. This place became my prison, even more so because I couldn't get *him* out of my mind.

Why couldn't he be someone I've come to hate for the right reasons? Them being that he kidnapped me, assaulted me, and traumatized me forever.

Instead, I hated him because he stirred my dormant desires to life. Showing my dirty secrets could turn real. He made me hate myself for the awakening he put me through. I was changed forever, knowing no one would make me feel the way that man did ever again.

Except Xi.

The crazy man who decided that he and I would be forever and that I didn't have a say in it. Having someone turn completely crazy with obsession for me. Isn't that what I've been looking for?

I'm disappointed that Xi didn't show up tonight. I had plans for us, but I finally fall asleep knowing that I can go back to him tomorrow. That he keeps me safe. That his love is what keeps me strong right now, and that one night in here on my own means nothing when I can be safely back in his arms in only a few hours.

Nothing specific awakens me. Probably the same fear and anxiety that hindered me from falling asleep.

There's no noise, no movement. Nothing touching me.

And yet when my eyes sluggishly open, heavy from sleep, I gasp at seeing a tall form standing at the foot of my bed.

My blood freezes as I jolt into a sitting position and plaster myself against the expensive cushioned headboard behind me. Only I don't scream, because deep down, I recognize him.

Xi is just standing there, observing me. I sleep with a small light on now, and the warm glow illuminates his body. My stomach churns when I take him in.

He's wearing a black suit, his hands in the pocket of his slacks. His black jacket is ripped at the shoulders, like it was too small and he did a sudden movement with his arms. His tie is undone, hanging over a white button-down covered in blood.

Covered. In. Blood.

It's drenched in it.

He's bleeding, and that's the only alarm ringing in my head right now.

"Oh my God, Xi," I whisper in panic. My instinct is to push my duvet off and throw my legs over the bed so I can run to him.

Except the moment I grasp the covers, his husky voice reaches my ear. "Don't move." It's a low, threatening rasp. The kind that stops me instantly.

I've never heard his voice like this. Xi is moody, obviously. He can never spare a smile, and everyone gets on his nerves.

But me.

I'm special, and I know it. It's what made me fall in love with him in the first place. How he has always been different with me. The effort, the protection he bestowed over me. Even during the times he protects me from himself.

"A-are you okay? You're bleeding," I whisper with concern.

"Not my blood."

"Whose?" I gasp.

"Why didn't you tell me the brothers threatened you?"

A silence falls over us, only disrupted by the sound of me working to swallow the sand in my throat. After we broke up, I deemed Ethan and Elliot's threat void. Since we got back together, I completely forgot about it.

His threatening form slowly walks to the side of my bed, getting closer to me. My window is now behind him, the light of the moon casting his face in shadow. A shiver crosses my body, the scene too similar to the night of my birthday.

"Can we turn the light on," I murmur. "I—this is making me feel uncomfortable."

"Why. Didn't. You. Tell. Me," he says through gritted teeth.

"Because you should never negotiate with terrorists," I say with a confidence I didn't know I had. "If there's one thing I know, it's that you don't give in to threats. If I'd told you, you would have done something about it, and I didn't want you in more danger with them than you already seemed to me. They talked to *me*, and I made the decision that they wouldn't get to us. What is it they even want?"

Ignoring my question, he leans over me, pressing a hand on the mattress by my hip. My eyes dart down to it and back up at him. "You thought they wouldn't get to us?" he sneers.

I gulp, nodding and understanding I must have been very wrong about that decision.

"Of course, they'll never get to you, cupcake. You live in your pretty castle and you had your North Shore knight protecting you. They would never get to you because your daddy would shield you. Build a fort with stacks of dollar bills if he had to."

"Stop," I rasp, feeling tears spring in my eyes and attempting to swallow them down. "Talk to me and tell me what happened. I'll accept my mistakes and make it right, but don't put up walls between us."

His other hand comes under the cover, wrapping around my thigh. "They didn't get to you, Alex. But they got to *us*."

In a sudden movement, he pulls on my leg, dragging me down until I'm lying on my back and gasping at the violence of his gesture.

He grabs both my wrists before I can react, pushing them above my head as I twist.

"Xi," I groan, his grip painful.

He reaches for his back pocket, and I feel my eyes round when I see metal glinting in the moonlight. I cry out when he wraps the first metal cuff to my wrist. He roughly grabs my other arm, forcing me to fold in half. Dread seizes me when I feel him slide the second cuff around my other wrist. The gradual clicking becomes painful as it pinches my skin. As soon as his hands leave me, I sit up with my back against the headboard. My wrists are cuffed behind my back, and a wave of sickness overcomes me.

"Us," he repeats. "You know? The people who don't have the money to protect themselves."

"Stop," I bawl. "Stop thinking no one ever got to me. That's not true. Xi, undo these. I'm not...I'm panicking," I wheeze. "With what happened here—"

"Ah," he cuts me off with a cold voice. "Yes, *that*."

The silence is back, only measured by the beat of my heart pulsing in my ears. It's hammering in my head, ready to explode.

"You're scaring me," I admit in a barely audible whisper.

My thoughts swirl in my mind, trying to make sense of why he's doing this.

"It's unhealthy to keep the truth from your significant

other." He presses a knee on the mattress, getting closer to me. The smell of blood on his shirt makes me gag.

"Since I know what you were keeping from me, I think it's time we put everything on the table."

My worried gaze travels up and down his body. My heart cracks my ribs as it tries to burst out of my chest, awaiting the sentence from my judge and jury.

"I've been trying to tell you, baby. I promise I tried. But it was never the right time. I was too scared of losing you." He runs his knuckles over my cheek and pushes strands of hair out of my face. "You're so beautiful when you're scared. Those eyes...they truly can't hide anything from me. That's how I knew I could push you the first time."

The smirk appearing on his face is terrifying. I was not built to see this side of Xi. It's reserved for his enemies, and I'm just not strong enough to take him on.

"Stop," I plead. "Please...I'm scared." My quivering voice is a mix of terror and disorientation. I'm racking my brain, attempting to get a grip on what happened tonight for him to make the decision to destroy us.

"How do you think I could fall for you so quickly?" he says low, his hot breath warming my cheeks. They're cold due to the blood draining from my face. "I was already consumed by you. From the moment we met, Alex, you had me wrapped around your finger. I tried to forget you. I tried to leave you alone. Seven months...do you know how long that feels when you've become completely obsessed with someone? And then you came to the North Shore that day. You walked into that shop...and it was fate bringing us back together. I know it was."

I'm trembling from fright, my body knowing this runs deeper than a quick scare. I whimper as tears start falling down my cheeks.

"How do you think I knew you liked being degraded when we'd barely met? Surely it should have warned a smart girl like you that I knew you from before."

I shake my head vigorously, squeezing my eyes shut.

"God, it's so good having you back in this position. That's what I missed. The *real* fear."

No. This isn't happening.

"Open your eyes, baby," he says as his thumb wipes tears away.

I blink my eyes open as I feel his knee pulling away from the bed.

"How did you never recognize me, Elisabeth?"

An uncontrollable whimper spills out of me. And when he pulls out a gun from the back of his jeans, my mouth opens, ready to call for help.

His finger comes to his lips as he presses the gun against my forehead, his whispered words calm as the sea on a beautiful day.

"Don't scream."

He's in the exact same position as that fateful night, except now I finally see my aggressor clearly.

It's the face of the man I love.

32

XI

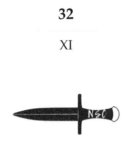

Young, In Love & Depressed AF – Call Me Karizma

"Why?" she sobs.

The tears on her face should break my heart. But it's already in pieces from my best friend's death.

I did a lot of thinking before coming to Alex's house tonight, and I've reached two definite conclusions.

Had she warned me about the brothers' threat, I would have been more vigilant. I would have watched my back, been more aware they were coming for the people I love.

The second thing that came to light was that Alex and I were never meant to last. We're not just different; we live in separate realities. I can't keep going with the lies. I can't keep living a life worried about what repercussions my actions will have on her well-being. There is no protecting Alex if she's with me. She will always be in danger. She wants me to leave behind a life that's entirely who I am.

Brutal and deadly.

A life where the people I care about could be gone the next day. Revenge never stops; violence is endless. It was nice to dream about what else I could do for a while, but every dream must stop when it turns into a nightmare. You have to force yourself to wake up and face what life really is: a game of survival.

And *that's* why.

I'm about to explain that to her when she speaks again, her words taking me by surprise.

"Why did you tell me?" Her trembling voice racks my chest, pinching at my heart. "You could have kept it from me. Forever. I could have loved you till death had you just kept it to yourself."

"What about after death, baby? When we have no choice but to drop our masks and reveal our secrets?"

She ignores my question, shaking her head as she sniffles. Her nose twitches, the cutest fucking thing known to man.

"What, then?" I insist. "You have to know who you're dealing with before I take you to hell with me."

"You're the only one going to hell," she hisses.

I smile warmly at her. For someone who's been wanting nothing but to see me smile, I know she finds no reassurance in it now.

"Heaven is overrated, cupcake. You'd hate it."

I use the gun to smear the tears on her face and watch her flinch. "I told you because you need to know who I am. If you choose to love me after that, that's your responsibility. *You* putting *yourself* at risk. Life is made of choices, right?"

Her beautiful hazel eyes blink up at me. "Don't say this to me," she whispers. "No one could love another knowing what you've done." Weirdly, there's more guilt in her voice than shock.

Almost like...she *has* been loving me knowing what I've done.

I lean closer to her, making sure we're facing each other entirely. "I know, Elisabeth. That's the whole point. We're going to move on from each other and return to our lives from before we started dating. Extinguish that love, baby."

I spent seven months trying to get Alexandra Delacroix out of my head. Seven months forcing myself to never contact her, never go back to the scene of the crime, never try to get back into her life. What if I contacted her and she ran to the police? I couldn't act on my obsession from that night or run to her and tell her about the powerful connection I felt running between us. And then she walked into that shop, coming straight to me like a gift from God. When she didn't recognize me, I knew I was never letting her go again. Until I realized being with me meant she could simply die any day.

I move my gun down her chest. It slides easily against the silk camisole she's wearing. I let it disappear under the covers until I'm able to press it against the silk covering her pussy.

She gasps, the sound beautiful.

"I almost told you several times. I wanted you to know who I really was. I wanted you to love me despite it. To make things right." I stare deep into her eyes. "But there's no going back from that..." I pause, not sure what I expect from her. Probably to contradict me. "...right?"

She remains silent, keeping her thoughts to herself. Almost as if she's punishing me, and not for having committed the unspeakable but for voicing what I've done to her.

I press the barrel harder. "Don't," she whimpers.

"I'm afraid I have bad news for you, Elisabeth."

"Stop calling me that," she groans, shifting as she tries to escape my gun.

"But that's what he called you, isn't it? Your kidnapper."

She shakes her head as her eyes shut, like wanting to ignore the truth. That the man who put her back together is the same man who had broken her.

That I'm her kidnapper *and* her savior.

The person she's afraid of the most protected her.

Her illusion of safety has shattered to pieces.

I rub the gun between her legs and watch as she bites her lower lip, attempting to suppress a soft moan. "I know your secret, Elisabeth. I know your body. I knew it when I took you from your home and made you come against your will. I knew it when I drove you back to the safety of your room that night after your party. I knew it when I leashed you with my belt. How did you expect me to stay away when I was fully aware of our compatibility, even when you didn't know who I was? You love being degraded. You love the humiliation of being forced to do debasing acts. And, fuck baby, do I love degrading you."

Pulling my weapon away from her burning core, I use my other hand to rip her shorts off. She cries out when I grab her hips and move her so she's lying right in front of me, her ass on the edge of the bed.

"Should I check how wet you are for me?" She shakes her head, pulling at the cuffs. They're crushed between her lower back and the mattress now.

"Why are you asking?" she spits at me. "I thought you only *took*."

"I take with you because I know that's what you like." Keeping my gun trained on her head, I spread her legs, putting a knee on the edge of the bed between them. "You would hate me if I didn't push you to your limit, baby." Her pussy's now spread open before me as I press my thumb to her clit. She shudders, her breath faltering. "You would throw me away like you did your ex. That boy couldn't give you what you craved. You needed *me* for that."

"I crave these things because you broke me in the first place," she says between clenched teeth.

Without a pause, I slap her pussy harshly. She yelps and I press the gun against her forehead. "Lies get you punished. *Lies* broke us. Mine and yours. Now face the fucking truth. You were this way before me. I might have changed you that night. I might have shown you that you *needed* it, but your dirty fantasies started before I kidnapped you." I use the tip of my middle finger to spread her wetness. She's soaking. "Am I wrong?" I press inside, slowly, until she can't hold back her moan.

"No," she whispers.

"That's right. Now stay quiet while I fuck you like the little whore you are. Then we'll deal with the rest."

"Xi..." she gasps as I push a second finger inside her. She lifts her head despite me pressing a deadly weapon against her skull. Her eyes shine with fire and death. "*We're over*," she hisses through gritted teeth. "*Fuck. You.*"

All I can do is grin in response. My beautiful princess is finally showing her teeth. My pretty flower has grown thorns, and I couldn't be more satisfied.

"I'm so proud of you," I tell her softly. But, slowly, I drag the gun from her forehead, down her damp cheeks and press it against her flattened lips. "Now, say sorry for disrespecting your owner."

I can read the resounding *fuck you* in her expression, except she can't say it, or she risks me slipping the barrel of my gun into her mouth.

I curl my fingers inside her dripping pussy, pressing against her G-spot as I move in and out of her. Her small gasp gives me access, and I push gradually inside. The fear is so evident on her face, even as she narrows her eyes in hatred.

She moans when I quicken my movements, thrusting my fingers roughly and making her thighs shake. "Say sorry, baby. Be my good little pet and beg your owner for forgiveness."

It only takes a few more seconds for her to moan a loud *sorry* as her eyes roll to the back of her head.

"That's my good girl." I pull out of her, relishing in the way she mewls in desperation around the gun.

I cup her sex and move the gun inside her mouth, forcing her to suck on it. "Who does this belong to, Alex?" I rasp, the tips of my fingers grazing her entrance.

"You," she sputters around the barrel.

"I own all of you, baby. Don't I?"

She nods, and as she hears the sound of me undoing my slacks, she presses her pussy against my hand. "Please..." The muffled sound is music to my ears.

I know we're over. I know there's nothing left of us...but how can I accept it when her entire being matches mine like we were made for each other. Everything that is her belongs to me.

"Your body is mine," I grunt, pressing the tip of my dick to her entrance.

She nods, her eyes squeezing shut as I start to push. "Your soul is mine. From the moment I took you from this exact bed, you became mine." I slowly move inside her, her wetness welcoming me and her body shuddering under me. "You were mine when you came to the hand of your kidnapper."

The first thrust shifts her body up, sliding on the mattress as she groans around the gun. Her chest is heaving. Sweat is dampening her throat. I trace my fingers around her hard nipples through the silky fabric covering them. One after the other, I watch her writhe under me, moving her pelvis to try and fuck herself on my dick.

I'm deep inside her, still.

"Your heart belongs to me, baby. And mine to yours. It did the moment I walked back into that burning house. I set the fire myself only to save you from it. That's what I'll do over and over again, Alex. I'll save you from the fires I start. I'll protect you from everything."

What am I saying? This is meant to be the end.

Pulling back, I slam into her with force. She moans, and I start moving my hips in tandem with the gun in her mouth. "Suck on my gun like it's my dick, baby."

And she does. Because there is no one else in this world that matches my brand of crazy like Alexandra Elisabeth Delacroix. For every single curveball I throw at her, she throws it back tenfold, matching my insanity with her need for darkness.

I watch her head move around my gun and pull it back, only for her tongue to swirl around it and for her to take it back into her mouth again.

"Fuck," I pant. My thrusts become merciless. "You're the most beautiful woman I've ever seen." I push harder inside her, grabbing her legs and wrapping them around my hips. She presses back against me, moving in rhythm together with me. My heart is racing, not from the fucking, but from knowing that this is the last time I'll have her this close to me.

The last time I can allow myself to love Alex fully and let her love me in return.

I shove the gun further into her mouth. "Swallow," I order roughly. Her eyes light up with lust, and I pinch one of her nipples as I increase my pace. She comes around my dick as she attempts to swallow the barrel of my gun. Her pussy tightens around me, sending waves of pleasure through my entire body and forcing me to explode inside her.

There's a long silence as we both catch our breaths. Then, I pull the gun away from her mouth. I just want to fall onto her trembling body. I want to hold her close and caress her hair.

But she already knows what I'm here for.

"I'm guessing you want me to take you to my dad's office now," she pants.

I pull out and grab her shorts, putting them back on her.

"Yes. Get up," I say roughly as I grab her by the upper arm and hoist her up. She whimpers from the violence of my gesture, her knees buckling as I finally get her to stand. I hold her, gazing down at her.

Her eyes flutter shut, and she takes a deep breath. When she opens them again, there's something in them I've never seen before, and I can't pinpoint what it is.

"You're heartless," she rasps.

"And yet you love me. Tell me what that says about you."

She doesn't deny it, and we both accept it as the irrational yet straightforward truth.

"Come on," I say softly. "Don't make this harder on either of us."

I help her walk to her bedroom door, and once in the hallway, she guides me down the stairs, my grip on her arm gentle but firm.

Downstairs, Tamar is waiting for us. She's not the kind of girl who would often come and commit crimes with me, but I brought her tonight in case I need to breach through some computer security to get what I need.

Tamar looks at Alex and then at me, her worried eyes forcing me to toughen up.

"Alex," she whispers. "Are you alri—"

"She's fine," I grunt in answer. There's no space for feelings right now.

There's light shining under the door to her father's office, a straight line illuminating the three of us in the darkness of the house.

"He's up," Alex panics, shuffling back into me.

"That doesn't change anything." I put a hand at the back of her neck, guilt threatening to rip me apart.

I'm in love with this woman. And yet I've been the source of her grief from the moment we met.

I put the gun to her temple.

"Xi," Tamar hisses quietly. "What are you doing?"

My head snaps toward hers. "I need you to trust and listen to me, Tam." To Alex, I whisper, "I'm only doing this to scare him. I won't hurt you. I promise that on my life."

"You've already hurt me beyond repair," is her only answer.

I take in the pain, knowing I deserve it.

I open the office door and put my hand back on her neck. I take a deep breath as her dad's head lifts from his laptop.

"Senator Delacroix." Every single emotion running through my body mere moments ago, everything Alex can make me feel is gone. I'm cold as a stone. As dead as the lives of the people I cut short.

"What the hell is thi—"

"Shut up," I cut him off in a harsh tone. "It would be a shame for your daughter to take a bullet to the head just to protect your pride."

Tamar closes the office door behind me as I keep Alex in

front of me. I feel her shaking, but I'm sure she's not crying. No, I finally fucking did it. I made her as dead on the inside as me.

She's spent weeks attempting to light up my soul with her bright light. Instead, I snuffed out the flame inside her. Killed it with my own brand of darkness. How ironic for someone they accuse of being an arsonist.

"Sit over there, Senator," I say, pointing at the sofa with my chin. I nudge Alex, forcing her to sit there too. Tamar locks the door to the office and keeps the key with her.

"I'm going to have a look around. You two stay put."

I don't bother tying up Delacroix. His phone is on the desk, so he's got no one to contact, and he can't go anywhere. He's not strong enough to take me and there's also the threat of his daughter's life. So I'm safe. Plus, Tamar is keeping an eye on them.

It takes me less than a minute to find the safe he keeps hidden under the wood flooring. I've robbed enough houses to know where to find money and secrets.

"Code," I say simply. I don't want to be here any longer than necessary. Not because of the risk of getting caught, but because I can't take the betrayal on Alex's face. Every time my eyes dart to hers, my heart bleeds.

I swallow past my taut throat, my patience thinning by the second.

"The fucking code, Senator," I repeat. "Before I blow your daughter's brains out. It's a bitch to clean off. Trust me on that."

The glare he gives his daughter bothers me. It accuses her instead of me. It puts the blame on the woman with her hands cuffed behind her back rather than the man holding the gun.

Victim blaming at its finest.

I grab Alex by the hair, making her cry out as I drag her off the sofa and onto her knees in front of her father. My hands are shaking doing this, and I have to try my best to calm myself so Delacroix doesn't catch it.

"The. Code. Now." I seethe as I press the gun to her temple.

His nostrils flare. "Your fucking boyfriend, huh?" he says, looking down at her. "Now you know why he was dating you." The disgust in his voice curls my stomach.

"You knew?" she gasps.

"That you were seeing a thug from the North Shore? I know everything, Alexandra. You're the one stupid enough to think you can hide anything from me." The fucker dares look down at the queen she is.

"The code!" I bark as my gun goes from her to his forehead. "If you don't give a shit about her life, maybe you like yours a bit more?"

"2371A"

"Atta boy."

I kneel by the safe and open it. All that's inside is a burner phone. I grab it, but it's locked. This man clearly only uses this for things he doesn't want anyone to know about. Murder maybe. That would be useful.

"What is that doing here?" Delacroix grunts. He plays the shocked part well.

"Let's do this again," I huff. "Password."

"I don't have it," he says right away.

"Don't bullshit me."

"That phone...that phone shouldn't even be here. My security guard keeps it, and the password, from me. For instances like this. I can't give a password I don't know. He doesn't stay at night." A beat before he adds, "It looks like we're stuck."

"Do you think you're talking to the fucking rookie gangster of the year?" I growl. I give the phone to Tamar. "Be quick."

She pulls her laptop out of her backpack and sits at his desk. I stand behind her, watching her work while she starts attempting to breach the security barrier.

We're both focused on the laptop screen when the sound of a slap and Alex's whimper forces Tamar's fingers to freeze on the keyboard.

Glancing up, I see Alex on the floor, her cheek red and her eyes brimming with tears.

"You disgust me," her dad hisses with fury, now standing up in front of her.

I knew I was safe from him. I hadn't realized Alex was the one who wasn't.

"I'm sorry," she whimpers as he towers over her. She curls onto herself, attempting to make herself smaller in front of him.

"Your mistakes are going to ruin my entire career, Alexandra. He might as well shoot you because I'm going to kill you myself otherwise. I spent so much time on you. What for? So you could turn into the biggest disappointment of my life? You don't want to find out what happens when you're not useful to me anymore."

Am I fucking hallucinating right now?

"Dad...I'm sorry..."

"You *fucked* a man who is going to destroy everything I worked so hard for. You let him use you. Take you for a fool. Did you honestly think anyone could love you? *You*?" he barks. "I can see his cum running down your leg! Girls who can't be ladies are put with the whores, Alexandra. Is that what you want? For me to throw you out and give you to my friends, who'll show you what it's like to be used like a dirty slut?"

I stride to him as he rears his hand back to hit her again. Grabbing his wrist, I stop him. He turns around, scowling at me as Alex whimpers from fear.

"Mr. Delacroix," I drawl with a deadly calmness. "Hit her once, and we'll call it an unfortunate mistake. Hit her again, and I'll set your house on fire with you in it." I lean in slightly since he's much shorter than me. "And that's if I'm feeling kind."

He tries to jerk his arm from my grasp but doesn't compare to my strength. Not even a little bit.

"Alex," he rages. "I swear to God you better call this thug off or else—"

"I must warn you," I growl. "I can only take so many threats to my woman's life before I start losing my shit." I grab his tie. "That's a nice tie you have here. It would be a shame to end up hung by it."

As I watch sweat drip down his forehead, I realize that for the first time since I've met Alex, she doesn't try to stop me from being violent. She defended her dick of an ex when he was in the wrong, and she's the first one to say she hates violence. Yet, right now, she's watching me manhandle her father with wide eyes and in complete silence.

And that's when it hits me.

The lack of self-esteem. The fear. The people-pleasing. The infinite sorry's. The *bruises*.

All of it was deeply rooted. All of it was instilled by her own father.

The man who was meant to love her unconditionally, abused her. Who knows for how long.

"Sit down," I order her dad, my tone deadly. This time, I undo Alex's cuffs and put them on him. I give her the gun and train it on him. "He moves, you shoot." I glance at him. "You're only alive right now because I might need you."

Alex's bright, wet eyes dart to me, and against all odds... she nods. She sits on the opposite armchair and keeps my gun on the man she truly hates.

"Xi," Tamar grabs my attention. I stare at Alex for a few more seconds, her gaze stuck on her father and power in her eyes.

I walk back to my friend, and she shakes her head. "It's nothing," she whispers so he can't hear us.

"What?"

"It's a burner phone, but there's only one conversation on it, and...it's nothing. Just some normal texts."

I lean over her from behind, looking at her screen.

And how I wish it was nothing.

I read silently, knowing exactly what this is.

Tamar sighs. "It's just him asking some art dealer for a painting. Unless that painting is stolen, he's just talking about the cut the dealer will get. Vito Luciano can't use any of that against him."

"It's not a painting," I rasp, barely believing my eyes.

"It is. Look, *pick it up after midnight on February 14th. We'll be away on vacation for Valentine's day, so let yourself inside the house.*" She mumbles some other things that have been texted. "Then the art guy asks how much he should ask for. Delacroix says *two point four million nothing more. Your cut is one million.*" She pauses for a second. "That's a huge cut for an art dealer."

I run my hand against my face and rub my eyes. I can hardly believe what I'm seeing.

"It's not art," I repeat, feeling sweat running down my back. I've seen a lot of shit in my life. But this...this I never thought I'd see.

"What is it, then?"

My voice is barely audible because I struggle to believe it myself. "It's Alex."

My best friend's eyes leave the screen to look up at me. "I'm...confused."

I straighten up, feeling the room tilt from the shock. I round the desk, standing in front of it with Tamar behind me and our hostages in front of me. "You motherfucker orchestrated the kidnapping of your own daughter."

Tamar gasps as Alex turns to me, pale as a ghost. "What?"

Delacroix doesn't say anything.

"Dad?"

"He's out of his mind," he replies casually.

"Why would he do that?" Alex asks me, utterly confused.

"For sympathy. So people would talk about it. Career boost...who fucking knows what else?"

Tamar jumps back in. "This doesn't make sense. How could you know him asking to pick up a painting means, *walk into my house and take my daughter.*"

"Because I'm the one he hired."

The silence stretches for so long, I have to take a look at Tamar to make sure she's still alive.

My best friend stares at me with wide eyes. She never knew what I'd done. "Please, tell me you didn't spend Valentine's Day kidnapping a young girl..."

"She was eighteen."

"...and then dated her."

"None of this was planned. In February, it meant a million dollars for NSC. Obviously, nine months later, she means something else to me."

"I don't...I can't...Xi, you're *not* a kidnapper."

I cock an eyebrow at her. I've kidnapped and tortured many men, and she knows it.

"I mean of *innocent people*," she hisses. "What the hell went through your head?"

"We were desperate."

"Who was with you? What did you do with the money?"

"Logan, his brother, and Racer. I never got the money because the cops got to the house. I now know it was Delacroix who sent them after us since he was tracking his daughter. The fucker never intended on giving us any money. He just wanted to show the world he could rescue her. He wanted some publicity."

Delacroix looks at me and back at his daughter.

"He's lying," he tells her, the lie slipping through his teeth like a snake through the grass.

In a swift movement, I grab the gun back from Alex and press it against her dad's forehead. "Don't call me a liar. I've come clean to your daughter about my mistakes. It's time you do the same. Tell her."

"Dad," Alex whimpers. "Please...I don't want you to die. Tell me the truth."

His panicked eyes dart from her to me multiple times. "People's opinion was that I wasn't a family man. That I was incapable of love. They thought I was cold toward you and your mother. I needed to gain their trust back. I needed to show I would do anything for my daughter."

When Alex talks again, she's right next to me. There are no tears on her face. She's not shaking anymore.

"That's right." Her voice is low, controlled. "So you sent Xi and his crew to kidnap me and hold me for ransom." Her tone freezes me to the bone. It's like nothing I've heard from her before. It's like that glint I saw in her eyes earlier. So lethal.

"You let me stay in a filthy house with a dangerous man who assaulted me. You let him torture me until it'd been long enough for people to see you cry about your daughter. And *then* you came to get me back. If people knew how you 'took care of me' afterward. That you wouldn't even look at me. That you locked me in the same room I was taken from, while I was having panic attacks about that night. You let me cry until I passed out. You only got a nurse when you walked into my bedroom one morning and thought I was dead. You let my trauma get worse. You let it turn into PNES. You let me *die* on the inside."

"You're a slut who came when her attacker fingered her!" he roars. "That's not my daughter!"

The shock makes me take a step back. He watched the whole video.

"I did," she says, almost proudly. She fake pouts and presses her tits together with her upper arms. "He was just so good at it, Daddy."

"You disgusting whore." He spits at her feet, and I press the gun harder against his forehead.

"Do that again, and I will make you lick it off the floor."

"He'll do it, Dad," Alex chuckles. It's so cold. "Xi is a *bad* man." And it's my turn to be on the receiving end of her sharp tongue. "You and your friends took the role so seriously, didn't you? Such good actors. Pretending you didn't know whose house you were in. Pretending it was a *simple* home invasion so I would do everything you said."

I lick my lips, racking my brain. What is she doing?

Her hard eyes narrow when she insists, "Am I right?"

"Yes," I say simply, taken by the power she's wielding over us.

"Well, would you look at that? Look at the men I'm surrounded with. A father who abused me since I can remember. The only thing he taught me was how to hide bruises with makeup. And a boyfriend who lied to me all along about being the man who had traumatized me."

She looks at Tamar, her cute little smile back on her face. Except it's as fake as they come. "No wonder a woman loses her mind, eh?"

"Alex," I say tentatively. "Are you okay?" Her behavior is not her. She's not *herself.*

There's a pause before she hisses. "Of course, I'm not fucking okay."

This woman scares me. This woman sounds powerful and in control. It's a new version of Alex.

I think I love it.

My thoughts are cut short by her dad bursting into laughter—a genuine, maniacal-sounding laugh.

"Poor boy, don't you see what she's done?"

My brows furrow. I look at him, and when I look back at Alex, the confusion dissipates. She's smiling at me like the devil would to a sinner's soul he's about to snatch. It's eerie and, oh, so fucking sexy.

"She orchestrated this whole night," her dad keeps on laughing. "What a little cunt you are, Alex."

And I finally understand.

I understand that my beautiful girlfriend has been playing me.

She duped me into thinking I was in control tonight when she was the mastermind.

I felt it in her room earlier, but I didn't trust my gut. I didn't believe my sweet Alexandra could turn against all of us.

You could have kept it from me. Forever. I could have loved you till death had you just kept it to yourself.

"How long have you known?" I ask her calmly.

33

XI

Mastermind – Taylor Swift

Alex was not surprised when I told her the truth. She didn't want to hear it because she wanted to keep us in a bubble of ignorance. She never wanted me to confirm something she already knew.

No one could love another knowing what you've done.

She hates herself that she does. She kept it to herself and carried on loving me despite knowing.

"How long?" I repeat.

"Since the night I found out you were part of NSC."

I shake my head, hardly believing what I'm hearing. She was aware all this time. She...she told me she loved me, and she already knew.

"Since the night at the warehouse? How? My eyes? My voice? Did you finally remember?"

She shakes her head. "Trauma is a bitch. I never recognized your eyes or your voice because so many things about that night are unclear. Although maybe that's why I always thought your eyes were so mesmerizing or why I felt so comfortable with you. Perhaps, subconsciously, I knew you were the one who had changed my life."

I have to physically swallow the information she's giving me. "If not that...then how?" I insist.

"You have a tell, do you know that?"

I feel my eyebrows lifting. My hand is sweaty around the gun, my arm starting to shake from holding it out.

"Every time you lie." Her tongue darts to her two front teeth, and I recognize it as exactly what I do. "Do you remember when I asked if there was anything else you'd lied about?"

Like it was yesterday. She was trying to break up with me.

Her tongue grazes her teeth again as she repeats the lie I told her. "*No, baby. You know everything.*"

I close my eyes, hating myself. Opening them again, I watch helplessly as she grabs a fistful of my t-shirt.

"And then I saw them." She lifts it to show my lower abdomen. "The three scars. The only thing I remembered about the monster who had kidnapped me."

My eyes flick down and I lick my lips. I made sure to never take my shirt off in front of Alex. I didn't want to do it until I was ready to tell her everything. But the night she learned about NSC, I was too focused on not losing her. I didn't realize I was topless when she left. I didn't realize she saw the scars.

Flashes hit me so hard I sway.

I'm excited for your dad's birthday party, Ella.

Alex is the one who brought up the topic of Gerald Baker's birthday party. She pretended it was an accident, that it slipped. She had Ella invite me so it wouldn't be obvious she was desperate for me to come.

"You wanted me here tonight," I murmur.

I look around at Tamar, still sitting at the desk, the phone right there. Delacroix was shocked when he saw it in the safe.

"You're the one who put the phone in the safe."

"This morning." Her devilish smirk is magnificent.

She's just standing there, right next to me, her gorgeous blonde hair disheveled, her cheeks red, and her hairline damp from sweat. Still, everything is in her hazel eyes. They can never hide anything from me.

She is so beautifully powerful at this moment.

"You knew...you knew your dad orchestrated your kidnapping," I rasp.

"Yes," she says calmly.

I open my mouth and clamp it shut. I take a second and ask, "H-how...Why?"

"You're at a loss for words, so let me help," she says condescendingly. "The moment I realized you were my kidnapper, I decided to use you since you clearly have no conscience." She looks at her dad and then at me again. "You men are so malleable, it's a joke anyone ever put you in power. The day I learned you wanted dirt on my dad, I found it myself. And oh my, what a surprise when I saw my progenitor was the one who hired you to break me." She cocks an eyebrow and tilts her head to the side. "Do you understand your role now?"

When I blink at her, she laughs mockingly.

"Let me make it simple for you two. One of you has abused me my entire life, and one of you is a violent criminal. Here I am, in the middle, used by the both of you. All I had to do was get you," she looks at me pointedly, "in the same room as him," she nudges her head toward her dad, "to witness what he does to me. We were broken up—because you're a dick—so it would have sounded suspicious

461

if I suddenly invited you, didn't it? I played the heartbroken girl part for a few weeks so it'd sink in. So you'd become more obsessed than ever, holding onto any branch I offer, even if it's a twig. I brought up the birthday party, and *look at that!* Xi is desperate to come."

She puts her hands to her cheek, pretending to be an actress playing a dramatic role. "*Oh, no, please don't come.*"

"You checked if I was going to work late tonight," her dad murmurs to himself.

Her sharp eyes turn to him.

"Well, yes. Initially, I was going to bring Xi to your office after the party and announce that we were together. Then I was going to slowly watch you lose your shit."

Her mouth twists, showing that it didn't work out as planned. "But then he didn't show up. My hopes died until he broke into my room in the middle of the night *again*. I could see something was wrong. Something had changed. And the poor boy admitted everything to me, so I immediately reminded him why he was using me in the first place."

I'm guessing you want me to take you to my dad's office now.

She manipulated me just like I did her.

"The result was the same." She shrugs her shoulders. "We were all alone in the office. Then I had to get you to hit me. Which isn't hard, is it, Dad? I spread my legs a little and showed you his cum running down my thighs. And there you were, showing your true self. Now Xi saw it. He saw some old bruises you left on me, too. He knows you're the one who hired him." She winces, her little face scrunching up, and shakes her head. "Doesn't look too good for you, Dad. That man is crazy for me."

She turns to me, vulnerability shining in her eyes. "Imagine falling in love with the person who broke you," she whispers. "Imagine...being able to get past it and hating yourself for it while at the same time finding it impossible to stop that awful flow of true love you feel slithering through your veins."

Her eyes dart around my face, moving between mine like following a game of tennis. "Isn't that the saddest thing you've ever heard?" she rasps.

I shake my head. "It's the most beautiful thing I've ever heard," I whisper.

The corner of her mouth tips into a winning smirk. "Make it up to me, then."

"What?" I ask, completely taken aback.

"Dad," she says, almost innocently. "Let's play one of our games. What does the Latin word *mors* mean?"

Delacroix pales.

"Dad?" she sing-songs without even looking at him.

"D-death," he stutters.

Her gaze goes to the gun and back to me, her voice lethal. "That man has made every single second of my life a living hell. Now pull that trigger and avenge me."

My heart explodes, beating so loudly in my ears I can barely hear Tamar's voice behind me.

"Xi, don't."

Alex's eyes narrow on Tamar, ready to annihilate anyone who dares stand in her way.

"He's a senator. Do *not* kill that man."

"Listen to your friend," Delacroix blurts out.

Except my eyes are on Alex.

"You did all this so I would kill your dad?" I ask, completely incredulous.

"Yes. Because it turns out I'm too weak to do it myself." She flutters her eyelashes at me. "I'm just a woman, after all."

Tamar stands up suddenly, the clattering sound of the chair falling behind her resonating in the room.

"Xi, if you do this, you're going straight to prison. For life."

"It wouldn't be the first man you kill for me. I would be careful if I were you, though. Think about the cleanup or Tamar's right: your years in prison will be long and painful." Her smug smile gets to me. Her controlling tone wrapping around me.

I'm a sucker for this woman's power, ready to fall at her feet like a knight offering his protection to a queen.

She glances at her father one last time. "I just wanted to be *enough*, you know?" For a second, her innocence and vulnerability ring through the room again. "I just wanted to be enough." And she's back on me. "Do it." Her order is soft, even as her eyes are sharp. They're knives digging into me and killing my resolve.

I would do anything for her. I stare deep into her eyes, seeing her love stronger than it's ever been.

And I pull the trigger.

Bang!

34

ALEXANDRA

The Heart Wants What It Wants – Selena Gomez

It's not ugly. Xi pulled away from his head and shot his chest instead.

Right in the heart.

He was looking straight at me when he did it.

My dad's body falls back against the sofa he's sitting on, and it's only when I see the blood seeping from his chest onto his expensive rug that I realize what I did.

"Oh my god," I gasp. The smell of burnt powder and blood makes me gag. "You...you did it."

He grabs the back of my neck and forces me to look up at him.

"You didn't have to put all this elaborate plan in place," he growls. "You could have just *asked*."

I smile at him. Pride feels so warm in my body. It makes me tingle. It turns me on.

"What would be the fun in that?" I sneer. "It's not so nice to be used by the person you love, is it? To be oblivious to the control they have over you."

He shakes his head, and I smile to myself. I can still fit a Taylor Swift song to my situation. I'm on my *Vigilante Shit* right now, and people are paying for their mistakes. "Alex, I love you. I'm desperately in love with you. I would do anything for you."

"And you have. *Now*, we're even. Now, I don't feel like a stupid girl who got used."

"You two are completely insane." Tamar's voice is a shocked, choked sound.

We turn to her. "It's called love," I chuckle. "Just our version of it."

"He's going to get arrested," she snaps.

"Tamar," he says, his hands now holding my waist tightly. There's a strong desire in his eyes. They're burning with lust. "Go get her mom."

Despite her disagreement, Tamar runs out of the room. The second she's gone, his lips crash on mine, his tongue pushing inside my mouth, and everything inside me explodes. My knees buckle, but he's holding me up. My hands are shaking when they come to grab his t-shirt. I can't breathe, but who needs air when you're being kissed that way? It's soul-shattering, so poignant I can feel his fist around my heart, forcing it to pump warm blood through my veins.

When he pulls away, he murmurs, "I've never been so proud of you in my life."

Only when I sniffle do I notice the tears raining down my cheeks.

"I love you, Alex," he breathes out as he pulls me to his chest. "I love you with everything I am."

Squeezing my eyes shut and forcing drops to fall from the corner of my eyes, I nod, acknowledging his words. And despite not wanting it—despite wishing for everything and anything but that heartbreaking feeling—I rasp, "I love you too."

"Good girl," he sighs with relief. It's as if there would have been no point in all this if I couldn't have added that I still loved him. Everything tells me he would have grabbed that gun and pointed it at his chest had I not made it worth being alive.

"Tamar is going to take you to your mom's car now. She'll be in there waiting for you."

When a small gasp escapes me, he presses his thumb to my bottom lip, mesmerized by it. "I want you to tell her what your dad did to you. The truth about the abuse. All of it. Then I want you to explain exactly what happened tonight. Your plan. What I did. Everything."

I feel my brows furrowing as I look up at his face. "I don't understand."

"There's nothing to understand, only the truth to tell."

"But what about you—"

"Don't worry about me. Now go, baby."

"My bunnies," I whisper. I think deep down I know Xi so well that I can imagine what he's about to do to this entire house.

"Fucking hell, Alex," he chuckles, like remembering who he's facing. "I'll take care of your bunnies. Don't worry."

Tamar is back before I know it, and she grabs my hand, pulling me. "Come on, Alex. Every second we waste is a second closer to chaos."

Xi kisses the top of my head, his eyes already longing for me. Does he not see my heart attempting to crawl out of its cavity so it can stay with his?

Does he not understand I would kill anyone for him too?

Tamar guides me outside. My mom is standing by her car, wearing a silk robe. Her eye mask is pushed up to her forehead, and she runs to me when she sees me.

"Alex," she cries out, her hands coming to rest on either side of my face. She checks my face and the rest of my body. I'm shaking and must look pale because she asks, "Are you alright, sweetie?"

"I'm okay." I nod sternly. "Get in the car."

I help her into her car, and I don't even know who's driving. All I know is that she holds me close to her chest and her beating heart calms mine.

I don't know where we're driving to, but I do know she's holding my hand, and that's all that matters right now.

The adrenaline disappears as we get further away from the house, the fear choking me. Suddenly, having my mother near me is something I didn't realize I would need so much. And when she asks what happened for the tenth time tonight...I tell her.

She cries with me when I share the abuse her husband put me through. I see the guilt in her eyes when she realizes the extent of the things she didn't see. And when I tell her my own dad had orchestrated my kidnapping to benefit his reputation and win the sympathy of the public, I feel her heart fissuring.

"I should have known," she rasps.

"How?" I snort. "He was so good at making me terrified of telling anyone."

"Because he tried on me once." My eyes widen and she caresses my swollen cheek from when he hit me earlier. "He stopped as soon as I threatened to leave him and take my money with me."

Of course. My dad's entire career, hell, his entire life

relied on my mother being a billionaire with a famous name.

"But you've been married for so long. Surely he was entitled to some of it by now."

She snorts. "Give your mother some credit, Alex. I'm not such a fool that I would marry a man as power angry as him without a prenup."

My mouth falls open. I don't know my mom, only from afar. I'm a stranger to her as much as all the people she invites to her Gatsby-like parties. I always took her for a weak, looked-after wife. That so long as someone made the decisions for her and she could have her fun, she wouldn't bat an eyelid.

But she's smarter than I thought. Or at least not a complete idiot.

"Why did you stay with him, then? You have everything. You didn't need him."

She can hear the desperation in my voice because her eyes close softly for a few seconds. "At first, I thought I loved him. Then we got married, and what I thought was love quickly disappeared. By then I was pregnant. Life flashes before you when you age. You blink, and your baby is eighteen and you still never got to know her. You're with a man you hate, but you don't want to be the horrible mother who broke her family." Her eyes dart around my body before she talks again. "Of course...I had no idea. I should have, but I didn't because..." Her voice dies, and she swallows.

"You never wanted me, did you?"

"Your father is a master manipulator," she admits. "The moment he saw my love fading, he was always on me. And suddenly, you were here."

I lay back, looking at the ceiling of the car. Tears fall down my face for something I've known all my life.

"Alexandra," my mom says as she puts her hand in mine. "I love you."

I drag in a shaky breath but refuse to turn to her when I hear her voice wavering. "I was not a good mother to you. I never wanted to be a mother at all, but this doesn't change the fact that I love you with all my heart. I don't expect you to forgive me for not seeing what was right under my nose, and even less for the hurt I've caused by not caring for you like a mother should. But I don't need your forgiveness to start fixing the pain I've caused."

I sniffle, a relief coming over me. All I've ever wanted was for her to see me. For one of my parents to tell me they love me. I'm not ready to create a bond with her, but I will take what she has to offer.

I turn to her and nod. She smiles through the tears on her face, and I tell her something I've never told her before.

"Mom..." I feel my chin trembling, the realization of what I've done catching up with me. "I'm scared," I force past the tightness in my throat.

"Oh, baby," she sobs. "Mommy's here."

I lay down in the car, my head on her lap and hand in my hair.

"I love you, Alex," she sniffles. "I'm sorry."

For the first time in my life, I feel safe in my mother's arms. The adrenaline crashes, and I'm asleep before we reach our destination.

35

ALEXANDRA

The Night We Met – Lord Huron

I watch a duck make its way from the lake shore to the water, five ducklings following behind. From my bedroom's wooden balcony, I have a perfect view of the lake. We have a private deck that gives us access to the crystal-clear water. Nothing on the horizon but water and far, far away, the shadow of the cliffs I know belong to the North Shore.

It's snowing today, a white coat decorating the beautiful surroundings. Evergreen branches are heavy with snow, and the ponds surrounding the lakes are frozen. Soon, the lake will freeze too, and our fellow billionaires and millionaires will come to ice skate on the thick ice.

"Miss Delacroix." The deep voice startles me, stopping the flow of condensation coming from my mouth and into the cold air.

I turn around to find Vincent, my mother's personal bodyguard, standing by the French doors leading to my bedroom. In the last two weeks, Vincent has been the only one allowed in our lake house.

Security surrounds it, worried that anything could happen to us now that my father is dead.

An accident. That's what it's been ruled as.

It seems my father fell asleep in his office with a cigar in his hand and the thing set the whole place on fire. Only my mother and I escaped, leaving a *beloved* Senator behind.

There was not enough left of his body to know he died of a bullet to the chest before Xi lit up the whole place.

He has many ways to make a body disappear, but fires burn when Ziad is angry. And God knows he was fuming at my dad for hurting me.

I haven't seen him since. We've been captive in our own home while the reporters surround our property like vultures. While the coroner was working and deciding what had truly happened. The second it was ruled an accident, my mom had her assistant organize the funeral.

Two weeks. She gave her no more than that. She doesn't want to give any more time or energy to a man she now loathes. The same assistant wrote a statement from *his grieving family* that went out in the newspaper. Mom made no other appearances.

She's too angry. Too busy trying to make it right by me. I have never seen my mother like this, so attentive and loving. It's a speck of light in the darkness surrounding me.

"Miss Delacroix," Vincent repeats. "It's time to go." I notice just now that he's holding my oversized, blacked-out sunglasses. I need them to make sure everyone thinks I'm crying.

It's strange how the little guilt I had turned into pride over the last few weeks. How I realized being free of my father was worth every nightmare I've had since. I'm certain his ghost will disappear because he can't hurt me anymore.

I grab the glasses Vincent is handing me. Today, I chose

my own clothes for a public appearance. That had never happened in my life. My dad had always done so, forbidding me to wear heavy makeup and look like a whore.

I'm trembling under the black, knee-length lace dress I'm wearing. I grab the black faux fur coat on my bed, my hand itching to wear the fuchsia leather jacket I have next to it.

Vincent must notice because he says, "One last time, Miss Delacroix." When I turn to him confused, he adds, "Just pretend one last time. Then you can be yourself forever."

I understand he knows everything, and I'm surprised my mom told him, wondering what their relationship truly is. How close are they?

His words stick with me as I button my coat.

Then you can be yourself forever.

And isn't that the problem when you don't know who you truly are?

My father has dictated me my entire life. I only know a couple of things about my taste and personality. I love fuchsia and Taylor Swift. But I don't know who I am as a person. I relied on my dad for that. I had no choice but to.

The press follows our car closely as we make our way to Stoneview Cemetery. They're forbidden to follow us past the gates, but it doesn't stop them from hurling questions at us as we walk the few yards from where our chauffeur is dropping us off and to the entrance.

"Miss Delacroix, is it true you took drugs in college?"

My mom holds me closer, slipping an *ignore them* in my ear.

"Mrs. Delacroix, you seem awfully close to your bodyguard...did your husband confront you about it?"

I take her hand in mine and give her a small smile. "I hope that's true," I whisper before eyeing Vincent.

She blushes and shakes her head. "Don't be silly."

"Miss Delacroix! Miss Delacroix!" When I don't respond, the man insists, "Elisabeth!" I freeze at that name. He jumps on that. "Is it true you're dating a gang member from the North Shore of Silver Falls?"

I don't know. Is it? I haven't heard from Xi in the two weeks following my dad's death. I didn't message him since he changes numbers so often. I knew he wouldn't receive it after such a huge event.

Vincent nudges me, silently telling me to keep going until we're safe behind the gates. I nod at Ella and Peach as we walk past the rows and rows of seats. They're sitting in the middle with their parents. Her brother Luke is here too. So are Christopher Murray and his parents. It's a small town, and most of us know each other. Camila is sitting near the front with the Diaz family. Her mother was one of my father's many attorneys.

His funeral lasts forever. Speeches after speeches about how much of a good man and fair politician he was. The national anthem, a flag folded on his casket, and finally, after forever standing, sitting, and standing again in the snow under the umbrella Vincent is holding above my mother and me, he is put to rest.

I have never felt so relieved in my life. Because nothing would have stopped him but death. If for a bullet in his chest, he would have tormented me forever. I would have never lived. I would have only been an extension of him.

Everything comes to me at once. The fact that I hate knee and ankle-length dresses. That tulle is a horrible material, itchy and too innocent looking. That I love short skirts and dancing. Finally, It hits me in the chest that I hate politics and all the classes that come with it. That I love using the word *thing* when I can't describe something.

Lightning strikes me when I understand how much I want to be closer to my mom, even though we barely have anything in common. I want to hear about her love for art and stick my fingers in the gooey paint. I want to jump in a puddle and soil my dress. I want to scream at the top of my lungs that sometimes I'm a lady, and often I'm a whore for the man I love.

I want to find Xi and tell him how much I love him.

That when I'm ready again, when I've found the woman I truly am, I will be ready to love him fully.

Tears fall down my cheeks, and I hope everyone thinks it's for my dad. Because no one gets to understand how free I suddenly feel. This is for me only.

We go through rounds and rounds of condolences, hugs, and formal handshakes. It's never-ending, and I've never been a good actress. I hope everyone takes my silence and indifference as shock and grief. It's only when a man in an all-black suit comes to shake my mother's hand that my attention comes back to the present.

"Fleur," he says low. Everything about him screams criminal in the most elegant way possible. His hard face doesn't have an ounce of empathy, and his black eyes dart to mine before returning to my mother.

He's with a tall woman in a midnight-blue suit. Her hands are crossed behind her back and her green eyes dart everywhere, so aware of everything around us she must be dizzy. She has long red hair, like Peach, but unlike my best friend, there's nothing friendly about her.

"I apologize," he says to my mom. "That it ended this

way." No condolences. Only an apology heavy with meaning.

My mother shakes her head, the shadow of a smile twitching at the corner of her mouth. "The result is more or less the same."

He eyes me again. "Minus innocence," he adds in a murmur, his eyes stuck on me.

"Thank you for coming," she cuts the conversation short. "I'll be in touch."

It's only when everyone is gone, and we're crossing the cemetery that I ask, "Who was that?"

She doesn't need me to tell her who I mean.

"His name is Vito Luciano. He's an old friend of mine."

Everything is instinctively clear in my head. No need to use your brain when your gut tells you the truth.

"Mom, did you...did you—"

"Ask the head of a criminal family to find dirt on your dad because I wanted to ruin his career?" She pauses, clearly checking my reaction. When she deems she can trust me, she continues. "Yes. As I told you before, I hated the man. I promise you on my life I had no idea how Vito was proceeding about it."

Shocked, I swallow heavily. Xi was asked to kidnap the daughter of a Senator by the man himself. That girl was me.

My mother asked a mafia man for info on my dad, Vito asked Xi, and Xi used me.

We've come full circle to the insanity of the lives we live, the intricate bonds between the billionaires of Stoneview and the crime families around us.

Xi and me? We're just pawns in bigger games.

"Why?" I ask with a strength I've come to understand is a new part of me.

"I wanted to divorce him. He didn't. Your father was a

master manipulator, and there was only one way out. I waited until you went to college, thinking I could keep you out of it. I was wrong, and I'm sorry."

I give her a tight-lipped smile. "I forgive you, Mom. I would have done anything to get rid of him too. In fact, I have."

"We have our whole lives for you to forgive me truly. For everything." She wraps an arm around my shoulders and walks me toward the gates.

Just like in the movies, I notice a tall, dark shadow leaning on a tree at the back. Too far to have heard anything from the funeral, close enough to keep an eye on me.

Xi looks handsome in a black suit. It doesn't fit who he is, but he is beautiful, nonetheless. His arms are crossed over his chest, strong muscles threatening to crack the seam of the suit jacket. He must be freezing without a coat.

"I'll meet you at the car," I tell my mother. Her eyes follow my gaze, and she nods.

I take my time walking to Xi, delaying the inevitable.

"Hey," I finally say, facing the giant in front of me.

"Hey." His voice is the same as it always is, devoid of emotions. They seem to be stuck in his eyes, swirling with the different shades of brown—Tiger's eye stone.

The first thing that comes to mind is fixing my mistakes. Something unfixable. "I'm sorry about Zara." His sad eyes meet mine. That's the last thing he was expecting. "Billie told me. And I want you to know that had I known...had I been able to grasp how dangerous it was to withhold information from you, I wouldn't have. You were right, it's not my world and I knew nothing. I'm sorry you felt you failed her. I don't think you did." When his confusion starts being clear on his face, I add, "I think you live in a place torn by a war you can't control, and you can't save everyone around you."

He takes a deep breath, his eyes dampening. When he swallows, the tears disappear without having had a chance to fall.

"How have you been?" I ask.

"I should be the one asking you that question," he chuckles dryly.

"Do it, then," I snap a little too hard. I can see he likes it, the determination in my voice.

"How have you been?"

"Better than I thought," I admit. I pause, taking him in, breathing in the familiar scent of his cologne mixed with the hints of turpentine. "But I miss you."

His eyes darken with sadness. "I miss you too." Another heavy pause, during which he pushes off the tree and takes my hands. "Alex," he rasps. "I want you to know that I've officially left NSC."

My eyes widen, my mouth falling open.

"You were wrong," he adds.

"Wrong?"

"I'm not heartless. I know I'm not, because..." he licks his lips, "because, how do I love you if not with my entire heart?"

Tears prickle at my eyes because this is not how this was meant to go. I shake my head. "Xi...I don't think we should keep seeing each other. Not for now."

His grip on me tightens.

"I know what I did was wrong, Alex. I know...I know I lied. But you knew, and you chose to stay."

"It's not about the kidnapping. I'm in love with you despite that."

"Nothing is the same in my life without you in it. I can't

go back to something that isn't me anymore. My heart doesn't belong to NSC. It belongs to you."

Running a hand through his hair, he looks away and back at me, grabbing my hand again, holding both in his gigantic palms. He puts one against his chest and takes a deep breath. "Do you feel that? I feel like I've had to fake being alive for so long I had forgotten that I was barely surviving. With you, I'm finally learning how to breathe. You're my oxygen, Alex. You're my everything."

"You're my everything, too," I rasp.

"Then there should be no issue. I took a job with Dickie. I'm painting. I want to change my life around. For you. For us."

"I'm happy you figured it out," I say honestly. "But I need to do the same."

He doesn't even let me breathe to keep going. "Tell me what to do, and I'll do it. Tell me how long you need."

"I can't give you a timeline—"

"How long," he grates through clenched teeth. "I need to know when you'll come back to me."

"I can't say. I'm barely learning to be myself. I want to be someone outside of my dad's puppet. I want to discover myself. I want to know I didn't do all of this because you had taken over my entire being, that I also did it for myself."

He inhales through flared nostrils, attempting to control himself. "I need you," he exhales. "Make me a better man, baby. *Please.*" The desperation in his eyes almost causes me to break.

"Make yourself a better man, Xi. And I'll become a woman with a mind of her own while you do that."

"What if...what if you don't come back." His throat is tight; I can see it. I can hear it in his fragile voice.

"Then it wasn't meant to be, I guess." I swallow the same

tautness in my throat. I can feel our hearts beating in unison. I can feel the thread that links my beating organ to his.

My hand is still on his chest as the grip on my wrist tenses. "If I could go back to that night. The night I took you from your home...If—" his voice breaks. "If I'd known I could lose you, I would have kept you to myself. I would have never let you go."

A genuine smile spreads onto my face. "That's not true." I press my hand harder against his chest. "It beats too hard for me, that big heart of yours."

Going on my toes, my lips brush his before I leave a featherlight kiss on them. I step back, but he still holds me.

"Give me a Taylor Swift song," he says with a hint of humor. "Just to make it all better."

I need to leave before he shatters my resolve.

"*Afterglow.*"

He lets me go, and I whisper the most famous three magic words before walking back to the car.

Once inside, I break.

Tears come crashing and falling while my heart shrinks and pumps poisonous regret into my veins.

I sacrificed the love of my life for a chance to become whole. If this backfires, there will be nothing left of me.

"Sweetie," my mom consoles me as I burst into tears. She holds me as the car drives away. I turn around only to see Xi run out of the cemetery and after our car until he understands there's nothing he can do. The anguish on his face ends me, and a sob explodes out of my throat. I watch Xi become a small point on the road until we turn onto another street.

By the time we reach home, I've calmed down, my mom holding me close to her.

"Is there anything I can do?"

I'm about to say no when something comes to me. "Actually, yes."

She looks at me, expectant, as a buzzing resonates in my chest. "I would like you to help a friend of mine. He's looking at a career in art. He's a painter."

"Of course, sweetie. Anything."

My mom has enough contacts in the art world to make or break anyone.

"That friend of yours," she says softly. "Do you plan on seeing him anytime soon?" Of course, she knows exactly who I mean.

I shake my head. "Not until I've learned to fully love myself."

EPILOGUE

ALEXANDRA

Miss Americana & The Heartbreak Prince – Taylor Swift

Three months later...

"Happy birthday!" Ella screams as she runs into the lake house. I suffocate in her arms, the fuchsia balloons she's holding bumping against my head. Behind her, Peach walks in carrying a huge, white-frosted cake.

"If it's not chocolate, I'll kick you out," I announce as Ella lets me go.

"Chocolate with vanilla frosting. Boring like your ass," she laughs.

I turn around and slap my ass. "This ass is anything but boring."

"Fine, you win. Your ass is great. Happy birthday, bitch," Peach cheers.

"Is your mom here?" Ella asks politely.

"Kitchen. Come." I take the cake from Peach and lead them to the kitchen. We like being by the lake, so we stayed. Mom is using the insurance money to rebuild the old house, but she doesn't want to live in it anyway, so she's going to sell it.

She's been enjoying our extended retreat at the lake. Especially since Vincent is keeping us company.

"Hi girls," Mom greets them. "I'm so glad you're here to celebrate Alex. Can you believe my baby is turning nineteen?"

I roll my eyes, pretending to be annoyed.

"She's so focused on her studies, we barely see her anymore," Peach pouts. "Us turning up here was the only solution."

Since changing my major from politics to early childhood education, I've loved my studies so much that I always have my nose in a book. My friends are used to seeing me study all the time, but not enjoying myself, so they try not to distract me.

During the Christmas break last year, Xi Ep sent us to volunteer with children from vulnerable backgrounds. I was at a community center on the North Shore, spending the holidays helping kids with their homework and organizing activities for them. That's when I fell in love with the job.

I found my true calling spending time with those little babes and took the initiative to change my major as soon as I returned to SFU. My mom fully supported me and I'm now on my way to becoming an elementary school teacher.

"You're so dramatic," I tell Peach.

"If I was dramatic, would I be here today? No, I would be mad at you."

There's a short pause, and they all look at me, clearly expecting something from me.

"What?" I ask, clueless.

When they see I'm completely lost, Ella says, "If I *were*," to Peach.

"Damn, I didn't even hear it," I chuckle as I brush it to the side. "Can we open my presents?"

"Lunch first, maybe?" my mom suggests.

"Fine." I let out an exaggerated sigh that makes them laugh.

It's only my mom, my two best friends, and me at home. And Vincent, of course, who's always near my mother. He lurks in the kitchen doorway, watching her with heart-shaped eyes.

The most unprofessional bodyguard I've ever met.

We enjoy our lunch together, eat cake and open presents. Ella got me a Tiffany's bracelet that should definitely be gifted to a partner rather than a friend, but I accept it with joy. Peach got me a gigantic vibrating dildo since *I don't get out of the house nearly enough to find dick.*

My cheeks flush as my mom explodes in laughter. "She's not exactly wrong," she snorts.

"You should come to some Xi Ep parties," Peach insists. "It's so much better now that the older sisters respect us."

I shake my head. "No, thank you." I left Xi Ep the first week of January, when we got back to college. I've come to know myself better, and I'm not a party girl. I'm not a sorority babe who enjoys alcohol and men. I respect my best friends for staying and forging solid friendships with the sisters, but I've discovered I am indeed a stay-at-home-with-a-good-book kind of girl. Especially now that I get to enjoy whatever book I want rather than the ones my dad forced me to read.

My mom and I have been enjoying buddy-reading sexy romances, and I've discovered a new passion. My favorite thing to do in the evening is to put Taylor Swift on and read a book by the fireplace.

"Thank you for my gifts, girls. I love them."

"Especially mine, right?" Peach winks.

"Speaking of massive dongs, how's Wren?" I ask.

She ignores my question. "Should we go ice skate?"

"Well, maybe Alex can open my present first?"

My eyes round. I don't remember the last birthday my mom gave me a present herself. She usually sends someone to buy it and give it to me, or gets it mailed to me when she's away partying with artists in Europe.

It's a simple square envelope with my name on it. I open it with trembling hands, my heart already sensing what it could be.

You are cordially invited to the Fleur Delacroix Art Gallery for the opening night of our new collection:
A love that lasts forever
Please, join us for an evening of cocktails and canapés while discovering our rising artist of the year; XI (Eleven)

In the hopes of seeing you there,
Fleur Delacroix

I didn't need to read the *eleven*. I know that's the name Xi uses as an artist, but I'm glad he made sure it was specified on the invitation.

"Mom," I breathe out, practically choking on emotions.

"You don't have to go," she says soothingly. "I just wanted to give you the invite. It's the first exhibition we have at the gallery this year. That man has worked hard, and his talent should be seen and appreciated by everyone. Including you. I already know it's the one and only time he'll be at such a small gallery. He will sell and be off to bigger and greater things in the art world."

A feeling of pride wraps around me. It's warm and electrifying. Xi's art is going to be on display in a gallery for the first time. How could I not go?

"I can't wait to see Harper," I say bitterly, making everyone around me laugh.

In the last few months, Harper has been interning with my mom as she finishes her studies. I know she's been working at the gallery and undoubtedly has been spending time with Xi.

"Sweetie, you look stunning," my mother says as I walk into her gallery. I'm wearing a short, satin cocktail dress. It's sleeveless, the bodice stiff and tight to my body, while the skirt flares from my hips down. It's all white, with specks of fuchsia. It looks like someone threw drops of pink paint at me, so I thought it was fitting. My fuchsia stilettos fit the style perfectly. And, of course, my signature lipstick.

"Thank you," I smile tightly as she hands me a glass of champagne. My stomach is twisted, my skin damp from the anxiety of seeing the man that left a hole the size of the universe in my heart.

What a crazy feeling to have found myself and learned to love the person I am, yet still know something is missing. Especially when I know exactly what that something is. Or rather, *who* he is.

"Let me show you around." There are already people here sipping champagne and eating fancy canapés. Not many, though. My mother's gallery is highly selective, and very few people get invited to opening nights. Only individuals who truly know about art. Specialists who can take an artist to the next level, collectors who would pay hefty prices for an exceptional piece of art.

My mouth falls open when I see the first canvas. It's beautifully abstract, and yet something about it feels familiar. I can't place it, though. The background is a midnight blue with specks of silver gray. A black figure mixes with so much pink paint it has a 3D effect on the canvas. XI is signed at the bottom right, engraved in the paint. The piece is titled *The first time.*

My eyes almost bulge out of my head. Not because of the price of $15,000—this is nothing for my mother's gallery —but for the small note on the side that says *sold.*

"I...am I late?" I ask out loud.

"Only by half an hour," my mom replies casually.

"This is sold," I say, pointing at the painting.

"Oh, half of them are sold."

"What?" I gasp. I look around, searching for Xi, but I can't find him.

"He's at the back." Mom puts a hand on my shoulder. "Opening night nerves and all. Let me show you the rest."

The backgrounds change, but the main colors stay the same, a black shadow and a flooding of so much pink it's thick and hard on the canvas. The titles take my breath away.

The party.

The night she fell in love.

The breakup.

The punishment.

The mastermind.

The heartbreak.

Seven canvases all depicting an undeniable bond between the shadow and its lover.

I'm sweating by the time my mom and I finish our walk.

My dress feels tight, and I need some fresh air, but what I need the most is to see Xi.

The air is sucked out of the room the moment he walks in. Everyone rushes to him, crowding in as they congratulate him. He looks handsome, wearing a midnight blue suit that goes so perfectly with his bronze skin tone.

I smile, filled with a pride I can't describe. His hair is a bit longer than the last time I saw him, practically reaching his ears. It's thick and silky as it's always been. His five o'clock shadow is perfectly trimmed, and his eyes shine with pride.

My smile falters when I see Harper next to him and drops completely when I notice his hand at the small of her back. My ears start ringing as I fear I might pass out in this constricting bodice.

I should have never come.

What the hell am I doing here?

The flute in my hand crashes to the floor, startling me and making me jump back.

"I'm so sorry," I mutter. A waiter hurries my way, but I insist on helping him pick up the shards. I go with him to the kitchen as I feel my skin splitting from the broken glass I'm holding—the perfect excuse to disappear.

The second the double doors to the kitchen close, I release a painful sob.

"Oh my god," the waiter panics. "Miss Delacroix, your hands."

I drop the glass in the trash and rinse my hands. It's only a few cuts. The kind waiter passes me a cloth, and I press it against my wounds.

"Are you alright?"

I nod, knowing perfectly well I can't share how I truly feel with a stranger. How my hope that Xi would wait until I was ready to see him again has been crushed under Harper's expensive heel.

"I'm so hungry," I admit.

His eyes widen and he looks around. "I can get the chef to prepare something for you."

"Please," I nod. The truth is, there's no way I'm going back out there, and I know there's no exit through the kitchen.

I sit on one of the steel tables and wait for my Philly Cheesesteak. I'm not truly hungry, but I'm polite. I eat it slowly, drink a glass of orange juice, and wait.

The waiter goes in and out of the kitchen all night, until he comes to me. "Miss Delacroix, the gallery is about to close. Everyone is gone. I took the liberty to tell your mother I'd call a taxi for you. I assumed you wanted to be alone."

"Thank you," I murmur. "I'm sorry for hiding in here all night."

"Anything you need, Miss."

I jump off the steel table and nod goodbye to him and the cook. The main lights in the gallery are off when I walk out. Only the tiny LED fixings above the paintings are on.

I am such a hopeless romantic, it's a fucking joke. All the romance books I've been reading lately have been getting to my head.

I feel no hate, just disappointment in myself. The man was in love with me, and I told him to leave me alone. He asked me for a timeline, and I gave him none. It could have been a day. It could have been forever.

I brought this on myself.

I look at the painting titled *The first time.* I could have sworn...

Never mind.

Spinning around, I gasp at the shadow standing behind me. I retreat, but his hand wraps around my arm, stopping me before I bump into the painting.

"Hi, cupcake."

My heart squeezes at the sound of his voice. My entire body electrifies, firing up from the exact spot he's holding.

"H-hi," I stutter.

"You came." His smile is dazzling, something I hadn't realized I missed until right this second. How could I not? It's the rarest and most beautiful thing in the world. A diamond hidden in the most precious caves. Inaccessible to mankind.

"I did." I scratch my throat. "Congratulations. This is all...breathtaking. I—I'm sure you and Harper must be over the moon."

"Harper? I painted them. Give me some credit."

"Of course," I blurt out. "You're an incredibly talented artist. I've always known that. I was just...trying to say I'm happy for you both. I'm sure she inspired some of your work. It's beautiful."

A love that lasts forever.

I want to die on the spot. I want the floor to open and swallow me whole. My heart can't take any more of this.

"Harper is my manager while she interns with your mom," he says calmly. But there's something in his tone. Confusion?

Brushing it to the side, I keep going. "Bold to date and work together," I chuckle. "But good for you." I can't help the slight cynicism. I'm not as sweet as I used to be. I mind a little less about what people think of me. I don't care about pleasing everyone anymore. And fuck, I'm not happy. Surely that shouldn't come as a surprise to him.

He narrows his eyes at me until clarity crosses in them.

His face hardens, and frustration makes him tighten his hold on me.

"Are you insane?" he growls.

"Insane? I'm being kind enough to not burst into tears and put you in a situation. I just saw the man I'm hopelessly in love with with his new girlfriend. Give me a break, will you?" I snap back.

Excitement flashes in his eyes, like he loves that I'm fighting back. Still, he's fuming.

"What's the color on the paintings, cupcake?"

"W-what?"

He flips me around, a hand on my waist and another that comes to grab my jaw. He forces my head up slightly, making me stare at the painting.

"The predominant color on every single canvas I've painted in the last five months. What is it?" he says low.

"I—"

"Look," he hisses. "Look and answer the fucking question."

"Pink," I force through a wince. His grip is deadly. "It's pink."

"It's fuchsia," he growls in my ear. "In fact, it's hot pink. You were never that good with colors, but I know my muse. I know you more than you know yourself, Alex."

My heart explodes in my chest, my knees buckling. He holds me, turning me back to face him. "I've given you enough time. One more minute and I'll implode, do you understand? Life is made of choices. So make it. Choose me. Choose *us*."

My eyes fill with tears, my breathing erratic.

I nod, for I'm incapable of uttering a single word. Instead, I slam my lips against his.

And for the first time, I feel Xi's hands trembling as he

holds me. Like he feared truly losing me tonight.

"I have to show you something," he says in-between kisses as we tumble inside his house. We cross through the kitchen and a side door, and he takes me to the small backyard. There's a shed there. He unlocks the door and drags me inside. There are countless pots of paint in here. Fuchsia, or hot pink I guess, is the main color everywhere.

"Obsessed much?" I laugh.

"You have no idea," he growls as he rids me of my clothes. I'm naked in less than a minute. Fully dressed, he grabs a huge pot of paint and empties it on a white canvas lying on the floor.

"What are you do—" My words die in my mouth when he takes off his clothes. It's pretty clear what he's doing. He strides towards me, and I stop him with two hands on his chest. I take a moment to appreciate the god lusting after me.

"Xi," I say cautiously. "What is *that*?" I point at the tattoo at the crook of his neck. It's on the curve that leads to his shoulder. "Is that–"

"From when you bit me? Yeah."

"You got the marks of my teeth tattooed on you?"

"I needed the reminder. The reminder of when I fucked up. Of when you hated me. The pain. I will never forget that I hurt you."

My stupid heart skips a beat because I can't help but feel a sense of ownership knowing he tattooed me on him. Knowing that for the last few months, every time he looked in the mirror, he saw me.

My hands drag down to his abs and to the three scars. I graze them with the tip of my fingers.

"You never told me what happened."

"Billie's boyfriend stabbed me for burning his house down."

"Excuse me?" I choke.

"It's a long story. One that isn't nearly as beautiful as ours, cupcake. I love you, do you know that?"

Everything we've been through together comes crashing into my mind at once. But the only thing that stays as my thoughts storm around in my head is an indescribable feeling of completion.

"I love you," I rasp as I look up into his eyes.

He fists the hair at the back of my head and chokes me with a kiss. Before I know it, he pushes me to the floor...or so I think, until I feel cold wetness on my back.

We're on the canvas.

"Who owns you, Alexandra?" he whispers against my lips as he comes on top of me.

"You do," I breathe out.

"That's right. Open your legs."

I slide my legs open, feeling the paint smudging under me.

"Keep your eyes on me." He lowers himself, grabs my ass cheeks, and presses his mouth to my hot core.

"Fuck!" I scream as he eats me out like a starved man. "Xi..." I moan.

"I missed your taste, baby."

He spends infinity licking and nibbling at me, keeping the rhythm only he desires and making me writhe under him.

After making me orgasm from his mouth and tongue only, he comes up and grabs my hand, placing it on his chest. He closes his eyes and takes a deep breath.

"Do you feel that, baby?"

I feel my eyebrows pinch in the slightest.

"I can finally breathe," he exhales.

The way Xi makes love to me that night is like nothing before. He takes his time, making me come over and over again. We fuck until the paint is practically dry and I can't keep my eyes open anymore. He makes me repeat that I belong to him and him only, and I love it. We take our time like we've got forever together.

And I think we do.

I wake up in his bed, but he's not there. After showering, he carried me here and we both fell asleep in each other's arms. I slide out of bed and call out his name, but he doesn't answer. Over the last month, he finished redoing the entire house, and it's absolutely gorgeous. This man can indeed do wonders with his hands. And don't I know it.

He must be back in the shed. I put one of his oversized t-shirts on and go to the backyard. Well, it's more like a side yard since it's on the side of the house. We can see the main road from here, and if it weren't for the small wooden fence, it'd link directly to the front yard. I open the shed since it's unlocked and walk in. On the floor, the painting is finished. He's left the background white, and the pink art of us fucking for hours is covered with drops of black.

"What's our Taylor Swift song?" I startle, turning around to find him leaning on the doorway, arms crossed over his bare chest.

"Oh, baby," I scoff. "I don't associate songs with people. The rules are that they have to fit situations."

"The rules? You made your own rules, *and* you make sure to respect them? You're still such a good girl, aren't you?"

I shrug. "I can be a good girl with a dark, manipulative side for the people who mess with me."

He licks his lips. "I'm in love with both sides, but I don't think I want to meet mean Alex again. She's scary."

"Don't fuck around, and you won't find out."

That makes both of us laugh.

"Come on." He approaches me slowly. "You know you love breaking the rules for me. Give us a song."

I sigh dramatically. "Fine. *Miss Americana & The Heartbreak Prince.*"

"You didn't even have to think. You totally already had that song for us."

"Shh. Keep the mystery alive."

"Am I Miss Americana then?"

"Yes," I nod, keeping the joke going and biting my lip so as not to laugh. "And I'm the Heartbreak Prince."

"Of course you are," he chuckles. He grabs something in his back pocket as he adds, "I've got a present for you. It's your birthday, after all."

He shows me his closed fist and opens it when he brings it near my face. A necklace hangs from his finger.

I gasp. "That's my grandmother's necklace. Xi, how..."

There's a flash of guilt in his eyes when he says. "I had kept it with me. I've had it for a year. I got it fixed for your birthday."

I blink up at him, shocked. "You had it since..."

"Yeah."

"Why?"

"For the same reason I went back into that abandoned house to save you. Because of the connection I felt. Because of the spark of interest that grew into the biggest obsession of my life. Because of you."

There will never not be a strange feeling between us

when we think about the night we met. On my eighteenth birthday...when he kidnapped me. But my nightmares began disappearing when I started sleeping next to the man who haunted my nights.

I turn around and present my neck as I lift my hair. He attaches the necklace, and I grab the locket my grandmother had given me.

"Thank you. It's my second favorite present today. My first one was you."

I feel his arms wrap around my waist from behind. The smell of turpentine mixes with his soap from the shower we took earlier. He was working while I was sleeping.

"Do you like it?" I know he's not talking about the necklace.

"I love it," I murmur. "Abstract is beautiful. What will this collection be?"

"This is the last piece of *A love that lasts forever*." He nestles his head in the crook of my neck, inhaling my skin.

Goosebumps rise everywhere on my body. The idea of being his muse seems eccentric, and yet I love it so much.

"But I thought you finished that collection."

"No, it needed one last piece. One I won't sell."

"Oh. Why?"

"It means too much to me. Look again," he says softly.

I narrow my eyes at the painting, looking for a clue.

It's signed XI at the bottom right. Next to the canvas, he wrote something on a piece of paper.

The night she chose me.

The end.

ELLIOT

Alexandra Delacroix notices the second our car parks in front of Xi's house. She gasps, her eyes rounding with fear. She's wearing a large t-shirt that must belong to her boyfriend. Ethan cuts off the engine as she runs inside.

I grab the gun in the glove compartment and load it.

"Patience, brother," he says calmly.

My stepbrother and I don't always have the same way of doing things. He's quiet, composed, *patient*.

I'm a ticking time bomb. Especially since we've started looking for our ex-girlfriend.

Two years ago.

If that's not being patient, I don't know what fucking is.

He pushes the gun down with a hand on the barrel. "He's coming."

Xi bursts out of his house, topless and with his own gun tucked into his jeans. I can see the three ugly scars he still has from the time Caden stabbed him.

Things have changed since then. Caden and Billie Scott fell in love despite being from different crews. Xi got over his stepsister and found himself a rich Stoneview girl.

But something stayed the exact same: Jade is impossible to find.

Ethan and I get out of the car in tandem. I round the front of the car to face the man who has what we want.

And then our passenger gets out as well.

"I'll be doing the talking," Caden says just before Xi walks into earshot.

The NSC boy doesn't bother with formalities. He stops just short of barreling into us and eyes us one after the other, his nostrils flared and jaw clenched.

"Emma and Kayla had a talk," he growls low. "This very house is on neutral territory. Keep me out of your shit because I've left it all behind. Did you fuckers not get the memo?"

The two women at the head of our opposing gangs rarely discuss anything, yet Kay did make us aware of the new rule. Xi Benhaim is out, and his house has turned into neutral territory. It's crazy what love can do. I wonder what Emma offered for Kay to agree. Both are ruthless businesswomen.

What they didn't anticipate is that Ethan and I don't give a shit about their little truce. We want to find the woman who betrayed us, and Xi has the information we want.

"Same," Cade chuckles. "Isn't life on the right side of the law just so boring? I'd give anything to stab a fucker three times in the stomach again."

Xi narrows his eyes at his lifelong enemy.

"But Billie won't let me." My best friend sighs dramatically. "And you know what they say; Happy wife... happy Caden King when he makes her scream his name. Or something like that."

Cade's attempt at taunting Xi doesn't even make him

blink. The man is so taken by Alex Delacroix I don't think he remembers Billie's last name.

I'm ready to start threatening him, maybe even his girlfriend standing by the window and watching us with the clear order to stay inside the house.

Before I can say anything, he addresses Ethan and me.

"I want you to know that if sparing your life wasn't in the deal Emma made with Kay, you would both be six feet under for what you did to Zara."

"Fucking do it," I sneer. "Just try."

"No," he says sternly. "It's part of the deal, and I'm a man of my word. It's keeping me out of this war, and that's all I want. My life is about protecting the woman I love, not avenging the dead."

He lifts his hand, showing us a ripped piece of paper he's holding.

"That's where Jade is hiding. I'm going to give it to you and never see your fucking faces again. Is that clear? Come near me, my woman, or my family, and you'll wish you were never born. Deal or no deal." He shoves the piece of paper into Ethan's chest, my brother barely catching it in his big hand, and walks back to his house.

Completely unafraid, like an invincible man. He just turns his back to his enemies.

"Love truly fucks a man up," I say.

"In the best way, my friend," Caden smiles. That fucking creepy smile he does so well.

I look at the window again, watching Xi wrap a hand at the back of Alexandra's neck. He watches us until we go back into the car and disappear.

Ethan gives me the crumbled paper, and I unfold it as he rounds the corner and drives us back to Kings' territory.

Elliot

420 Old Montauk Highway, Montauk, NY

"What the fuck?" I mutter to myself. Ethan stays silent, waiting for me to continue. "She's in Long Island."

"Long Island?" he repeats.

"Fuck," I chuckle to myself. It turns into a laugh until I can feel tears at the corners of my eyes. When I can finally breathe again, I become so serious one would think my dog just got run over. "The fucking bitch found a sugar daddy to escape us." She always knew how to slither her way into men's beds for her own benefit.

I watch Ethan's jaw work from side to side. "Huh. Looks like we're going on a road trip."

To be continued...

ALSO BY LOLA KING

STONEVIEW STORIES

(MF Bully):

Giving In

Giving Away

Giving Up

One Last Kiss (Novella - includes spoilers from Rose's Duet)

ROSE'S DUET

(FFMM why-choose):

Queen Of Broken Hearts (Prequel novella)

King of My Heart

Ace of All Hearts

NORTH SHORE STORIES

(interconnected standalones):

Beautiful Fiend (enemies to lovers)

Heartless Beloved - (good girl/bad boy)

Delightful Sins - (MFM enemies-to-lovers) Coming November 2023!

Lawless God - Coming 2024!

ACKNOWLEDGMENTS

Thank you to my readers for allowing me to share this world with you. Every book, this universe gets biggers, new people join us (real and fictional), and I am eternally grateful for your support in this journey.

Thank you to my king for being the better half of me. Your love carries me through everything. You wiped every single tear when I wanted to give up, and you keep pushing me when I don't even want to. I love you.

Thank you to the team behind me as we all know releasing a book would be impossible without you: My assistant Nikki, my alpha reader Lauren, and my beta reader Kat.

Thank you to the amazing ladies from VPR for all your help. Valentine, Ratula, Amy, Kim.

Thank you to my girlfriend, Jess...oh the angry, frustrated texts you received for this release. Thank you for your support, baby.

To my crazy family who is the most disorganised family in the world and yet manages to take care of me while I spend days and nights writing and editing...damn thank you, guys.

To my best friend who spent a week at my house to witness the insane schedule I keep to make this happen and forgave me for all the time we couldn't spend together.

Printed in Great Britain
by Amazon